EMPIRES OF BRONZE
SON OF ISHTAR

by Gordon Doherty
www.gordondoherty.co.uk

GORDON DOHERTY

Copyright © 2019 Gordon Doherty.

First Edition

The author has asserted their moral right under the Copyright, Designs and Patents Act, 1988, to be identified as the author of this work.

All Rights reserved. No part of this publication may be reproduced, copied, stored in a retrieval system, or transmitted, in any form or by any means, without the prior written consent of the copyright holder, nor be otherwise circulated in any form of binding or cover other than that in which it is published and without a similar condition being imposed on the subsequent purchaser.

EMPIRES OF BRONZE: SON OF ISHTAR

Also by Gordon Doherty:

THE LEGIONARY SERIES

1. LEGIONARY (2011)
2. LEGIONARY: VIPER OF THE NORTH (2012)
3. LEGIONARY: LAND OF THE SACRED FIRE (2013)
4. LEGIONARY: THE SCOURGE OF THRACIA (2015)
5. LEGIONARY: GODS & EMPERORS (2015)
6. LEGIONARY: EMPIRE OF SHADES (2017)
7. LEGIONARY: THE BLOOD ROAD (2018)
8. LEGIONARY: DARK EAGLE (2020)

THE STRATEGOS TRILOGY

1. STRATEGOS: BORN IN THE BORDERLANDS (2011)
2. STRATEGOS: RISE OF THE GOLDEN HEART (2013)
3. STRATEGOS: ISLAND IN THE STORM (2014)

THE EMPIRES OF BRONZE SERIES

1. EMPIRES OF BRONZE: SON OF ISHTAR (2019)
2. EMPIRES OF BRONZE: DAWN OF WAR (2020)

GORDON DOHERTY

Writing stories is my dream job. It's also a lonely business, and a tough one too. This book wouldn't exist without the help and support of those kind enough to offer it. Sarah, Mum, Ben, Alun, Lilias, Gavin, Leni, Judith and Jeremy, Dave & Olly the dog at Climb Scotland – here's to you.

Having had the bright idea to write about one of the least-understood eras of history – the Hittite New Kingdom – I quickly realised that I would struggle to get the project off the ground without some expert guidance. Step forward Mr. Joost Blasweiler: your in-depth knowledge and enthusiasm have gifted this story its wings.

GORDON DOHERTY

HISTORICAL FOREWORD

Note: historical detail is discussed at a finer level in the author's note at the rear of the book. A glossary is also located there should you wish to familiarise yourself with Hittite terminology prior to beginning the tale.

Over three thousand years ago, before iron had been tamed, before Rome had risen, before the ashes from which Classical Greece would emerge had even been scattered, the world was forged in bronze. It was an age when Great Kings ruled, when vast armies clashed for glory, riches and the favour of their strange gods.

Until the late 19th century, historians thought that they had identified the major powers who held sway in the last stretch of the Bronze Age: Egypt, Assyria… Ahhiyawa (Homer's Achaean Greece) even. But there was another – a fourth great power, all but lost to the dust of history: the Hittites.

Hardy, fierce masters of Anatolia, utterly devout to their myriad gods, the scale and wonder of their world is only now shedding its dusty cloak thanks to the tireless work of archaeologists. The Hittites ruled from the high, rugged plateau at the heart of modern-day Turkey, commanding a ring of vassal states (most notably Troy) and boasting a dauntless army that struck fear into the hearts of their rivals. Their Great King, titled *Labarna* and revered as the Sun itself, was every bit the equal of Egypt's Pharaoh, of the trade-rich King of Assyria, and of the brash lords of Ahhiyawa.

The Hittites were there when the Bronze Age collapsed. They bore the brunt of the cataclysmic events that destroyed the great powers, threw the Near East into a centuries-long dark age and changed the world forever.

This is their story…

GORDON DOHERTY

THE GREAT POWERS OF THE LATE BRONZE AGE (CIRCA 1300 BC)

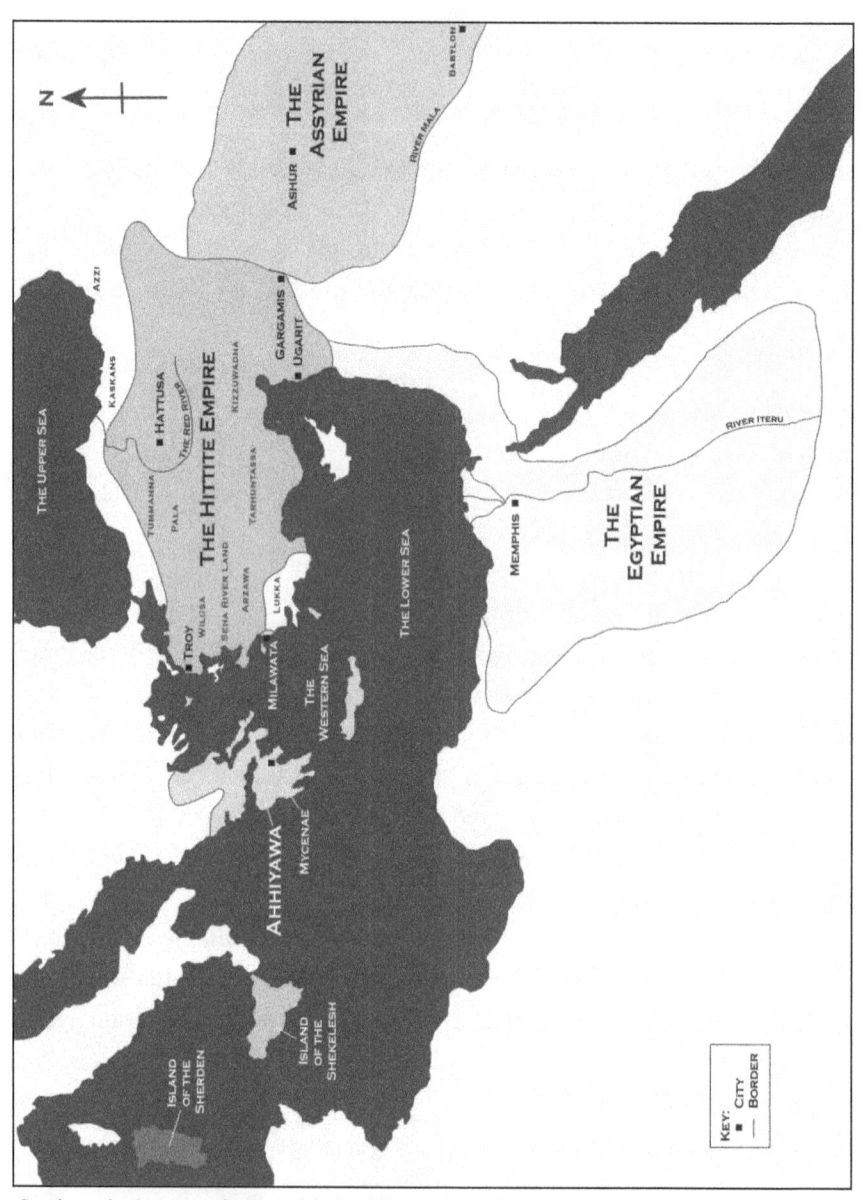

See the author's note to the rear of the book for further rationale/detail, particularly surrounding the terms 'Hittite' and 'Empire'.
Note that full and interactive versions of this and all the diagrams & maps can be found on the 'Empires of Bronze' section of my website, www.gordondoherty.co.uk

THE HITTITE HEARTLANDS AND THE LOST NORTH, REALM OF THE KASKANS

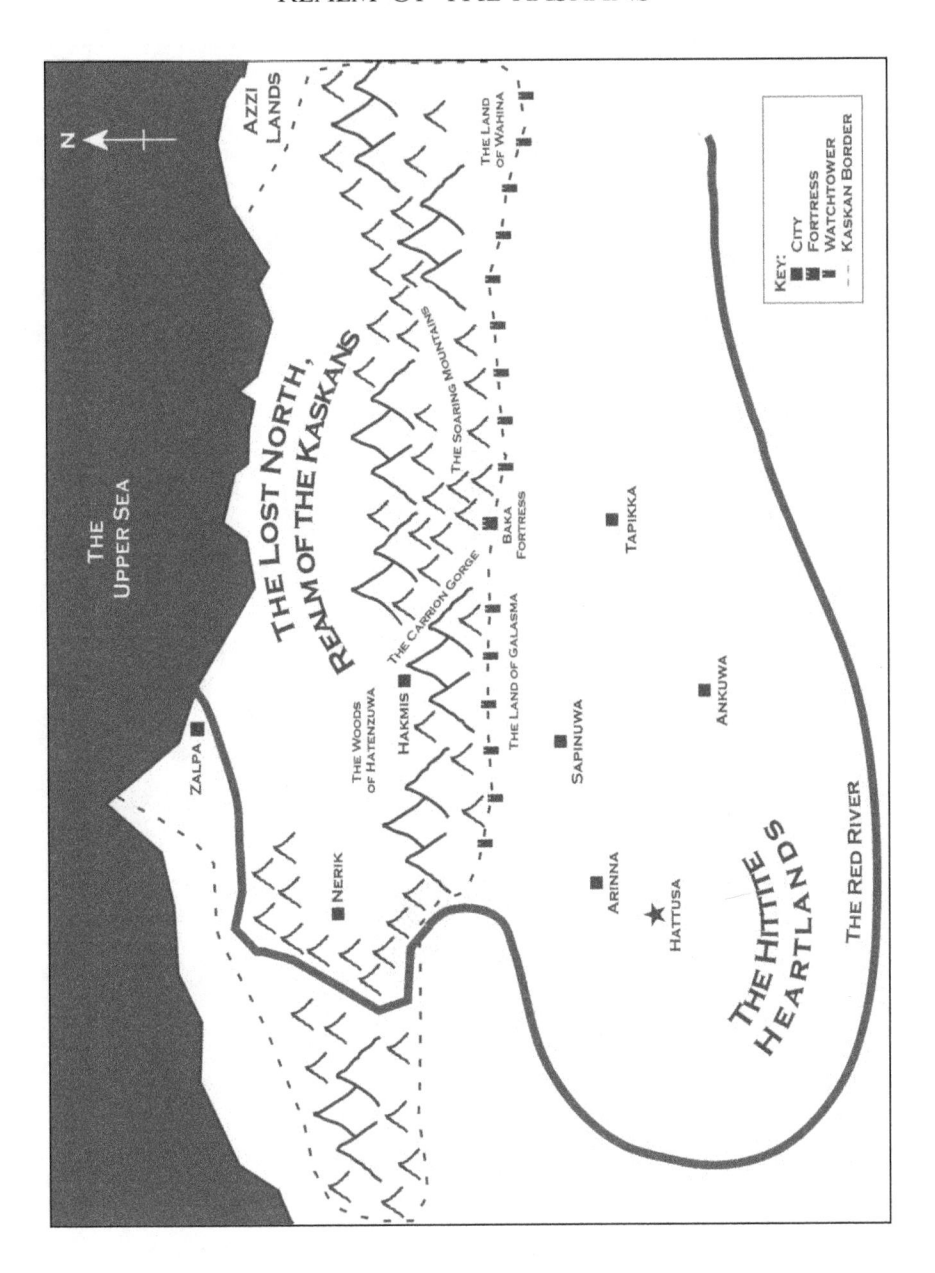

GORDON DOHERTY

THE CITY OF HATTUSA
As seen from the West. Artwork courtesy of Simon Walpole.

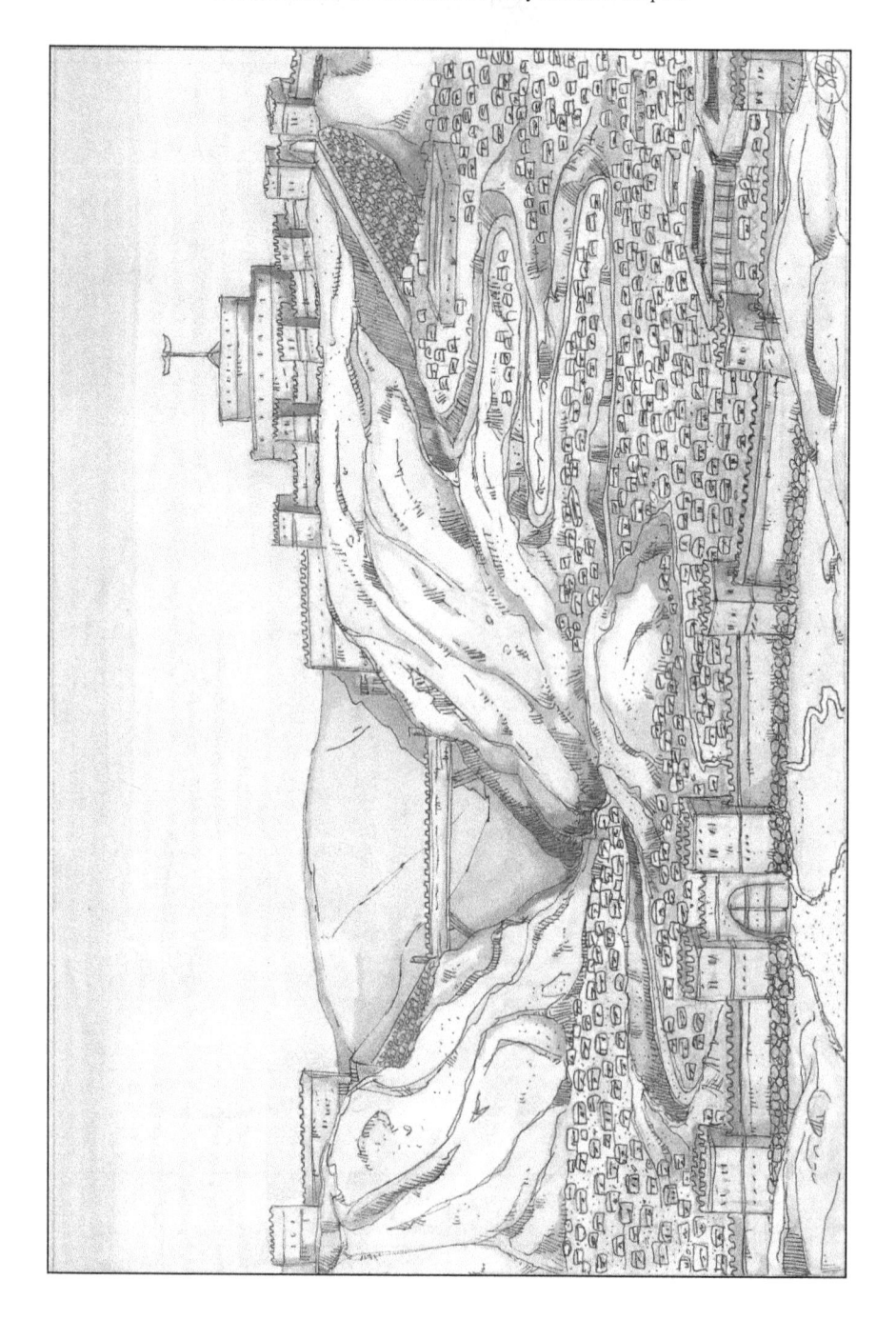

EMPIRES OF BRONZE: SON OF ISHTAR

MAP OF HATTUSA

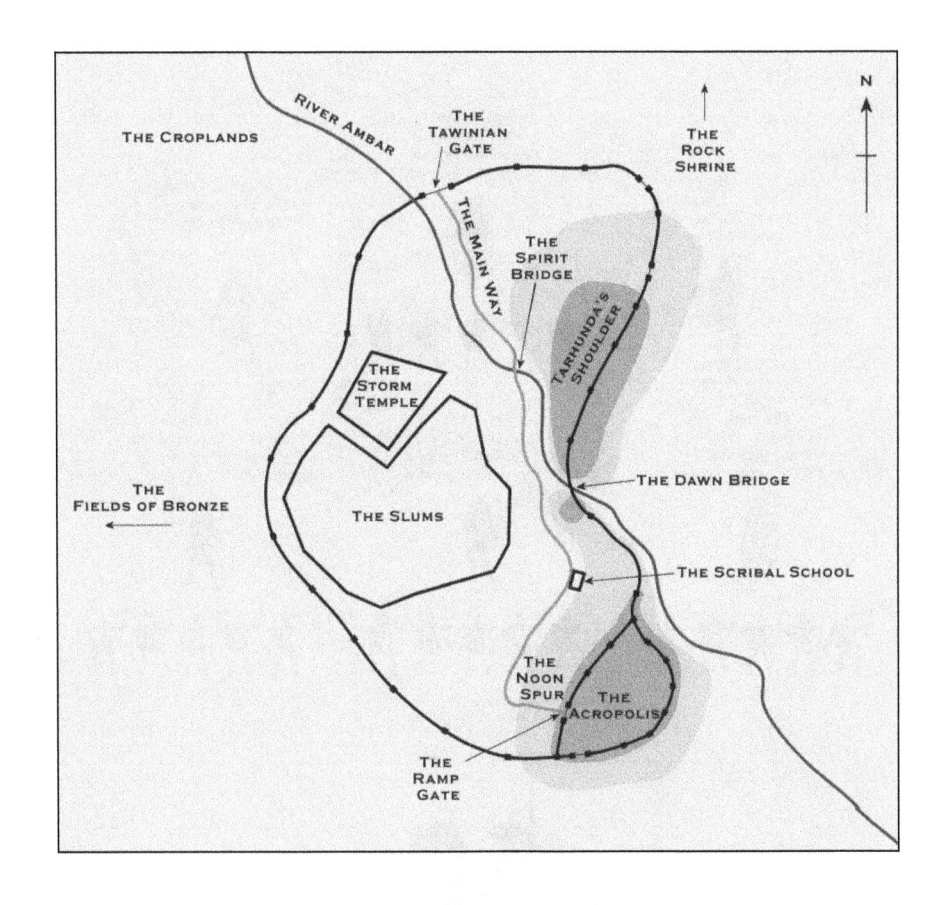

GORDON DOHERTY

THE ARMY OF THE HITTITES

See the author's note to the rear of the book for further rationale/detail.

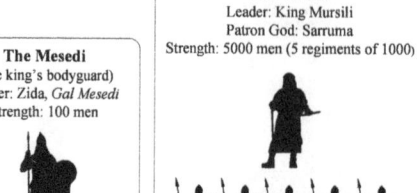

The Mesedi
(The king's bodyguard)
Leader: Zida, *Gal Mesedi*
Strength: 100 men

The Wrath
Leader: King Mursili
Patron God: Sarruma
Strength: 5000 men (5 regiments of 1000)

The Golden Spearmen
(The palace guard)
Leader: —
Strength: 50 men

The Fury
Leader: Prince Muwa
Patron God: Aplu
Strength: 5000 men (5 regiments of 1000)

The Storm
Leader: General Kurunta
Patron God: Tarhunda
Strength: 5000 men (5 regiments of 1000)

The Blaze
Leader: General Nuwanza
Patron God: Arinniti
Strength: 5000 men (5 regiments of 1000)

The Lords of the Bridle
Leader: Colta
Strength: 400 War Chariots

PROLOGUE

HATTUSA, CAPITAL OF THE HITTITE EMPIRE
1315 BC

'Last night I dreamt of skeleton hawks,' said the bald, waxy-skinned priest. 'They banked and swooped above the Storm Temple, clutching hale nestlings in their talons. Shrieking, maddened, they cast the young down, dashing them on the cold, hard ground. It was a dream of death.'

King Mursili sank to one knee, deaf to the bleating words, every sense instead fixed on the ailing newborn in his arms. His long, night-black hair hung like a veil as he dipped his face towards his feeble son, his tears spotting on the babe's blue-tinged lips.

'Hattusili?' Mursili said, his throat thick and raw. It was a name of strength, a name of famous predecessors. 'Hattu?' But the babe's every breath grew shallower. The king looked up, towards the birthing stool before him. Slumped upon it was his beloved Queen Gassula, naked, skin greying and stained with her own blood, as frail as baby Hattu. Mursili had witnessed such traumatic births before... and the burning pyres that followed. 'No. Not my queen... not my boy,' he begged the ether.

'My dreams foretold this, My Sun,' the priest persisted, his eyes reflecting the light of the tallow candles and sweet frankincense flickering on the stone floor around the stool. The storm outside raged as if to underline the claim: lightning scored the night sky, thunder shook the heavens, a gale keened and rain lashed the purity hide sealing the stony birthing chamber's outer door. 'And Hittites should always heed their dreams.'

The words tore Mursili back to reality. His head snapped round to pin the priest into silence, the winged sun-disc on his silver circlet accentuating his angered brow. Then he looked up and around the ring of others. The midwives gawped at him uselessly, their arms wet with blood to the elbows. The augurs too could only look on fearfully. 'Do *something*,' he growled. His gaze snapped onto the Wise Woman. 'Repeat the prayer to the Goddess of Birth.'

But the withered, yellow-toothed hag was impassive. 'The rites have been recounted, *Labarna*. Repeating them will achieve nothing.'

'Then slaughter another crow, another lamb,' he demanded.

'Those slain already were enough,' the Wise Woman drawled. 'The Gods will not be pleased at senseless butchery.'

Mursili shot to standing. 'The Gods? They have *abandoned* me.' He stared at the high ceiling of the chamber, thinking of the skies above and the thousand divinities of his sacred land. 'Is there none who will spare me this tragedy? *None?*'

'Be careful, My Sun,' the Wise Woman advised. 'Such appeals can echo far into the void…'

'I will give you anything,' Mursili cried, ignoring her.

'My Sun!' the priest beseeched him.

Mursili shouldered him away. 'Spare their lives, spare them from the Dark Earth, and I will honour you.' He lifted the ailing baby Hattu aloft like an offering. 'My child will honour you. Hear me!' he roared.

Silence. Nothing but the pounding of rain. He slumped with a deep sigh. A midwife took baby Hattu from him and the well-meaning priest rested a hand on his shoulder. 'You must entrust them to the healers now.'

Mursili made to protest, but as he swung to the priest a fog of exhaustion passed over him. Spots swam across his eyes. He swayed and almost fell, only for the priest and others nearby to catch him.

'My Sun! You must rest,' the priest wailed. 'It has been three nights since last you slept.'

A fresh protest welled in Mursili's throat but died on his tongue as another wave of fatigue washed over him. Steadying himself, he saw the *asu* healers lifting Gassula to a bed near the birthing stool, while a cluster of others placed Hattu on a towel-clad bench edged with jars of curative waxes and potions. *The Gods are silent,* he thought, *and so men must decide the fate of my beloved ones.*

'My Sun, please, take leave of this room and rest – for a time, at least.'

'Perhaps,' he snapped. Staring through the fog of exhaustion, he let the priest guide him from the birthing chamber and through the palace. 'But you will summon me as soon as anything happens,' Mursili said as they came to his bedchamber. It was an order, not a request.

The priest assured him, and in moments he was alone. Numbly, he lifted off his circlet, prized off his boots and cloak and lay down, beset with worry and uncomforted by the soft linen bedding. There was not a chance that he would sleep, he was sure. But when the tallow candle by his bed guttered and died, exhaustion crept up on him like an assailant, tossing a black veil of oblivion over his weary mind. It was a deep, dreamless, restful slumber.

For a time...

And then the dark oblivion parted like drapes. He realised he was standing on cold, rough ground, a finger of dire, grey light shining down upon him as if from an unseen moon. All else remained in shadow. Was this a dream? Was he alone in this strange nether-world?

The answer came in the form of a growl. A deep, throaty, inhuman growl that dripped with menace. When a lion prowled across one edge of the gloomy finger of light, its leathery, black lips peeling back to reveal yellow fangs dripping with saliva, Mursili clasped in vain for the hunting spear he did not possess. He started to back away when a second growl from behind him turned his legs to stone. The two lions began circling him watchfully.

And then a third figure emerged from the ether before him: an impossibly tall woman, sun-kissed and naked bar a silver necklace of an eight-pointed star and a diaphanous scarf around her broad waist. Her dark locks tumbled around her heart-shaped face, then on to cover her bare and weighty breasts. But she was no woman, for her legs below the knee tapered into the gnarled talons of an eagle. And sprouting from her back were shuddering cascades of feathers – wings!

At once, he understood. The goddess of many names: Inanna, Shauska...

'... *Ishtar*,' he whispered, wide-eyed, dropping to his knees. He thought of everything this goddess represented. Love, fertility... war. And of her reputation as the bearer of bittersweet fruits.

'My-my pledge was sincere,' he stammered, understanding this dream now. His pleas had been heard. 'Save my queen and my child... I will do anything for you as will they.'

With a glint in her cat-like eyes, Ishtar walked around him, hips swaying. Her talons clacked on the dark ground as she went. 'Only one can live,' she replied with a throaty purr.

Mursili balked. Had he misheard her? 'I... I don't understand.'

'I can heal Gassula or Hattu, not both. One must journey to the Dark Earth. So who is to die, King Mursili: your queen or your boy?'

What had she said? The words stabbed like a knife into Mursili's heart. The bittersweet fruit had been offered. 'I will not choose,' he said.

'Then both will die... ' she hissed, receding into the blackness.

'No... *no*,' Mursili begged, one hand outstretched. 'How can a man choose between his wife and his child? Guide me, help me at least.'

She halted at the edge of the grey light. 'I see two futures,' she said. 'In one, your wife regains her strength and grows old with you. Yet her life will be an unhappy one, spent by the Meadow of the Fallen, weeping over baby Hattu's bones. When she is on her death bed she will tell you she wished she had died along with the babe. It will crush you.'

Cold pins pricked Mursili's heart at the mere thought of his sweet Gassula in such torment. 'And... the other?' he asked cautiously.

'In the other, Gassula's pain will be short. She will perish, but Hattu will never have known his mother and so he will not grieve for her.'

Mursili hesitated then whispered: 'And if... if Hattu lives, will he lead a good life?'

Ishtar remained silent for a moment, and Mursili thought he noticed something of a smirk on her lips. At last, she parted her arms, closed her eyes and began to sing in a voice of molten gold:

A burning east, a desert of graves,
A grim harvest, a heartland of wraiths,
The Son of Ishtar, will seize the Grey Throne,
A heart so pure, will turn to stone,
The west will dim, with black boats' hulls,
Trojan heroes, mere carrion for gulls,
And the time will come, as all times must,
When the world will shake, and fall to dust...

She opened her eyes again. 'This I foresee, if Hattu lives.'

Mursili's eyes darted as he combed over the words of the song. It made little sense, apart from one line: 'The Son of Ishtar, will seize the Grey Throne,' he croaked. 'You speak of *Hattu*?'

'Yes,' she purred, 'it has been some time since Hittite Kings and Princes took up swords against one another. But if Hattu lives, he will be your fourth son. Four sons... and just one throne to inherit.'

'Hattu would turn upon his own kin?' he searched Ishtar's face in desperation.

Ishtar beheld him with a doleful look. 'It will begin on the day he stands by the banks of the Ambar, soaked in the blood of his brother.'

Mursili recoiled at the thought. 'No, never.' He raised a shaking hand, one finger wagging, briefly daring to show his anger to the goddess. 'This is a trick!'

She stretched to her full height, wings extending, lips receding to show sharp fangs and her eyes suddenly ablaze like coals. 'Enough!' the goddess bawled like a vengeful dragon so as to make the ether of the shadow-world tremble around him. 'Make your choice, Great King of the Hittites. Who is to die?'

There was only one answer, but the words stuck in his throat. Yet he knew in the pit of his heart that if Gassula was here in this foul dream, she would give that same answer.

Heartsick, he whispered at last: 'Save my boy.'

He woke and sat bolt upright in his bed, lashed with sweat. A flicker of lightning illuminated his chamber for an instant, and he saw the ancient and vividly-painted carvings of the gods on the opposite wall, Ishtar amongst them. Nearby thunder pealed as the essence of the dream crept across his flesh like a winter chill. 'A dream and no more,' he muttered, before he remembered the words of the priest and that most ancient mantra: *Hittites should always heed their dreams.*

Suddenly, the muffled voices of the birthing staff – raised and urgent – echoed through the palace. At once his head snapped round to the sound. In a panic, he rose and stumbled barefoot through the unlit passageways, jagged flashes of lightning his only beacon, until he barged back into the birthing chamber, eyes wide, maddened.

All stared at him, all speechless. Gassula lay on the bed, her eyes gazing into eternity, lips blue, chest completely still. A crying midwife cradled baby Hattu – the babe equally lifeless.

'Queen Gassula passed into the Dark Earth a short while ago, My Sun,' she wept, 'and the boy stopped breathing just a moment ago.'

'No,' Mursili whispered, stepping forward to take Hattu. He held the tiny form to his chest and stared at the ceiling of the birthing chamber. 'This is not how it was supposed to be,' he cried. 'You made me choose. You *made me ch-*'

Thunder cracked directly overhead, drowning him out and shaking the chamber. In the same instant, the gale outside gained immense strength, the purity hide stretched over the chamber's outer door bulged inwards and then one edge snapped free, the pegs holding it there spinning across the room. The tallow candles roared and spat at the sudden intrusion of storm-wind and driving rain. The birthing staff shrieked in fright, their robes and hair rapping as they backed away.

But King Mursili did not move despite the scourging rain, for the tiny bundle in his arms suddenly convulsed, then took a full gasp for breath.

Baby Hattu cried out at last, in time with the storm.

TWELVE YEARS LATER…

CHAPTER 1

SHADOW PRINCE
SPRING 1303 BC

The alder woods north of Hattusa were still and tranquil. The noonday sun blazed in the cloudless, pastel-blue sky and all was quiet but for the croaking cicadas and the occasional drumming of woodpeckers.

When a branch near the southern treeline shuddered, a flock of song thrushes scattered. A muscled arm reached up to still the branch. Bagrat the amber-haired Kaskan scout fell to one knee, eyeing the pale-walled hillside city beyond the forest.

As a youth, fireside yarns about this place had stoked his dreams. Hattusa, the rocky heart of the enemy realm, where the Hittite King lived in a high palace, well-appointed with precious relics and smoking pools of molten silver. Since his boyhood, he had helped topple the walls of many Hittite cities. But this was a city like no other. Such stout walls, such high towers... too high, surely?

The trees behind him rustled again. He swung round to see a stout and tall warrior with a tangled mane and beard, both rusty and dashed with grey. He was crowned with a bronze cap, a glaring lion's skull fused to the metal, the two fangs stabbing down to serve as cheek guards. A fine black leather breastplate engraved with a swirl of silver hugged his torso and he wore a vicious double-headed axe across his back.

'Lord Pitagga,' Bagrat quailed, 'you should stay back from the open country. If the Hittite patrols see you then...'

Pitagga ignored him, turning his hunter's eyes on Hattusa. He lifted one foot up on a rock and rested his arms across his knees, a ravening half-grin pulling at his lips. 'I do not fear the Hittite soldiers, scout. And I will show that.' He lifted and wagged his finger once at Hattusa. 'And this... *this* will be my reward,' he patted Bagrat's shoulder, 'yours too. Aye, before winter comes, those walls will tumble, the streets within will run red... and not a soul will be spared.'

Bagrat felt a shiver of excitement at the grand claim, his earlier misgivings suppressed. Such was Pitagga's gift. The Lord of the Mountains could inspire the twelve tribes of the north like no other. He looked at Hattusa again. Perhaps it *was* possible...

From behind, somewhere in the woods, a distant scrape of rock sounded. Alarmed, Bagrat's head snapped round, peering through the trees. Nothing. Then he noticed how Lord Pitagga's gaze looked not into the woods but above.

A sheer-sided ridge of silvery granite protruded from the heart of the forest like a shark's fin. The shaded southern side was etched with a grand scene of the Hittite divinities: Tarhunda the Storm God wore a high, thorn-studded hat and stood upon the shoulders of the twin bulls, Serris and Hurris. The carving was ancient, cracked, dotted with falcon's nests and threaded with vines. Bagrat was confused for a moment, then he saw what had drawn his master's eye.

Scaling the rock face high up there was a lean, dusky-skinned boy... a Hittite boy, wearing just a pale linen kilt. He was merely a dot by the Storm God's neck. And even from here it was clear he was in trouble.

Pitagga's half-grin widened. 'Into the woods, scout. I haven't shot my bow in months...'

***

Hattu's limbs trembled with fatigue. His odd eyes – the right one hazel and the left one smoke-grey – were fixed on the Storm God's lower eyelid. It was high above. Too high. But there was nothing else. His inky hair traced along the nape of his neck as he switched his head to and fro. No other way up.

Despite all his training, he glanced down: the forest floor seemed impossibly distant; the fallen trunk he had vaulted over down there now small as a twig. When a gentle breeze tugged at him, his belly flooded with ice water. His numb fingertips and toes tightened on the meagre crimps he clung to. At once, he wanted nothing more than to be on flat, safe ground, to be Hattu the scribe, Hattu the forgotten son of the king. Just as terror looked set to overcome him, a welcome voice echoed from the brume of memory, the voice of his brother, Sarpa: *Master your doubts, and you will master the climb.*

Hattu closed his eyes and marshalled his ragged breaths as best he could, slowing them and feeling his rapping heart slow with them. He remained, nose-to-nose with his fears, until the storm within steadied. When he opened his eyes again, the fog of panic was gone.

He looked up towards the groove of the Storm God's eyelid again. 'I can do this,' he insisted. He glanced to his right side, seeing the faintest wrinkle in the rock at waist-height there.

Keeping his breaths slow and steady, he drew his right leg up towards the wrinkle, the left foot and toes quivering with the strain of his entire body weight. His right instep scraped over the wrinkle twice before finding the merest purchase. He looked up to the Storm God's eyelid once more, a thousand voices screaming in his head, telling him he was wrong.

But Sarpa cried above the naysaying clamour: *Be brave. Open up the climb. Rise!*

With a cry, he put all his strength into his right leg, pushing against the wrinkle, thrusting upwards. He reached above until his fingertips curled over the rounded lip of the eyelid and a gasp of sweet relief escaped his lips. He swung his left leg up to wedge his foot into a thin, vertical crack on the god's cheek, then grabbed the edge of the upper eyelid with his left hand. Now fear and euphoria battled in his breast. *Up, up... up,* he mouthed euphorically as he continued to ascend, using the many thorns in the Storm God's high hat like a ladder... until the uppermost one crumbled away in his fingers.

No...

Dust puffed into his eyes, his fingertip hold fading to nothing. His hands clawed in vain for purchase and found none, his body peeling away from the rock face, into the void.

No, no, no, NO!

In the throes of terror, he heard a piercing shriek, saw a streak of white and hazel plumage, a sharp beak and a pair of lethal talons. The falcon swept past, releasing the end of a vine from its claws. Hattu grabbed the vine with both hands, his body jolting as his fall was halted. He hung there for a moment, mouthing a prayer to the gods through shaking lips. Then, by walking his feet against the rock face he used the vine to climb the last stretch in a hurry. And when he reached the grassy top of the ridge he tossed both arms gratefully onto the flat and levered himself up.

He heard himself laughing as his mind and body settled. The peril of the climb was now a treasure. He sat, cross-legged, tucking his hair behind his ears then tying a strap of leather around his brow to hold it there. His gaze swept across the land: across the forest and the chiselled heartlands of the Hittite Empire, veined with sacred rivers and ancient tracks, on to the hazy blue point of infinity where sky met land. The mystery of the horizon thrilled him and saddened him at once.

He had never been allowed to journey far – never beyond these woods and certainly never to the horizon. He recalled the previous summer, watching Father leading the Hittite Army from Hattusa, off to the west to fight and win the Arzawan War. The king had taken his two eldest sons with him: Muwatalli the *Tuhkanti* – Chosen Prince of the Hittite Empire – and Sarpa, next in line to the throne. Hattu had been left behind in old Ruba's scribal classroom to write out – ironically – the Epic of Gilgamesh and his far-flung adventures. And in autumn, he had watched again as the army had returned, victorious. Muwa and Sarpa had ridden with the king in a chariot parade through the city. Father and scions, as one. The memory stung him now even more fiercely than it had done then.

Cursed Son, a wicked voice hissed in his head.

He blinked hard to stave off the voice, then drew open the small leather bag roped to his belt, lifting, weighing and checking the pale, brown-speckled falcon's egg he had collected halfway up. *Intact,* he realised, mustering a degree of cheer again.

The air was again pierced by another shriek, coming right for him once more. He held up a stiff, level arm. The falcon who had brought him the vine swooped down and settled on the dark-brown leather bracer on his forearm, keening again and again.

'Enough, Arrow, enough,' Hattu chuckled. He looked from her black eyes to the egg in his other hand. 'This? It's for Atiya. It was from an abandoned nest,' he reasoned, 'just like the one I found you in – but abandoned for much longer: no chick will spring from this egg.' Another impertinent shriek. 'Ah, you don't care about the egg, do you?' he realised, rustling in his bag again to produce a fat worm. No sooner had he held the specimen up than it was gone, the shrieking blessedly silenced as the falcon gulped down the meal. But the void of stillness and silence was all too brief.

Cursed Son! the voice snarled this time.

It was the voice of many: of palace staff, of soldiers, of citizens in the lower town. *The Cursed Son,* they whispered as he passed, thinking he could not hear them, *he who cast Queen Gassula into the Dark Earth.* And the gossipers dispensed with whispering when one of his three brothers died of plague in his sixth summer. *Death follows that boy*, they said openly, an edge of fear in their voices.

Unconsciously, and as he had become accustomed to doing when in company, he pulled a few locks of hair round from behind his ear to let them drape over his odd, smoke-grey eye. It did not change who he was, but it usually meant fewer people recognised him.

He stroked Arrow's head until the dark thoughts eased. When they did, he noticed something: several *danna* away to the south a cloud of terracotta dust had risen, the plume working its way towards Hattusa. Arrow's head rose too, suddenly alert. 'More strange princes for the Gathering. Best we return to the city also,' he sighed, standing then lifting and flicking his wrist lightly. Arrow took off at once, heading in a straight line towards the capital with a parting shriek.

Hattu set off down the less-severe northern side of the ridge and was soon making his way through the shady alder woods, the dry bracken crunching under his bare feet. He came to the chalky banks of the River

Ambar, a vivid turquoise ribbon that ran through Hattusa and all the way out here. More a series of falls, pools and gentle rapids than a true river, its waters were sacred. He waded across, the thigh-deep water as chilly as the day was hot, and up onto the far banks. There, he froze, his breath held captive.

A whisper of movement nearby?

His head turned like an owl's, but all was still and silent. Yet when he faced forwards again, something snagged the edge of his vision once more. Something *had* moved. A glint of bronze, he was sure. Only warriors wore bronze. Warriors... and bandits, or worse, *Kaskans!* Those rugged brigands from the Soaring Mountains who took delight in defiling and toppling Hittite temples... who took Hittite heads as trophies.

Another crunch of bracken. Closer.

His heart thundered faster even than that weightless moment when he had fallen from the ridge. 'Who's there?' he called out, feeling afraid and foolish at the same time.

Silence.

He took a step towards the forest path, timid as a fawn.

Whoosh... twang.

Suddenly, Hattu was still. He stared at the reed arrow shaft quivering in the dirt before him. His limbs almost buckled under him until he saw the fletchings: silver and white striped feathers from a greylag goose. Instantly, his fear evaporated and a broad smile split his face. 'Muwa?' he cried, looking this way and that.

With a crunch of bracken, Prince Muwatalli, Hattu's eldest brother, emerged from the shade of a nearby oak. At sixteen summers, Muwa towered a good two heads over Hattu, his thick, wavy, coal-dark locks gathering upon his muscular shoulders. His jaw was square like a man's and his broad, flat-boned features were handsome and hale – if Hattu resembled a fox, then Muwa was a lion. He wore a black cloak, a dark kilt and a shining white, silver-scaled vest – the ancient armour of the Chosen Prince. Muwa slung his cherry wood bow across his back and stalked towards Hattu. But his usually ice-bright eyes were shaded by a frown. 'Walking the woods alone?' Muwa said, his gaze on the tell-tale scrapes and cuts on Hattu's hands and feet. '*Climbing?* After Sarpa's fall?'

Hattu's neck and shoulders prickled at the invisible cloak of shame that settled there. 'I... I,' he started.

Muwa held up a finger, silencing him, his eyes shooting suspiciously to the nearby trees.

'You hear something too?' Hattu whispered. Only now he noticed the pair of Hittite soldiers lurking further back, behind Muwa. They were dressed in belted, white knee-length tunics and pointed, dark-brown leather helms with cheek guards, aventails and bronze brow bands. Their long dark hair hung loose to their waists, animal teeth knotted in their locks. They held their spears two-handed, eyes alert as if expecting danger.

'Word came in this morning of a small Kaskan band roving in these parts,' Muwa replied, relaxing just a fraction as his suspicions faded.

Hattu shivered, despite the hot sun. 'Father will be angry with me.'

'Father doesn't know. Ruba went looking for you when you didn't turn up at the Scribal School this morning. He saw you sneaking down to the city gates... but decided it would be best for your sake only to tell me. Ruba is old and forgetful these days, Hattu. He was lost with worry that you would come to harm.'

Hattu's shoulders slumped.

Muwa crouched by the arrow and worked it free from the dirt. He held up the bronze arrowhead and blew the dust from it, checked the shaft for straightness then tucked it away in his belt quiver. 'More importantly, you are my brother, Hattu,' he said, rising again. 'Were something to happen to Sarpa and me then you would be Father's last heir. You must not roam alone like this.'

Cursed Son! the voice screamed. Hattu's head flopped forward. He could do nothing right, it seemed.

Muwa's mood loosened a little and he wrapped an arm around Hattu's shoulders, giving him a reassuring squeeze. 'Come, Brother, let us return to the city before anyone notices. The Gathering is set to begin before the afternoon is out.'

***

Pitagga crouched behind the smooth river rocks. His fingers itched to seize his axe and to rush the two young Hittites. *Princes, no less. King Mursili's heir and the odd-eyed runt too!* He screamed inwardly, imagining the pair's heads on poles, back at his mountain villages. But the two Hittite soldiers escorting them were keen-eyed, regarding every inch of the woods around them. He had lied when he told Bagrat that he did not fear Hittite soldiers, but that was not what mattered. What mattered was that the scout believed him... that the multitudes of the north believed him. They would come together soon enough, fight for him, and deliver to him the heads of the Hittite King and all his heirs. He saw in his mind's eye once more the city of Hattusa ablaze, the streets stained with blood.

'Before winter comes... ' he vowed once more.

Then, with a whisper and a waved hand, he and Bagrat darted away, through the trees to the north, back towards the Soaring Mountains.

***

After trekking half a danna upstream, Hattu, Muwa and the escort soldiers emerged from the alder woods. Their eyes snapped at once to the imperious city ahead.

Hattusa!

Built around a craggy silver hillside cleaved by the Ambar River valley – narrow as an axe-wound – the capital was ringed by a curtain wall the colour of pale sand, studded every fifty paces or so with square, fort-like towers. Tiny forms of sentries milled along the tower tops and the battlements, their pointed, bronze spear tips and helms like flames, flitting in and out of view behind the smooth, triangular merlons.

Wrapped within the walls was the rising jungle of the lower town: a maze of mud-brick temples, homes, workshops, taverns and turquoise pools set on natural and quarried terraces. Crowds swarmed like ants through the streets, upon the flat rooftops and across the vine-like bridges straddling the Ambar.

The silvery peaks either side of the Ambar shimmered like treasure in the sun. The southernmost and tallest tor served as the city acropolis, crowned with the great citadel, a fortress within a fortress. A thick pole jutted from the roof of the highest building – the twin-storied throneroom known as the Hall of the Sun – bearing a bronze, winged sun disc, gleaming in the spring sky.

They followed a wheel-rutted track through the farmlands that lay before the city: golden fields of wheat, spelt, sesame and barley dotted with sweating, kilted men and women in simple sleeveless robes and headscarves busy binding early harvest stalks into sheaves. Oxen harrowed fallow fields while sheep and goats grazed in green meadows. They passed beekeepers lifting drawers of sun-gold honeycomb from hives and young milk maids pouring clay vases of chalk-white goat milk into storage urns.

As they approached Hattusa's walls, the dirt track became a well-worn, paved path, alive with the clatter of ox-drawn carts and jabbering voices. The arched Tawinian Gates soon loomed over them – tall as four men with the towers flanking it another two men high again. The gates were open, but the queue to enter the city was long – a hectic contraflow of people, animals and wagons shuffling in and out under the hard eyes of sentries on the ground and atop the gatehouse. Hattu saw the sentries stiffen suddenly, theirs and the eyes of the many falling upon Muwa.

'*Tuhkanti!*' they hailed him. The sentries pumped clenched left fists in the air in salute as the crowds parted like curtains to let their Chosen Prince enter his city. Muwa rewarded them with a slight nod of approval.

Hattu kept his head down as they passed under the gatehouse, sensing the many eyes upon them. They gazed at his older brother in awe. But he felt something else in the stares that strayed onto him: something cold and resentful. Indeed, one plague-scarred, greasy-haired, gaunt boy eyed him with disgust. He tugged a lock of hair round under his headband to cover the smoke-grey eye.

He heard one of them mutter: 'See where the Cursed Son walks? Always in Muwatalli's shadow.' *Muwa's shadow,* he felt the term sizzle like a brand on the back of his neck.

'It is like magic, Brother, the way they part before you,' he said to Muwa as they entered the lower town. 'They respect you. They love you.'

Muwa snorted, patting his silver cuirass. 'It is my title they respect,' he said, flashing Hattu a quick smile. 'And... those in the crowd, ignore their bitter words. Cast aside our stations for a moment.' He tapped his own breastbone then Hattu's as they walked. 'In here we are brothers, equals.'

Hattu smiled and gazed ahead as if the compliment had been unnecessary. In truth it had been like a salve. They walked up the paved main way, lined with bright markets and taverns and thronged with yelling merchants, sweating workers carrying baskets on their heads and lumbering wagons bearing precious ingots of tin and copper. The air was rich with the scent of charcoal, baking bread and malting barley and the less pleasant reek of dung and sweat. The way led over the Spirit Bridge, the Ambar's packed banks below thick with women washing garments and men gathering clay. On the far side of the bridge, the road snaked steeply up the base of the acropolis mount. They wove past the tablet house and the Scribal School, on across the Noon Spur – a quarried terrace that only ever saw sunlight from midday onwards. Soon, they reached the final approach to the acropolis: a broad, flagged, earthen ramp. The gates at the top were sheathed in bronze, and the colossal stone lions either side gazed down upon them with black-painted eyes.

Home, Hattu mused despondently as they climbed the steep ramp. When they neared the citadel they were greeted by two elite soldiers. A *Mesedi* – one of the hundred chosen warriors who served as the king's bodyguard – stood resplendent in a bronze scale corselet, leather kilt and a high, bronze helm. Beside him up there was a white-robed Golden Spearmen – from the fifty-strong acropolis guard unit bearing the gilt spears that gave them their name. These two warriors saluted then hauled at ropes and the Ramp Gates groaned open to let them in.

As soon as Hattu stepped through the shadow of the gatehouse and onto the carmine-red flagstones of the acropolis, his senses were assailed. The air was thick with the aroma of wine and roasting meats and the clamour of shrieking laughter and highborn argot. Strangers lurked in the shadowy colonnades, clustered near the palace and by the polished-stone edge of the sacred pool. Some were pale-skinned, some dark as night.

Some were daubed garishly in strange dyes, others clad in lurid gowns and most dripping with jewels. There were bragging rich men and their wives, slaves, sycophants, holy men, champions and warriors. From the royal harem, fiercely-painted women leaned from the shuttered windows, eyeing the fattest and richest foreigners like cats planning to corner mice. And amongst the outlanders stood members of the *Panku* – the tall, proud, Hittite nobility who gathered often before the king to lobby and squabble over affairs of the realm.

Hattu found his gaze being dragged from one spectacle to the next, until it settled on a trio of men standing high and clear of the masses, up on the steps by the tall doorway to the Hall of the Sun. Each was a cousin of the king, and each looked over the gathered masses with deliberately cruel eyes. At once, Hattu felt his mouth grow dry as he always did in the presence of these men.

There was Zida, *Gal Mesedi* – chief of the king's hundred bodyguards – lean, tall and sinewy, wearing a flowing red cloak held in place by a fierce silver hawk brooch. His lips moved almost imperceptibly, whispering suspicious words to the one nearest to him.

General Nuwanza, the square-jawed Master Archer, had the powerful chest and upper arms of a bowman. Dressed in just a kilt and boots, he nodded slowly, his gaze following Zida's direction. Nuwanza's night-black, sharply receding hair was gathered in three tails that sprouted from his crown. His brow was creased in concern, his black, wiry eyebrows drawn together in a V. There was someone in the crowd these two disapproved of. Hattu felt a crumb of sympathy for whoever that was.

But the third figure standing by the hall's entrance sent the sharpest of chills through Hattu. General Kurunta dragged his lone, mean eye – the remains of the other masked behind a tattered, leathery patch – over the crowd like a scythe. His bald, umber-skinned head was dipped a fraction. The braid of silver hair sprouting from above his right ear hung down the side of his face to rest across his chest like a scorpion's tail. He was clad in a leather kilt, boots and crossbands that hugged his bare, teak-hard chest – the hilts of the two swords sheathed on his back jutting up behind him as if he was about to sprout wings. There was something in the way he stood, feet apart in a stance of power, shoulders tensed as if ready to reach up and snatch out his twin blades... the man reeked of menace. The people of Hattusa spoke of Kurunta One-eye in whispers. The breaker of men, the master of infantry, some said. The vengeful general, others dared to say: for what man would not seek revenge, whose king had ordered the taking of his eye?

Kurunta's gaze swung across the masses and halted, pinioning Hattu. Hattu felt an icy lance of panic in his breast, not sure what to do, where to look.

'Ah, refreshments,' Muwa said, taking two clay pots of foaming barley beer from a passing slave girl and handing one to Hattu. 'Here: I find it a good way to avoid speaking to bores,' he said, then quickly sucked on the reed straw when one dignitary swung round to engage, eyes bright and mouth primed to offer some gushing monologue.

Hattu chuckled and took a sip of his own beer – bitter and refreshing – as he scanned the sea of strange faces.

'Brothers,' a voice cut through the crowd.

'Sarpa,' Muwa and Hattu replied in unison as the king's second son barged towards them, his honey-gold eyes sparkling and his head freshly shaved as was the way of the templefolk. At fifteen summers, he was as tall as Muwa but nowhere near as muscular – his face gaunt and angular. He pushed between two dignitaries with the aid of a crutch. At the sight of the stick, Hattu felt that familiar spike of guilt: Sarpa had been following in Muwa's wake, training as a soldier, accompanying Father to war. Until last autumn, when he had taken Hattu on a climb. It was a short climb – only eight times a man's height, but it was damp that day. Hattu had slipped, and Sarpa had caught him only to fall himself, shattering a hip on the rocks. The limb had healed but now Sarpa's gait was shambling at best, and his military days were over. Now he spent his time serving as a priest at the Storm Temple in the lower town.

The three brothers embraced. Hattu winced inwardly: *I'm sorry, Brother...* When they drew apart, he smiled to mask his true feelings.

'How was it?' Sarpa whispered to him. 'The climb,' he clarified with a grin, seeing Hattu's confusion. 'I see the rock dust under your fingernails.'

Hattu smiled genuinely this time. 'It was incredible. My heart was fit to burst with pride when I reached the top.' He thought of the falcon egg in his satchel and added: 'Is Atiya here yet?'

'The priestesses will be here soon,' Sarpa smiled.

Then, from the high end of the citadel grounds, the thick, metallic *clash* of a gong sounded. All heads turned to the Hall of the Sun. With a rumble of feet the crowds poured towards the towering throneroom's entrance. The Gathering was about to commence.

Hattu beheld the tall doorway. Of all the hard faces and doubting eyes out here, it was the judgement of the man inside he feared most of all.

CHAPTER 2

THE GATHERING
SPRING 1303 BC

Crowds took their places on the benches lining three sides of the hall, a dozen Mesedi and Golden Spearmen standing watch before them. The chatter faded towards a whisper and all eyes turned to the semi-circular, stone-carved dais at the hall's western end, as if guided there by the broad fingers of reddening, late afternoon sunlight that shone in from the high arched windows. Atop the dais were two limestone lions passant, each with one paw raised as if ready to stride forth, and they bore the seat of Hittite power upon their backs. The sacred Grey Throne was deliberately plain: fashioned from cedar and cold-hammered rivets of iron – a stubborn, hoary metal that fell from the skies.

King Mursili sat upon the royal seat draped in a blue linen robe – the silver, winged sun circlet on his brow the only kingly trapping on his person. As a final, reverberating clash of the bronze gong chased the remaining whispers from the hall, he glanced at the polished bronze sceptre resting on the right arm of the throne. His reflection stared back at him: his eyes glazed and pouchy, his expression melancholic and his face wide and jowly. Even his once sleek, dark locks were now riddled with spidery white strands.

Life as *Labarna* had been hard, devouring his youth like a leech. An endless succession of rites and rituals in honour of the Gods had him trekking eternally across the Hittite heartlands to its holy cities. And when the Gods were appeased, war quickly filled the gaps. And through it all, one name had echoed eternally in his heart.

Sweet Gassula, he wept inwardly.

At first he had blamed the midwives, then he had exiled the augurs, and he had even raged at his late stepmother who had chosen the birthing staff. His anger had been like a ravening, insatiable predator, for a time. He realised his eyes had settled on one face in the crowd: the one he had chosen over his wife. Hattu, upon whom his grief had fastened, festered and grown into something misshapen and cruel. The boy's odd eyes were wide and fearful. He was barefoot and dressed in only a scuffed, threadbare kilt, his hair tousled – in stark contrast to his flanking brothers, the tall, princely Muwa and the lame but still-majestic Sarpa.

Ishtar, ever-present in his thoughts since that dark night, spoke from somewhere deep within: *It will begin on the day he stands by the banks of the Ambar, soaked in the blood of his brother.*

He barely noticed that silence had long taken over from the faded gong until something snagged his attentions: someone shuffling uncomfortably down on the bench to the right of the throne, like a cat pawing at its feeding bowl trying to attract the attention of its owner. It was his Great Scribe, Ruba, his owl-eyes fixed on the sceptre, his winged eyebrows rising in concern.

'My... My Sun,' Ruba said, his voice tremulous.

Zida, sitting on the bench beside Ruba, rolled his inky eyes, chuckling darkly with Kurunta and Nuwanza.

Ruba shot the military trio a sour look then turned back to the king: 'We should get things underway as soon as we can.'

'You wish to hold court in my place, Old Goose?' Mursili whispered back. He loved Ruba, but the old fellow was like a nagging concubine at times. Ruba dropped back to the bench and shook his head.

Lifting the sceptre in his own time, Mursili drew a long breath and swept his gaze around the room, meeting every eye. 'My loyal kings, your presence gladdens me,' he lied. 'Arinniti the Sun Goddess, and Halki, God of the Grain, have been kind, for our fields are thick with crop this year. Together, we trade our wares and make for a stronger world.'

He settled the sceptre across his knees, indicating that the tributes were to commence.

First came the King of Ugarit, a thriving market town – the trade hub of the world, some would say – perched on the coast of northern Retenu, not far from the Egyptian borders. This alliance was a vital one, ensuring the Hittite merchants who travelled there received good rates on the vital tin ingots, wine, oil, flax, timber and much more. The king's skin was dark as old leather, telling of his life under the unforgiving eastern sun and contrasting sharply with his white cap and cape. The crowd rose respectfully as he crossed the black flagstoned floor and climbed the stairs towards the throne, the echoes of his footsteps rising to the high ceiling like the flapping wings of scattered doves. Bowing at the neck, he offered Mursili an ostrich egg, silvered and dotted with jasper and beryl. 'My Sun, I bring you this treasure. And outside waits a wagon with five hundred golden shekels and two fine silver cups.' His words of tribute and a description of the gift were recorded by junior scribes – Ruba's underlings, their hands a blur as they tapped their reed styluses at woodpecker-like speed into their soft clay tablets.

'Most generous, Brother King,' Mursili replied. 'May the gods continue to bless Ugarit's fleet with good trade winds.'

The King of Ugarit bowed again as he left the plinth.

Next came the Lukkans from the fertile southwestern lowlands. Their yellow-cloaked chosen chieftain shuffled up the semi-circle of steps, his soft leather slippers squeaking and his feather headdress swaying and shuddering like the tail of an ungainly peacock. He held out a hunting bow – a fine piece made from ash and ibex horn, the handle dotted with pearl and the ears fashioned as serpents' heads. 'May this bow fell game for you with your every shot. Or,' he added with a toadying look, 'strike down the encroaching armies of your enemies.'

The oily words were intended to please, but Mursili felt angry, like one who has a stain on his gown pointed out to him before a group of friends. He fixed a false look of equanimity on his face and replied: 'No bow could strike my enemies and their forces: they cringe, far beyond my borders.' It was a lie, but a necessary one.

A series of vassal kings approached and the gifts stacked up. Next came the purple-cloaked Trojan King. Mursili's decorum wavered and it was all he could do to stop his face breaking into a rare smile.

'My Sun,' King Alaksandu said with regal poise. Then his resolve failed and he added with a whisper: '*comrade.*' A smile marched across his face – as bright as the gold and silver banded scale vest he wore. The King of Troy and ruler of the western vassal state of Wilusa was Mursili's age but far fresher-faced. He carried his helm – crested with a stiff, curled tail of leather like a coiled whip – underarm, wore his nut-brown locks combed back from his brow without a parting and his short beard was expertly groomed to fill out his handsome face. His green eyes shone like gems. 'It has been too long.'

'Aye,' Mursili replied, 'though longer for me than for you – I seem to have aged forty years since last we met and you are still but a young man.'

Alaksandu started to laugh, but stifled it when he sensed the many jealous eyes around the hall scrutinising the interaction.

'He brings no gift?' one gull-voiced member of the crowd called out.

Alaksandu's face hardened for just a moment. 'I, Alaksandu of Troy, Laomedon of Wilusa, would not dare enter My Sun's halls without bearing gift,' he addressed the crowd then turned back to the king. 'On Hattusa's southern approaches wait eighty sorrel-red stallions, broken and trained upon the plains of the Scamander. Forty chariots they will pull for you. Forty reasons for any who dare even *look* upon your borders to think again.'

Mursili allowed a smile to play on his lips as he dipped his head fractionally to show his gratitude, first to Alaksandu, then to the Trojan King's wife, Placia, who stood back down in the crowd with a contingent of Trojan guardsmen. The last time he had seen her she had been heavy with child. Now, she carried a babe in her arms.

Alaksandu spotted Mursili's interest. 'Just as I bear two names, we have given him two also: Podarces... and Priam. The augurs give us mixed messages,' he whispered. 'They trouble me with their words. But I have faith in the Gods: my boy will grow to be strong and wise, and he will preside over a glorious time for Troy and her allies.'

As Alaksandu spoke, Mursili noticed Hattu, just beyond the Trojan King's shoulder, shuffling where he stood.

The west will dim, with black boats' hulls,
Trojan heroes, mere carrion for gulls... Ishtar whispered.

Mursili smiled to mask his disquiet. 'Good fortune to you and your beloved, friend,' he said, 'always.'

'Always,' Alaksandu genuflected and turned to leave.

The next to ascend the throne dais was an odd one, his skin the shade of river clay. He was slender, shaven-headed, and sported a jutting, squared beard that hung to the copper pectoral necklace on his bare chest. His wore a pale linen kilt and a shawl covering his back and shoulders. The fellow's dark eyes held a hint of something parlous and untamed, there and not there at once – like the glimpse of a serpent swimming in a deep, black tarn.

Egyptian, Mursili realised, shooting a look to Ruba, whose face was creased in confusion as he scanned his clay tablet of attendees. Egypt was no part of the Hittite world. Indeed, the colossal empire at the southern edge of the world was just the opposite – probably the biggest rival of the Hittite realm alongside the avaricious Assyrian Empire.

'Great King Mursili, *Labarna,*' the fellow said. 'I am Sirtaya of Memphis, messenger of your Brother King, Pharaoh Horemheb, Lord of the Two Lands, Son of Ra, Horus of Gold.'

Mursili beheld him with a carefully blank expression. Rumour was strong that Pharaoh Horemheb spent his days revolutionising the mighty desert armies in preparation for war. More, in recent summers there had been raids on the southeastern vassal land of Amurru – one of the Hittite throne's most tenuous possessions. Brigands, most said, desert raiders and no more, others claimed. But why, then, had some of the captured raiders been in possession of Egyptian gold? Mursili's chest tightened. With every passing season the prospect of a Hittite-Egyptian war grew like a gathering black pall.

'My master offers you this... ' Sirtaya held out an elephant's tusk, finely polished. Mursili studied the piece, admiring its beauty but uncertain what the odd markings on it were supposed to be. He thought of the rare elephant herds roaming in the Hittite heartlands and felt a pang of sadness that such a creature had died to provide this oversized trinket. But, he thought as he turned an appraising eye on the Egyptian dignitary, did this gift offer hope? Might war be avoided?

'While I did not expect Pharaoh to be represented at this gathering, I appreciate his fine gift. And in excha-' he halted, now understanding the markings. They were a depiction of lands and rivers and great seas. Not just the Hittite realm, but all to the west, east and south as well. Egypt was marked out at the bottom of the etching, yet it had no borders. Where currently the Egyptian realm touched the Assyrian Empire and Hittite lands in the patchwork of vassal kingdoms known as Retenu, this chart showed no such boundaries, with all Assyrian and Hittite holdings contained inside the Egyptian domain... like conquered subjects.

'It is a map,' Sirtaya advised Mursili through a well-practiced smile.

Mursili's heart hardened, the glimmer of hope vanishing. He stared into the envoy's eyes for a time before speaking again. 'And what does my Brother King ask of me in return?'

Sirtaya's eyes narrowed. 'Pharaoh requests a small gift of iron... iron of heaven.'

Mursili might have laughed had the tension not been so high. His blacksmiths had strived fastidiously to craft the few divine meteorites that fell upon Hittite lands into daggers and axes. Seven such weapons were locked in the royal armoury – hard blades, harder than bronze, but they were brittle and useless as true weapons. Still, they were rare treasures, and he would be damned if he was going to gift one to his enemy.

'Do this, and he will send you,' Sirtaya continued, his veil of servility slipping, 'a vast shipment of tin. With it, you could make many jackets of bronze armour. A prudent investment... ' his eyes traced the taunting markings on the tusk-map '... in these *dangerous* times.'

Mursili's jaw worked at the twin meaning, anger broiling within him as Sirtaya's lips twitched in triumph. He leant forward briskly on the throne, primed to rise. He could set Zida, his two generals or any of the finely-armed guards loose upon this dog. He could hang the beggar from the city walls and let the crows peck at his eyes. But the thunder in his heart steadied, the gods guided him, and he knew what he had to do.

'Your master needn't have bothered sending me tusk-etchings,' the king said in a low, steady burr. 'I have scholars of my own who can draw our borders... with far greater accuracy. And extra weapons? I have no need for them. Have you seen my divisions in their pomp? They shine and clatter, heavy with sharpened bronze of their own.' He inhaled slowly through his nostrils and sat tall upon the throne. When he spoke next, each word was like the slow, deliberate strike of a smith's hammer: 'Pharaoh will have no iron.'

Sirtaya's face fell in disgust. 'You reject Pharaoh's request? Surely you know his wrath is legendary?'

Mursili let a weighty silence past. 'Oh yes, I know. And so too, I am led to believe, does the Hittite nobleman, Tetti.'

Sirtaya's head retracted at the apparent non-sequitur. 'What?'

'Tetti was a loyal and good-hearted member of my Panku. A friend, a comrade... and a damned fine envoy. Two years ago I despatched him to Memphis to speak with Pharaoh,' Mursili's eyes darkened under his dipping brow, 'yet he never returned. Some say he now languishes there in a cell, beaten, naked and forgotten.'

Sirtaya's lips receded over his gums in anger. 'Such words blacken my master's name. When Pharaoh hears of this affront, you know what will happen.'

Mursili, Great King of the Hittites, glowered at him. *War?* he mused. *War is an inevitability. It is only a question of when, as you have proved today. And when it comes, it will be the cruellest war ever waged, and the Gods will gather to watch.* He sucked in a deep breath, and boomed: 'Pharaoh *will* surely hear of this, but not from your poisoned lips. Just as Tetti never returned to me, neither will you return to Egypt.'

Sirtaya's face fell blank for an instant, then – at the slightest movement of Mursili's index finger – a pair of Mesedi lunged up the steps and seized the Egyptian by the shoulders. Gasps and whispers filled the hall.

'Take him to the Well of Silence,' Mursili boomed, standing. The grim underground gaol lying east of Hattusa would provide the brazen messenger with an eternity of darkness and quiet with which to reflect upon matters.

Sirtaya spat some jagged volley of oaths in his native tongue, struggling to free himself from the grasp of the Mesedi as they dragged him down the steps, until Zida rose from his place by the throne and strode over to whack him over the back of the head with a small cudgel. As the Egyptian's limp form was dragged from the hall through a small hatch-door, the whispers of the crowd exploded into a babble of shock and intrigue.

With a sharp clap of Mursili's hands, the din ceased.

'Loyal Kings, remain here with me,' he said, struggling to control the still-strong tremor of rage in his voice. 'The rest of you, I bid you outside to the feast.' He gestured towards the doorway, beyond which a skirl of pipes had struck up.

***

Hattu slunk quietly out of the hall amongst the masses – all gossiping avidly about what had just happened. Ranks of long, low, food-festooned feasting tables now lined the twilit ward. People took their places and the entertainment began: acrobats and dancers spilled across the centre of the feasting area, bearing torches, ropes and hoops. The pipers now belted out a fast, frantic tune as the acrobats took to leaping and twisting, setting light to the hoops and diving through them. Two dancers held a rope taut between them while a third edged along it on his toes.

As Hattu made his way around the spectacle, a painted man at one of the feasting tables stopped talking and stared at him as he chewed on a leg of goose, grease staining his chin and food-scum clinging to his teeth.

Would you dare glower at the Labarna or my brothers like that? Hattu thought to himself.

Another fellow took a long gulp of expensive Amurrite wine, eyeing Hattu over the rim of his cup, then whispered something to the painted one. Hattu read his lips over the skirling pipes.

The Cursed Son, the man said, but in Sumerian, an ancient language. The painted one nodded in agreement, then scraped up a handful of honeyed nuts and shovelled them into his meat-stained maw, crunching into them with a dismissive laugh.

The pair probably expected that Hattu, a prince, knew nothing of the tongue. It was, after all, the job of a scribe to understand and translate the many languages of the world for their kings and people. For the first time in a while, Hattu silently thanked the Gods – and Ruba – for his confinement to the Scribal School.

'You eat like pigs, and smell like them too,' he whispered in Sumerian as he passed the pair.

The two gawped, faces blanching further under all the paint. A brief glow of pride burnt off Hattu's anger.

An arm wrapped over his shoulders. 'Ah, Brother, there you are. Come, let us sit,' Muwa said, guiding him through the chattering throngs and clacking cups towards a table. Hattu looked up, seeing the empty benches there. 'Why there?' he started, then saw exactly why: on the opposite side sat the young Priestess of Poverty, Atiya.

She toyed nervously with the braided tail of black hair that hung from her scarlet headscarf and sat across the breast of her pleated temple robes. The amber hoops she wore in her ears shook gently as she shot timid, dimpled smiles around the crowd, and the copper moon amulet on her chest sparkled in the torchlight. She was closer to Muwa's age than his, but it never felt that way. There was something about Atiya that instantly lifted his heart. Perhaps it was her sepia skin, or maybe her eyes: full, sable pools. Atiya's parents had been killed by the Kaskans years before, and he had always felt a need to protect her.

As they approached the table, Hattu felt himself shrink in his step, suddenly self-conscious. Why on earth had he not first returned to his chamber in the palace to find a pair of boots or a clean tunic? His bare, grazed and grubby chest and arms looked even scrawnier when set against the many older boys and men suited in ceremonial armour.

Atiya hadn't noticed them approaching yet, so he tried to mimic Muwa's tall, confident stride, pushing his shoulders back and tilting his head up a little to give him a fraction more height, throwing his legs out with each stride purposefully. She noticed them then, eyes widening in delight.

'Muwa!' she said, standing. 'And, er…' her beaming smile grew lop-sided and she tilted her head, 'Hattu? Why are you strutting like a deranged peacock?'

Muwa burst into laughter and Hattu's face creased in anger. Few spoke to the two princes with such candour. 'I, no, *he*,' he pointed to Muwa as if to blame him but his words died in a tangled stutter. Atiya stretched over the table to accept Muwa's embrace and the delicate kiss he placed on the back of her hand. Hattu felt a fiery spike of injustice at this and at the coquettish look she gave his older brother. He stretched out to embrace her too, but found he was a little too short to reach, and had to make do with the motherly kiss she planted on his head instead – the kind offered to a child who has just settled down after a tantrum. *But damn,* he thought, slumping onto the bench, *is this the Gathering or the Humiliation of Hattu?*

A panicked shriek sounded from the acrobat display: one of the fire dancers was rolling on the ground, his kilt ablaze. The crowd offered the fellow sympathetic laughter, one man deigning to toss his cup of wine over the thrashing wretch, who then suffered the ignominy of staggering away, kilt reduced to ashes, exposed buttocks burnt angry red. *Aye, well, it could be worse,* Hattu grinned.

Next, a troop of bulging wrestlers came on, dressed in just loincloths. They coated their skin in oil, tied their hair up in tight knots and proceeded to twist seven spadefuls of agony out of one another with a series of grunts, cracks and pops of bone and cartilage. Hattu turned away and gazed over the fare on offer: sweet loaves, slabs of pure white goat's cheese peppered with chopped coriander, joints of goose and venison, figs, ruby-red pomegranates, chunks of honey in the comb and rows of foaming beer cups and huge urns of wine. Hunger swept away his annoyance. He reached over to take a sweet loaf – still warm – pouring a little oil on it then breaking it in two and biting off a chunk. Syrupy, soft and fragrant, it instantly reinvigorated him.

He wondered what he could talk to Atiya about. She was already in conversation with Muwa, intrigued by his recent trips to the southern cities. He spotted some hen's eggs on the table, and this suddenly reminded him of his efforts that afternoon. He rummaged in his bag and presented the falcon egg across the table like a prize. But Atiya was oblivious, for Muwa had offered her something first.

'For you,' Muwa said, pressing a white linen purse into her hand. She pulled the cord and out fell a small silver brooch in the shape of a lion's head, its eyes picked out with twilight-blue lapis stones. The Elder Priestess and a few others nearby cooed in wonder.

'I cannot accept this,' Atiya gasped.

'You cannot refuse,' Muwa replied instantly, closing her hand over the piece. 'It was crafted in faraway Troy, by the hand of King Alaksandu's finest silversmith – more delicate than anything the artisans of Hattusa might sweat, solder or hammer. I had it commissioned whilst in Troy last year, during the last months of the Arzawan War. King Alaksandu brought the finished piece with him today.'

'Muwa, you make me burn with embarrassment: I am not worth such a treasure.'

Muwa grinned, cocking his head slightly until she smiled. 'Oh it was worth it – if only to see you smile.' Atiya clasped the brooch to the breast of her robe, looking around timidly as if expecting someone to scoff at her.

Muwa began to recount some other memories of his time fighting in the west. 'The Arzawan War was gruelling,' he mused with the poise of a seasoned warrior, swishing his wine cup and gazing into the distance as he described the battles and the distant lands. Atiya seemed lost in his words.

Hattu found himself drawn into Muwa's tale also. Talk suggested the Chosen Prince would soon lead a division in his own right – as a general like Kurunta or Nuwanza. This was Hattu's twelfth summer, and Father seemed loath to be in his presence, let alone discuss his future.

Muwa flicked his head to one side and clicked his tongue as he concluded his recollections. 'Aye, it was a hard-won war. But the Arzawan League is gone.'

'Thanks mainly to you,' Atiya said. Her fawning words were belied by the playful glint in her eyes and the way her ruby tongue played with a small gap in her pearl-white teeth.

Muwa reddened ever-so-slightly 'Well, I don't mean... I... I,'

Atiya looked at Hattu now, winking to share her mischief. Hattu's heart soared at the momentary attention. Then she noticed the falcon egg.

'My goodness, what a comely shell,' she cooed.

'It is for you,' he said, sounding unflustered in comparison to Muwa.

'He found it out in the woods – when he should have been at the Scribal School,' Muwa clarified, reaching to ruffle his younger brother's hair, but Hattu ducked out of the way, stretching over to place the egg in Atiya's hands.

'It will not hatch,' he said, noticing how warily she held it. 'I found it whilst climbing,' he started, then raised his voice a little, casting Muwa a sideways glance, 'at the top of a ridge. A *high* ridge.'

'Hattu? You must be careful,' she shot him a reproachful look. 'Men have fallen to their deaths from those heights.'

'It was worth it to see you smile,' he said, hoping Atiya wouldn't spot the obvious imitation of his brother's line.

Atiya laughed, but shuffled awkwardly. 'Muwa, Hattu… I…'

Sarpa hobbled up behind them, resting his crutch against the bench and scooping his hands over his brothers' shoulders. 'Brothers, what Atiya is trying to say is she thinks you are but a pair of goats.'

Hattu chuckled and Muwa shot him a quizzical look: 'Goats? Funny you should choose to liken us to goats,' Muwa said. 'Did you ever tell Atiya about the time when you were a boy and you tried to ride on a goat's back?'

'No,' Sarpa said, straightening up and plucking a cherry from the table before hobbling away promptly.

'The goat threw him,' Muwa smirked, raising his voice so Sarpa would be sure to hear, 'tossed him into a trough of dung.'

Atiya laughed then eyed both. 'But Sarpa is right. Stop bringing me things. I need nothing. If you have to bring gifts, then bring them as offerings to the temple grounds – the Gods are more befitting of them than I.'

'In the eyes of some, perhaps,' Muwa said, rising and taking Atiya's hand to kiss it once more. 'Now, I must leave you – Father asked me to eat swiftly then rejoin his talks.'

Hattu watched as his brother returned to the Hall of the Sun. For the brief moment the tall doors were opened, he heard raised voices within, the conversation sharp and salty. When the doors banged shut, Hattu felt a great sadness.

'And how is Arrow?' Atiya said, mercifully drawing his attentions back to her. She could read him like a clay tablet, Hattu realised.

He looked over to the royal palace at the north end of the acropolis – where Arrow had made a nest on the sill of his upper floor bedchamber. Old Ruba's beloved pony, Onyx, was tethered underneath, and seemed to be engaged in some conversation with Arrow, he nickering, she screeching. 'Ah... no doubt hungry,' he confessed. 'I will be back shortly,' he said, gathering up some strands of meat and rising, warmed again by her smile.

He traipsed on towards the palace. It was largely dark and silent, but something caught his eye: the high balcony at the southwestern corner of the royal dwelling. He had never been on it or in the dark adjoining room. The Black Room, as it was known, was always locked. Father never allowed anyone to enter that chamber. He had even beaten Hattu for approaching it. He gazed up at the balcony sadly. Then he was overcome with a chill: for up there he saw some dark, rippling shape – writhing like a living shadow, floating. The movement faded, then all was still again. He had seen the likes a few times before.

Just what was up there? He had asked Ruba once, and the old tutor had replied:

The king's demons live in that high room.

With a shiver and a nervous gulp, he eyed the palace wall, contemplating a climb up there to see these demons for himself. But the plasterwork was recent and utterly smooth. Even the best climber would be confounded. When he had pressed Ruba again on what was up there, the old tutor had replied: *You will have to ask your father, lad.*

But how could he ask his father about the Black Room, about *anything*, when the king despised him so, left him out of everything? Overcome with angry defiance, he swung round to glower at the Hall of the Sun with a sour eye, thinking of Father, Muwa and the many kings within. The doors were locked, two Golden Spearmen standing vigil before them. His eyes drifted to the corner of that building: unlike the palace, there were creases in the stonework foundations and full wrinkles in the mud brick section higher up, leading to one of the high-up, arched windows that lit the hall. This, he *could* climb.

If Father won't invite me to the talks... he mused with a recalcitrant half-smile.

It was as if a spell was upon him. He scuttled over, hugging the shadows until he reached the foot of the throneroom walls, then up he went. A moment later he was halfway up, the climb easy and the holds regularly-spaced. He began traversing sideways, over the grand doorway and the heads of the oblivious Golden Spearmen then up towards one high window.

He clambered onto the dusty, broad stone sill, settling there, peering down into the Hall of the Sun like a crow. Muwa and twenty-three uniquely-dressed monarchs and lords were gathered around the foot of the throne in an arc, facing the throne dais. Two Mesedi and Zida stood before the platform like a screen. General Nuwanza, the coal-haired colossus, stood at the side of the hall with a trio of sentries. But where was the demon, Kurunta One-eye? Hattu wondered.

He leaned ever closer, searching the hall for the missing general, when a shard of loose stone scraped under his foot and a tiny puff of grit and dust spat out from the sill, toppling down into the throneroom. Instantly, the eyes of the Mesedi, Nuwanza, Zida and the king shot up like flaming arrows, about to be loosed. He ducked down and lay still with fright.

***

Mursili saw nothing but starlit darkness up there. Zida gave him a shrug, but kept his tapered eyes on the window for a moment longer. The king returned to his thoughts, rubbing his temples, still trying to put shape to what had occurred with the Egyptian 'diplomat'.

'The Egyptian borders must be reinforced,' Prince Muwa repeated urgently.

Mursili half-nodded. With the crowds gone, it was a time for stark truths. His thoughts shifted to the other great threat in those lands. 'And what of our frontier with the Assyrian Empire?' he muttered, glancing down at a young Hittite nobleman who had travelled from the southeast.

'The fortress of Gargamis watches over the River Mala ford like a stone giant. Viceroy Shahuru's garrison is small but skilled, and he sends his thanks to you for your gift of chariots,' he replied. 'But the Assyrians… they, like the Egyptians, are not for accepting our presence there.'

He scanned the arc of men and found those he was looking for: the allied kings of Ugarit, Nuhashi, Amurru and Kadesh – each vassal commanding a small army and a small buffer territory in northern Retenu, each a vital protector of the precious tin route. He recalled and cringed at his hubris-fuelled words to the Egyptian earlier on.

And extra weapons? I have no need for them. Have you seen my divisions in their pomp? They shine and clatter, heavy with sharpened bronze of their own.

The truth was far bleaker: tin reserves were scarce, perilously so.

'I count upon you, loyal kings, to be my eyes in the east, to keep the tin trade route open, lest my bronzesmiths' forges grow dim and cool.'

Zida seemed a little perturbed by his stark words in front of these unreliable kings. 'Our mine at Kestel, just a half moon's ride to the south, still holds some tin, My Sun. We are not *entirely* dependent on the trade routes through Retenu.'

Mursili gave his Gal Mesedi a dry half-grin. *The last attainable seams at Kestel were mined generations ago. Remember what happened when my father tried to dig further, to the deepest seams?* Regardless, he let Zida's tactical fiction resonate. 'Perhaps. But in any case, the southern edge of that land must be watched carefully. Should the Egyptian Pharaoh prove as brave with his actions as he is with his words and clumsy theatre, then I must know as soon as possible.'

The leathery-skinned King of Ugarit answered first. 'It will be done, My Sun.'

Mursili made a faint noise of agreement, then his thoughts swung from east to west. 'And what of Western Anatolia?' he asked King Alaksandu.

Alaksandu stood tall, clearing his throat. 'Unrest prevails, My Sun. Ahhiyawan brigands roam the Seha River Lands, encroaching on

Wilusan territory as if there is no code of law.'

Mursili felt the rising heat of agitation. The myriad city states across the Western Sea – Mycenae, Pylos, Thebes, Sparta, Tiryns, Ithaca, Argos and many more, dotted across the rocky, broken and strange peninsula known as Ahhiyawa – had formed some sort of warlike coalition.

The feather-crowned Lukkan Chieftain stepped forth, eager to air his view: 'They use the coastal city of Milawata as a bridgehead. They dream of taking all Anatolia, My Sun.'

'As long as Troy stands in their way,' Alaksandu thundered, 'the states of Ahhiyawa will never truly call Anatolian soil their own.'

'You underestimate the Ahhiyawans,' the Lukkan Chieftain replied curtly. 'They make alliances with strange sea warriors from the distant, dark western islands.'

Alaksandu's nose wrinkled. 'Still, they will never best my navy.'

'Enough,' Mursili said, a little more tersely than intended. 'I understand. The south and east suffer the covetous eyes of the King of Assyria and the Egyptian Pharaoh. The west is ripe for another rebellion – invasion, even.' He sighed through his nose.

'Now, of the north… ' he directed this question to a small, mop-haired, bearded and pig-eyed man who hadn't spoken yet. This was Darizu – the *Bel Madgalti,* Lord of the Northern Watchtowers. He wore a knee-length Hittite robe and nobleman's jewels in his ears, yet he was not a Hittite but a Galasman – a small but pithy tribe who helped man the northern frontier and work the precious lead mines of those lands. While his father had been a stout master of those borders, Darizu was as yet unproven. 'Pitagga and the Kaskans are quiet at least?'

The truth was those twelve mountain tribes were like a spear lodged in the northern flank of the Hittite realm. For generations they had called the Lost North their own – the once-great Hittite cities of Hakmis, Zalpa and Nerik had for too long lain in tumbled ruination, their Gods disgraced, Kaskan mud-dome shanty towns erected amongst the fallen stones, their swines foraging amongst the tall grass that sprouted through the toppled temples. Too numerous to conquer, too devious to outmanoeuvre, the best a succession of Hittite Kings could hope for was to contain the Kaskan threat.

Darizu's nervous pause was enough to send Mursili's heart plummeting. 'Bel Madgalti,' Mursili reiterated, 'of the north?'

Darizu gulped. 'Pitagga rises against you, My Sun. I tried to tell you before the Gathering beg-'

'Tell me *now*,' Mursili demanded.

Darizu licked his dry lips. 'He struck the northern towers in the first days of spring. A stretch of the beacons and turrets have been toppled. I only knew of the breach when I smelt the smoke one morning. I watched them herding masses of Hittite families, captured soldiers and droves of oxen and sheep back north, towards the pastures of Wahina.'

'You *watched* them?' Mursili said softly. 'From where?'

'From the fort-city of Tapikka. From m-my balcony,' Darizu stammered.

'The polished stone balcony designed by my chief architect?' Mursili mused. 'High above and safely within Tapikka's stout walls?'

The Galasman's face drained of colour, leaving just a red glow of embarrassment around his cheeks.

'What of the garrison I provided you? Three hundred men and twenty chariots I stationed in Tapikka,' Mursili said. 'Enough to ward off a few Kaskan raiding parties, surely?'

'This was not just a few raiding parties, My Sun. They moved like an army, they-'

Mursili glared at him, pressing for an answer to his original question.

'I despatched the garrison in pursuit of the Kaskan forces,' Darizu said meekly. 'They... they were slaughtered. All of them.'

'Yet you survived?' Mursili observed dryly. 'Oh, I see: you despatched your forces but remained on your balcony to *watch* and see how they would fare. Brave,' he said, curling his lower lip and nodding fiercely, 'noble. Your father would have been proud.'

'I have failed you, My Sun,' Darizu bowed and dropped to one knee.

The northern towers were breached. Men and beasts had been stripped from Hittite lands. Mursili almost felt the rupture in the vital defences like a gash in his own shoulder. Left to fester, infection would set in and soon spread. The Kaskans would return, probing further south. The heartland cities and their surrounding and precious crop meadows would suffer destruction and plunder. More men and herds would be lost. Famine and unrest would soon threaten.

Trouble burgeoned in every direction, it seemed. The Hittite Army – twenty thousand strong and the dread of the battlefield when mustered in its entirety – could only be in one place at any time. That it consisted of four divisions was a playful bait, a tidy solution for a mind untrained in military matters, for to send a single division of his forces to each beset border would be akin to answering the wrathful roar of each enemy army with a yelp. No, the divisions of the Hittite army had to move as one and conquer, united. Perhaps one division could be left behind to protect Hattusa, but what destination for the other three?

To send the army west to crush the fresh troubles in those recently-pacified lands, or to lead them southeast to ward off the bold Pharaoh, or east, to keep the Assyrians in check. *No, only a fool would fight faraway demons when one hovers behind his back,* he mused saltily. The Kaskans were the most immediate of the great threats: with Pitagga and the mountain men perched like black crows just north of the Hittite realm, there was no luxury of choice.

He rose from his throne. 'Before the summer is past, the pastures of Wahina will quake under our boots. Our captured people will be liberated and returned to their homes. Pitagga and his Kaskans will be crushed: the Lord of the Mountains will become the Lord of Ashes and Bone.' He looked down at the kneeling Darizu. 'And when we march, brave watcher from the balcony, you will march at our head.'

***

Hattu, watching the discussion like a wary cat, hung on his father's words just like the foreign kings. The *Labarna* possessed an aura, a commanding backbone to his every word that made the room his own. To maintain such a presence in the face of so many doubtless shrewd individuals, Hattu thought, was surely the quality of a true king. He envied early signs of those same virtues in Muwa, and bemoaned the lack of them in his own nature.

But the moment of awe passed. He saw now what would happen in the coming days: Father, Muwa and the high generals would once again lead the divisions to war, a bronze beast that would crush the Kaskans and free the captive Hittites... and he saw his own future, in the quiet rooms of the Scribal School. He sighed and turned away from the hall to face the night and the acropolis ward – now rippling with increasingly drunken forms, the tables scattered with bones and crusts of bread.

He backed one leg down from the sill, stretching to find the thin gap between the stonework below, then worked his way down – silent and unseen just as he had ascended, halting only to shoot a triumphant look at the two Golden Spearmen at the throneroom doors, oblivious.

'Curse them and the rest of the army – *hurkelers*, one and all,' he muttered. A hurkeler – one who engages in sexual congress with an animal – was the favourite curse word of the soldiers. At least, it was the one Hattu always heard the acropolis guards muttering under their breath when they were ordered to do some tedious or unwanted task. 'Aye, hurkelers!' he enthused.

A sense of smugness was just building, when something clamped around his shin and shook him like an earth tremor. He gasped and scrabbled to keep hold of the stonework, only to be torn from it. He fell his own height and crashed onto the red flagstones of the courtyard, winded and startled.

Glowering down at him was a bald, one-eyed nightmare incarnate, scowling, inhuman, his single silver braid hanging like a whip.

'Kurunta?' he gasped in a whisper, shaking free of the man's grasp.

'We're all hurkelers, you say?'

'I, I -'

'You, you?' Kurunta mocked, his top lip twitching in disgust.

'I didn't mean to cause any trouble,' Hattu stammered.

'Then you should have done as your father bid you and stayed at the feasting tables. You were not invited to the talks, *boy*.'

Hattu wilted under the general's gaze and blunt accent which contrasted sharply against the more polished tones from the throneroom.

'You hate it when they call you that name, don't you?' Kurunta spat, eyeing him with a scowl that showed every fine line on his face. '*The Cursed Son.*'

Hattu felt the words like a stinging lash. He stood up and shot Kurunta what he hoped was a fierce look.

'If you hate it so much then why do you persist in feats of idiocy like this?' he gestured sharply up and down the outer corner of the throneroom walls. 'Your father wants you to have no part in the affairs of the military, don't you understand that? For your own good, *boy*, stay in the Scribal School with that wittering old goose, Ruba.'

Kurunta took a step towards him, radiating threat. Hattu took one step backwards, panicked.

Kurunta stamped a foot, flicked his head towards the palace, and issued a *tssss!* as if chasing away an irritating cat. Hattu turned and ran, stifling hot tears of shame.

CHAPTER 3

LAND OF WRAITHS
AUTUMN 1303 BC

King Mursili's heart thundered in anticipation of battle, his bronze scales clinking as he ran, his eyes fixed on the point where the grassy brow of the hill met the cloud-streaked Wahina sky, his mind conjuring the image of the Kaskan force on the other side. The telltale glow of a fire had been sighted here during the night and they had moved to close upon it even before dawn. It had been an arduous campaign, but Pitagga had been cornered, at last. His warriors would be smashed and the Hittite people he held captive would be liberated.

Beside him, the eager Zida and the trembling Darizu of Galasma stumbled along. Behind him came the Wrath Division. Up, up they went with the dull clatter of spears rattling into place beside shields, the clicking of arrows being nocked to bows…

Mursili crested the banking first, his tall bronze battle helm catching the sunlight, spear in one hand and his battle blade in the other. He leapt over the brow, his long, grey cloak trailing in his wake. 'May the Gods rush before us!' he cried. The wall of spearmen erupted in an echoing cry and the skirling battle pipes exploded in a buzzing song of battle… only for the world to fall silent again.

The cries faded, the rumble of boots died to nothing, the pipes sagged and fell quiet. Mursili gazed across the barren field before him. Not a soul to be seen. Just the charred remnant of a colossal campfire. A tremulous whimper of relief escaped Darizu's lips. Mursili shot him a winter-cold look.

Then, across the plain, a similar embryonic war cry rose from the woods there. The ranks of the Wrath Division bristled, Darizu wailed... then many sighs and curses escaped as the Fury Division burst from the trees and slowed, equally bemused. Prince Muwa, leading them, gazed at the smouldering bonfire and then across at his father.

A third shrieking song of war erupted and was swiftly cut short as the Blaze Division arrived on the western edge of the plain. General Nuwanza, the strapping Master Archer and leader of the Blaze, cast his gaze across the empty plain. He shot Mursili an exasperated and mildly reproachful look and held out his palms to either side.

'Aye, bowman, you were right, we should have waited for our scouts to report back first,' he muttered. A black plume of smoke and a trail of bootprints had lured them here. Their haste had been foolish, in hindsight.

'Where are they?' Zida grunted, hurling his spear into the soft earth where it quivered, his red cloak swirling around him in the breeze. 'What are we hunting: men... or wraiths?'

Mursili eyed the hoof and boot prints in the worn grass. A host of some sort had been through here recently. But who, and how large, and where were they now? His eyes narrowed and he combed the horizon, suddenly feeling not like the lord of an avenging army, but like a rabbit in the sights of an archer.

'My Sun,' Zida said, his voice low.

Mursili turned to see his Gal Mesedi lifting something from the ashes of the fire on the end of his spear. A string of blackened beads and a charred skull, brutally halved. The beads were Hittite. The skull had been split by a Kaskan axe. A chasm of an eye-socket stared at him and the teeth grinned horrifically. Some of the captured Hittites had found liberation of another kind.

***

As night fell, Zida and the Mesedi set about erecting the royal pavilion while the army marked out the camp and set up their bivouac tents. King

Mursili sat before a fire stocked with birch wood, his retinue alongside him. He looked into the embers and could not help but think of the grim find from earlier that day. His advisors had counted the remains of eighty charred bodies. A fraction of the people captured from Hittite lands. Where were the rest? Where was Pitagga? Somewhere deep inside his mind, he heard the Kaskan Lord laugh long and loud.

'That is three false hopes dashed to pieces,' Nuwanza reasoned, chewing on a chunk of charred river bream on the end of a stick. 'They were at the lakeside village, apparently, until we got there and found nothing but abandoned huts and a lone captive, hanging by his neck from the mast of a fishing boat. They were camped by the woods, until we arrived and found only another captive staked through from groin to mouth and shorn of his tongue and guts. Then today, we risked disaster on the premise of a glow of fire in the night.'

'Yet we have nothing else to go on,' Prince Muwa mused.

'Then we should return to the heartlands, to Hattusa,' Nuwanza replied. 'Winter is but a single moon away and the passes will soon be blocked with snow. It would be folly to maroon ourselves in these parts until spring.'

A regimental chief from the Wrath Division interrupted upon hearing this: 'And it would be dangerous to leave Hattusa in the hands of Kurunta One-eye for too long, My Sun.'

Mursili looked up and shot the man a long, silent glare that almost knocked the officer to his knees. Awkwardly, the man took his leave with some muffled excuse and a curt bow. Mursili gazed into the flames, the man's meaning irking him.

Kurunta's Storm Division – devoted to the almighty Tarhunda – had been left in Hattusa to guard the capital and its approaches. A fool's choice, he had heard people whispering, for just one of the Storm's five, thousand-strong regiments was mobilised – the men of the other four deemed too vital to be taken away from the otherwise under-tended crop fields or from garrison duties in the other major heartland cities. Imprudent also, some had suggested, to leave the 'vengeful general' in charge of the capital. From the depths of his mind and despite his will to keep the memory supressed, he recalled the sucking, squelching sounds of Kurunta's eye being scooped out, the animal grunts of the men pinning him to the ground and performing the punishment and the utter silence of Kurunta himself. He closed his eyes, shaking the memory away.

'I cannot leave until I have found my people,' Mursili concluded. 'It would be victory for Pitagga were we to return to Hattusa without having given him battle or liberated those he shackled and led from our lands.'

Darizu the Galasman, sitting opposite the king, hung his head in shame.

'Perhaps that's the way he wants you to think?' Nuwanza reasoned, his eyes locked onto the fire, then switching suddenly to Mursili. 'You have sensed it too, My Sun, I know you have: a feeling of being toyed with. Last night when we slept at the camp on the high plain, I lay awake and watched as a feral cat bounded back and forth with a mouse in its mouth. The mouse was fine, alive and all, but I could see in the tiny creature's black eyes that it knew that things were far from good. It is time to take the army home, My Sun.'

Mursili sighed. He had ignored Nuwanza's words too often recently, and every time, the shrewd general had been proven right. It was in an archer's nature, he realised, to wait, to measure, and never to shoot without absolute certainty of a clean strike. 'Home, you say?' he said, breaking off a chunk of offered bread and chewing on it absently.

'We have triumphed in part,' Zida added, stopping in his efforts to raise the tent. 'We can detach a thousand men, perhaps, to rebuild the broken watchtowers here, further north than before, to reclaim Wahina as our own.'

'Let us take the soil of Wahina as a blessing from the Gods, and look to next year,' Muwa agreed. 'The men are growing weary of this campaign, Father.'

Mursili looked around him, seeing that the ranks were not busy wrestling, drinking and bantering as usual. Many sat in silence, way worn and no doubt thinking of their loved ones. The balance of the argument was tilting, until he noticed a commotion near one end of the camp. A clutch of spearmen wrested a trio of men in from the darkness of night. Zida laid down his hammer and pegs, letting the part-erected pavilion slouch, taking up his spear instead. 'What's this?' he said keenly.

Mursili rose, Nuwanza and Muwa doing likewise. The king peered at the apparitions being brought to him. Three men with the heads of bulls, it seemed. An army of chill-footed ants raced across Mursili's skin.

'What the?' Prince Muwa gasped.

But as they drew closer, the firelight showed them as no monsters: they were men – warriors – but in the oddest garb. To each of their helms were affixed two horns. The middle one of the three reeked of charisma, and was clearly their leader. His eyes were pale blue, his skin fair and his narrow nose and lips were almost sculpted. His hair was thick and flaxen like the noonday sun, tumbling from the back of that remarkable helm. He wore a green-painted, armless scale corselet with a wide gold band clinging to his right bicep, and plate-sized copper rings dangled from his ears. He carried a fierce-looking trident – which Zida swiftly denuded him of as he was brought before Mursili.

'My Sun,' a Mesedi said. 'The scouts found these three on the nearby hills. They were staked out by an ants' nest.'

The crawling death, Mursili thought, *one of the Kaskans' favoured ways of despatching their enemies.*

A momentary silence gripped the crowds who had gathered round.

'This one asked for an audience with you,' the Mesedi escorting them added, nodding to the central stranger.

The leader of the odd trio's eyes widened as he beheld Mursili. 'Lo-ord of Hit-tite?' he said in a jagged accent. Clearly the Hittite tongue was not his native language.

Mursili appraised the fellow for some clue of his origins, while Zida hissed in the newcomer's ear. '*Labarna,* Great King of all you see around you. Now bow before him. You will address him as My Sun.'

The stranger obediently sank to one knee, dipping his head. 'My Sun,' he said, 'I am Volca, from the Isl-and of the Sher-den.'

Mursili's eyes narrowed.

Nuwanza leaned in close to whisper: 'The Sherden. A tribe from far, far to the west. Beyond Troy, beyond even the dark islands of Ahhiyawa. I have only heard traders and adventurers speak of them before.'

Volca looked up at Nuwanza now. 'This true. We only passed the Ahhiyawan coastlands near end of journey to get here.' The throaty hiss and the way he pronounced *Ah-hee-yaaa-wan* lent a mystical air to his words and seemed to chill the night just a fraction. 'My men and I travel long, long way to come to My Sun. Sailed towards the dawn for many moons,' he swept a hand across the sky as if outlining their voyage.

'A mercenary? Did King Alaksandu not warn us of his like?' Muwa whispered. *'The sea warriors from the faraway western islands.'*

The slightest twinge on Volca's lips suggested he had heard – and understood – this. 'Some of Sherden are pirates, this true,' he agreed, the copper rings in his ears jangling as he spoke. 'But I am not. I carry trident, not cutthroat dagger. Indeed, I loathe sight of blood,' he grinned, his teeth shining like the gold band on his arm, 'particularly my own.'

'What do you ask of me?' Mursili said.

'Bread, broth and the chance to serve a good king. Nothing more.' He held out a hand either side to his two companions. 'I bring you no treasure or army, but I hope to offer you knowledge and advice.'

Zida laughed a single barking laugh. 'What can you tell the Great King of the Hittites about his own realm?'

Volca shrugged. 'I know where Kaskan army is. They were ones who tied me and my men to ants' nest.'

Silence. A thousand captive breaths.

'My Sun, now is not the time to change your thinking.' Nuwanza started. 'You were on the verge of ordering the march ho-'

Mursili held up a hand, cutting him off, then crouched to be level with the kneeling Volca. 'Tell me… '

CHAPTER 4

FROM THE SOARING MOUNTAINS
AUTUMN 1303 BC

Hattu took Atiya's hand as they edged sideways along the narrow shelf of rock, halfway up a silvery crescent of bluffs, a few *danna* north of Hattusa. He glanced up, seeing on the cliff wall a giant and bold etching of the *Haga*, a mighty, two-headed eagle – a stamp of Hittite power, a symbol of heroes. The sight sent a frisson of excitement through him: they were nearly there. His climbs and ventures like this had been a much-needed contrast to what had been a quiet spring, summer and autumn in the Scribal School, like gold thread in a dull grey garment.

The fresh morning wind cast up a playful russet storm of leaves from the ground – the height of four men below, causing Atiya to whimper.

'Don't look down,' he whispered, squeezing her hand. 'Look at me.'

She gulped and smiled, her free hand switching from the rocky wall at their backs to her red headscarf, which the wind threatened to steal away. 'You promised me wonderful things, Hattu.' She said with a tremor in her voice. 'This… isn't quite what I expected.'

'This isn't what I meant. You'll see, soon. I promise,' he smiled.

Within a few steps, the ledge widened and there was a small gap in the cliff wall at their backs – as if a giant stonemason had chiselled into the stony redoubt. Atiya gasped, turning, peering through the gap. 'What is it?' she whispered.

'It is invisible to the eye from the ground. I only found it when I last came out to climb,' Hattu winked, then took her hand and edged through the gap, leading her with him. The tight gap became a narrow corridor, through which their every footstep echoed. The corridor widened and then yawned open to reveal a round, green, stone-walled hollow – like a giant washing bowl, sheltered from the autumn winds high above but open to the sun's heat.

Dust motes floated languorously in the air as he led her across the soft, lush grass on the hollow floor. He let Atiya's hand slip from his and watched as she walked almost on her toes, turning, eyes drinking in the scene: at the far end of the hollow, a tall, terraced waterfall fell in sleek, glossy sheets over smooth stone into a cerulean tarn. A fine mist rose from the fall, iridescent haloes of sunlight growing and changing in the air before them. Dragonflies hovered just above the water's surface, capriciously darting from one spot to another. The pebble-smooth banks of the tarn shimmered in the sunlight, and where it was wet, patches of glistening lichen had grown in delicate shades of sorrel and cream. Cherry trees and honey-scented broom lined the edges of the water. But the real wonder lay up above.

'Look,' he said.

She tilted her head back and looked up with him. Hawks, falcons and eagles banked and soared in the zephyrs, plunging down into the hollow then swinging up again.

'Wondrous, isn't it?' Hattu grinned.

'I dream of such places,' Atiya whispered. 'So... beautiful.'

'Aye, it is,' Hattu agreed, his eyes on Atiya.

With a flutter of wings, Arrow swept into the hollow and came to a rest on Hattu's bracer, then looked up at the heavenly dance.

'Are the big birds putting you to shame?' Atiya teased Arrow.

Arrow extended and shook her wings in impotent fury.

'She can swoop and dart with the best of them,' Hattu laughed, linking arms with Atiya and coaxing Arrow onto her wrist. 'When she was a nestling, I taught her to hunt,' he said, unravelling a long ribbon of light-coloured linen and tying one end around a fat earthworm. Holding the other end, he ran until the linen billowed up into the air behind him.

Arrow's head dipped, her eyes locked onto the prize on the ribbon's end. She shot off to catch it, only for Hattu to sweep his hand sharply, bringing the floating ribbon round and away, the worm safe. Arrow keened in disgust, but did not give up the chase. Round and round they went before the falcon got her prize. Next, Atiya took a turn. Hattu stood behind her, guiding her arms to hold the ribbon correctly, then running with her. 'Now, flick your hand up and…yes!' Atiya squealed with delight as the ribbon fluttered and leapt up into the air. She spun and ran, leading Arrow in a merry dance.

At noon, they sat on a carpet of soft moss. Hattu lit a small fire to cook a rabbit and they ate it with flatbread and drank berry juice, watching the concert in the sky. Arrow joined the winged masses above and they talked – of simple things, of silly stories from past play, of dreams for the future. She told him how the Elder Priestess at the Storm Temple had hinted that she might one day be appointed the keeper of the holy silver effigy of Tarhunda. He recited for her part of the Epic of Gilgamesh. When at last they fell silent, Hattu gazed wistfully northeast. Atiya once again read him like a tablet.

'The king and Muwa will return from Wahina unharmed, I am sure of it,' she said.

Hattu felt ashamed for a moment. In truth he had been thinking not only of their welfare but of the injustice of it all: left behind again while Father and Muwa chased glory in distant lands.

She squeezed his arm, then gazed through the corridor of rock in the rough direction of Hattusa.

'Aye, we should be getting back,' he mused.

After edging off of the cliffs, they made their way across the exposed hills, the fresh autumn wind buffeting them again. About half a danna away from Hattusa, they passed the great Rock Shrine; the place resembled an ancient crown of grey stone, pushed through the earth from below, its sides etched with scenes of the Gods. The ring of natural, fin-like shards sheltered a small and very sacred area within – where kings were buried, where gods were honoured, where highborn men and women were joined in marriage. He unconsciously reached out and took Atiya's hand.

Arrow, following, came swooping down and landed on his shoulder, shrieking. 'Food? You've eaten plenty – any more and you won't be able to take flight.' Yet on she shrieked, not at him but at the sky behind. 'What's wrong?' Hattu cooed. He glanced back but saw nothing.

Ahead, the bulky outline of Hattusa rose into view. The outlying croplands were nearly deserted for the coming winter, with just a few farmers busy repairing their homes. One man was sitting on the roof of his mud-brick home with his three-legged dog, enjoying the heat from a small brazier. The fields themselves were stripped bare, the grain having been carted into the city and stored in the pits atop Tarhunda's Shoulder – the smaller tor opposite the acropolis mount.

Without warning, Atiya halted, looking whence they had come.

'Atiya?' Hattu whispered.

'Something is out there,' she said, agitated like Arrow.

'We're alone,' he reassured her. The cool wind did its best to convince him otherwise.

Hattu took her hand again, carrying on towards Hattusa at a faster pace. He could not help but look back once more at the still and silent north – bleak hills and skeletal alder woods, deserted.

Suddenly, a loud, deep *clang* of bronze shuddered across the sky from Hattusa. The warning bell. A harbinger of some grave threat to the city. He had only heard it once before, some eight years ago. Then, he had been within Hattusa's walls and it had come to nothing.

'Hattu?' Atiya wailed, looking all around. Suddenly, the few people outwith the city walls took flight, throwing down tools and bolting towards the Tawinian Gate, well ahead of Hattu and Atiya. Arrow shrieked and leapt into flight, swooping towards Hattusa and coming back again in circles as if urging them on.

Clang!

Hattu saw the few sentries on Hattusa's northern walls pointing, gesticulating to the north, shouting to one another. He and Atiya broke towards the city in a stumbling half-run, Hattu looking back in the direction of this unseen threat. A sharp pain shot through his smoke-grey eye and suddenly he saw everything a little more clearly.

'What's happening, Hattu?' Atiya quailed as they ran.

'There's something in the woods…' he gasped, turning to run backwards.

Then he saw the strangest thing emerging from the trees: many hundreds of bobbing heads. Heads with long, flowing black hair, some with leather Hittite helms on. 'Our soldiers?' he panted, unconsciously slowing. But something was wrong with the sight: the heads bobbed high – higher than any man. When he saw the red ribbons of flesh and sinew that dangled from the neck of one of the heads, the riddle was solved. Hittite heads, right enough – severed and affixed on top of spears like grim totems.

Just then, the woods spewed forth a landslip of shapes – mountain warriors festooned with bronze and copper axes, swords and those foul spears.

'Kaskans?' Hattu gasped, seeing the many screaming mouths, manes of shaggy, tousled hair, unkempt beards and faces daubed with hideous bright streaks or handprints. They wore fleeces or rough woollen capes on their shoulders, with leather corselets and caps or headbands of brightly dyed wool.

How could it be? Pitagga and the Kaskans were in Wahina, right now being dealt with by the Hittite Army, were they not? This host numbered too many to count, and many more than the thousand soldiers of the Storm housed in Hattusa's Great Barracks. They swung and waved their weapons in the air like a bronze crop field, and they brought many rudimentary ladders with them, tall enough to scale Hattusa's walls.

'Run,' Hattu stammered, suddenly swinging to face the city and speeding up. 'Run. *Run!*'

He and Atiya now broke into a headlong dash towards the Tawinian Gatehouse – its heavy gates still wide open, the smattering of Hittite sentries there in disorder. Yet the gates seemed so far away and the Kaskans were bearing down on them like stampeding bulls.

Clang! the great bell tolled again, shaking the earth.

Then came the cry of the mountain men as the Kaskans came to within a few hundred paces of the city and broke into a fervent charge. And a terrible wail erupted from what sounded like a Kaskan ibex horn – low like a demon's growl then suddenly and jarringly high and deafening.

Clang! the great bell of Hattusa sounded in reply, this time barely audible over the Kaskan horn.

Hattu and Atiya sped, hand in hand towards the Tawinian gatehouse. But they were greeted with the sight of the last few field workers scrambling inside before the bronze-strapped gates swung shut, and heard the thick *clunk* of the locking bar within being lowered into place. He, Atiya and the three-legged farm dog were alone, outside, in the shadow of the gate like cornered sheep. Up on the battlements a sentry looked down on them, his face draining of blood when he realised what had happened.

'It is the Cursed… it is Prince Hattu – Prince Hattu is outside!' he yelled. But the few others on the walls barely heard – perhaps even chose not to, running to and fro, tossing spears and shields out across the battlements from the tower guard rooms.

'Open the gates,' Atiya cried as the din of the onrushing Kaskans seemed to swell up behind them.

'Those gates will not open now. Not for anyone. Come,' Hattu said, twisting towards the small, triangular alcove dug into the bedrock under the walls, just left of the Tawinian Gates. All had been taught well the location and purpose of the postern tunnels around the city – wide enough for a single man to pass in or out – or a boy and a girl.

But he felt Atiya's hand slipping from his and, with a twist of her ankle and a cry, she fell. Hattu swung round, his hair sweeping across his face, the smoke-grey eye sharp like a blade on her – sprawled, a few paces back. The swell of Kaskan warriors coursed towards her. She was struggling to rise, her face gaunt, terrified, mouth open, wordless in panic, eyes screaming for help. The foremost of the charging Kaskans – a red-bearded monster of a warrior – was bounding in her direction, just thirty paces distant, a fire-hardened club gripped and readied to stave in her head.

'Prince Hattu,' the sentry shouted down from the walls, 'get into the postern tunnel – *now!*'

Hattu twisted to the dark postern burrow and the small triangle of light at the far end. Safety within the walls beckoned. His smoke-grey eye ached again and he made out a shape through there, momentarily – a figure, part-silhouetted: a slender, aged man with odd eyes, wearing scribe's robes, shoulders rounded and head hung in timidity... alone; when he swung back to Atiya, there was another figure. Hattu started: a stranger, back turned to him, facing her and the Kaskans. Tall, broad, draped in a magnificent green cloak, crowned with a warrior's helm.

He lurched towards Atiya, hoping the stranger might help him save her. He stooped swiftly to pick up a hand-sized, pitted rock as some means of defence. When he rose and bounded on, the stranger was gone, just as a shadow might vanish with the coming of the sun: it was just him and Atiya outside Hattusa's walls, with a multitude of plunder-hungry mountain men about to fall upon them. His stomach flipped over at the sight of Red-beard, leaping across the last stretch behind Atiya, club raised, face agape in an animal cry.

With a wild swing, Hattu hurled the rock at Red-beard's face. The warrior's bloodthirsty leer vanished in a puff of scarlet mist, a crack of nasal bone and a roar. The Kaskan fell in a thrashing mess. Hattu stooped, ducking under Atiya's midriff and hoisting her across his shoulders. For a heartbeat, he was faced with the rest of that tidal wave of frenzied creatures from the northern mountains, before he pivoted round with a puff of dirt and dust and lumbered as best he could towards the postern tunnel. A rain of stones, spears and thrown axes battered the rim of the tunnel as he rushed inside, the three-legged farm dog coming with them.

For a moment there was nothing but near-blackness and the odour of musty, damp air, alive with the clatter of his feet and weak cries from Atiya. Then his eyes adjusted, with a little help from the pale, algae-streaked wash that coated the corridor walls and smooth floor: the passageway was just high enough for him to carry Atiya without ducking, leading them under the walls and into the city. Footsteps rapped – his own and many heavier ones in pursuit. His breath came in panicked gasps. The pursuing Kaskans' breaths came with anticipatory growls – one of them scraping an axe along the wall as he went, filling the postern with the most awful, demonic screech.

'Hattu!' Atiya wailed, the tremor in her voice enough to tell the story of the swiftly gaining Kaskans behind.

'I will draw out your guts while you still live, Hit-tite scum,' the lead pursuer said in an acid hiss.

Hattu put everything into his run, his grey eye fixed on the bright triangle of light ahead. With a sequence of loping strides, he spilled out and into blinding daylight again, just inside the lower town wall. Instantly, a group of citizens pulled down a pair of heavy, bronze-strapped gratings over the postern opening, a pursuing Kaskan slamming against it a trice later, only to be driven back by a pole, thrust through the grate. Moments later and he and Atiya would have been stuck in that tunnel.

All around him was chaos. He staggered, barged one way and another by a frantic contraflow of rushing bodies, deafened by screams and shouts from every lane and building in the lower town.

'The dread Lord of the Mountains is here, at our hallowed walls!' a priest screamed, aloft upon the balcony of a nearby shrine.

Hattu's veins flooded with ice-water. 'Pitagga *is* here?' he gasped, the certainty that Father and Muwa were right now in the land of Wahina putting that rogue down now crumbling like stale bread. 'How can it be?'

Atiya was wrenched from his shoulders by two women in the swaying crowds. 'She has turned her ankle. Take her to the healer, take her deep into the city – far from the walls,' Hattu cried as the women carried her off. And she was gone. Just then, from the muffled din of roars outside the walls, a sharp, thrumming noise cut through. An instant later came the punch of something hard and sharp hitting something else soft and wet. A shadow passed over Hattu as a sentry flailed backwards, swatted from the wall tops, a Kaskan axe embedded in his breast. He landed with a crunch on his back before Hattu, shuddering, convulsing, shield and spear falling from his dying grasp, thick gouts of blood pumping from the atrocious wound. The stricken soldier's wide eyes met Hattu's, his dying look one of confusion and terror. All around them, a rapid, irregular drumming struck up – a storm of missiles from the Kaskan masses battering down into the lower town streets: axes, rocks, slingshot, javelins and blazing, pitch-soaked arrows. In every direction, the hail mowed down bodies: A goat, shot through the eye and an innkeeper, struck in the throat. A woman fell, back peppered with arrows. A young girl dropped dead, struck on the head by a rock and a man pierced by a pitch arrow ran, screaming, ablaze like a living torch.

When a javelin stabbed into the ground by Hattu's feet, he stumbled back, seeing that few – too few – sentries were upon the walls: a company of one hundred at most along the Tawinian Gatehouse and the abutting sections of curtain wall. Most were pinned – crouched behind the merlons, their hide shields taking a battering from the hail. A dozen more were struck down in a bloody mizzle, one pirouetting from the defence, face torn open by a slung pebble, hair and limbs flailing, his dark red leather helm flung from his crown. And then came a far uglier hail: a cascade of severed Hittite heads – tossed from the tips of Kaskan spears – came thudding down, rolling through the dust, long hair flipping as they went. Hundreds upon hundreds of them. One came to a halt by Hattu's foot: a soldier of the northern watchtowers, he realised. Another head was a woman's, and another an elderly man's: some of the captives carried off to Wahina?

A leader of ten barged past him, guiding his scant troop of bronze and leather-clad spearmen towards the sturdy mud-brick stairs that would take them up onto the battlements. No sooner than the captain had climbed the stairs than a thrown rock took him in the temple, crushing the bronze brow-band of his helm and cracking his skull, sending him staggering on and over the merlon. A terrible scream sounded from outside and a puff of red shot up where he had landed in the Kaskan swell. The rest of his ten climbed onto the walls more guardedly, but an instant later, a clatter of timber on baked mud-brick sounded as ladder tops swung into view along the battlements, shuddering and creaking, the Kaskan cries growing louder, nearer.

Hattu's body was wracked with a shuddering fear that came in waves, each more violent than the last. His mouth drained of every last drop of moisture as he backed away, sensing the swell that was about to burst into view over the wall. He looked behind him, across the Ambar and halfway up the acropolis mount, to the Noon Spur and the Great Barracks. Where was Kurunta One-eye and the garrison regiment? Surely the bell had been heard there too? *Surely.*

Suddenly, he recalled the whispers of drunk men near the open tavern by the Ambar. *The king gouged out Kurunta's eye. One day, the vengeful one will have his redress...*

An animal cry sounded and Hattu turned back to the wall as the first of the Kaskans leapt from the ladder-tops and onto the battlements with an ululating shriek. The man's copper sword struck across the back of one Hittite warrior, blood blossoming across his long, white cloak from the strike before he fell to one knee. He tried to rise but a torrent of crimson boiled from the wound and he collapsed. Many more Kaskans flooded onto the wall tops and the meagre resistance crumbled. As the enemy began rushing down the wall stairs and dropping down into the lower town only paces from Hattu, the few Hittite soldiers there were quickly despatched. Hattu backed away, overcome with fright.

And then a mighty *boom* shook the air. Hattu saw the ancient Tawinian Gates shudder, dust crumbling from the gatehouse's mud-brick upper, the few sentries holding out up there disappearing under a hail of missiles. *Boom!* again – now the gates bulged violently and a spidering crack shot across the curtain wall either side, chunks of plaster toppling into the town and merlons breaking off and falling outwards. *Boom!* with a shredding crunch and a shower of splinters, the bronze tip of a ram burst through. Another few strikes and the famous old gates would be kindling.

'Pull back – to the Spirit Bridge,' one voice yelled.

Hattu saw a Hittite soldier, face and tunic smeared with dust and blood, standing atop one home, waving the citizens and the few remaining wall guard back from the fray, towards the thick bridge that crossed the River Ambar. It would serve as a bottleneck – a last redoubt to prevent the Kaskans spilling through the lower town entire and up towards the Royal Acropolis.

'Fall back to the br-' the soldier's words ended with a wet gurgle as a spear whooshed up and tore into his chest. A gout of blood leapt from the soldier's mouth as he clutched at the shaft, then he pitched from the roof and crunched onto the ground. Moments later, a trio of flaming torches were hurled into that building and the home was swiftly ablaze, the skyline stained orange and undulating in the heat of the blaze.

Crash! and the Tawinian Gates burst inwards. Kaskans flooded into Hattusa's streets.

Hattu spun and ran, haring along the main way. Shooting glances behind, he saw Kaskan warriors loping along in his wake. He dipped his head and put everything into his flight. But when a dull whirring grew louder and louder he looked back once again, only to pull his head to the side, the spinning dirk aimed for the back of his skull shearing a lock of hair and whirling on into the side of an abandoned ox cart. The streets were thick with Kaskans now: they threw over bread and grain carts and pinned down women, tearing off their gowns and deaf to their pleas for mercy.

'Hit-tite dogs,' one warrior roared in a spirant, throaty breath as he knelt on the chest of an old market trader, hoisting a weighty rock then bringing it down, crushing the old man's head like a watermelon.

There was one who stood out like bronze studs in a leather shield – fiery-bearded, broad and tall, clad in a black leather cuirass and crowned with a fearsome lion-skull helm. Pitagga, Hattu realised at once. This was the ambitious lord who had united these oft-infighting mountain people. Pitagga stalked forward steadily. He carried a double-headed axe, twirling it with devious intent.

The Lord of the Mountains caught Hattu's eye and the murderous look was enough to throw his stride. Catching his toe on a flagstone, Hattu was catapulted to the ground, smacking down on his jaw and shoulder and then rolling. Dazed and prone, he shook his head and tried to right himself, only for his spinning vision to come together and sharpen on the sight of Pitagga a stride away from him, axe rising, the baleful eyes complemented by a yellow-toothed rictus.

The axe blade hammered down for Hattu's thigh. He swung his leg back just as the blade shattered the flagstone underneath, sending up a shower of dust and stone across Hattu's eyes. Blinking, he staggered to his feet.

'It is you,' Pitagga said, grinning a hunter's grin as his gaze flicked between Hattu's odd eyes. 'The climbing boy. The Cursed Son of King Mursili. The progeny who shames him so.'

Hattu stumbled backwards, the words gripping his darkest doubts like black roots.

'Perhaps it would be more fun if I were to leave you breathing, for now,' he said in a mocking tone, then stamped forward and sharply thrust his head down and forward like a ravening vulture – nose to nose so Hattu could smell his fetid breath, the lion fangs on his helm touching Hattu's face. '*Run,*' he hissed, then brought the back of his hand across Hattu's cheek.

Hattu's head filled with a shower of lights as the brute's knuckles raked across his face. He scrambled and sprinted on up the main way, his mind in pieces as Pitagga's tormenting cackle rang out behind him. His cheek felt like it was on fire and seemed set to burst. He ran and ran, oblivious to the chaos all around him. But one voice cut through the din.

'Help... *help!*' it cried from one side of the street. Hattu saw there the doorway of a house – blocked by an abandoned cart. A boy's face peered out from within, his eyes wide like an owl's. Hattu noticed the lad's gaunt, plague-scarred features and thin, slicked back hair. It was the one who had recoiled in derision from him at the city gates in spring as he and Muwa had come in from the woods. 'Please,' the boy begged.

Hattu grabbed the cart by the handles and hauled it clear. The boy scrambled out.

'Run,' Hattu pushed him to get him going.

'Thank you,' the boy panted, then melted into the lanes with the many other panicking citizens. Hattu ran too, black smoke scudding across his path until he finally came within sight of the short, wide, Spirit Bridge. Not a soul stood there waiting to defend the choke point. Nothing. Nobody. Just a cacophony of screaming and shouting on the far side and the fleeting glimpses of citizens rushing to and fro – generally on up the main way towards the Noon Spur and the acropolis and the protection those heights might offer. Panicked, heart-sick, he ran across the bridge, looking this way and that as he went, the din of the pursuing Kaskans rising swiftly behind him. *Father, Muwa, where are you? The enemy is here, in our home.*

Hattu was halfway across the bridge when the thunder came. From further up the main way sounded a low, dull clatter of boots moving rapidly in time, the source obscured by the kink in the road and the rising maze of houses hugging the way's sides. Hattu slowed, wondering if he was about to run into a second wave of Kaskans coming through the other side of the city. The air around him thickened and crackled like in the moments before a storm. Then a single voice, a noise like a bellowing ox, split the air:

'Men of the Storm… raise your *weapons!*'

Hattu stumbled onto the southern banks, awestruck at the cry.

Then came the reply: a deep, reverberating cry of one thousand voices that caused the bridge and the streets of Hattusa to shiver: 'Tarhunda, God of the Storm, coat my heart in bronze!'

Like a pack of baying hunters they came, at a jog, round the bend in the main way. Hittite spearmen. Their pointed, leather helms jutting, faces fixed in animal rictuses, dark hair in tails that jostled and lashed behind them like those of angry lions, bodies clad in stiffened linen or baked leather cuirasses, shields bound in dark leather or raw, black and white cattle skin – covering them neck to thigh, spears trained like fingers of judgement. Twenty-wide, they filled the road, and forty such ranks advanced in perfect order behind them. *Crunch-crunch-crunch,* the rapid din of their upturned leather boots was unrelenting. The rightmost soldier on the front rank held aloft a wooden staff topped with a golden lightning bolt – the symbol of the Storm Division.

One figure broke through to run proud of their front, head dipped, lone-eye ablaze, silvery braid swishing, teak-hard chest bulging under his leather crossbands. Hattu tried to get out of Kurunta's path, but could not escape his gaze. 'You?' Kurunta gasped. 'Get back, boy, *back,*' he swiped a hand towards the side of the main way. That was enough to send Hattu stumbling out of their way, letting the lone regiment of the Storm Division take up its position, spilling onto the near half of the bridge like a plug.

At the same time, a clutch of Storm archers burst into view, clambering like spiders from a disturbed nest up onto the rooftops around the bridge, around two hundred in all. With no armour or weapons bar their composite bows and twin quivers looped over their backs, they were spry and sped into position on the lips of those roofs within moments, nocking arrows to their bows, those nearest the edges kneeling so others behind them could stand and shoot too.

From the southern banks, Hattu watched, panting, as the wall of spearmen slowed to a walk on the centre of the bridge. Kurunta stepped up on the wooden rail on the side of the bridge, flush with the front line. Reaching over his shoulders with both hands to draw out and raise the twin, curved blades there, he reprised that ox-like howl once again:

'This sacred bridge *must* be held,' he cried. Just as they had moved in unison, they stopped as one, a wall of shields and spear tips, blocking the wide bridge as firmly as any stone redoubt. Then he gestured to the archers on the rooftops. 'Shoot down any hairy *hurkeler* who tries to ford the river.'

With a vociferous roar, the Kaskans now exploded into view and flooded onto the northern end of the bridge, erupting in a thunderous roar. Pitagga remained a safe distance back, climbing atop the side of a stone cistern and pointing his double-headed axe like a preacher's finger.

'Where is your Great King, your *Labarna*, your Sun?' Pitagga cried out, as if the city of Hattusa itself was listening. 'Ah, he is chasing my shadow, faraway in Wahina,' he bellowed with laughter then continued in a gurgling cry, swinging his axe forth: 'Forward. Topple their temples, take their treasures, spill their blood! Leave their sacred city no more than a dark stain like the rubble-heaps that are Zalpa, Hakmis and Nerik – upon whose soil my pigs now shit.' The Kaskans surged across the bridge with a roar.

'To the Dark Earth with these dogs. *To the Dark Earth!*' Kurunta screamed, his din just besting the enemy cry before it was drowned out in a riotous clash of bronze blades clanging upon the bridge's midpoint, men screaming, shields sparring and the crisp whistle of many arrows being loosed from either bank.

Hattu watched as the two forces vied for possession of the bridge like herds of clashing bulls. Hittite spearmen lashed their lances forth without mercy, the leaf-shaped tips splitting Kaskan armour, plunging into enemy throats and limbs. The Kaskans were no less fierce, their axes swinging rapaciously, crushing Hittite skulls, gouging into shoulders and cleaving men's bodies deeply – so deep that the blood that spurted from the wounds was black, not red. Pitagga waved more and more warriors onto the bridge. As the Kaskan push intensified, the Storm soldiers suffered, being driven back one step and then another. One Hittite sank to his knees, blood erupting from his nose and mouth and an axe embedded in his forehead. Another toppled like a felled log, sideways, pitching over the side of the bridge and plunging into the Ambar, turning the sacred waters red as he floated face-down towards the culvert by the shattered Tawinian Gates.

Suddenly, a stray Kaskan arrow skated off the flagstones of the main way, just by Hattu's ankle. He ducked down behind an abandoned potter's cart, then edged his head out to glance across the water: Over one hundred Kaskans were wading across the river, under the covering shots of their archers. Hattu's blood was suddenly laced with cold realisation: the bridge was about to fall and the river was close to being traversed. He edged his head out from the cart again and saw a braid-bearded, wading Kaskan in the near shallows, just a few paces away. The warrior locked eyes on Hattu, turning his blood to ice.

'Loose,' the Hittite archer captain yelled from the roof of the smith's workshop. A moment later, a concerted volley spat down upon the near Kaskan and the others following. With a series of thumps, thuds and groans, many slumped into the water and were carried off downriver by the gentle current. The braid-bearded giant took an arrow in the cheek: blood tumbled down his face and beaded in his beard. The huge warrior somehow waded on for a few paces, as if his body was slow to register the mortal strike, before he too succumbed and sank into the water. Suddenly, the few unhurt warriors mid-river slowed, doubting the wisdom of their approach, abruptly deaf to Pitagga's cries of encouragement from the far bank.

And in that same instant, like a changing wind, the clash on the bridge turned too. Hattu saw Kurunta in the midst of it, leaping in battle-fury, shieldless, his silvery braid of hair swinging. He elbowed a Kaskan in the face before turning on his heel to drive one curved blade into the collarbone of a stocky foe and then bring the other sword slashing across the belly of a sprightly one. Three splashes sounded as this doomed trio staggered to the edge of the bridge and fell into the river. He saw Kurunta's face contort, mouth agape as he cried encouragement to his soldiers. Over the din of dying men and clashing weapons, he could not make out the words, but he saw that they certainly worked: for just a heartbeat later, the Kaskan push faltered and the Hittites edged forward.

But then a hand slapped on his shoulder.

Hattu felt his heart leap into his throat. He swung round in fright, only to see Sarpa, panting, shaved head beaded with sweat having hobbled from the walls of the Storm Temple. 'Brother, you should have stayed in the temple strong room.'

'I was on the temple roof and I saw you out here, so close to the fray.' Sarpa said, his eyes darting over Hattu, one hand reaching up to trace over the swollen, grazed cheek where Pitagga had struck him.

'I'm fine,' Hattu insisted, pushing his brother's hand back from the stinging wound. 'And the Kaskans are losing, look.'

A few snatched breaths passed and true enough, the first Hittite step forward became a second then a third. Soon, they were almost at a slow, grim march, the front rank a blaze of jabbing spears and curved swords. Kurunta leapt clear of the push, up onto the bridge's edge again, driving them on with his words and his pointing blades: '*Forwaaard.*'

'Some thought King Mursili was a fool when he set off for Wahina and left Kurunta behind,' Sarpa grinned. 'But I doubt they will question his loyalty again. He's saved our city.'

Hattu saw Pitagga on the far bank: the Lord of the Mountains' hubris was draining, head switching in every direction for some way of turning the tide. 'Still, you are right, we should draw back,' Hattu said. But before the words were fully out, he saw Pitagga lift a small throwing axe, then with a flash of bronze, hurl it across the Ambar.

'Sarpa!' Hattu cried. But his brother was too slow to move. The axe spun and hammered into the back of Sarpa's neck, wedging side-on and deep just above the collarbone. Sarpa staggered, honey-gold eyes wide in shock. Black blood pumped from the awful wound in gouts, and Sarpa's head tilted to one side, almost peeling away from his shoulders, his dying breath coming as a choked rasp.

'Brother,' Hattu cried, lunging forward to halt Sarpa from toppling down into the Ambar. A hot, shower of blood sprayed over Hattu's face and torso: the coppery reek branding itself on his memory forever. His brother's blood-slick body slid clear of his grasp and crashed into the waters. Hattu fell to his knees, hearing the Kaskans roar in delight as Sarpa's corpse was carried out into the centre of the Ambar.

'We have the head of a prince as our prize,' he heard Pitagga howl from across the water.

In a blur of tears, he saw the Kaskan leader's men over there poking their spears into the current, then hooking poor Sarpa out like a fish, hoisting him. Pitagga seized the body by the scruff of the collar and brought his great double axe slicing down to sever the last tendons that held Sarpa's head in place. The Kaskan lord held the Hittite prince's head aloft and he and his men howled as if it was some sort of victory. Yet it was short-lived as their attempt to take the Spirit Bridge crumbled moments later. In a trice, Pitagga had turned away from the river with his 'prize', fleeing with his personal guards.

A moment later and the last resisting Kaskans on the bridge broke too, turning, all sense of cohesion vanishing as they spilled back from whence they came, some trampling or barging comrades out of the way. Pursued by the men of the Storm, the remnant of the horde was soon just a dull rabble, surging back into the black smoke clouds of the lower town ward, charging through the ruins they had created, leaping over the dead they had stolen life from, fleeing through the ruined Tawinian Gate. A breath of wind swept some of the smoke away and revealed the full extent of the dancing fires, the wrecked mass of blackened or part-tumbled homes and the broken gates and listing, cracked walls. Hattu saw the three-legged dog, pining, tail wagging in forlorn hope as it stood over the prone, still form of its owner. He saw Sarpa's body and the red mess at the end of his neck.

'They took… his head,' he whispered, realising he was shaking, badly.

He barely noticed the figure striding towards him.

Kurunta's mottled skin was lashed with blood. Steam coiled from his bald scalp and torso as the sweat of battle began to evaporate. If this wasn't fearsome enough, his face was a crumpled ball of fury.

'Boy? What in the name of Tarhunda were you doing? I told you to get back. A moment later and-' his words ended abruptly as he saw the runnels of redness dripping from Hattu's face, soaking his tunic. 'Prince Hattu?' he said in alarm.

'It is not my blood. I am unhurt,' Hattu said with a tremor, then pointed across the river to the headless corpse. 'But Prince Sarpa is dead,' he wailed. Rivulets of Sarpa's blood snaked from Hattu's person, through the shingle and into the Ambar's waters. 'My brother is dead.'

Kurunta took a step back, his breath caged and his good eye wide as he realised what had happened. 'By all the Gods, no… it will begin on the day he stands by the banks of the Ambar…'

Hattu looked at the gnarled general, confused.

'… soaked in the blood of his brother,' Kurunta finished, his face draining of colour.

CHAPTER 5

SHIELD OF THE KING
LATE AUTUMN 1303 BC

Red dust rose from the age-old track like an ethereal serpent into the crisp blue morning sky. Almost nine thousand men marched southwards along it, back into the Hittite heartlands. They went without their armoured vests – carried instead in the mule and ox-cart train – but wore their bronze and leather helms and carried their spears and shields still as Hittite martial code demanded. Leather bags of rations and personal effects tied near the tops of their spear tips swung and they alternated between chants of prayer and coarser marching songs.

The singing stopped when they came to a clay altar by the left side of the route. The commanders bellowed an order to halt, and the regiments obeyed, taking time and care to leave small portions of bread by the altar – gifts to the God of the Road and a ruse to trap the evil spirits that many said lingered on that side. Others sent prayers up to the familiar hills ahead, for they were but a few weeks' march from Hattusa... from home.

Up on the cliff top that overlooked the procession of his army, two gleaming Mesedi stood guard by the royal carriage – a sturdy, bronze-banded, cedarwood wagon. King Mursili himself stood at the cliff's edge, shrouded in his dark-grey cloak, his silver-threaded locks dancing in the biting wind. An entire campaigning season, gone. *And what have we achieved?* His bones ached in the breeze – as if demanding he become an old man before his time. He let his tired eyes trace the bronze-scaled serpent of the Hittite army from head to tail as it set off again: leading the way was the Wrath of Sarruma – his own division, dedicated to and named after the Mountain God. Next came the Fury of Aplu – devoted to the God of the Dark Earth. Chosen Prince Muwa marched at their head, resplendent in his black garb and shining white silver cuirass. Next year would be the lad's seventeenth summer, and it showed: he was tall, strapping and strong... and he had certainly developed an eye for women. He had mentioned more than once how eager he was to return to Hattusa, to meet with the priestess girl. *Perhaps that is why he marches at such haste?* Mursili chuckled.

His eyes swung to the next division: the Blaze of Arinniti, Division of the Sun Goddess. He could see their fine ranks and their barking captains, but could not see General Nuwanza at their head. *Where is the bowman?* Behind the Blaze rode the bloated pack of sumpter mules, thousands strong, laden with bags of grain and salted meats. With them came a caravan of ox-wagons carrying the dread spearhead of his army: the chariots, disassembled and strapped down to the wagon floors. A pack of four hundred unburdened war stallions trotted alongside the vehicles and the fork-bearded Hurrian Chariot Master, Colta, walked with them, wandering amongst them, whispering to each of them like children. The horses and cars had gone unused. Wahina had been re-established as Hittite territory, a bite had been taken out of the Lost North, but only because the enemy that had rampaged there the previous year was gone, like an autumnal mist.

He felt a nagging, gnawing doubt – nebulous and persistent. It was like the dream that had plagued him all throughout this campaign: a dream where he wandered in an unfamiliar palace in search of the distant echoing call. *Father!* The call would lead him to the doorway of a room, where Ishtar would greet him with a warm smile, then direct him with an open hand to the opposite door and on along a corridor. Yet at the end of the corridor, he would find himself in the same damned room, the goddess there too, playfully guiding him down the same corridor. He grunted and shook the thought away – the mere memory of the dream maddening.

Father! the call from the dream persevered.

He thought of his youngest son, left back in Hattusa. Hot pins of guilt pricked his heart as he thought of the life he had enforced upon Hattu. He imagined his long-dead wife's face gazing at him in cold censure. 'I'm sorry, Gassula, there is no other way. At least he wants for nothing,' he whispered.

Nothing but his father's love, his wife's wraith replied.

Seeking distraction, he looked back whence the army had come. Wahina, that strange, bare land of endless green hills. Wahina, a land of shadows. Volca the Sherden had led them to a creek where he and his two men had heard rumour of the Kaskan masses, but ultimately, those sites were as bare as all the others and their quarry had continued to elude them. His eyes traced along the northern horizon and the jagged Soaring Mountains, grey-blue in the haze of distance: near-impenetrable rocky fortresses where Pitagga and his growing army had no doubt retreated to.

'I'll find you, you basta-' he stopped, wincing, clutching his left arm. A shooting pain on the inside of his bicep almost blinded him such was its ferocity.

'My Sun,' a voice spoke behind him.

'What?' he said tetchily, swinging round to glare at the two Mesedi, expecting to see Zida there with some bothersome issue. But he saw it was Nuwanza who had spoken. His ire faded with the pain in his arm – few men could remain angry in the bowman's company. 'I'm sorry, my friend. I was letting my thoughts get the better me for a moment there.'

'If it was only the odd fleeting moment, My Sun,' Nuwanza said, striding over to stand by the king and behold the north with him.

'We didn't even catch sight of him, Nuwanza,' Mursili snapped.

'Such is the Kaskan way. They know they cannot match us on an open plain, thus they melt into the trees and the hills and,' the veins in his temples under his V of hair stood proud, 'those damned mountains.'

Mursili's jaw worked, not satisfied. 'In days past they might have been content to do so, year after year: raid and retreat. But those we spoke to in the shanty villages by the pillaged cities did not speak of raiding bands.'

'Like ants, one fellow claimed, Kaskans moving in a single drove, many thousands strong, and more than one such force,' Nuwanza mused. 'My Sun, what if... if Pitagga has managed to...'

'To unite the twelve tribes?' Mursili finished for him. 'Then he must have promised them a fine prize for them to set aside their differences.' His brow pinched and he heard that call from the nagging dream again. *Father!* Instinctively, he looked south in the direction of Hattusa.

Nuwanza read his disquiet instantly. 'I sense something is wrong too, My Sun. We should hurry back to the capital.'

A clop-clop of horse's hooves cut off the exchange. The pair looked up to see Volca the horn-helmed Sherden riding on a mare, coming up the winding path by the cliffside to join them. The comical sight softened Mursili's hard thoughts.

'Warriors do not sit on horses, man,' he laughed, 'messengers, scouts and boys might, but not warriors.'

Volca slowed the mare and slid from his awkward sitting position on the beast's croup. He landed on the ground with a thump and stroked the mare's nose. 'I am not warrior today,' he said in his improving but still-simplistic Hittite tongue, with a wide grin that exaggerated his impeccable looks, gesturing to the thin linen tunic and belt he wore. 'My armour is stowed on mule train.'

No armour save for the helmet, Mursili thought but did not say. Volca had been a charismatic addition to his retinue: affable, knowledgeable and inspirational throughout the chase to pin down Pitagga. Yet never once had Mursili or any other seen him without that nightmarish horned helm. *Hiding a bald crown?* Mursili wondered with an inner chuckle.

'The danger is over, is it not?' Volca continued. 'You said we are now safely back on sacred Hittite soil, no?'

'Danger is pervasive,' Nuwanza said in a remedial tone. 'And we should neither be lax nor let our pace lessen.'

Volca shrugged, unimpressed. Then he nodded towards the snaking army down on the ground below. 'Prince Muwatalli is keen to lead march back to Hattusa. I thought we could ease off on our return – spend rest of day hunting then follow on?' he said, then turned away from the cliff edge and looked southeast to the run of bumpy foothills. He crouched by imprints in the dirt. 'The spoor of lion! I have heard many rumours of the creatures in these lands: deer, lynx, tigers, bulls, wolf and boar. Elephant, even.'

That smile again – enough to convince a harlot to pay for his company, Mursili reckoned. Volca handed him a drinking skin. 'I prepared some more of the Sherden root brew for you. Drink, wet your lips and whet your appetite for the thrill of the hunt.'

Mursili took the skin and sipped on the drink. It was deliciously sweet and spicy at once, invigorating indeed. He smacked his lips in satisfaction, his eyes following Volca's sweeping hand. 'It has been some time... '

'My Sun,' Nuwanza interrupted, 'perhaps a hunt could be organised for another day. It has been more than a summer since last the people saw their *Labarna*. Think of the throne...' he hesitated before adding, 'think of the soft beds and the wine... think of the harem?'

Mursili shot the Master Archer a fiery look that faded into a salty half-smile. 'Perhaps you are right.'

Volca's handsome features crumpled. 'Not even single catch – to honour Gods? Did you not tell me how dark skies gather over your city when the Storm God is not honoured?'

Mursili balked at this. It was an unwelcome seed of doubt that he knew would plague his every moment were something grim to occur. A deer hunt, perhaps, and then they could catch up with the army on the royal carriage. They could offer the beast up on the altar within the Storm Temple. Its meat would feed many weary mouths, so it would be no wasteful hunt. The Goddess Kamrusepa, protector of the herds, would approve.

'My Sun,' Nuwanza started to protest.

Just then, a faint drumming of wild hooves sounded, deep in the wooded vales of the foothills. The trees there shook. Volca's face opened up. 'The hunt is on, My Sun?'

***

A scent of pine spiced the air as Mursili stalked through a mesh of ferns and a frosty carpet of golden leaves and bracken, wishing away their every crackle and crunch. He silently thanked the Gods for taking up Volca's suggestion: never did the stresses of the throne drain as swiftly as when on the hunt. For the first time in so long he felt like a boy again. Shadowing him was a lone Mesedi – like Mursili, barefoot, stripped to just a tunic and carrying only a hunting spear and bow.

The two halted as they heard a shuffle of leaves and bracken just beyond a small, root-knotted ridge ahead. Mursili ducked and made eyes with his guard, who indicated his agreement: their prey was just ahead.

Mursili cupped his hands together and intertwined his fingers, then blew softly, imitating the whistling melody of a song thrush twice. Silence. Even the crunching footsteps of their prey fell quiet. Then, in reply, the chirruping bird call of one of the other two hunting parties: Zida and another Mesedi, or Volca and the two other Sherden.

'Only one repetition,' Mursili whispered to his Mesedi.

'Then the beast is watching, listening,' the bodyguard replied. 'We must wait, My Sun.'

An eternity passed, and Mursili's thighs began to ache. There was a rush of moving leaves then the shuffling beyond the ridge sounded different, heavier. He was about to give the call to abandon the hunt when, at last, the chirruping sounded again. Twice? 'The creature is at ease,' he mouthed, his usually pouchy, weary eyes alert and wide.

Aye, his guard mouthed.

Mursili rose, ghosting forward, catsoft on his feet, the Mesedi following him. They came to the tip of the rise, keeping low and as yet unable to see over it. They heard the call again – twice. Zida and Volca's lot in position, surely.

'Ready?' he mouthed to his guard. The fellow nodded. Mursili crouched a little lower to charge his legs with energy, made the double call to let Zida and Volca know it was time, then sprung up and over the parapet of ferns atop the ridge.

He barely heard the third, muted call from the woods.

At once he took it all in: a small glade, ringed with red-gold leafed poplars and carpeted in moss. The deer was nowhere to be seen. Instead, a great, grey mass dominated the centre of the clearing: ferocious ivory tusks, colossal legs and a scarred trunk. The cow elephant – huge and very old – instantly swung its great head to face him. He realised straight away what peril he was in – seeing its calves stripping and eating tree bark. She put herself between them and him.

Mursili skidded on the downward slope into the glade, arms lashing out to catch something to halt his descent. The Mesedi, just behind him, cried out. 'My Sun, come back, *come back!*'

But Mursili could only stumble and fall to his knees in the clearing as the elephant let out a deafening, trumpeting cry, shaking its head from side to side then stiffening its ears and tucking its trunk in below its mouth. *The prelude to a charge,* he realised, dread skewering his heart.

The elephant thundered forward and the ground rocked – akin to the tremors the Gods sometimes cast through the earth. As the creature ate up the short distance between them, Mursili scrambled back on his heels and palms… until his ankle became tangled in a vine – caught fast. The Mesedi guardsman bounded down the slope and past Mursili in an effort to defend his king, but the elephant swished its head to the left, goring the guard through the groin with her short tusks and tossing his haemorrhaging body up and through the poplar branches.

Mursili's body froze with terror as the elephant charged on towards him. The beast was but steps away when Zida and his man burst from the trees, haring for the gap between the elephant and their king. The creature thrashed its trunk towards the Mesedi guardsman, batting the fellow off his feet, sending him crashing into a tree trunk with the thick crack of breaking vertebrae, bringing a thick shower of golden leaves toppling onto the clearing floor. Then came brave Zida, sprinting from the far side of the glade, leaping before the creature with his spear readied for a battle he could never win. The spry Gal Mesedi ducked the elephant's swishing trunk and leapt back from its tusks but fell under its charge, a giant foot crushing his body on the clearing floor.

'No,' Mursili wailed.

Bodyguards dead, the king gawped as the elephant rose up on her hind legs, its forelegs ready to come crashing down upon him, to dash him into paste. He heard a million voices sing in his head: of glory, shame, love and hatred, then swung his arms up before him like a futile shield, knowing he was bound for the Dark Earth.

But instead of pain came a thud and a trumpeting cry from the beast. Mursili prised open an eye and saw the creature, still on two legs but now with a trident spear jutting from its left side. The cry cut right through him, and gave him the strength to draw an arrow from his quiver and cut through the vine entangling him, rolling clear just a moment before the elephant's feet smashed down where he had been. He scrambled back up to the lip of the rise and watched, astonished, as now a volley of two javelins plunged into the beast's flank. It swung round to face the threat. There, in the treeline, stood Volca and his two fellow Sherden warriors, crouched, upper bodies weaving as if ready to leap in any direction to avoid the elephant's counterattack. Having spent their spears they now drew their swords. The elephant trumpeted once more, then tensed to charge the Sherden pair.

'She is enraged; do not challenge her,' Mursili cried. 'Separate and run.'

But the shout barely had time to leave his lips before the elephant lurched towards the trio. Mursili's eyes widened, knowing the three there were as good as dead… until Volca, bounding like a deer, his handsome face spoiled by a feral grimace, leapt up and tore his trident free from the beast's flesh, then drove it up and into the creature's neck. It plunged deep and blood sheeted from the wound. The elephant emitted one more wail, its incipient charge instantly repealed and its legs suddenly bowing and bending. As the cow crashed onto its side, Volca stalked around it, his back straight, shoulders square, nostrils flared as he glowered down his nose at the felled giant.

A moment later and the glade was still and silent. Mursili descended into the clearing to stand by the elephant's corpse. Instinctively, he fell to one knee and placed a hand on the creature's forehead, between its haunted, lifeless eyes.

He noticed the other two Sherden moving over to the terrified calves, nocking their bows. 'By all the Gods lower your weapons and let them go,' he snarled.

'My Sun?' Volca said as the two small elephants backed away, trumpeting in terror and reluctant to leave their dead mother. 'You grieve for the monster and its spawn?'

Mursili spoke without looking up. 'We came for a deer. This beast has died for nothing and the Gods will not be happy. You could have let her run,' he added. 'If you three had parted she would no doubt have charged into the forest and fled with her young.'

Volca stalked round to the elephant's neck, placed a foot on its hide then wrenched the trident free with a grunt, sending a puff of blood into the air. 'We could not take the chance that it might come round on you again, My Sun,' he said, bowing, the faint red mizzle settling on his horned helm.

Mursili stood, his mind ablaze with the frantic few moments that had led to this grizzly conclusion. His brow creased as he thought of the signals. 'You made the double call – said we were good to move on the deer, why?'

Volca's face remained blank. 'We made no call,' he said, his eyes drifting to the mangled, ruined form of Zida – shards of white bone sticking through his pulverised, discoloured body, his tunic torn, the red cloak darkened with lifeblood.

'Zida made the call?' Mursili gasped.

'We saw him through woods. He made two calls to tell you to come, then became flustered and confused when he saw elephant. Didn't know how to signal danger to you. I tried to wave at him, to tell him: *stay silent,* but he made a third call regardless – but late, almost disastrously so.'

Mursili felt tears welling in his eyes as he beheld Zida's ruined body. 'He was a brother to me. Selfless, loving, always there.' He moved over to kneel by his chief bodyguard. A wet sigh slid from Zida's lips. He was still alive. The Gal Mesedi's eyes – flooded with dark blood – rolled with great effort towards the Sherden three. 'My... Sun... ' he started. His lips quivered, more words trapped there on the cusp of death, before his pupils dilated and the life seeped from him and into the Dark Earth.

'You were my shield, my protector,' Mursili whispered, unclipping the silver hawk cloakpin from Zida's breast and unhooking the red cloak.

Volca bowed curtly in the corner of Mursili's eye. 'I protect you for rest of journey home, My Sun. I be your shield.'

Mursili glanced at Volca and then at the corpses, the Sherden's offer barely registering. 'We should bury my men. Then we shall return to the column and journey back to Hattusa before the snows come.'

Volca nodded in agreement then clicked his tongue, sending his two Sherden warriors scampering over to begin digging.

CHAPTER 6

OATH
EARLY WINTER 1303 BC

The snows came early, blanketing Hattusa in a slow, relentless fall. A low cherry wood fire crackled in the centre of the palace hearth room, holding the sharp chill at bay. Hattu sat cross-legged on a goatskin rug before the ring of stone and the warming embers within. He looked up and around the walls, where the light from the fire threw flickering shadows from the red and blue painted stucco reliefs of prowling lions and imperious sphinxes, giving them life.

Then, when he closed his eyes, he saw only death. That wicked collage of memories that had deprived him of sleep since the previous moon: bearded warriors, blood, flashing blades. The screaming, the smoke, the stench. And then poor Sarpa. His head sank and he felt tears rushing to his eyes.

He caught sight of himself in the polished bronze mirror resting on the floor by the fire: his dark hair had been overly-groomed by a palace barber, scraped back into a tight, high knot that expanded like a jagged weed on his crown. His face was apprehensive, lips tight like the fading weal on his cheek – the mark of Pitagga's knuckles. His immaculate white tunic, forced upon him by the eager royal tailor, itched on his skin.

Soft, shuffling footsteps sounded on the stone floor. Hattu wiped his eyes and looked up. 'Ah, Master Hattu,' Ruba said from the hearth room doorway. An announcement seemed to be hanging on the old man's lips, but then the brightness in his eyes dimmed and he seemed confused as to why he had come.

'Come, sit,' Hattu gestured to the spot on the carpet by his side, eager to disguise the old scribe's embarrassment, 'warm yourself by the fire.'

Ruba wandered in and sat, muttering to himself, his face sagging and anxious. 'I fear my thoughts wander again. The candle does gutter…'

'Yet still your mind is sharper than any other in Hattusa,' Hattu said swiftly and firmly.

Ruba chuckled. 'Sharp enough to know what is happening to me.'

Hattu felt a thickening in his throat.

'It could be worse,' Ruba mused. 'I once knew a man who lived by the salt lake.'

Hattu's sadness receded as the prospect of another of Ruba's entertaining tales settled on his shoulders like a warm blanket.

'He was young, spry and sharp of mind. And such a strong swimmer. He would search the freshwater estuaries to gather smooth, bright stones he could sell at the markets. While others panned for stones and metals from the banks, he knew better: he would row his raft right out to the deepest part of the water, then tie a rope around his ankle, looping the other end around a heavy rock. With a knife clasped between his teeth, he would leap overboard and let the rock pull him deep down to the bed of the estuary. He said it was like diving into a treasure chest.'

'Like Gilgamesh?' Hattu said with a smile. 'In his quest for the thorny underwater weed that promised to restore youth.'

'Like Gilgamesh indeed,' Ruba grinned. 'This diver man would fill a sack with water-polished stones, precious healing weeds and sometimes even small ingots of gold, then cut the rope with his knife and shoot to the surface with his haul. Then one day, before a dive, a fisherman carelessly bumped his raft. They quarrelled and traded insults, but it came to nothing. And so he dived as usual, the rock taking him to the muddy bed.'

Ruba fell silent again.

Hattu wondered if the old man's mind had slowed once more. 'And what did he find this time?' he prompted.

Ruba turned to him, a wry smile on his face. 'I have no idea, for he never resurfaced. They found his raft. On it was a sack with his bread and water... and his knife.'

Hattu felt a chill on his skin and the urge to laugh darkly at once, imagining the diver's moment of cold realisation, anchored by his own volition to the floor of the estuary with no means of cutting the rope.

Ruba arched one eyebrow. 'Now it might have been the argument with the fisherman that caused the slip or it might have been something else... but that... *that*, is forgetfulness at its worst.'

Hattu peeled away the layers of the tale. Ever the pedagogue, Ruba often embellished his stories with as many lessons as possible. The detriments of a fiery temper, the foolishness of leaving only one means of escape, the folly of hubris. The old tutor had taught him so much: of the stars and the seasons, of the birds, blooms and trees of the land, of how the soil itself – the dry ground upon which they stood – had once been deep under a great ocean. He remembered tracing his fingers over the delicate relics Ruba had shown him – impressions of shells and long-dead sea creatures in shards of rock found right here in the hilly heartlands.

Perhaps the old man's wisdom might answer the question that had been lodged in his thoughts since the Kaskan raid. 'Tutor, when Sarpa was killed, General Kurunta... he was shocked, in a way I have never seen before.'

'The death of your brother shocked us all, Hattu,' Ruba said.

'No, Kurunta was saddened by what happened to Sarpa... but he seemed horrified by the sight of me standing there.'

Ruba's face lengthened, like one sensing bleak weather.

'He... he said something.' Hattu gulped. 'It will begin on the day he stands by the banks of the Ambar, soaked in the blood of his brother.'

Ruba's eyes slipped shut, his lips tightening.

'What did he mean?'

Ruba stayed silent for some time. Hattu wondered if the candle was guttering once more. 'They were not Kurunta's words, Hattu. They were the words... of Ishtar.'

Hattu's flesh crept. 'Of the Goddess? Of my protector?' Every year,

Father had bluntly commanded him to visit the small shrine to Ishtar in the lower town. She was his protective deity and so he would take pots of honey and wine to her altar. He thought of the great stony, lifeless eyes of the statue within, and it sent another chill through his marrow.

'On the night of your birth, she came to him.'

Hattu's flesh crept.

'She came to him in a dream and sang him a song,' Ruba said quietly. 'A song he never wanted to hear. A song he certainly never wanted you to hear.'

'What song?' Hattu snapped, fists balled, frustration rising. '*Tell me.*'

Ruba arched one eyebrow, turning to him. 'And I can understand why he is so reticent,' he chided. 'The fire within you is bright, perhaps too bright.'

Hattu uncurled his fists and lowered his voice. 'Please, Tutor, tell me.'

Ruba hesitated then sighed. 'Aye. My mind will desert me one day and then... so few will remain to tell you. Only Kurunta, Nuwanza and I know the song's words in full.' He gulped and looked around as if fearful Ishtar might be watching, before whispering:

'A burning east, a desert of graves,
A grim harvest, a heartland of wraiths,
The Son of Ishtar, will seize the Grey Throne,
A heart so pure, will turn to stone,
The west will dim, with black boats' hulls,
Trojan heroes, mere carrion for gulls,
And the time will come, as all times must,
When the world will shake, and fall to dust...'

Hattu's skin tingled, colder than ever as the verse washed around in his head. What did it mean? Then he picked out one part of it. *The Son of Ishtar, will seize the Grey Throne.*

'The Son of Ishtar? I... am the Son of Ishtar? These deeds are destined to be mine?'

Ruba sighed. 'The Goddess is a riddle, Hattu. You are a young man. Your actions will define your destiny.'

A patter of footsteps saw a palace servant lean in from the doorway. 'Master Ruba, Prince Hattu: one of General Kurunta's messenger-hawks has landed at the Tawninian Gate – a grey-feathered bird.'

Ruba's face lit up and he clicked his fingers. 'That's what I came to tell you: Kurunta and a knot of scouts set off this morning to clear the western approaches of snow and watch out for the king's return.'

Hattu's heart froze, knowing what Kurunta's grey bird meant. 'The king and the army have been sighted,' he said, his voice devoid of enthusiasm.

'They will be here imminently,' the servant nodded then left.

Hattu's stomach plunged. He imagined General Kurunta out in the blizzard, telling the king all that had occurred in his absence. By now, Father would know about the Kaskan attack... and about his part in it – at a time when he should have been in the acropolis grounds as Father had decreed. Had he obeyed the king, then Sarpa would not have risked his life to stray from the safety of the temple strong room. He rubbed at his eyes with a sigh.

'I will ride Onyx down to the Tawinian Gate and speak with him first,' Ruba said, reading Hattu's thoughts.

Hattu stood. 'And I will go across to the throneroom, for his reception. To face his anger.'

Ruba cocked his head to one side, confused. 'Hattu, anger is a false emotion, you know that, don't you? It is carried on truer sentiments that most men do not know how to express: the tavern brawler who fights only because he cannot bring himself to confess his love for his friend's woman; the shepherd who beats his animals with a cane only because he is heartsick for them, knowing he has not fodder enough to feed them through the winter; the soldier who slays men in scores because he cannot for one moment stop to face the reality of what he is doing.'

Hattu shook his head. 'My brother died because of me. Ishtar's foul verse... it is cursed. *I* am cursed.'

Ruba sighed and gazed past Hattu into the flames. 'Pitagga's axe took your brother's life, Hattu. Now, I should go. I will meet you by the

Grey Throne, soon.'

Hattu sighed. 'Tell me one thing, Tutor. This verse: was it alone enough to conjure Father's ill-feelings towards me?'

Ruba's eyes grew rheumy. He shook his head but seemed unable to speak for a moment, as if assailed by a pang of grief. He dipped a hand into his breast pocket. 'Your father made me swear never to let you have this. But now I know you must see for yourself.'

'Tutor?' Hattu whispered.

Ruba brought out a thick bronze key, placing it in Hattu's palm. Without a further word, he left.

Hattu stared at the key. Cold realisation – as cold as the metal – settled upon him. 'Is this...' he whispered, the words trailing off. He gazed up at the ceiling as if to see through it, then dropped his gaze to the hearth room doorway and beyond, the broad stone staircase leading to the palace's second floor.

He edged towards the stairs. Up he went to find not a soul up there. The shutters of the arched window on the landing had blown open, and snow had gathered on the sill and the floor there, the strange brightness that comes with snow part-illuminating the upper floor. As he made to close them, he heard the distant noise of cheering from the lower town, of chanting priests and droning Wise Women. Pipers began a sombre, ancestral tune too, braving the elements and preparing to welcome their *Labarna* home.

He closed the shutters and gulped, looking again at the key. Father would have to wait. He turned to the long, gloomy upper corridor and gazed along it: deserted, the wintry wind causing the shutters along its length to tremble. At the far end of the dark corridor, atop a short flight of steps, was the Black Room, forbidden to all. All he had ever seen of the room – the highest in the palace – was from outside: that high balcony. And, on just a few occasions, that weightless, rippling form upon it.

The Black Room, forbidden to all.

'Why?' he whispered. He touched a hand to his left cheek. The graze Father's rings had cut across his flesh – as painful as Pitagga's strike – had long ago healed, but the memory was fresh. The king's anger had been fierce that day – and Hattu had only been playing near the door.

How dare you. You must never tread near that room, never!

The Black Room, forbidden to all.

'But *why?*' Hattu muttered.

As if in reply, the winds outside grew strong, the shutters along the corridor chattered again. The black door rattled too, angrily. And long after the wind had calmed and the shutters had fallen silent, the door still shook ... as if there was something locked inside. Dead fingers stroked his neck.

Father's demons live in that high room... you can never enter.

'Why!' he hissed, railing against his fears.

The Black Room, forbidden to all...

And now he had the key.

He stepped forward ever so slowly. 'Banish me from the room, berate me, beat me if you will. But tell me *why,*' he whispered.

The timber floor bent under his weight, groaning sadly as he went. Icy breaths searched under his tunic from the cracks in every set of shutters he passed. On he went and on the Black Door rattled. He climbed the few steps at the end of the corridor, then froze as the Black Door suddenly fell still. He reached out with a shaking hand. The copper handle was deathly cold. He took a long, deep breath, then inserted the key and turned it. The lock shifted with a thick *clunk*. He twisted the handle and, with a moan of ancient, dried-out wood, the door opened.

The air inside the shadowy chamber was perishing and the dust thick. Just one set of recent footprints marked the dust on the cedar floor: Father's he realised, recognising the shape of the king's boots. A finger of gloomy light stretched across the floor, coming from the opposite side of the room – from the doorway that led out onto the high balcony. His gaze was drawn to that arched opening... and to the writhing, floating shape silhouetted there.

His blood ran cold as ice for an instant, before he sighed in relief and broke down in weak laughter. It was merely an old purity hide, pegged to one side of the balcony door; sun-bleached and frayed, rapping in the wintry breeze. More pegs and fragments of the veil were dotted around the rest of the doorway's edge, as if it had been ripped in haste long, long ago. He became deaf to the growing clamour on the main way outside, his attentions instead on the other contents of the forgotten chamber: a bed, a small table, a set of strange bronze implements, knives, pans and cushions. He lifted each one, examining it carefully: surgical tools of some sort, he realised. He was oblivious to the voices outside, on the acropolis. Then there were bones, small bones. He knelt, lifting one and realising it was the remains of a long-dead lamb, and the others were of crows. All this lay around a strange, curved stool. Realisation crept across his skin: he had seen the like before, in the courtyard at one of the villas on Tarhunda's shoulder when a noble's wife was in labour. 'A birthing chair?' he asked the ether. Alone, he could expect no answer.

But he was not alone.

The tortured creaking of the door falling shut behind him was the first herald of the unexpected visitor. The shaking, storm-dark voice was the next:

'So little I have asked of you, and in every way you have defied me,' King Mursili said.

Hattu swung round on one knee, his whole being ablaze with fright. The towering king was damp with melting snow, silvery hair plastered to his face, eyes alight with fury.

'I arrive at my city to find the gates in tatters, entire wards reduced to heaps of rubble. My second son... dead,' his thin lips struggled to contain an animal twitch. 'And then I return to my home... but instead of sanctuary I find my errant issue, railing against my every rule. Again, and again,' he said, his voice trembling, 'and *again!*' he thundered, then strode across the room, his ringed hand drawing away for a backhand blow.

Father's anger had always destroyed Hattu, more than any beating. Yet this time, Hattu felt a fierce spark of defiance, like that which had occurred on the day of the Kaskan raid, at the moment of the strange apparition of the green-cloaked warrior when he had saved Atiya. *Damn your anger, Father, I will not cower under it any longer*. He shot to his feet, his head held high as if preparing to take any blow that might come his way.

'I'm not afraid of you,' he said.

Mursili halted, shocked, the pair a half-stride apart, the king's raised hand juddering like a taut bow. Both held breaths captive. The king's eyes shone like wrathful embers. Nearly level with his own, Hattu realised; last winter, he had been just shoulder-high to his sire. At last, the fire in the king's gaze died and Mursili's malevolent hand fell limply by his side. His eyes grew rheumy, darting over Hattu. 'By all the Gods, my boy, it seems Kurunta and Ruba were right: you have grown in this last summer,' he muttered, then brushed past, out onto the balcony.

Hattu felt his breath return in short gasps, and realised his heart was racing like a maddened colt's. He twisted to the arched doorway with the rippling old veil, seeing his father out there on the balcony, back turned, fresh snow settling upon his shoulders. The king's head was dipped and he seemed to be clutching at one armpit in discomfort. Concerned, Hattu stepped out onto the balcony too, brushing a patch of piled snow from the balustrade with his leather bracer to rest his hands there. The king's moment of pain seemed to have passed, and now Hattu felt acutely awkward at having followed him out here.

From the vantage point of this veranda he could see almost all of Hattusa. Immediately below, on the acropolis grounds, men moved to and fro, taking horses to the royal stables, unhitching the king's carriage and towing it into the wooden byre in which it would winter. One guardsman carried Zida's red cloak, head bowed. The brave Gal Mesedi had perished on the campaign, he realised, his blood cooling.

With the leaderless Mesedi was a pale stranger wearing a long-horned helm – the likes of which Hattu had never seen before. Yet all of this was like a dull, distant buzz of gnats in comparison to the crackling air between him and Father.

'This is the room in which I was born, isn't it?' he said flatly, looking over his shoulder into the Black Room. 'Mother died in that bed.' He laughed once and without humour. 'She died and I lived. *That* is why you hate me.'

King Mursili lifted his surly gaze to one side. Hattu felt pinioned by it, his plucky words suddenly drying up.

'I've never hated you, Hattu. But I can barely look upon you without seeing my beloved and knowing... *knowing* that I chose for it to be that way.'

Hattu's face pinched in confusion.

'I chose for you to live,' Mursili said, the next words coming after a great struggle, 'and for your mother to die.'

'You... chose?' Hattu stammered.

The king traced his fingertips along a section of untouched snow on the balustrade's edge, as if handling a delicate treasure, sparkling crystals of ice falling away in a light shower. 'On the night of your birth, mighty Ishtar came to me.'

Hattu gulped, the verse coming to him.

'You and your mother were dying, so perhaps I should be grateful that she gifted me the chance to save one of you.' His light fingers curled into a shaking fist and he battered it down on the balcony edge, sending the snow plummeting in great lumps. 'But *damn*, it was no gift,' he shook his head, biting his bottom lip and closing his eyes. Tears tremored there, then he looked up and wagged a finger into the white-flecked ether as if reprimanding an unseen form there. 'Yet I did as you demanded. I made my choice.'

Hattu glanced out through the thickening snow with Mursili.

'I chose for you to live, Hattu. I did all Ishtar asked of me – declared her as your protector, offered her a place almost as high as Tarhunda himself.' He waved a hand down to the lower town where, by the snow-blanketed grounds of the majestic Storm Temple, the smaller but no less beautiful shrine to the Goddess of Love and War stood, a small cupola roof topped with an eight-pointed bronze star. 'All the time I hoped it might placate her,' he shook his head and let it loll.

Hattu suddenly felt the winter chill acutely. Ishtar's words and ways were renowned for their devious ambiguity, her every promise entwined with a curse. 'Like a sandal that trips the wearer,' he muttered, Ruba's teachings coming to him. 'Like a castle that crushes the garrison.' He hesitated, then thought of the wicked verse: 'Like the son that brings death and destruction upon his father's throne. The Cursed Son... the Son of Ishtar?'

King Mursili's eyes narrowed. 'Ruba?'

Hattu nodded.

'I made him swear not to tell you, but he seems to have forgotten his vow. Indeed, the old goose is more forgetful than usual when it suits him.'

Hattu's mind swirled. 'Ishtar's verse can have no bearing on things, can it? It talks of bloodied thrones and turmoil. But look at me: I am merely a scribe.'

'Are you?' the king said with a wry laugh. 'Ruba tells me you have been spurning your lessons more often than ever in this last year,' the king said. 'He says you have been taciturn and sullen.'

Hattu adopted a stony sincerity to tell his father what he thought the king would want to hear: 'I will work harder, Father. Whatever it is you wish me to become – a diplomat, a travelling envoy – I will see to it that my mind is strong for such a future.'

Mursili waved a hand. 'I didn't commit you to the Scribal School to train you as an emissary. I assigned you to Ruba's classroom because I wanted to protect you – because I was afraid.'

'Afraid?' Hattu said. The Hittite *Labarna* was a creature who evoked fear but never felt it. 'Of what?'

Mursili hesitated for a moment, the snow settling thickly on his eyebrows in a way that added years to him. 'Kurunta told me how dear Sarpa met his end.'

All at once the foul memories rapped back into Hattu's mind like a colony of bats.

'It will begin on the day he stands by the banks of the Ambar, soaked in the blood of his brother,' King Mursili recited in little more than a whisper.

Hattu shook his head and took a step back from the balcony. 'Ishtar's words are once again laced with trickery and insinuation. Sarpa died on the end of Pitagga's axe. That his blood poured upon me is of no consequence,' he said, drawing on Ruba's earlier words of support.

'Yet Sarpa's body lies in the Dark Earth, while his head is far to the north, no doubt staked like a trophy for Pitagga to admire,' Mursili said. 'Ishtar toys with men, but her words are rarely without substance.'

'Then you believe the rest of it? That I will slay princes and kings. That I will seize the throne... bring the *world* down around us? It was but a foul dream, was it not?'

'Hittites should always heed their dreams,' the king said in a low drawl.

Hattu's flesh crept. Father, Muwa and he were the last of the direct royal line. Not in his darkest nightmares could he envisage harming either of them. 'Ishtar is *wrong*,' Hattu snapped.

Mursili looked up and around them, eyes momentarily timid as a stiff wind cast the snow around in a sudden blizzard. 'Be careful of such words, Hattu.'

'But she is wr-'

Mursili pressed a finger to Hattu's lips, silencing him. 'Swear an oath to me, my son.'

'Anything, Father,' Hattu said.

Mursili took Hattu's hands in his own. It sent a warmth through Hattu that he only now realised had been eternally absent. 'My flesh and blood, my precious boy. Swear to me that never… never will you take up weapons against your family.'

'Never,' Hattu said without hesitation.

'And always you will stand loyally by he who sits on the throne.'

'Always,' Hattu agreed, pride swelling his heart.

Mursili stared into his eyes for a long time, and Hattu wondered what he was seeking. He thought of restating his affirmations, but remembered seeing his Father dealing with foreign kings in the past, never once repeating himself. It was all part of that magnificent, fearless aura. So Hattu said nothing more and held his father's gaze. Eventually, the pair turned to look out over the snow-cloaked acropolis grounds again.

'What lies ahead for me now?' Hattu asked after a long, shared silence.

'You tell me, Hattu,' Mursili replied, his eyes narrowing to crescents.

'As I stated. I will resume my schooling. I will fulfil Ruba's expecta-'

'From your heart, Hattu,' Mursili grabbed him by the shoulders so they were face on once more, shaking him. 'Cast everything out into the snow, everything but the voice… the voice in your *heart*.'

'You know,' Hattu said, his breath puffing between them. 'You know what I wish for.'

'Say it,' the king demanded.

'I… I want to be everything the son of a *Labarna* should be. I want to travel with you on campaign. I want to learn the hardships of the march. I want to be there to put my body before yours like a shield. Surely now it is imperative that I am trained? With poor Sarpa gone, only Muwa stands capable of succeeding you.'

Mursili flashed a wry smile. 'You seek the path of the warrior? Then it is as I thought.' He stood tall and turned away from Hattu, leaning on the balcony again and looking out over the lower town and off into the white wastes of the western countryside beyond. 'Were I to forbid you this, you would merely defy me, wouldn't you?'

Hattu said nothing, but both knew the answer.

Mursili sighed long and deep. 'Very well. When the snows have come and gone, when spring arrives, you will go to the Fields of Bronze.'

Hattu felt a shiver of disbelief. He had never set eyes upon let alone been to the great military academy, a morning's trek to the west. 'But my schooling with Ru–'

'You shall be trained in the arts of war just as Muwa was,' the king shot a sideways look over his shoulder at Hattu. 'As an infantryman and as a charioteer. But you should be aware: a Hittite Prince must show he is stronger and hardier than any other. You will be given no quarter because of your blood. You will suffer like the rest. For two long years: one as an infantryman, the next as a charioteer. I had to do this. Muwa too.'

'And it shows: the people look up to him,' Hattu replied. 'That is all I crave: respect – from others, aye, but most vitally from myself.'

King Mursili turned back to him and drew him into an embrace. Hattu felt his whole being glow in the bear-like hug. The smell of oil, smoke and the dust of foreign lands on Father's damp woollen cloak were so unfamiliar – this embrace itself virgin territory. 'I will do you proud, Father. I will do it all.' He thought of what remained of his small family: Father and Muwa, each utterly beloved. 'And our oath shall be like Tarhunda's bronze shield – unbreakable, sacrosanct.'

Mursili turned from the balcony, leading Hattu back inside. As they walked through the room, the king glanced over the forgotten birthing tools. 'So tell me: why were you outside the city walls – on the day the Kaskans came?'

Hattu thought it an odd question given all they had discussed. 'I took Atiya to the high hollow – where the hunting birds nest. It was a foolish thing to do.'

'Foolish? Why?' the king replied, a fond, distant look on his face. 'I took your mother there when we were young. She wept tears of happiness up there. I am the fool, for I never took her there again.'

***

The snow continued to fall as the light faded, and most within Hattusa had hurried back to their homes now that the king's return had been observed. But one figure braved the cold, padding around the Storm Temple's gardens. Atiya took to brushing the snow from a statue of two life-sized terracotta bulls pulling a copper chariot. Keeping them free of dust, dirt, frost and snow was a simple duty but one thought to draw much favour from Tarhunda himself and the many other gods.

'You don't need to do that now,' a voice called over from the shelter of a nearby colonnade.

Atiya turned to see the Elder Priestess there holding a tallow candle, shivering, beckoning her back to the kitchens and bedchambers. The thought of a hot bowl of stew and then the warm caress of her bedding did appeal, but sleep? That was a different matter: the nightmares since the Kaskan raid had been incessant. 'I don't mind,' she said, 'I can't sleep anyway.'

'I'll set aside some stew for you then,' the priestess sighed.

As the Elder wandered off, Atiya turned back to the monument before her, and realised she was smiling. Few made her smile. The Elder Priestess had been good to her since the Kaskan raid, since Prince Sarpa had been struck down. Sarpa had been a close companion, and she missed him terribly. She thought of young Hattu, shivering and drawing her robe tighter as she imagined what it had been like for him, to see his brother slain before him. Yet in the time since the raid, she had noticed something different about him: a callousness, a sobriety that had been absent before. Was he still a mere boy? Not according to her dreams.

That moment outside the walls, when she had fallen with countless Kaskans bearing down upon her, was where the nightmares always began. They ended every time not as nightmares but as dreams, with Hattu lifting her to safety – it was then she would awake, panting and startled. Frightened, yet comforted at once. The thought of his hands upon her, holding her firmly, carrying her to safety... yes, Hattu was another who made her smile.

And then there was another, one who had been gone so long...

'Brushing bulls is no way for a girl like you to be spending her evening,' a voice said. She turned to face Prince Muwa, swaddled in black robes, military boots and the shining white cuirass, crunching across the snow towards her.

'And sneaking up on templefolk is not the business of a prince, is it?' she said, trying to sound stern but failing, especially as a coy giggle escaped after her last word with a puff of breath.

Muwa's face split with a matching grin.

The pair embraced, giggling, her head buried in his chest. She hadn't seen him since spring, since he had gone north with the king in pursuit of the rogue, Pitagga. Atiya felt her heart lift and noticed how much more manly he had grown in that time: his long hair loose like a lion's mane around his broadened features. And his confident manner, still developing the last time they had spoken, now seemed rounded and natural – as if he had learned from the *Labarna* how to harness and command the very ether around him. There was a sadness in his ice-bright eyes too. It was a devastating mix and she felt breathless for a moment.

'I sang for you, at Sarpa's pyre,' she said.

Muwa's head fell for a moment. 'We were brought the news by outriders. Still, it seems unreal.' He twisted in the direction of the Storm Temple. 'Still, I see him in here, hobbling, smiling. Pitagga will pay,

Atiya. By the Gods he will pay.'

Atiya rested a comforting hand on his chest.

After a short silence, the darkness lifted from him. 'I brought you this,' he said, holding up a vial of clear glass, with a light green liquid inside. 'Perfume, made from the resin of pistachios,' he whispered. 'I bought it from overland Amurrite traders.'

'Muwa, I have told you before,' she complained, trying to hand it back.

He replied by kissing her hand. 'I've missed you dearly, Atiya. When Kurunta rode out to meet with the column and told of the Kaskan attack, I,' he faltered, his eyes misting over. 'I feared that you...' he let his head drop, his thick mane of hair tumbling round to part-obscure his face. 'I could not bear to lose you too,' he said.

'You still have your father and Hattu,' she reminded him.

'Yet it is only you I can think about when I close my eyes,' he replied instantly.

Like a lost girl, she felt her cheeks flushing at the words. A tingling glow rose from within, as if her heart was being stroked by a feather, just like that life or death moment when Hattu had saved her outside the walls, she realised. But then, it had been stronger and more intense, now it was slow and lingering. Muwa raised a hand to cup her chin, tilting her head gently up towards his, then leaned down and pressed his lips onto hers. Her heart raced.

'I missed you, Atiya,' he said as their lips parted.

'And I you,' she replied, somewhat dazed. It was the first time a boy's lips had touched hers. 'Hattu missed you terribly too.'

Muwa smiled. 'My brother found ways to keep himself busy, it seems. Fighting Kaskans? Gods, he had more excitement here than I did in Wahina chasing Pitagga's shadow.'

That memory of the Kaskan raid, of Hattu's first thought being to save her, to protect her, returned. The glow inside her grew too. And then the oddest thing happened, she felt a pang of guilt for standing here with Muwa like this. Muwa reached down to kiss her again, but she stepped back, smiling awkwardly. 'I'm so happy you're back, and tomorrow we can spend all day together – you can tell me of the lands of Wahina. But the elders will kill me if I don't finish clearing the statues of snow,' she lied.

Muwa's confidence seemed dented, and his smile grew a little lopsided. But he recovered well, bowing curtly and smiling warmly once more. 'As you wish. Until tomorrow.'

She watched him go, feeling guilty and confused. After the sound of footsteps faded, she returned to brushing the statue, humming a song to herself. It was a therapeutic task, and one best done alone.

But no, she realised, she was not alone. Sensing eyes upon her, she looked round, expecting to see the Elder Priestess there in the colonnade again, but it was deserted. Instead she noticed, through the copper fence bars nearby, a brave fellow trudging through the snow outside the temple grounds. He was strange, she thought, with short amber hair and a handsome, freckle-dotted face. A foreign trader of some sort, she reckoned. He smiled at her and offered a polite bow of the head. She returned a smile of her own then nervously went back to tending the statue. Yet she had the oddest feeling the stranger was still watching her.

'Men,' she cursed under her breath.

***

Muwa crunched through the snow, back up the deserted main way. When Atiya was a girl and he a boy, she had enthralled him with her energy and zest for life. Now, as adolescents, her beauty and her companionship had him spellbound. The mere thought of her brought giddiness to his mind and clumsiness to his actions.

A few times he shot a look over his shoulder. Something was awry. Not with Atiya – brushing at the bull statue. Nor with the odd fellow trudging past the temple fence – the only other soul outdoors apart from the fur-clad sentries on the walls. No, there was something wrong with *him*. Inside. It was a new sensation. Like the first taste of honey or the first sight of snow, he mused… no, for those things were golden and heady. This was like… like the first taste of sour milk, like the sting of a wasp… deep, deep inside. Then he realised what it was: for the first time in his life, someone had denied him that which he desired.

She rejected me.

He looked back once more, seeing Atiya and recalling the moment Father had told him: *one day, you will be Labarna. Until then, you are the Tuhkanti – and you will want for nothing.*

Indeed, Muwa had lived the life of an heir-apparent. Adulation, respect and reverence met his every turn. Harem girls quarrelled to keep him company just as men fought to be noticed by him on the battlefield. Nobody had ever denied him... until now.

And it only made him crave her affections more intensely than ever.

***

King Mursili walked along the heights of the fortified Dawn Bridge, the winged sun-disc circlet hugging his brow and his body wrapped in grey wool against the blizzard. He passed two shivering sentries posted there, who threw him clench-fisted salutes. He had given his chat with Hattu a day to settle, and now he knew what he had to do.

General Kurunta waited for him on the centre of the bridge, wearing just his leather kilt and twin baldrics strapped across his bare chest. 'You must be *melting* in that garb,' Mursili said glibly.

Kurunta swung to face him, his braided tail jangling in the wind. 'Eh? My Sun,' Kurunta saluted. 'I came at once. What concerns you?'

Mursili stood in Kurunta's lee, then shot a glance over his shoulder back up at the acropolis. He had the most dreadful feeling that – despite the roar of the storm – someone up there might hear them. 'It is more about what will concern *you*, old friend. Next spring, Hattu is to be trained.'

Kurunta's scarred, leathery face creased. 'The Prince? With the army?'

Mursili nodded.

'I don't understand, My Sun,' Kurunta replied. 'You've worked so hard all these years to confine him to the life of a scholar.'

'And you are one of the few who truly know why,' Mursili replied. 'You saw my boy by the Spirit Bridge, Sarpa's blood upon him. Scholar or otherwise, Ishtar's divination came to be... the first part of it at least.'

Kurunta's good eye searched the snowstorm moodily. 'Perhaps this is Ishtar's test.'

'How so?' Mursili asked.

'In recent days I have begun to fear what might happen should you and Prince Muwa come to harm. With no other trained heir, this sacred land would erupt in a thousand fires, My Sun. I remember the chaos of old – princes fighting princes. Pretenders slaying kings... does that not sound familiar?' His face was a war of doubt and certainty as he spoke. 'Maybe this is the fate of us all if Hattu is *not* trained as a true prince?'

Mursili smiled a tepid smile. 'You think Ishtar's game is to show me that my boy is the bringer of our demise... when he might actually be our saviour instead? You have always been an idealist. That is why men follow you without question.'

'My Sun?'

'I digress, Kurunta. In any case, all that matters is this:' Mursili's features darkened. 'When Hattu comes to you in the spring, you must... break him.'

Kurunta's good eye widened. 'Break him? I will not take offence because this comes from you, My Sun, but surely you must know I will do this without need for you to ask. Like any recruit, he will suffer. And I save my hardest moods for the princes: he will grow stronger or he will break, like a blade passing through a smith's fire.'

Mursili leaned a little closer. 'No, he *will* break. I want him to return to me after the summer, beaten, begging me to resume his schooling instead. It must be *his* choice – one that he will abide willingly. You will see to it.'

Kurunta searched the snow again. 'His time will be hard enough. The people whisper about him as they whisper about me. The other soldiers will reject him: you know what they call him?'

'The Cursed Son,' Mursili replied, his face lengthening. 'And that is why you must break him.'

'Then it will be done, My Sun,' Kurunta bowed from the neck.

CHAPTER 7

WELCOME TO THE STORM
SPRING 1302 BC

The spring sun blazed just above the eastern horizon, flooding the Ambar valley with golden light and casting the shadow of Hattusa's twin tors across the lower town. When an ox-drawn carriage rumbled from the Tawinian Gates and along the rutted track that intersected the croplands, many field workers turned to look. It was a fine vehicle: made of cedar wood, banded in copper, with bronze footplates and silver rails and handles. Not the royal carriage, but a vehicle from the acropolis nonetheless.

Within, Hattu felt the many eyes searching inside this small, shady box. They couldn't discern its occupant at such distance, surely, but he drew the linen curtain a little across the small window in any case, sinking back into the cushioned bench.

Two Mesedi sat across from him, their hair clubbed on the napes of their necks and their bronze helms resting across their laps. Big Orax and the remarkably hirsute Gorru – from a distance it seemed that his white tunic had black sleeves and black leggings to match – were two of Father's finest guards. The pair maintained stony, expressionless stares.

Feeling the need to further withdraw, Hattu tugged a lock of hair forward from his leather browband so it hung over his misty eye, as if it might somehow make the soldiers mellow towards him. When the carriage bucked as they crossed the small, rustic stone bridge across the stream emanating from the Spring of the Meadow – the seventh of

Hattusa's blessed water sources – he almost yelped in fright, much to Gorru and Orax's amusement. All morning he had been like this, unable to relax: his every step seemed clumsy and his breathing shallow. He had even snapped at the well-meaning Ruba, who brought him a wax tablet and stylus so he could practice his writing while he was away. *Away*, he thought, tugging the curtain back a little to see how far from Hattusa they were now. The city was shrinking, the familiar sounds and smells fading. He looked in the direction they were headed: the croplands had tapered off and now just rugged, hilly scrubland and wild olive thickets sprouted here and there, shimmering in the hot sun. The path was dotted with just a few men and boys too, trekking westwards with bags and a few with weapons, headed where he was.

Isn't this what I've always wanted? he wondered, a pang of dread trying to serve as an answer.

It was then that a cry sounded from the sky. He looked up to see Arrow gliding there. His heart surged at the sight and, instinctively, he thrust his left arm out of the carriage window. Arrow swooped, landing gracefully on the leather bracer. When he drew her inside the carriage, Gorru and Orax suddenly shuffled and sat a little further back in their seats, their hard, confident demeanours crumbling. When Arrow paced on the spot to settle her talons and then shrieked aggressively at the pair, Gorru grabbed the bench in fright and let out a strangled sound that might have been a scream, but was quickly covered up with a cough and then a harrumph of humiliation.

Hattu did all he could to maintain a straight face. He stroked Arrow's speckled neck. 'I have no food for you, girl,' he said, sadly realising that he would not see her again until winter, when the academy would break up over the cold season. Then he saw the tiny, polished, blue-green beryl stone in the shape of a teardrop tied to Arrow's leg. *Atiya,* he realised, recognising the piece as one of the jewels she often crafted at the temple.

Over the winter, he had taught Atiya how to handle Arrow, standing with her on the Dawn Bridge, sending the falcon out to chase voles, mice and rabbits through the snow-blocked eastern stretch of the Ambar valley. It seemed that the lessons had been sound, given she had managed to despatch Arrow to him like this. But she had been ever so serious the last time he had spoken to her. It was six days ago: they had met in the budding gardens of the Storm Temple. She had sat by his side at the edge of a natural pool there, tracing her fingers along the surface of the turquoise water. He had tried to make conversation: banal chat, nonsense jokes, even teasing her to the point where he thought she might push him in the pool. But she said almost nothing. It was at the end of that odd meeting that it had become stranger still. *I will never forget what you did for me,* she said, kissing him on the cheek and squeezing his hand before turning and running into the temple complex's interior without a further word.

'Return to her,' he said to Arrow, holding his arm outside again. 'Watch over her, aye?'

As Arrow took flight back towards Hattusa, Orax relaxed a little and Gorru muttered some oath at the bird under his breath. Hattu grinned as he threaded a lock of his hair through the tiny hole in the beryl stone, affixing the gem in his chin-length mane. The carriage climbed a low hill. When it came to the brow, Hattu felt a cold stone settle in his belly as he saw three huge shapes emerge from the gentle heat haze ahead, like spirits rising from a silvery pool: three towering stone *huwasi* – rock effigies, set a danna or so apart, each with lifeless eyes staring into infinity. One was of a warrior, feet set wide apart in a stance of power, bronze-headed spear clutched across his muscled chest; another was of an archer, kneeling, teeth clenched in a rictus, drawn bow pointed to the sky and strung with a bronze arrow; the last was of a prancing horse, its hooves and eyes picked out in bronze. He heard Gorru chuckle darkly and knew that this was it: the Fields of Bronze; the ancient training grounds where horses were broken... where *men* were broken.

As they drew closer, the silvery pool of heat haze obscuring the feet of the statues slipped away to reveal the sprawling academy complex. It was spread across a large oval of flat ground, hugged by a crescent of scarred, red-earth fells. It resembled an open, unwalled town rather than a fort, with an assortment of huts, byres, low, white-walled compounds and paddocks holding cantering warhorses.

He saw faint movement here and there, and heard stark, distant shouting and whistling, along with the *thwack* of missiles plunging into wood. Soldiers marched to and fro, their weapons catching the sunlight. Their sharp, urgent cries stirred a sense of unease in him, reminiscent of the day the Kaskans stormed Hattusa.

'Are you ready for this, Master Hattu?' Orax asked as they descended the gentle slope towards the academy.

Hattu swung round, the sudden dialogue after unbroken silence unnerving. He saw that both of the Mesedi wore a slight glimmer of mischief in their eyes – revenge perhaps for the intrusion of Arrow. He gathered himself with a deep breath as the wagon drew to a halt, right in the heart of the academy complex. 'By all the Gods, yes,' he lied.

This place would be his home now. Somewhere behind his breastbone he felt a welling sense of terror and excitement.

Then a voice in the darkness added: ... *destiny*.

***

His hubris melted like wax in the sun as soon as he stepped down from the carriage and into the stark light of day. The heat exacerbated the acrid stink from a nearby smith's furnace and the reek of sweat – from horses and men. Then there was the noise: a raucous clatter of metal and wood and incessant hectoring cries, not to mention the gruff laughter and clatter from within the ramshackle *arzana* house – a soldier's tavern and a brothel in one. As the carriage wheeled away back to Hattusa, a hot wind blew up around him, coating his skin in puffs of red dust, sending his hair dancing across his face. Regiments marched around him on the bare parade field. Scarred, knotted bodies, flint-hard faces and gritted teeth, everywhere. Two soldiers stood by the stone pool marking the Spring of the Soldier – the academy's main water source. They were dressed in kilts, their sweat-slick torsos scraped from some combat drill, sipping water from wooden cups. One nudged the other, nodding furtively in Hattu's direction. The other looked then straightened up as if he had seen a venomous snake. He saw other men's eyes flick towards him, heard them muttering. He couldn't make out what they were saying, but in his mind, he was sure every single voice whispered the same three words.

The Cursed Son.

He felt his heart quickening as he looked this way and that for something, *anything,* other than the hateful eyes. But they were everywhere. And even the high statue of the spear-warrior, wide-apart feet straddling the gatehouse of a low-walled compound just ahead, seemed to be glowering down at him, nostrils flared.

'Prince Hattusili?' a voice whispered. His head swung round: there by the paddock was the most unexpected sight... and the foulest stench. A boy with thin, greasy, hair, short and slicked back, stood by a mountainous pile of steaming horse dung, his face and grey tunic smeared with the stuff, a spade in his hands. 'I am Dagon, he said, 'you do not remember me?'

Hattu frowned.

The boy wiped some dung from his face and the sunlight betrayed the cruel plague scars on his cheeks.

Hattu now realised who it was: the boy who had been trapped in the house on the day of the Kaskan raid, pinned inside by a cart that had rolled across the doorway. The boy who had previously scowled at Hattu like all the others. 'I remember you.'

The boy stepped forward. 'That night, after the Kaskans came,' he said, shooting glances left and right as if wary of being seen talking to Hattu, 'I returned to my home to find it a pile of ashes. If you hadn't moved that cart...'

'I would try to help any Hittite in trouble and I'm sure you would have too,' Hattu reasoned.

Dagon shrugged. 'My father fought on the Spirit Bridge that day,' he said. 'He took an axe-blow to the leg and now he can only walk with the aid of a cane. He sent me here to make up for his absence from the ranks. I arrived yesterday – he said it would be better than living in the shanty hut in the slums that now serves as our home.'

Hattu felt the silence that followed weigh upon his shoulders. 'My father is seeing to it that all those homes are rebuilt,' he said at last.

'That is good to know,' Dagon smiled awkwardly. 'But, if I may ask, why are you here? They say you were destined to live your life in the Scribal School – never to be a true prince.'

'And I think I was, until now.'

Dagon's eyes widened. 'Do you know what rigours and horrors the recruits are put through?'

Hattu eyed the dung massif. 'I have a fair idea.'

Dagon suddenly fell silent, his eyes bulging before he stooped to officiously shovel more dung.

Hattu was confused for a moment, until purposeful footsteps thudded up then halted right behind him. He heard a rasping of breath being drawn in and exhaled through flared nostrils. 'If that shovel stops moving again, I'll *bury* you in that shit mountain,' a voice blasted, causing Dagon to flinch and then shovel frantically. 'And you,' the voice continued, a little quieter, addressing Hattu, 'what do you think you are doing, distracting this hurkeler?'

Hattu turned, mindfully, knowing who was there.

Kurunta was not tall, especially now Hattu had grown a little more, but the man dominated the space before him. The general's mottled face was bent in disgust, perhaps at Hattu's presence, perhaps at the stench of the dung. His good eye tapered and looked over Hattu like a butcher might eye a goat kid.

'General Kurunta, I…' he started, his voice giving out on him. 'I, my father sent me. No, *I chose* to come here.'

Kurunta's nose wrinkled a little more, then he pulled an affected look of mollification. 'Prince Hattusili?' he said with an exaggerated gasp, loud as could be to make sure every single soldier in the academy heard. If they hadn't recognised him before, then they certainly did now. Indeed, a troop of archers jogged past, shooting him narrow-eyed looks.

Kurunta leaned in a little closer, so only Hattu could hear. 'It is a rare thing to be given the chance to work with a prince. You will find the training that lies ahead… *most* enjoyable.' He pointed to the white-walled enclosure watched over by the statue of the warrior. 'The infantry compound will be your home now, the ranks of the Storm Division your family. You will look back and cherish the days when you were thin as a reed with soft, princely hands.'

Hattu felt a spike of anger, rubbing the fingertips of one hand across the calluses and chapped nails on the other – evidence of the three crags he had scaled in the tail-end of winter. And although his body was still lean, he was no weakling.

Kurunta cupped Hattu's chin and bent his head one way then the other, as if evaluating a mule. 'You're a meagre specimen, aren't you, Prince Hattusili? Perhaps some dung shovelling might strengthen those shoulders.'

Hattu's body shook with anger now. *How dare he?*

A hundred spearmen filed by, glowering upon Hattu, Kurunta's words calcifying their mistrust. Kurunta's face came so close their noses were touching and the general's forehead touched Hattu's. 'Welcome,' he grinned a shark's grin, then shoved another spade into Hattu's hands, 'to the Storm.'

***

The low moan of a horn spilled across the Fields of Bronze with the pink light of dawn, infiltrating the grounds of the walled infantry compound. Hattu woke with a yawn that turned into a long sigh. His head ached from the din of the horn and the previous day spent in the full sun, heaving spadefuls of dung with Dagon.

He sat up, the rough wool blanket sliding down to his waist and the spiky, uncovered hay of his box bed rustling and crunching under his weight. He rubbed his aching back. All along the length of the sparsely-appointed dormitory were some hundred other beds like his, occupied by slumbering or stirring shapes. They were boys like him, part of the army's annual intake of recruits. He even recognised one or two of them as boys he had passed in the carriage yesterday; at once he wished he had travelled here on foot like them. He had only been shown in here after dark last night, when they were all asleep already – though he had caught one or two eyes opening, watching him as he made his way to his bed. And when he had put his head down, he had heard them whispering. *Our luck is out, we have been burdened with the Cursed Son.* He had taken to thumbing Atiya's beryl stone and pretending to be asleep. Soon, thanks purely to his tiredness, he was.

The moan of the horn continued, unbroken.

'By the Gods, what *is* that?' he croaked.

'Make haste,' a voice screamed from outside as the wail at last faded. The shapes in the other beds were sitting up now, bleary-eyed and confused, like him. He heard a drumming of feet from outside – men in a great hurry. Hattu sniffed the air, expecting to smell smoke, such were the sounds of urgency. Instead, he caught a stale waft from under the blanket of a bed nearby.

'Hmmm?' Dagon grumbled, rising up on one elbow, eyes barely open.

'Outside,' the screaming voice continued, accompanied by a rapping on the dormitory door.

'Dagon, what's-' Hattu started, but a second moan of the horn began, drowning him out.

Dagon's eyes shot open. 'It's the Dawn Call. Get up, get up!' he yelped, suddenly awake.

All around him, the other young recruits were sliding from their beds, confused or still befuddled with sleep.

'Damned tunic,' one portly young soldier wailed, realising he had pulled on his tunic inside out. He tore it off then put it on again – *still* inside out. 'Halki's balls!'

As the horn's moan ended, Hattu swung his legs from the bed and dressed, unused to such a panicked awakening. He pulled on his linen kilt and tied his belt, then reached down for the stiff pair of soldier boots tucked under his bed. They were the only thing the clerk at the barrack store had issued him with yesterday evening: shin-high, tight around the ankle and upturned at the toes.

Turn your feet into bronze, these will, the clerk had laughed darkly.

The horn began a third long moan. Hattu tied the leather laces on his boots and rose as the cluster of recruits shuffled clumsily towards the dormitory door. They filed though a porch area, passing by the empty racks of what looked like a small armoury.

Hattu hesitated. 'No weapons?' he whispered to one of the boys passing him. The boy ignored Hattu and hurried on past him and outside.

'It's Kurunta's way of saying we are worthless,' Dagon replied instead as he and Hattu spilled outside at the tail end of the group.

The fresh morning air hit Hattu like a playful slap. Disorientated and part-blinded by the sun, he moved forward as best he could behind the others. When they halted, he did too – at the northeastern corner of the huge, low-walled compound. This place housed the core of the army: a single standing regiment from each of the four divisions. Tall staffs were planted in each quarter of the compound, each bearing a gold symbol on top: a torch for the Blaze, a clenched fist for the Wrath, a bull's head for the Fury and a lightning bolt for the Storm in this nearest quarter. Rows of long, pale-red mud-brick buildings like his own dormitory lay perpendicular to the compound walls, with a vast rectangle of flat, red dusty ground in the centre. The space was crammed with soldiers: perfect, hundred-strong squares of men, backs straight, jaws stiff, long, dark hair rippling in the breeze. They wore leather soldier boots, off-white linen kilts or tunics, stiffened linen or leather cuirasses and bronze-browed leather helms. In their belts they carried curved swords, vicious maces and small axes and in their hands they clasped hide-covered shields and high, skywards-pointing spears. The two rearmost ranks of each hundred wore bows and quivers too. Each hundred was fronted by a captain sporting a trailing, black plume on his helm that hung to the waist like a horse's tail.

Cries rang out from commanders in the other three quarters of the square, where the ranks began to dissolve and reform in different shapes: *Blaze of Arinniti – march! Fury of Aplu – form a wall! Wrath of Sarruma – present spears!* Every movement threw up a racket of echoes – boots, shields and spears in motion.

Nine not-quite-replete companies of one hundred Storm soldiers stood in this quarter, surrounding the hundred boys. They were each scarred and scowling, their long hair beaded with animal teeth or small talismanic jewels. This was the standing regiment of the Storm Division, Hattu realised, the remnant of the thousand veterans who had flooded from Hattusa's Great Barracks to battle the Kaskans on the Spirit Bridge. They gazed in silence out over the compound walls towards the eastern skyline as if impersonating the warrior statue. The flat-faced regimental chief in charge of this lot stood at the head of the rightmost company of one hundred, holding the staff topped with the golden lightning bolt.

Urgent footsteps beat up behind them and Kurunta burst into view. He came to a halt before the assembled Storm ranks, posturing like a rhinoceros waiting to charge, feet wide apart, head dipped. 'Storm Division... *atteeention.*'

With a sharp, martial clatter, the nine neat squares of veterans rapped their spear hafts into the dust and stood even more proud. The rabble of boys in the centre seemed to jolt at this.

'And now let us welcome our new recruits... *preeeeesent.*'

With a rattle of timber and crunch of dust under boots, the nine neat squares of Storm veterans swung so each was facing inwards at the recruits, levelling their spears, their distant stares now trained on the young men. Fierce, cold stares. Eyes innumerable. '*Ha!*' they cried as one.

Kurunta ignored his nine perfect companies to stride before the corralled gaggle of young men, the braided silver tail sprouting from above his ear jostling with each stride. Hattu only dared snatch glances from the side of his eye when the general's back was turned. Suddenly, Kurunta thrust his face into that of the plump recruit with the inside-out tunic. 'Garin, aye? I knew your father. He liked his food too.' Hattu heard a low whine from the boy, then a deep chesty chuckle from Kurunta. On he strode like a vulture around a carcass. One toothy lad who had only had time to partially dress – standing in his loincloth and wearing one boot – stared at the general, wide-eyed. Kurunta rushed for him and screamed in his face: 'See something you like?' he pulled his eyepatch up to reveal a pit of scar tissue and the small, black hole at the centre. Hattu looked away, hearing just a weighty crumple as the staring boy passed out.

Hattu heard the rapid stomp of footsteps coming his way and before he could turn towards them, a flash and zing of bronze brought one of Kurunta's twin blades to his neck. The cool tip touched his throat like the feet of a butterfly landing there. Kurunta gazed down its length, his teeth gritted and a low growl pouring from the gaps. Hattu dared not gulp lest the sword's edge pierce his neck.

'And you, *Prince* Hattusili,' the appellation couldn't have been more derisory. 'Last of one thousand men to crawl from your stinking bed. What an inauspicious start. Muwa, the *Tuhkanti* – a true prince – at least made sure to lead his band of recruits out on his first day.' He snorted. 'Muwa's Shadow, indeed.'

Now the nine veteran bands began to murmur. 'I told you, Chief Raku – it *is* him,' a soldier next to Flat-face the Regimental Chief whispered. 'See his eyes – one like mist? He brings his curse to the ranks of the Storm,' another claimed, the disguised hiss amplified by the compound's walls. Even some of the other divisions turned heads towards the announcement. The boys near him took a step away, some with that same baleful look. Only Dagon remained where he was near Hattu's side, his gaze on the ground before him as if struggling with his choice.

'Well, what have you got to say?' Kurunta demanded.

Hattu knew he was damned no matter how he chose to answer. 'I stopped at the armoury in the porch. I should have been swifter. I made a mistake,' he said.

'Aye, aye you did,' Kurunta replied, the words dripping with dark insinuation. He paced away from Hattu and strode before the recruits, then tossed up both swords and caught them overhand, before driving them down into the dust. 'You have the honour of standing here today and the privilege – the mere *chance* – to prove yourselves worthy. The First Regiment of the Storm lost many soldiers last year when the Kaskans came. Veterans working the farmlands were drafted in to replace some of them, yet still we are one company short of a thousand. And I see one hundred boys before me. Are you ready for what is to come?'

Silence.

'*Are you?*' he screamed.

The reply came in a thin and highly unconvincing mumble.

Kurunta chuckled darkly. 'You come here as lambs, weak, bleating, frightened. In the months to come each of you will be oxen and I will be your master: I will put your neck to the plough and, by the Gods, I will drive you until your heart *bursts!*' His gritted teeth creaked under the strain of a gleeful rictus and spit showered the air. 'When it is all over, we shall see who remains. Should you crumble, then you will spend the rest of your lives in ignominy. If you suffer it all as a Hittite should, then... *then* you will be lions. Your reward will be the chance to die for your country.'

While Kurunta spoke, Hattu couldn't help but notice the fierce and frantic drills of the other divisions. He saw from the corner of his eye a hundred of the Blaze Division, gnarled and knotted as if sired by Kurunta himself, each with a bird's talons painted on their hide shields.

'The Pitiless Ravens, *turn,*' the captain of that company bawled. They swung like a door, as one.

'The Savage Bastards... *brace,*' came another cry. This one was from a hundred of the Wrath Division, each with a fang emblem daubed on their hide shield. They stamped one foot in unison then dropped into a warrior's crouch. '*Ha!*' they cried.

'The Savage *Bastards?*' Hattu half-whispered, half-gasped, terrified and trying not to laugh at once.

'My Father said they are savage,' Dagon whispered in reply. '... and most certainly bastards.'

'And I call you,' a voice cut in, chokingly close, right behind and between Hattu and Dagon, 'the Hurkelers of Hattusa!' Somehow, Kurunta had yet again flitted round behind them unnoticed. 'Aye, that's right... when they're not shovelling shit, they're no doubt eyeing up the sheep and the goats.'

A burst of derisory laughter rang out from the veterans.

The general pulled away and now strutted past in front of them. He stabbed out a finger at Hattu as he went, not looking at his target but directing every other pair of eyes there. 'Now our pampered prince mentioned that he stopped at the armoury. No doubt expected to find a jewelled spear waiting for him there and a set of plush armour.'

More snorts of derision from the veterans.

'The first thing most recruits look for is a blade and a chance to play with it, but look at you – you would cut yourselves to ribbons.' Kurunta said, addressing them all. He came back to Hattu again. 'And the pampered prince – he would no doubt call for his slaves to show him which end to hold.' The veterans' laughter faded into a chorus of heckles and dark grumbling.

'In any case what a recruit must do is not take, but give,' Kurunta clapped his hands twice. 'Give his being, his body, his mind, his heart… to a life of soldiery. Our enemies call us the Wretched Fallen Ones. They say we eat animal bones and sleep on rocks. They mock our Gods and our way of life. But… damn them all… they fear us like their darkest nightmares.' Kurunta's face was twisted at its saurian worst now, his every word sizzling with zeal. 'And I cannot allow such a reputation to slip.'

From a squat red-clay building by the walls, a slave boy emerged, bringing with him a hemp wrap and a stool. The lad set the stool before Kurunta and unwrapped a small, polished bronze mirror with an ash handle, laying it on the stool. Then he dug out a pine implement and put it there too.

Hattu scrutinised the object. *A spindle?* he guessed, having seen women using these when winding flax by the Ambar.

The lad took the last item from the wrap. It was a square of bright, saffron-yellow material. He shook it and it unfurled, revealing itself as a long woman's gown. The boy then folded it in half and laid it on the stool too.

Silence.

Kurunta gestured towards the odd goods. 'You see here a woman's dress, do you not?'

Utter silence.

'DO YOU NOT?' he bellowed.

'Yes!' came a rather terrified reply.

'A mirror for applying coloured pastes to your skin, a tool for weaving pretty, soft garments… *princely* garments.'

More laughter from the veterans, now comfortable that Hattu was here to be mocked.

Kurunta wagged a finger, eyeing each of the boys. 'So you make your choice. Walk from this compound and back to your homes…' he glanced at Hattu, 'or your palaces… where you can live the soft life of a woman. Or you can take the Soldier's Oath today.'

Kurunta's top lip twitched like a hidden wolf watching passing deer, seeking the weakest. 'But know that whoever takes this oath then breaks it later, spits in the eye of the *Labarna* and the Gods. He will know no mercy... ' Not a soul spoke. The only noise was the *crunch crunch* of Kurunta's boots as he strode to the compound gates, bashing them open with his shoulder and thigh. The general stood there, in the shadow of the gatehouse and the warrior statue.

'Make. Your. Choice.'

Kurunta's one-eyed gaze pinned Hattu like a glowing copper rod, almost ordering him and him alone to leave. The cicada song grew shrill, almost deafening.

Then the one-booted toothy boy who had fainted came to. Bewildered and still wracked with terror, he rose and hobbled away from the group, across the dust and then sprinted out through the gates, flinching as he passed Kurunta.

'Anyone else?' Kurunta bawled as the toothy boy's uneven footsteps faded to nothing.

A doubting voice screamed inwardly at Hattu, almost shoving him towards the compound gates. His smoky eye ached, and he saw in the shadow of the gatehouse an ethereal form of another – that meek, round-shouldered scribe, face in shadow just as he had seen at the postern tunnel on the day of the Kaskan raid. The imagined scribe held out a hand, as if offering to escort Hattu home. And the ethereal scholar was not alone, Hattu realised with a shiver: for up on the roof of the officer's quarters by the gate, there was another – another Hattu knew was not real. It was the strange vision of a green-cloaked warrior he had also seen at the Kaskan raid. This figure was crouched on one knee, the cloak hanging around him like a shroud and a battle helmet obscuring most of his face. The shadows hid this one's face, but Hattu was sure he was being watched like a hawk.

'Courage comes in many forms,' Kurunta said in a low drawl. 'It takes a brave man to admit that he is not suited for certain things.'

Hattu felt Kurunta's words like hooks in his skin, drawing him towards the gates. But neither he nor any other moved. The vision of the scribe vanished as did that of the watching warrior.

'Good,' Kurunta said at last, drawing the word out and pulling something akin to a smile, letting the gates close. 'Now let me take you on a journey, a journey to the edge of madness, the place where soldiers are born,' the general said, his cruel face twisting when his gaze met Hattu's, 'and craven hearts are broken.'

CHAPTER 8

THE EDGE
SPRING 1302 BC

Under a hot noonday sun the hundred boys, kilted and booted, scrambled up the steep red-earth fells that rose behind the Fields of Bronze. Russet dust puffed into the air with every footstep and their breaths came in gasps and croaks.

Hattu felt his hurried breakfast of bread and yoghurt surge up his gullet, but each snatched breath held it back. Sweat droplets sprayed from him with every juddering step as the scree littering the climb ensured that every stride upwards was accompanied by a slow slide back down.

'Come on: Up, *up!*' Kurunta bawled, already a good ten paces ahead of the fastest recruit. 'By the plague-boar who spawned you, you'll be doing this every day, so you'd better get used to it.'

Those in front of Hattu renewed their efforts, sending dust spraying back into his face. He closed his eyes and forged on, grasping for purchase at the hardy green shrubs that speckled the slope. This frantic scramble was nothing like the careful but continuous strain of a climb; this felt designed to make a man's heart explode. Blessedly, he reached the top of the fell before that happened. A gentle breeze touched him, not cool but a little fresher than the stifling, still air down on the low ground of the compound. He sank to one knee, panting.

The recruits all around him were flagging too, some dropping to the ground, others bent double and spitting, slender torsos gleaming with sweat and patches of caked dust. The portly boy, Garin, was worst off, back arching as he vomited like a cat. Only Tanku, a burly and dark-skinned lad with his long hair shaved at the sides, had reached the top a respectably short distance behind Kurunta, but even he was coated in rivulets of sweat.

Hattu looked all around. Up here, the pastel sky seemed infinite. These fells stretched off into the western horizon and to the south he saw the broad, ancient track that stretched east and west across the Hittite domain. Behind him to the east, he could see the Fields of Bronze down below: the compounds, paddocks and barns there swirling in a silvery heat haze. Beyond, he could see all the way back to Hattusa – just a hulking, sun-bleached mass near the eastern skyline – and far, far away to the north he could even see the great Soaring Mountains, their snowy peaks shining like white flame in the sunlight.

A dull babble of voices from other parts of the fells caught his attention: companies of bowmen, spearmen, and slingers were dotted around the heights, marching along tight hill-paths, running along high ridges, tossing rocks to one another on lofty flats and leaping over well-worn timber and rock obstacles.

'The hot season has begun, and so the ranks come up here – where it is cooler – to train.' Kurunta explained. A flash of bronze on an adjacent hill betrayed a company from the Blaze Division, the hundred crouching within a bitemark-like section of crumbled hillside. All the boys' eyes turned to the sight. The Blaze warriors had removed their leather helms, clutching them underarm so the sunlight would not catch the bronze brows. Meanwhile, an equal number from the Wrath Division jogged across the hilltop above the bitemark, two abreast. Their heads were switching this way and that warily.

'Heh,' Kurunta grunted, swinging one booted foot up onto a rock and resting his palms on his hips, his good eye alight with interest as he watched.

Hattu watched the hidden Blaze captain rise slowly from his haunches to steal a glance up at his prey. As the hundred of the Wrath passed his men's hiding place, the Blaze captain shot up with a shout: 'For the great Sun Goddess!' The Blaze ranks sprang from their crouches, out of the bitemark, bounding up the short stretch of slope towards the flank of the Wrath men, dark hair flowing in their wake. The Wrath ranks cried out, swinging their hide-shields and bronze-headed spears to face the flood of men coming for them. But a discordant rattle of Blaze spearheads clattering against Wrath shields brought it to an end. The Blaze soldiers whooped in delight at the victory won by those mock-killing strikes. A moment later they embraced with their disappointed Wrath counterparts, clasping arms and slapping backs.

'Warriors…' Kurunta said, pointing at the nearby infantry melee. Then he swung his finger across the hundred boys, '…scum.' He paced before them, scowling down his nose at Hattu more than any other. 'Unworthy scum. *They* carry sharpened bronze, *they* don the garb of soldiers, because I trust them, the king trusts them… the Gods trust them. You? *You* are barely fit to clamber up a gentle hillside, let alone carry a weapon. Now, every company of one hundred needs a name.' He pointed at the veteran groups on the other hillsides. 'The Scorpion Brotherhood, the Dark Sons, the Cruel Spears… You? I shall call you… the Hill Pups.'

Tanku was the only one to visibly take offence, a thick vein in the shaved sides of his scalp bulging, but he did not dare challenge the suggestion.

The thick *plonk* of a water skin being relieved of its cork had all heads turning towards Garin. The chubby recruit halted, the skin a finger's-width from his lips, his guilty eyes looking this way and that.

Kurunta brought his sword round in a flash. The flat cracked against Garin's hand, and the water skin splatted onto the ground, leaking its precious contents into the red dust. 'I told you before we left: *no* water. Did you not understand what I meant when I told you that I am now your master, the will of your king?'

Garin nodded hurriedly, gawping up at Kurunta, cupping his swatted hand under his armpit.

Kurunta's face creased in what might have been a smile, but probably an evil one. 'You know what they do up on the acropolis when someone offends the *Labarna*?'

Garin trembled.

'They treat him to a lovely meal, and a fine beverage to wash it down,' Kurunta purred.

Garin's face lifted in pleasant surprise. Everyone else wore looks of confusion.

Apart from Hattu, who had seen the punishment once before: when a Lukkan slave brought King Mursili bread and fruit-water. The Lukkan had a mean-eye and clearly resented his role – even though it was a relatively comfortable one. That day, he had made the mistake of neglecting to wash his hands before bringing the king's food, his fingernails caked with black dirt and scum. He had been seized by the Mesedi and subjected to the age-old penalty for such carelessness. Hattu's stomach churned in disgust as he recalled the stench from the plate of steaming brown fare the slave had been forced to eat – delivered straight from a palace official's bowels – and the cup of equally foul, warm, yellow liquid the fellow had washed it down with, gagging, retching, eyes bulging from his head and tears streaming down his face as he was forced to finish every last mouthful.

'Well I have a meal brewing in here, boy. A lovely, hot meal that will fill any plate,' Kurunta said, patting his belly and then hitching his crotch, 'and any cup.'

Garin's face darkened in realisation and he dropped his head.

'So, if you want water, then you must look to your prince,' Kurunta said.

Hattu suddenly snapped to attention, conscious of all eyes on him. 'What, how?'

'There's enough water to slake a hundred thirsty mouths, down there,' Kurunta said, calmly pointing back down the slope. There, barely discernible in the heat haze, two men were ferrying buckets to and from the Spring of the Soldier, filling them. Kurunta gave them a wave, then leaned towards Hattu. 'Go, fetch... or your comrades go thirsty.'

Hattu saw the pale, sweat-streaked faces, the dry cracked lips, the baleful eyes now hopeful, pleading. He looked downhill at the pole the two men down there were preparing like a yoke, each end laden with one full water bucket. 'But I, I can't-'

'You are a prince, are you not?' Kurunta gasped. 'Is it not your wish to be stronger than the rest? Go, fetch. Your limbs will grow sturdier for the repetition and the extra burden.'

Hattu saw the boys' gazes harden. Only Dagon offered him any encouragement, the plague-scarred lad nodding once, furtively.

'Go!' Kurunta snarled.

Hattu backed away, then turned to the slope. The descent was swift but taxing, his quadriceps and hamstrings soon trembling with every jarring stride. He stumbled to a halt near the two soldiers.

'Ready?' the pair said immediately, straining to lift the pole by its ends as if preparing to harness an ox. Hattu stammered, still catching his breath from the descent: 'I... I... '

'That's a yes,' one of the soldiers said.

The pair placed the pole across Hattu's back. The two water buckets on it pressed the pole down into his shoulders fiercely, squeezing precious air from his lungs. He shot his hands up to either side to balance the pole, the water buckets at either end swaying and sloshing, a little spilling from the sides. A moment later, the soldiers tied another two full buckets to the pole and one of them whistled gaily as he topped up the ones from which the spillage had come. Hattu staggered to adjust his footing, his arms trembling. A third pair of buckets nearly broke him. It was like carrying an awkwardly-shaped, writhing, grown man.

'You'd better be going,' one of the soldiers said, giving him a shove in the back. Six sploshes of water escaped and he nearly went sprawling, but he threw out a foot to stabilise himself, then another, then another on up the slope. The first strides were challenging and slow. The next few were utterly crushing. Everything was pulling down and back, and with his hands on the pole, he couldn't even reach down and pull on the shrubs and roots for purchase. The extra weight meant every footstep sunk nearly shin-deep into the dust and scree. He craned his neck to see up the hill and realised he was barely a quarter of the way up. Kurunta stood in a wide-footed pose, hands on hips, glowering down on him. The rest of the boys stared down too, dry-mouthed, eager. Hattu heard only the rattling of his desert-dry breath and the thumping of his overworked heart. It felt as if a glowing coal rested at the bottom of each of his lungs. The sun crackled on his skin and now every small step was an ordeal.

'I... I can't,' he croaked.

Silence. Just the staring wall of faces up at the top of the slope.

He focused on them until the edges of his vision grew black. Another step, and bright colours popped and flashed. Another step and he could see nothing. Suddenly, the weight was gone, a chaotic sensation of falling replacing it. He tumbled over and over, back downhill, the red dust going up his nose and in his mouth and more thorny roots scoring his skin.

He came to a halt at the foot of the hill, coughing dust, his leg dripping blood where a root had torn it open. The pole lay just uphill from him where he had fallen, the buckets on their sides, their precious loads spilt and seeping away into the red earth. The two soldiers laughed, one tossing the other a small silver shekel bar to settle a bet.

'Try again, Prince,' Kurunta bawled down from the heights.

Hattu felt a surge of nausea, and the very thought of standing, let alone climbing a hillside with a ridiculous burden, almost brought up the contents of his stomach.

'Try again, or your comrades will not drink until sundown,' Kurunta continued. Now a chorus of worried voices erupted. 'Come on: get up!' they cried, their words edged with anger.

Hattu pushed himself to his feet, his head instantly swimming. 'The pole,' he croaked, asking the two soldiers for their help. One's eyebrows arched in surprise, and he took the shekel back from the other's palm.

Hattu braced as they re-filled the buckets, then loaded each one onto the pole again. He took two steps towards the base of the dusty slope, then toppled face first. A chorus of jeers rang out from the heights above as he cast off the poles and threw up.

'No water for you today,' Kurunta concluded. The jeering intensified. 'Such a shame. Prince Muwa managed to beat the Water Ordeal and bring water to his comrades. I can see why they call this one Muwa's Shadow.'

***

That evening, the moment the sun dropped to touch the western horizon, Kurunta gave the order for them to descend to the academy grounds.

Hattu staggered downhill and over to the low, round cistern by the Spring of the Soldier with the rest of the recruits. The other boys fell to their knees, drinking frenetically, lashing handfuls of water across their dust-coated faces and hair. Hattu saw a space by the edge of the cistern and stepped towards it, only for big Tanku to elbow him out of the way with a snarl. So Hattu waited until the others were done then drank alone. He drank and drank until his gut ached from the sheer volume, then threw water over his face and hair and slid down to rest his back on the edge of the cistern, eyes closed. He brought the lock of hair with the teardrop-shaped beryl stone round from his shoulder and toyed with it, trying to forget about the day, to block out the gruff chatter of soldiers passing here and there and the inebriated caterwauling and clacking of cups coming from the arzana house. He spirited himself to the high hollow with the cerulean tarn, Arrow on his shoulder, Atiya by his side.

When he opened his eyes he saw Kurunta standing in the gateway of the infantry compound, twisting a splinter of wood in his teeth, glaring at him. *What have I done?* He suddenly realised. *I asked for this.*

***

As the days passed, spring turned into summer and the unforgiving Hittite heartlands baked. Every day, the Hill Pups were roused at Dawn and fed a breakfast of goat's milk and bread with a single pot of honey to share. Shortly after, they were put through the rigours of the training field – running around a track, leaping over fences, crawling along ropes tied between two high posts and scrambling through tight earth tunnels. Only when it came close to midday – the time when farmers, citizens and even mangy dogs would be taking respite from the sun and sleeping in some shady refuge for an hour or two – Kurunta would lead the hundred up the fells. And every single day, Hattu was tasked with descending the hill to haul water buckets to the summit in that furnace-like heat. Every single time, he failed. His muscles had strengthened as Kurunta had suggested, that much was true, but he had never once reached the halfway point of the water-burdened climb before exhaustion took him. He either passed out or sunk onto one knee, knowing there was nothing left in him. He had tried to carry one bucket to the top at a time. Kurunta had let him reach the top with the first before snatching it and pouring it out. *One ascent, six buckets,* the general had growled gleefully.

One day, exactly a moon after he had arrived at the academy, Hattu descended the hill at Kurunta's order and came to the two smiling soldiers and the water pole. He eyed the sight as if he had just tasted sour beer, but said nothing. Today, he would broach the halfway point, he affirmed. It was a crumb of focus – something to stave off the madness of it all; the hill could not be bested with such a burden, surely? Yoked with the water poles, he began the climb. Up, up, dust, rasping breath, skin on fire, muscles burning. He even found himself taking a few steps beyond the halfway point. But then came the thud of his knees into the dust and the chorus of exasperated jeers from above. He squinted uphill, seeing Kurunta up there, smirking. The dog had set him an impossible task and he knew it.

Now let me take you to the edge of madness, the place where soldiers are born... and craven hearts are broken.

Hattu felt a fresh wave of vigour. With a groan, he forced himself to his feet again. Kurunta's smirk faded and the boys up there cried in hope. He took one, two, three steps. Then blackness fell like an executioner's blade. One of the soldiers from below climbed up to rouse him, pouring a bucket on his face and slapping him. Hattu sat up and gratefully gulped the remaining water. 'Thank you,' he said.

'I wouldn't be thanking me,' the soldier said coldly, his eyes flicking to the hilltop.

Hattu stood, shakily, seeing the wall of faces up there, twisted in anger, enviously eyeing the water dripping from Hattu's chin.

'You'd better get up there,' the soldier said, dragging the pole and buckets behind him back downhill.

Hattu hiked up the rest of the slope, his brain throbbing and his limbs trembling. When he reached the summit, Kurunta snorted and turned away from him. 'No water... again.'

'Sir, let them drink,' Hattu rasped.

Kurunta swung back and shrugged. 'Why, so you feel better about letting everyone down? I don't think so.'

'Sir, please,' he insisted.

'Half-rations tonight for all of you,' Kurunta barked matter-of-factly. 'You can thank your prince for that in a moment.'

Hattu felt his blood run cold. *No*, he mouthed as he saw the faces of the other recruits fall, then twist into cruel glares, all fixed upon him.

Kurunta broke the wicked spell by putting two fingers between his lips to issue a shrill whistle. A trio of Storm soldiers brought over a bunch of spear poles – devoid of bronze tips – and a stack of shields. 'Now, split into two teams of fifty and face each other in a line… it's time to see how easily you buttercups bruise,' Kurunta purred, slitting the string holding the poles together and tossing them one by one to the boys.

Hattu caught one spear pole: it was heavier than he had expected and rough to the touch – enough so that it did not slip in his grasp. He slipped into place on one line of fifty. Dagon was by his left side and Garin on the right. He eyed the boy directly across from him in the opposing line of fifty. A little shorter than him but definitely sturdier too. An even match.

'With the infantry, it is all about holding shape. As two men working together in a forest melee, as a company of a hundred standing in square, anchoring a chariot manoeuvre or as part of an entire division, standing together in a line across a desert plain, you must stay on your feet and work together, as a unit. Sometimes it is fitting to charge, to sprint. Other times, you must measure your foe and approach carefully, slowly, retaining an ability to defend yourself as well as strike at him. Spear and shield epitomise this balance perfectly. Take a shield, see for yourselves.'

The trio of Storm soldiers began handing out the shields. One covered in tanned, dark brown cowhide was thrust into Hattu's hands. It felt solid, but lighter than he had expected. It covered him neck to thigh, with the sides curving inwards like a lady's waist. For a moment, he became lost in a brief and inappropriate reverie of Atiya.

'Now rest your spear against the right side of your shield, like so,' Kurunta said, showing them the correct grip and battle stance: left leg forward, right foot anchoring, spear held in the right hand and the shaft resting against the 'waist' of the shield.

Hattu followed suit, lifting his shield a little to place the spear there. Almost by accident, the edge of Dagon and Garin's shields clacked against his own, with their spears poking from the almond-shaped gaps between the touching edges. It was the same all along the line.

'See? Like the scales of a lizard and the quills of a porcupine,' Kurunta chuckled in satisfaction. 'Now, your task is simple,' he said, drawing a line in the dirt with the end of his boot behind each team. 'Drive the other side back. Capture the hilltop as your own. As soon as any one member of either side falls back over their line, the game is over. It is a test of strength and a lesson: that any group of soldiers is only as strong as their weakest link. Don't let it be you,' Kurunta said. The general then stroked his chin. 'First, though, let's mix things up a little. You, move here. You, there,' he said as he rearranged the opposite team, drawing the short stocky recruit away to another spot in the line. Hattu soon understood Kurunta's game: now it was Tanku – the burliest of all the recruits – directly across from him. The boy's lips, blistered and scabbed from the tortuous denial of water, lifted like an angered mastiff's.

'What are you waiting for?' Kurunta bawled. '*Charge!*'

With a clamour of shouts and panicked shrieks, the two opposing walls of recruits surged together. Hattu swung up his spear pole as he and Tanku bounded for one another. *Crack!* their shields and spear shafts met and Tanku's face was a finger's width from his own, teeth clenched. After that instant of collision, the pair fell back. *Whack!* They clashed again. This time Tanku's brute strength won out, driving Hattu back towards the line. Hattu saw he was but paces from falling over it. 'You're finished here,' Tanku growled, '*Cursed Son!*'

Hattu knew he only had one option. In a trice, he released the tension on his shield and spear pole and swung away from Tanku like an opening door. Tanku's incredible momentum sent him flailing forward, across the dirt line and onto his face.

The struggle amongst the other boys ebbed as they saw what had happened. Confusion reigned. 'Have we won?' Garin asked. 'No, Tanku fell over *their* line,' another insisted.

Hattu was caught between offering Tanku a hand to get to his feet and seeing what Kurunta had to say about it all, when Tanku rose and hooked a ham-like fist across his face. A shower of white light shot across Hattu's eyes and he spun wildly away, crashing into the rest of the boys.

'You *wretch*,' Tanku cried, the veins on his shaved temples pulsing like angry worms. 'I've had enough of you. You don't belong here. For an entire moon I've been starved of water from morning till sunset because of you. Tonight I will eat a pitifully small meal because of you. No more... *no more!*' he screamed then leapt at Hattu. Hattu braced. Dagon leapt between them, only for someone else to punch Dagon. A moment later and two boys – Sargis, a beanpole of a lad a good head taller than Tanku, and Kisna, a hawk-faced recruit with jaw-length hair – pounced on Dagon's attacker. In a few breaths, the two groups of fifty had dissolved into a sprawling mass of flailing arms and legs, young men thrashing on the ground, yelping as others collapsed on top of them. Some had dropped their spear poles and taken to using fists and feet. One had pinned another to the ground and was vigorously punching him in the crotch over and over – the pinned one's wails growing steadily more piercing. Hattu saw the livid face of Tanku, stranded like him on the opposite side of the melee.

'Oh dear, sweet, Lord of the Storm,' Kurunta boomed, striding around the ruckus, hands clasped behind his back. 'This is surely the sorriest shower of dogs I have ever been burdened with. Enough... *enough!*'

The fighting pack broke apart, the recruits panting, spitting blood, moaning, warily cupping wounds – the boy with the pulverised crotch wearing a haunted look.

Kurunta weaved between the two fifties in a figure of eight. 'If I took you into battle today, I would be digging a hundred graves tonight. Training is over for today.' With that, the gnarled general turned and strode away, his silver tail jostling as he made his way down the red-earth slope back towards the academy far below.

***

That night, Hattu sat on the dormitory porch, alone. A hearty aroma of spiced carrot stew wafted from inside the sleeping quarters. He looked over his shoulder: the porch armoury was now stocked with the poles and shields they had been given that day. A burst of laughter erupted from inside. He saw the boys there in the orange glow of tallow-light, eating their half-rations, drinking and bantering – Garin telling them some tale about his pet cats and their antics back home in Hattusa. They were exhausted but undeterred. He, it seemed, was as hated as Kurunta.

When he noticed a veteran from the neighbouring dormitory walking nearby, carrying a basket of bread, his belly growled fiercely. And an idea sparked in his mind. *Perhaps there is one last chance to make things right,* he wondered.

He tugged his hair round to hide his smoke-grey eye, then jumped to his feet and ran over to the soldier. 'Can you spare me a few loaves?' he asked. The soldier looked him up and down, then shrugged. 'In exchange for what?'

Hattu patted at the hair hanging by his ear, then drew one lock around and pulled from it the only thing of value on his person: 'this stone is beryl,' he said, untying it and offering it reluctantly.

The soldier eyed it then took it, not quite believing his luck, handing Hattu three rounds of bread.

'Thank you,' Hattu said. His hair slipped back from his smoke-grey eye as he said this, and the affable soldier's face drained of humour.

'You?' the man said, then hurried away.

'Aye, me,' Hattu whispered in reply to the space the man had been occupying.

Hattu took the three loaves back into his own dorm. The chatter amongst the boys fell away as they saw him. 'I… I brought you these. To make up for the ration cut.'

Silence.

Sargis and Kisna, the two who had helped Dagon during the brawl earlier that day, licked their lips, eyes fixed on the fresh loaves. Garin's belly growled in an unfortunately-timed protest.

Every other recruit in there followed Tanku's lead, glowering at

Hattu.

It was only when Dagon stepped forward as if to accept the loaves that another boy cut in, stepping out before Dagon, facing Hattu. 'Well, the son of the king spoils us tonight,' the boy sneered, snatching the bread from Hattu's arms. 'Three whole loaves? We are *truly* grateful.'

Hattu gulped. Dagon had slunk away into the shadows. The hard stares of the others remained. He backed away and left them to it, returning to the porch. He slumped to sit once more and gazed up at the sky, sprinkled with a silvery sand of stars. *If a man travels far enough – the stars themselves will change*, old Ruba had taught him. He made out the great Hunter – the constellation in the shape of a man drawing a bow. *Aye, old tutor, that may be. But as things are, I will likely never find out*, he mused, looking eastwards in the direction of Hattusa, thinking of the Scribal School.

'Why am I here?' he sighed, looking over at the small lodge by the compound gates where Kurunta slept – his snoring almost shaking the building. He noticed that the compound gates were open. *Odd*, he thought, usually they were closed and barred. Realisation dawned: there really was nothing stopping him from leaving. And there, in the shadow of the gatehouse, he saw the vapour-thin mirage of the round-shouldered scribe, staring at him, beckoning him. A bout of laughter sounded from inside and the last crumbs of conviction fell away at that moment. He began to rise from where he sat. 'Perhaps it is time to go home,' he said sadly.

'Who are you talking to?' a voice replied.

Hattu started, then looked round to see Dagon emerging from the dorm. 'Myself,' Hattu said, 'I think.'

'I brought you this,' Dagon said, handing Hattu a steaming bowl of carrot stew.

'I can't,' Hattu waved a hand. 'It's my fault the ration was halved.'

Dagon chuckled. 'Halki's balls it was. That was Kurunta's doing.'

'Not in their eyes, it wasn't,' Hattu muttered, flicking his head towards the dorm.

Dagon looked inside with a sigh then sat down and gestured for Hattu to do likewise.

Hattu lifted one side of his mouth in a pathetic attempt at a smile as he sat. 'Be wary of sitting next to the Cursed Son,' he said.

Dagon laughed nervously. 'I know how it feels,' he said. 'To have every smiling face turn sour when it looks upon you.'

Hattu saw how he traced a fingertip over the deepest scar pits on his face as he said this.

'When I was nine summers, my mother never tired of telling me how handsome I would be when I became a man. That autumn, I fell ill with the plague. I survived, as you can see, but life is different now. Some people avoid me as if I still carry the pox. Mother isn't quite so effusive about my looks any more.'

Hattu sensed the boy's awkwardness, but felt a great warmth inside at this – the first civil conversation he had enjoyed in a month. 'I was certainly pleased to see you that first day I arrived.'

'When I was arse-deep in horse dung?' he said, brightening up. 'Ha! Then, it seemed like torture...'

'Now,' Hattu finished for him, shooting a sour eye at the shadowy outline of the red fells, 'I'd pay to shovel dung all day long.' He picked up the bowl and took a spoonful of carrot stew. It was thin but salty, warm and flavoursome and instantly gave him a sense of wellbeing. 'Thank you,' he said.

Dagon said nothing. Hattu ate in silence for a while before the boy spoke again. 'Do you remember the first day I saw you?'

'No,' Hattu lied.

'It was at the Tawinian Gate on the day of the Gathering: you and Prince Muwatalli were entering the city. I remember scowling at you then. I did it because others did. I'd heard the things they said about you: that the Dark Earth stalked you and those close to you. I thought it was the right thing to do. Since then I've learned to think for myself,' he jabbed a thumb over his shoulder. 'To the pits with that lot.'

'To the pits,' Hattu smiled.

Dagon returned inside and Hattu remained where he was to the rest of his meal.

A while later, the dormitories were silent, the tallow lamps within extinguished. A hunter's moon cast a pale light across the still night, and

Hattu remained by the porch. Once more, he saw the meek scribe in the compound gateway. Rising, he stretched and walked towards the vision. The scribe vanished as he approached. Outside the compound, the grounds of the academy were devoid of movement. Crickets croaked and a drunk soldier lay slumped by the door of the arzana house. Looking east, he saw the few sentries posted near the academy's perimeter, standing around braziers. Now the ethereal scribe was there, one finger coiling and uncoiling, summoning him – further east. Hattusa was only a few hours' walk away. Safety, peace, sanctuary from this ritual humiliation.

'Would they stop me,' he mused aloud, looking at the sentries, 'if I simply left now?'

The idea seemed sweet, soft and seductive. He found himself walking towards the perimeter. By morning he could be visiting Atiya. He could groom Arrow in the comfort of the acropolis halls. He took another few steps closer to the sentries. What would Father think? What would the people say about him now: the Cursed Son or the Craven Son?

'To the pits with them,' he said – the words coming from deep within. It was only now he realised he had stopped in his tracks. 'And to the pits with you,' he repeated at the ethereal scribe.

He turned away from the academy perimeter, swinging back to face the red fells instead, eyeing them moodily. 'I can do this,' he whispered. He took a deep breath then set off at a run towards them, ploughing up the lower slopes, undaunted, his eyes on the top. Atop the hills, he fell to his knees, panting in a sliver of moonlight. It was not the climb that was the challenge, he realised, but the heat of day and the burden of the water. 'How can a man better the divine sun and the weight of the sacred water?' he gasped into the night.

Silence.

His eyes fell to the flat, boot-marked fell-tops before him. The moonlight betrayed a lone ant scuttling across the dust, bringing with it a tiny chunk of earth and placing it down by a red boulder. The first part of a new nest, he realised. 'Poor creature,' he said, guessing that the ant was separated from its swarm. Alone, it could never build an entire nest. An impossible feat.

'I have more in common with you than my soldier-kin, it seems.'

CHAPTER 9

THE MOUNTAIN WOLVES
HIGH SUMMER 1302 BC

Summer grew hotter by the day. One sultry evening, the officers met in the command building by the paddocks. Once their planning talks were over, a few remained, drinking and chatting.

General Nuwanza eyed his colleagues, the unanswered question floating between them like bad wind.

'Volca? He is a shrewd one,' Colta answered first, smoothing at his forked beard.

'Shrewd?' Kurunta scoffed. 'He is a bumptious fool with a voice like a chisel.'

Nuwanza roared with laughter. 'Then I am lucky to have spent little time with him.'

Kurunta gulped at a cup of wine and slammed it back down on the table – the sound echoing and drawing surprised looks from the few other officers in there. Kurunta shot them all a sour eye then turned back to Nuwanza. 'Who taught him to speak our tongue – Ruba, was it? The old goose wants stringing up for that, for Volca never shuts up now. On and on, riding over my every attempt at a sentence and echoing my ideas to the king with a boldness that seems to cover up the fact they were *my* bloody ideas in the first place. Even his apologies – rare as they are – seem offensive. And that helmet – who… *who* wears a ridiculous helmet with bull's horns like that all the time?'

'An arsehole in the king's retinue. Who'd have thought it?'

Nuwanza chuckled again.

'He's not Hittite... not even from the vassal lands,' Kurunta moaned.

'Nor was I,' Colta said with a raised eyebrow, now tugging testily at his beard. 'When I came here I was a mere Hurrian beggar. The king could have cast me aside but he did not.'

Kurunta's shoulders slunk and he sighed. 'I meant no offence, Old Horse.'

'The worst thing you can do is let his behaviour get under your skin,' Nuwanza suggested. 'Find a way to tolerate him.'

Kurunta shook his head, spreading his fingers on the surface of the table and rolling his shoulders. 'But he's everywhere. When he's not at the king's side, he's lurking around the palace like a ghost.'

'True,' Colta mused. 'Always seems to be in and out of the scullery.'

'The cellar kitchens?' Nuwanza said, his V-shaped brow drawing together. 'If he's caught down there with the slightest speck of dirt on him then he'll be eating a plate of turds for his evening meal.'

Kurunta's eyebrows leapt up at the prospect. 'And I'd happily supply the ingredients,' he said with a happy growl. 'And it seems he's impressed the king so much that he and his two cronies have been initiated into the Mesedi.' He snorted in derision. 'What next?'

'The two cronies are worse,' Colta reasoned. 'Drunkards! While Volca skulks around in the cookrooms, those two cavort with the harem girls – full of wine and acting as if they are royalty themselves.'

Nuwanza chortled. The two other Sherden were scrawny and pale versions of Volca. Each was uglier than the other and they certainly were not sharp thinkers like their leader.

'Braggarts, they are,' Colta rasped, any trace of humour draining from him. 'They boasted about their bravery the day they saved the king from the rampaging elephant. Belittled poor Zida while they were at it: crowing about how our old friend was overcome with fear at the sight of the beast and how they had to step in.'

Nuwanza laughed no more. 'Zida was many things,' he said in a low voice, 'stubborn, miserly, foul-tempered... noble, strong as a bull and fast as a lion. But never, *never* was he craven.'

Silence reigned for a moment.

Kurunta poured each of them a refill of watered wine from the mixing bowl, then drank his share in one gulp. 'We'll ask Zida what really happened when we each enter the Dark Earth.' He let a wry smile lift one edge of his mouth. 'Perhaps there the tight-fisted swine may even see fit to buy us all a drink at last?'

The three shared a bout of fond, gentle laughter. Soon after, Colta stood to depart and Kurunta followed, leaving Nuwanza alone. As the humour died he felt a niggling sense of untidiness in his thoughts. Something about the conversation just shared seemed askew. He stroked his bottom lip and searched his recent memories until, like a key sliding into a well-oiled lock, he remembered. King Mursili had told him of the elephant hunt after returning to the main army column.

Zida is lost, the king had said. *He charged into the path of the elephant – knowing it would crush him, but knowing also it would buy me a trice within which I might save myself.*

Whatever the Sherden drunks were telling the acropolis harlots was a lie. Zida had not been frozen with fear. And then another memory rose to the surface. It was of the time he and Zida had been on a patrol to the city of Arinna. On the way there, they had come across a bull elephant stricken with sickness, agitated and trumpeting near the edge of a stream to which the approach was rocky and steep. The elephant was trying to step down the uneven surface but for some reason kept pulling back. Zida had approached, slowly, obliquely, not getting too close, then slid down to the stream to fill a leather bucket with water and bring it back up, placing it near the elephant. Now the creature moved closer, plunging its trunk into the bucket and drinking it dry. A few bucketfuls later and the creature was calm. Zida stroked its trunk, then sank to his knees to draw from its foot the long thorn that had prevented it from negotiating the rocky slope to the stream. Many men were overcome with fear on sighting elephants, and rightly so. Zida was not one of them.

Kurunta's earlier rant came back to him now.

It seems he's impressed the king so much that he and his two cronies have been initiated into the Mesedi. What next?

The words took root in the Master Archer's mind. His high forehead furrowed and his pensive eyes stared long and hard into his wine.

***

Another month passed and Hattu ran up the red hills most nights. Someone was leaving the compound gates unlocked, and Hattu found it difficult to resist the call of the night. He took to carrying rocks in his hands to make the scramble tougher at first, then small bags of rocks, then sacks, slung over his shoulders. And once up there, he sought out stretches of scarp and bluff to climb and clamber over, still with the rocks on his back.

Your limbs will grow sturdier for the repetition and the extra burden.

'Aye, but damn they will,' he panted, flopping onto the hilltop, barefoot and sweating. His body was like knotted rope in places where muscles had developed. He flexed his shoulders, encouraged by their newfound breadth. He was still lean, but by the Gods, he was getting stronger. Calluses lined his feet and his palms, and his mind too, he was sure, but the challenge of carrying a sack of rocks was not as great as the burden of six full water buckets – not even close. Still, the daily humiliation continued. Today, Tanku had come close to losing his cool again. And the truth was, Hattu wouldn't have blamed him for it. There had to be an answer, a way of stuffing Kurunta one-eye's ridiculous Water Ordeal down his throat… there *had* to be.

The faintest scratching noise caught his attention. His eyes searched the moonlit dust until he pinpointed it. He laughed once in surprise when he saw there a slim, waist-high mound of earth. The ants' nest was taking shape. The scratching sounded again and the lone ant scurried over with a piece of red earth on its back, climbed the mound and placed its cargo on the tip. Back and forth the ant went, constructing the final parts of its nest. Hattu watched, enchanted, for some time.

He approached the nest, beholding it as if it might share its secrets with him. As he drew closer to it, he knelt, tracing a finger through the shallow furrow from which the ant had been lifting earth. The palest sensation on his fingertips triggered a sudden realisation. He looked down, lifting a little in between fingers and thumb, rubbing it, the granules falling away. At once, he was in Ruba's classroom again, trying to make sense of the old man's chalky etchings on a slate. *The sacred earth itself is alive: veined with life.*

The moonlight caught his eyes as they flicked to the edge of the hill and the academy below. He saw the eternal dung heap, studded with a few spades, then he saw the ring of stone that marked the Soldier's Spring. Finally, he looked back to the shallow furrow of earth upon which he knelt.

A broad smile crept across his face.

***

The moon waned, vanished and waxed once more. Another month where every night, Hattu ran to the red heights. Nobody saw what he was doing up there, but some heard faint scraping noises, over and over. And every day under the boiling sun, the recruits ran up the hillside. They trained hard, then watched Hattu struggle and fail in Kurunta's Water Ordeal.

One day, Hattu and the hundred Hill Pups spilled from the dormitory at the first wail of the Dawn Call. They snatched up their poles and shields and fell into place on the muster area in moments – even before some of the veterans had done so. And now they were all well-drilled enough to have dressed in time, each in linen kilt and leather boots. A few of the recruits shared triumphant looks. Hattu, however, felt the ache in his back and shoulders from his night endeavours, and his mind was foggy from little sleep. He glanced down, seeing his fingernails were still packed with red earth.

Stay strong, he told himself.

Kurunta stomped before them with a face like a dark nightmare, as if angered by their improvement. 'Dog-ugly curs,' he muttered under his breath. Hattu wondered if the general even realised he emitted such thoughts aloud. 'Three months of my life I've had to put up with you. Three months of my life I'll never get back,' he added, then reluctantly raised a hand and clicked his fingers. An ox wagon emerged from the gated armoury building near the compound's southern walls, its wheels grinding on the dusty ground as it made its way over to the recruits. Hattu saw upon it heaps of dark, polished leather, bronze studs and off-white cloth.

'Now that I've dragged you bastards this far, I am obliged to see how you fare with weapons in your hands.' He and a pair of Storm soldiers unbolted the back end of the wagon and lifted out a bundle of swords – hilts bound in leather, bronze blades curved like Kurunta's twin swords but not as long – and tall, honed spears. '*Real* weapons. And because I just *know* one of you will stab yourself... I must also provide you with armour.'

Hattu felt his mouth dry out as the general thrust a pair of weapons into his hands, his face uplit by the lustre of a leaf-shaped bronze spearhead. Kurunta hesitated for a moment, not letting go of the arms, emitting a low, grumbling sigh.

'You can trust me, sir,' he said.

'When you bring water to the hilltop for your comrades, then I will trust you,' he scoffed, then stepped away.

Hattu watched him go, eyes narrowed.

'First time you have held a sword?' Dagon asked, examining his blade.

'Aye,' Hattu said, gazing at the leather pommel and the blade's keen edge. It was light but solid in his hand. He slid the blade through his belt by his left hip so it hung to his thigh.

Another Storm soldier shoved a white linen tunic and a dark leather cuirass into his arms. Dagon had been given a padded linen vest instead – a single, lighter layer, and more supple, providing just as much protection. Hattu pulled on the tunic then the pair helped one another slide the armoured corselets on over each other's heads, securing them by tying the buckles at the sides. Hattu's leather vest was stiff, uncomfortable and too big for him, and it bit at his collarbone.

An instant later he was deafened by a scraping noise as something was thrust upon his head: a toughened leather helmet with a bronze brow band, the leather cheek guards and aventail settling around his face and the nape of his neck. He could smell the old leather and the sweat of men who had worn it before him and a trace of a sickeningly familiar, evil, coppery stench. *Blood?* He suddenly wondered if it had been taken from a fallen soldier. Indeed, he noticed Dagon's helmet bore a dark stain and a score that had nearly torn through the leather.

The soldiers then handed out savage, fanged maces and small, glinting bronze axes to each man. Hattu received an axe, and eyed it for a moment: the curved head had two large circular holes – a means of sparing every scrap of precious bronze – and the back edge had three jutting prongs.

Kurunta strode before them, grinning like a glutton locked in a bakery. 'Now you will experience a true run to the top of the fells. Biting, heavy armour and splinters on the hands, *lovely!*' More groans and disbelieving whimpers. Then he smirked at Hattu. 'And then you can enjoy a nice, refreshing cup of water when we're up there.'

The ascent to the top of the fells was every bit as painful as Kurunta had predicted. The armour chewed at their skin and trapped the heat of the day against their bodies. Once up there, they were given but a moment to catch their breaths before combat training began. First, they took to running an obstacle course – leaping over rocks, ducking and rolling under raised logs and dodging around poles, all with their armour and weapons anchoring them. After that, they mock-battled, now clashing bronze weapons instead of wooden poles. Hattu and Dagon partnered-up to spar. The spears were heavier with the additional weight of the bronze tip and tang, and they found that keeping the weapon level was hard enough, let alone manoeuvring it into a position where they might strike. Next, they fought with swords. These were light as air in comparison, and the blades clashed over and over as they and the many other pairs of boys fought to tap the flat of their blade against their opponent's chest, scoring a 'kill'.

'Balance, *balance,*' Kurunta screamed, striding amongst the sparring lads with his hands clasped behind his back. 'You can have all the strength in the world, but if you have the spryness of a pregnant elephant your head will end up as an ornament in a Kaskan mud house.' Hattu felt Kurunta's eye on him more than once. As much as he loathed the general, his only means of hurting the man was to defy him. And so he marked Dagon with a 'kill', then Garin too, then Sargis. At noon, only ten boys were left fighting and not yet 'killed'.

'Meh,' Kurunta grumbled and shrugged as he eyed the remaining boys. It wasn't quite the praise many had hoped for.

In the noon heat, he then split them into two parties, one 'patrolling' a rocky outcrop that rose like a skywards-pointing finger, the other tasked with outmanoeuvring the patrolling lot and claiming the finger for themselves. Kurunta climbed up the finger and sat upon it like a vulture, watching it all.

Hattu was in Tanku's patrolling fifty, with Dagon and Garin. It was just like the exercise they had witnessed between the Blaze and the Wrath men on their first day up on the hills, he realised. They shot glances to the rocky finger, then all around. The other fifty remained unseen, so they moved in a tight circle, round and round the finger. The ground nearby was pitted and uneven, and each of them remembered well how the Blaze soldiers had hidden in such a crater before stealing up on the Wrath men's flank.

Under the full sun, they were tiring, fast. 'They'll never come at us while we move like this,' Hattu said to Dagon. 'Wherever they're hiding, they'll just wait it out. They're in the shade and we're not. When we slow and tire, then they'll have us.'

Dagon nodded slowly.

Hattu flicked a finger to the wide, shallow natural trench in the earth that led right up to the rocky finger. A pile of rocks lay at the near end of it. 'That's the easiest approach: the other fifty will come for the rocky finger that way. On the next circuit we'll pass unseen by those rocks. We should fall in behind them, wait in the shade – turn this exercise on its head.'

'Tell Tanku,' Dagon said.

Hattu's lips shifted to one side. 'Anything I say to him, he'll reject out of hand.'

Dagon smiled wryly, winked at Hattu then jogged forward to mutter in Tanku's ear. The big recruit's eyes moved this way and that as if piecing together the idea in his own mind, then he turned round and whispered to the others. 'On the next pass, we stop by the rocks, aye?'

'Aye,' the rest said in a hushed agreement.

Dagon fell back to Hattu's side, grinning.

They fell into the shady lee of the rocks. Their parched breaths subsided and then there was a silence. Hattu felt a terrible doubt grip him: what if the other fifty spotted the trap and stole up on the rocky finger from the other side? But then: *crunch, crunch, crunch.*

He edged his head from the shade of the rock pile, seeing the shadows of approaching, scuttling men. Tanku saw it too and held up a finger, then swished it down. The fifty burst from the shade by the rocks and fell upon their startled opponents. Weapons clacked on shields and curses mixed with laughter.

Victory, Hattu mouthed, eager to share the momentary elation with his team. But he felt a molten gaze on his neck and turned, seeing Kurunta glowering down upon him, his silvery braid dancing in the weak breeze atop the rocky finger.

'The shade by the rocks – that was Hattu's plan,' Dagon panted as the clamour subsided.

Hattu swung round, seeing Tanku's face fall. The big recruit shrugged. 'Aye, well, good for him. Best he finished this early so he might just have enough energy to bring us our water,' he said without a trace of humour.

Kurunta half-climbed down the rocky finger then leapt down onto the hilltop with a dusty thud. 'Indeed. Thirsty work, that. Prince Hattusili, if you would,' he gestured from the edge of the hilltop down to the wagon with the water pole. Grunts of dismay sounded from the recruits. They knew what would happen now.

Hattu eyed them all for a moment. The image of the dauntless ant played over and over in his mind. He glanced past the gathered recruits, seeing the now-complete ants' nest a little way behind them. *No task is impossible, as you have shown me, little friend,* he thought.

'Are you awaiting a litter and some slaves to carry you down there, eh?' Kurunta snapped.

Hattu carefully set down his spear, shield, helm and sword. He started to untie his armour when Kurunta added: 'keep the cuirass on – unless it's too much for you?'

Hattu bit his lip and re-fastened the leather straps, then turned away to jog down the dusty slope. *One-eyed bastard!* He growled inwardly as he stumbled down the fells. He kept his footing thanks to his now rope-like hamstrings and bronze-hard quadriceps, and managed to stand tall as he reached the bottom and strode over to the usual two sneering soldiers who had the water pole ready for him.

The pole was loaded onto his shoulders with three buckets at either end.

'Off you go,' one of the soldiers said with a lazy chuckle.

Hattu turned away from them. Up he went, feeling the weighty pole and its six buckets crush down upon his shoulders and steal his breath, trample his spirits. Then he looked up, seeing the baleful looks of the Hill Pups.

Today, they will drink. Just over halfway up, his feet began to sink deeply into the dust then he stopped, dipping to his knees. The recruits groaned. Tanku spat on the ground and turned away, cursing. Hattu looked up, sweat running across his face. He stepped out of the yoke-pole, lifted one bucket off and poured it into the dust. Then he did the same with the others.

'What in the name of Halki's arse are you doing?' Kurunta howled. 'Start again.'

Hattu fixed his gaze on his one-eyed tormentor, and calmly lifted the yoke pole and six empty buckets back onto his shoulders, then climbed with ease, up, up and onto the hilltop.

'Did you hear me?' Kurunta screamed in his ear.

'I heard you on that first day,' Hattu replied calmly. 'You challenged me to bring water to my comrades.'

'Aye, water, not empty buckets,' Kurunta roared.

Hattu walked past him and stopped by a flat, wide rock on the ground, stooping to rummage in the brush at one side of it. Standing again, holding a spade and a length of rope concealed there, he met every pair of eyes. 'Today, you will drink,' he said flatly. He dug the spade under the rock and planted a booted foot on its bronze shoulder. Levering hard, the rock lifted, and with a twist, he shifted it to one side.

Now the watching eyes grew wide, drawn to the dark hole under the rock. Hattu took one of the empty buckets from the yoke pole and tied the rope to its handle, then lowered it down. As he did so he thought of every night, every moment of back-breaking digging. He thought of the uncertainty: the cool, moist earth he had found in the ant's furrow suggested water might lie underneath, as Ruba had taught him, but there was no guarantee. A month of doubts and toil, then last night, he had struck water. A splash sounded some way below, scattering his thoughts, bringing him back to the searing-hot day. He drew the bucket back up – brimming with water from an underground vein of the Soldier's Spring – untied it and walked past Kurunta.

He heard the one-eyed general grumble: 'You dirty, devious hurkeler...' as he calmly handed the bucket to Garin, the nearest of the Hill Pups, then turned back to the well. 'I will stop if you wish me to, sir,' he said to Kurunta, 'but I have completed your orders. The objective was to bring water to the men, wasn't it? One ascent, six buckets?'

Kurunta growled like an angered cat and flicked his head towards the well. Hattu drew another few buckets and handed them round, then sat near the rest as they drank. He asked for no water for himself. When Dagon handed him a cupful, Hattu noticed the cold eyes of the others upon him, Tanku's in particular.

'Drink it,' Tanku said, looking off past Hattu towards Kurunta, now standing with his back turned, too far away to hear – he hoped. 'Before Kurunta drowns you in it.'

A dull rumble of callus laughter broke out at this.

'And if he doesn't drown me then I fully expect a turd on a plate for my evening meal tonight,' Hattu said.

Tanku snorted once in dry humour at this and the others laughed too – guardedly.

'Water,' Dagon said, lashing a cup over his dusty skin. 'Tomorrow, and every other day, we have water while we're up here. Is that not a fine thing?'

The others murmured in relieved agreement.

But Kurunta cut it short, swinging back to face them all: 'Tomorrow? No,' he said eyeing Hattu askance. 'Tomorrow, we try something different.'

***

That evening, with the rudimentary well complete and the Water Ordeal broken, Hattu considered rewarding himself with a long, uninterrupted sleep. But as darkness had fallen, the whispers in his mind began to fight fiercely against his sense of achievement.

Cursed son! they shrieked, enraged that he had dared to defy them.

And so the notion of a night scramble – the only place the whispers could not be heard – came to him. As soon as the others were asleep, he rose and sped up the red hillside under a waning moon, crickets singing and a lone owl hooting. He found a dusty crag up there and scaled it, reaching the top and taking a moment to gaze up at the stars, to spot the constellations and to catch his breath before setting off back for the infantry compound again.

When he returned to the barrack house, he slowed, seeing a lone figure standing by the door. Tanku, Hattu realised. He approached cautiously, hoping Tanku would go back inside before he reached the door. But the big, burly lad was not for moving. Hattu considered waiting out of sight, but when his heel ground on a patch of dirt, Tanku swung round like a sentry on duty. His eyes were like moons, his face tight with terror. When he saw Hattu, his demeanour darkened. 'You?' he said waspishly.

'Aye, me,' Hattu said, edging past the big lad.

Tanku caught his arm. 'That water well was… a pleasant surprise. And the sortie too – I suppose I owe you gratitude of some sort for that.'

Hattu nodded awkwardly. 'You should sleep, you know,' he said, 'you will need your energy for tomorrow, for whatever Kurunta has planned for us.'

Tanku shrugged. 'I don't need to sleep.'

To Hattu, the words rang distinctly untrue, and the black rings under Tanku's eyes supported this theory. He saw how the big recruit's gaze kept darting into the shadows of the barrack room, to his deserted bed a few strides inside. Confused, Hattu peered there also. No, the bed wasn't deserted: in it was a small, dark, eight-legged shape. When the spider scurried suddenly, Tanku snatched in a breath, almost leaping back from the doorway as if the tiny creature could spring at him from there.

An intense urge to laugh grew in Hattu's belly. The burly, fearless Tanku – the champion recruit, destined to lead men one day – was afraid of spiders? He checked the laugh, seeing the raw terror in the big lad's eyes. Silently, he stepped inside, plucked the spider from the bed and tossed it outside through one of the shutters – big Tanku peering inside to watch like a nervous child.

'Until morning,' he said quietly to Tanku, before stepping over to his own bed and turning in.

***

Kurunta roused the Hill Pups before dawn. Hattu awoke from a deep, thick sleep to find the general shaking him violently with a dog-snarl on his features. 'Time to rise, Prince,' he hissed.

With a few coughs, pained emissions of wind, bewildered groans and muted words of confusion, they shuffled from the academy grounds in the cool darkness in their armour and carrying their weapons, following Kurunta to the south. They crossed over the broad track that linked Hattusa with the eastern and western extremes of Hittite lands. As dawn broke like a golden hawk, spreading its fiery wings across the sky, they climbed a long, slow path up a grey-green mountainside to the tune of the rising cicada song.

'Keep moving, hurkelers,' Kurunta grunted, 'You'll just *love* what I have in store for you today.'

Hattu glanced to Dagon, who shot back an equally bemused look.

The ascent steepened sharply, and a distinctly cool breeze swirled around them. Suddenly, a flurry of gasps rang out. Hattu looked ahead, craning his neck like the others. The slope levelled out onto a plateau of sorts, about halfway up the mountainside. Up there, glaring sombrely down upon them was an ancient stone huwasi – far taller than the warrior statues back at the academy grounds. This was a towering effigy of a man sculpted from storm-grey limestone, veined with white. Bearded, he wore a tall, conical helm and braved the cutting winds, bare chested with just a scaled kilt covering his waist and thighs. His feet were apart as if marching, right arm raised with the fist clenched in salute. The grass up there was bent almost flat and they could hear the forlorn moan of the wind, passing around the statue.

'Sarruma, the Mountain God,' Hattu whispered almost in time with the many other recruits, his hair blowing across his face as he beheld the effigy, worn smooth in places by centuries of wind, snow and rain. It had probably been erected by the earliest Kings of Hattusa, Hattu guessed.

They slowed behind Kurunta as they arrived by the foot of the huwasi, the wind buffeting them. By the statue's base there were shards of clay vessels, age-old libations of beer made to the Mountain God. Wordlessly, the recruits took to unhooking the small leather bags tied near the tips of their spears and breaking pieces from their bread ration, laying it by the deity's feet. Hattu made his offering, then looked behind the statue: a few paces beyond, the plateau was riven in two by a wide, jagged fissure. A rocky spur jutted out like an arm, stretching part-way across this ravine. Its surface was almost flat and smooth – well-polished by rains. On the far side of the ravine lay a shorter, stumpier arm, pointing back. But a gap existed between the two tips – as wide as a tall man lying prone, arms outstretched, he reckoned. He approached the ravine edge and heard a tumultuous roar of rushing water. He stretched his neck to glance over the edge, seeing the knots of white water and clouds of foam and spray down there, so far below that it made him dizzy. Jutting from the furious water were black fangs of rock, worn smooth like whetted blades. Hittite lore told that every stream, pond, river and lake marked the edge of one of the many passages to the underworld – the Dark Earth – and right here and now, Hattu understood why.

'Be careful, Prince,' Kurunta yelled, slapping his hands onto Hattu's shoulders from behind.

Hattu wailed, eliciting a chorus of mocking laughter from the others. He drew back, skin prickling with the ebbing fright and rising humiliation, while Kurunta strode up to stand on the neck of the near spur and turned to face the recruits. 'This was once a natural bridge, so the elders said, part of a path that led to the good tracts of shallow pasture in these low mountains: ideal for grazing horses and cattle in the arid summer months. Now, the bridge is broken – no use to herdsmen. Soldiers, on the other hand… '

'A recruit will jump and a soldier will land on the other side,' Dagon whispered by Hattu's side. 'My father told me about this. I didn't believe him.'

'Ah, our first volunteer,' Kurunta said, his face brightening.

Dagon emitted a syllable that suggested he wasn't so keen.

But a chant struck up – gleefully orchestrated by Kurunta – and the recruits quickly formed the walls of a makeshift corridor, leading to the nearside spur of the broken bridge. Dagon gulped.

'You're strong enough,' Hattu whispered. 'The gap is wide but not so wide. I know you can do it.'

Dagon gulped again and flashed a timid look of thanks to Hattu, then set down his shield and weapons, unbuckled his linen vest and prised off his boots so he wore just his loincloth. As the chanting grew more rapid, Dagon crouched, his right leg slightly proud, then sprang forward. He raced out onto the rocky spur and leapt. Hattu's stomach clenched, the chanting faded. Silence but for the moaning wind. Dagon flailed through the air, legs cycling as he went. *Thud!* He landed on the far spur with a stride to spare, then staggered on to the safe ground on the other side, turning round, eyes wide, mouth agape.

A reticent cheer rose up from the recruits, each more concerned about their turn. Hattu offered him a swift clenched-fist salute while Kisna tossed Dagon's arms and armour over to him.

Next went big Tanku. He stripped down to his loincloth and began by stretching his legs, bending his well-toned torso one way then the other, eyes fixed all the time on the broken bridge. There was an air of utter confidence about this lad, a sparkle in his eyes that suggested he already knew he would have no trouble making the leap. A stark contrast to his boy-like fear of the spider the previous night, Hattu thought. The chanting grew again as Tanku crouched like a lion about to spring, then launched himself forward, building into a ferocious sprint, stride lengthening as he struck out onto the jagged spur. The chanting faded again as a hundred breaths were sucked in at once, and Tanku's ham-like thigh muscles tensed, every sinew stretching and spending the momentum of the sprint as he leapt high and fast, legs astride, then tucked his calves up behind his thighs, arms aloft as if to cut through the wind.

Thud!

He landed soundly with three strides to spare, his legs uncoiling so his feet met the stony spur on the far side at a jog. Turning, he swept his eyes over everyone on the other side of the ravine, his hair billowing across his face. He took to beating one fist against his breast then punched the air and let out a wolf-like howl. Those watching on the other side erupted in a chorus of cheers.

The recruits lined up one after the other, each facing their own fear and leaping out across the void, the dread morphing into elation as each landed safely. Tanku's wolf howl caught on too, each emitting their own version. Gradually, the corridor of recruits on this nearside shrank until there were only a handful left. Hattu felt his heart beat faster and his limbs shudder. Best to go now, than to be last, he reasoned. But as he put forward towards the run-up, Kurunta blocked him with a hand. 'Not yet,' he growled, 'for a prince, it must be different. You must show that no level of fear will stand in your way.' He was unfurling a square of black cloth from his belt as he said this.

Sargis, Kisna then Garin went next in his stead. The chant struck up as Garin knotted his long black hair into a tight tail. The plump recruit had lost weight since his enlistment, but he was still ungainly in his stride and carried more bulk than he ought to. Hattu thought of his night scrambles and knew that being lean and spry offered a huge advantage. But timing and judgement were equally important. 'Measure your stride,' Hattu said quietly to Garin as the boy prepared himself. 'Get as close to the edge of the spur as you can before you jump.'

Garin shot him an irritable, nervous look. 'I don't need your advice,' he murmured.

Hattu shrugged and backed away.

Garin surged forward, his feet pounding onto the spur. His toes met the end of it and he launched himself. *A perfect stride,* Hattu thought. But Garin's leap was poor, with little elevation. The held breaths this time turned into a cacophonous series of alarmed cries. *Thud!* Garin landed, belly-first, *just* on the edge of the far spur, his legs thrashing over the void. The cries faded to a chorus of relieved laughter as Garin scrambled like a spider to safety.

Now just Kurunta and Hattu stood on the nearside.

Hattu turned to Kurunta. 'Now can I jump?'

By way of reply, a sudden, stark *crack* rang out. All heads shot to the edge of the far spur where Garin had landed heavily. A section of shale, about the width of a man, broke away from it and tumbled into the abyss. Silence. Then a *splash* where some of the loosened material had met with the angry waterway far below.

'The jump is... wider,' one boy shouted across from the far side with a tremor in his voice.

The words sent a cold fear over Hattu.

Kurunta turned his head to glare at Hattu, his lips peeling back in a foul-toothed smile. 'You want to take your turn? Certainly,' he said triumphantly. Just as Hattu began to stretch his legs, Kurunta held up the square of black cloth and walked behind Hattu, wrapping it over his eyes and tying it behind his head. 'Sir?' Hattu said, eyes switching to and fro in the sudden blackness.

'Now watch, Hill Pups, as your prince demonstrates his superior courage,' Kurunta boomed, ignoring Hattu. 'He can jump higher and further than any of you, and he can do it with his eyes closed.'

A refrain of derisive mutters sounded.

'You expect me to jump when I can't even see?' he said as Kurunta oriented him towards the spur.

'Afraid, Prince?' Kurunta cooed.

Hattu felt the wind turn cold as winter. His legs felt like water and even the thought of the ravine's unseen proximity made him feel sick and dizzy. His breathing grew ragged and short, and a stinging panic rose from his belly to his breast then coiled around his throat as if to choke him. All the fears of falling that had plagued his climbs came to him at once like a multi-headed demon.

'I will understand if you'd prefer not to make the jump,' Kurunta continued, resting his hands on Hattu's shoulders. 'Just ask me to send you back to Hattusa tonight, and you need not do it. You can take off the blindfold and set yourself at ease. No more danger, no more fear.'

In his mind's eye he saw that which the cloth blocked out: the void and the spurs, but there were just two people there: the shadowy, green-cloaked warrior across the jump and the round-shouldered scribe here, beside him.

A fiery defiance overcame him. 'Curse you, sir,' he said through clenched teeth, shrugging Kurunta's hands from his shoulders, then setting off for the spur like a deer.

He heard a gasp of shock from the gnarled general, but pounded onwards. He had watched all the other boys, noticed their speeds, counted their strides. Five strides took him onto the spur, then he felt the surface underfoot change: soft, smooth. Another three strides to the precipice. The ball and toes of his right foot met the rugged edge of the spur perfectly, then... he leapt.

Soaring, he heard only the roar of the wind. It seemed too long – endless: had he missed the far spur and was he right now plummeting towards the black rocky fangs below? Wretched terror shook him, only to be swept away by a bone-rattling crunch as he slammed down onto the end of the far spur, then rolled over and onto the safe flat ground.

He stood up and tore the blindfold off, tossing it into the ravine, shooting a fiery glare back at a gawping Kurunta, then eyeing each of the recruits likewise. There was no round of cheers, no wolf-howls, just a stunned silence. 'I jumped not to prove I am stronger, faster or more courageous than any of you. I jumped because I want to be one of you, no more.'

A few grumbled in disagreement. Some were still stunned. Tanku gave him a grey look, but said nothing.

Kurunta leapt across like a springing cat, landing beside Hattu and for a moment, looking like he was about to brain him. Instead, he spat on the ground. 'You jumped... ' he said, shaking his head. 'You actually jumped.'

'You were certain I wouldn't,' Hattu replied.

Kurunta beheld him for a moment longer. 'You remind me of me when I was young. I was stupid too,' he scoffed, then jogged past the recruits, leading them on uphill.

'He's running out of ideas,' Dagon whispered to Hattu as they went, a wry eye on Kurunta.

They came to a mountain brook, gurgling and narrow. Kurunta halted there, shooting an exasperated eye across the Hill Pups. 'So who knows of the River Ordeal?' he said.

The hundred young soldiers gulped, each sure that whatever it was, it would be unpleasant.

Moments later, they were in the white-cold waters in only their loincloths, neck-deep. Hattu sat beside Dagon, both boys with their arms clutched around themselves, shivering, teeth chattering, lips blue. The cold was insufferable, penetrating to their bones, frosting their marrow, clouding their minds. Kurunta, striding around them on the banks, seemed utterly unmoved.

Garin rummaged underwater with one hand then fell aghast. 'I... I can't feel it,' he stammered. 'It's disappeared inside me!'

'It was never that big anyway,' Kurunta remarked calmly, before covering one nostril and blowing a blob of rubbery filth from the other. 'So remember, the first to leave guarantees half rations for the lot of you tonight,' he reiterated. 'The choice is yours: blue balls or empty stomachs.'

'This is nonsense,' Tanku contested. 'One of us must leave first, so the punishment is guaranteed.'

Kurunta strode round the edge of the brook to crouch by the burly recruit. 'This is nonsense... *Sir*,' he corrected. 'And you are right, you will be eating half-rations tonight regardless. The test is to see who will break first, choosing to end their own suffering at the cost of their comrades' wellbeing.'

Hattu caught Tanku's eye. The big recruit was as blue as the rest of them, and for a blessed moment, the pair were in accord. 'If we all rise at once, then the suffering ends and no one person has to take the blame.'

Tanku's teeth stopped chattering for a moment. 'But damn, you're right.' He rose a little, waded into the centre of the group and waved his hands up. 'Up, get up. If we all get out at once...' he repeated Hattu's words. There was a moment of uncertainty, then the hundred rose onto their feet, made a careful few steps to the brook's edge and stepped out more or less together.

Kurunta said nothing. His withering gaze was enough. 'Get your clothes on and be ready to march.'

They filed down the mountain again, retracing their steps. When they came to the broken bridge of the Mountain God, it had lost something of its aura. Broken as a bridge, broken as a challenge. The boys leapt across one by one, giving fresh wolf-howls as they landed. Hattu, blindfold-free, relished the leap this time, then turned to watch Tanku – last to make the jump.

The big recruit's confident demeanour was as striking as the first time, his long legs eating up the run-up and the ball of his foot coming down perfectly on the edge of the far spur. Then the mountainside echoed with a thick, stark *crack!*

Tanku's face fell, just like the end of the far spur – the section under his kicking foot snapping off under his weight just as he launched himself. The shard plummeted into the void. Tanku shot across the gap, flailing, his face widening into a cry of horror as he fell short and disappeared into the abyss.

'Gods!' Kurunta cried, lumbering over to the edge of the ravine, staring down. The hundred sped to look over the edge too, some kneeling, some on all fours.

Hattu felt a cold sense of horror for the boy's end. An enemy, but a decent lad behind it all, he reckoned. Then he heard a weak cry.

'Ah... Argh... I ca-can't hold on!'

Hattu stretched his neck out a little further then saw it: Tanku, clinging by his forearms to a glistening, wet wart of rock poking from the ravine-side, the height of two men below the edge. His wrists and elbows were bleeding and the rest of his body dangled over the gnashing rocky fangs and thrashing waters.

'Spear!' Kurunta demanded, snatching the first lance offered. He slashed the tip of the spear off with one of his swords then fell prone at the ravine-edge, holding the shaft down. 'Grab it,' he called down. Tanku stretched one hand up but the end of the spear fell short of his reach. The momentary effort caused his other forearm to slip and he was nearly gone, were it not for his sudden grabbing of the wart of rock with just his palms.

'Rope?' Kurunta called over his shoulder, face red like an angry crab, eyes bulging. No reply.

Hattu knew Tanku was as good as dead. But already, he had mapped out the slight indents and creases on the ravine side. He pulled off his boots, helm and vest and slid his legs over the side, clinging to the edge, feet searching for the first hold.

'Hattu? What in the name of Tarhunda's crotch are you doing? The rock is wet. Get back up here,' Kurunta croaked, still trying in vain to stretch a little further down with the spear pole.

Hattu's foot found the hold. He shifted one hand to a slight ledge, then stretched his other foot down. Another lip of rock – wet as a fish – and he went lower. It was just like that black day when he and Sarpa had been climbing. Over-brave, he had scaled along a wet section of bluff like this. He had nearly died for it, and poor Sarpa's hip had been shattered saving him. *Give me the strength for this, Sarpa,* he muttered inwardly.

Within a few moments, he heard Tanku's pained breaths. He scaled down until he was directly over the burly recruit, then halted, checking his grip was good. It was not, the stone slimy and smooth where the water had worn it away and the holds shallow, but it would have to do.

'Climb,' he panted down at Tanku. 'Use my leg like a post, climb up.'

Tanku's face was wrinkled in terror, now only his fingertips holding him from doom, but even they were slipping. Hattu recognised the look: fear, a land where all the senses blurred and nothing made sense. '*Tanku!*' he yelled. This seemed to snap the boy from his trance. The big lad stretched up, clamped a hand to Hattu's shin, then hauled himself up until he had a hold of Hattu's shoulders.

'Hurry,' Hattu strained, feeling his fingers slipping in the slimy holds.

'All the Gods be with you,' Tanku panted as he clambered on over Hattu to grab Kurunta's spear and scale to safety.

'Take the spear!' Kurunta roared, louder than a thunderstorm. Hattu looked up to see the puce-faced general thrusting the spear end at him now. He sucked in a few deep breaths then rose to the next pock-shallow hold, before clasping the wooden shaft and clambering up. It all happened in moments, and then he found himself being hauled to safety, falling onto his back on the plateau, the sound of the hundred recruits cheering and whooping, threaded with guttural, blistering curses from Kurunta.

A hand clasped Hattu's, bringing him to his feet, then raising his arm in the air. Hattu realised it was Tanku, who emitted a piercing wolf-howl, gesturing for the others to do the same. Hattu felt the ground shiver under him such was their din. He saw the eyes of his detractors: different now, glinting with esteem. He realised a smile was creeping across his face. A moment later, and he joined them, turned his face to the sky, wet hair draping between his shoulders, and howled with all the air left in his lungs.

'Unbroken by the River Ordeal. Undaunted by the red fells or this mountain bridge,' Tanku panted. 'We are soldiers now,' he yelled in delight.

Kurunta's curses only became fierier now. 'I'll tell you when you're a company of soldiers. You're the Hill Pups and the Hill Pups you'll remain.'

Dagon lifted Hattu's other hand, howling too.

Hattu opened his mouth, hesitating for a moment when he saw Kurunta's lobster-pink features shaking with rage, then carrying on regardless: 'We are the Mountain Wolves!' he cried out joyously.

***

Some days later, Kurunta was stricken with some gut illness that saw him confined to the latrine pits. All within the Fields of Bronze could hear his ox-like oaths that came with every gastric expulsion, and any who dared look the crouching general in the eye when they went to the pits themselves – if they could brave the foul stench – was threatened with dismemberment. So for a blessed few days, the Mountain Wolves were assigned to archery training instead, on the broad ranges near the foot of the red fells, under the auspices of the kneeling archer statue.

The cool, shady air of the fletcher's workshop was pleasant on Hattu's skin, and alive with flecks of sawdust, floating in the golden curtain of sunlight from the roof hatch above. New unstrung composite bows of horn and wood hung in high racks, confined there for the long year it would take for them to fully dry and bind. The pleasant scent of freshly hewn poplar and cherry wood contrasted with the stink from the bubbling vats of glue and decomposing webs of animal skin at the far side of the archery workshop.

Only twenty or so men of every hundred would carry archery equipment, but every soldier was expected to know how to maintain a bow and shoot one, and so the recruits were gathered around the academy's Master Archer, who sat hunched over his workbench, demonstrating how to fletch an arrow. While General Nuwanza had the broad build of a bowman, he also had a gentle manner about him, a calm, methodical way of describing intricate detail.

'And the feathers are applied in a specific pattern,' Nuwanza explained. His dark, wiry eyebrows matching the shape of his sharply receding hairline. 'It takes three feathers to fletch an arrow. Three feathers, three gaps in between,' he said holding up three fingers to underline each statement. 'One of the gaps is bigger than the other two,' he said, deftly applying a touch of glue to a third goose feather with a brush, then pressing it onto the end of the nearly-complete arrow shaft, then holding the arrow up, end-on, to the gathered recruits and pointing to the bigger gap. 'The feather opposite this bigger gap is called the cock-feather. Always this should be pointing away from the bow when you nock it to your string, to allow a clean shot.' He hooked a bow from a lower rack on the wall, tied the string around one horn-tipped end, then expertly looped that end over the front of an ankle and placed his other leg before the bow's midpoint and bent it round, bringing it under tension until the free ends of the bow and string met. Despite the great strength this required, his hands barely shook as he calmly tied the string into place. He lifted the bow then broke off a chunk of yellow beeswax from the cake sitting on his workbench, and proceeded to wipe the wax up and down the bowstring in long, expert strokes.

'Never let your bowstring dry out,' he said, taking up a patch of leather and rubbing the wax into the string. 'And be sure to work the wax in well so the string absorbs it. The heat of your hand through the leather is enough for this.'

Nuwanza moved over to a rack on the wall behind the recruits, who turned like flowers following the sun. The archery master appraised each of the young men's height and shoulder-width. He plucked out a bow from one of the high racks and gave it to Tanku, then gave a smaller lad one from the lowest rack, and so on. Hattu took his and the string Nuwanza gave him, then stepped back and tried to repeat the stringing routine. What Nuwanza had done effortlessly took Hattu six tries. Garin managed to bring the weapon under tension only for it to slip from his grasp, one ear of the bow thwacking him in the genitals.

'Every man should have a bow that, when drawn back to the ear,' Nuwanza demonstrated, lifting the weapon and pulling back the string as if there was an arrow in place, 'causes your hand to tremble just a little. This means the horn and sinew in the bow are fully compressed and gives the perfect balance of power and accuracy. If your hand shakes too much, take a smaller bow. If you cannot draw back to your ear, take a larger one.'

Along with the others, Hattu drew his bow back – it came all the way to his ear. Truth be told it was an almighty struggle. He eyed the smaller bows in the rack and saw Dagon and Garin doing likewise. There was a tense moment where none of them wanted to be the first to take a weaker weapon. Nuwanza strode forward and took up the smaller bows, giving one to each of the three. 'There is no shame in choosing the weapon that makes you a better archer,' he said. 'Remember, one day your life may depend upon it – and who would be impressed to look upon you struggling to pull a bow that is too powerful for you? Only your enemy, who will be laughing as he looses his own arrow for your heart.'

Nuwanza strode past them, beckoning them, his three tails of hair swishing between his powerful shoulders. They followed him outside into the afternoon sunshine. Hattu saw that a company of twenty veteran archers were lined up at the near end of the dusty archery field – their hair scooped back tightly like Nuwanza's so as not to blow in front of their bows.

'What are they shooting at?' Dagon asked nobody in particular.

Hattu scoured the undulating heat haze across the field. There was nothing but dust until the red fell slopes began a good three hundred paces away.

'Ah, look,' Tanku cooed, pointing. There, at the far end of the field, rested four cross-sections of tree trunk, daubed with dyes to make coloured rings.

Hattu gasped. 'That's impossible.'

Nuwanza, hearing this, shot him a wry smile. 'Nock,' he barked.

The veteran twenty reached over their shoulders and plucked arrows from their quivers, affixing the grooved channel at one end to their bowstrings.

'Raise,' Nuwanza said.

Twenty bows rose up almost in unison, all canted to the same slight angle, all tilted to the same trajectory. Highly-stressed horn and wood groaned as they each drew their strings back to their ears. Nuwanza did this too, the veins in his forearm bulging under the immense tension of the bow.

'Loose,' Nuwanza howled. With a hiss like a rising flock of birds, the arrows leapt forth. Then, silence. Hattu frowned. It was as if they had melted into the heat haze… only for a thick chorus of *thock, thock, thock* to herald missiles hitting timber. Hattu strained to see the targets again, and when the heat haze bent once more, he saw the arrows there – or maybe their shadows – quivering in the coloured rings. Instantly, he wanted to dispense with sleep, food, water and everything else, just to learn and harness the skills of these bowmen.

'How can you hit a target you can barely see?' Hattu asked, directing the question at Garin.

But it was Nuwanza who answered. 'It is not what you see, it is what you know,' he said, tapping a temple. 'All men of the army are taught to shoot at a set of fixed distances. Then, only one man need scout the enemy and call out the appropriate range: it means we can shoot over hills, in the black of night or in the melting heat of day and know we will strike our targets.' He turned to the twenty archers and bellowed: 'Short – loose!'

With a flurry of nocking and bows rising a lot less than before, twenty arrows hummed into the air and came thwacking down into the dust, almost in a line, around one hundred paces away.

'Mid-range – loose.' Thrum... *thwack!* Another perfect line two hundred paces away.

'You see?' Nuwanza said.

For the rest of the afternoon, the archery master had them practice their draw, also showing them how to stretch their arms and shoulders before and after to avoid strain and cramp. For the last few hours of daylight, they emptied quiver after quiver into yellow targets drawn up at short range. In truth, it took all of Hattu's strength to draw the bow enough to achieve this distance and his accuracy suffered as a result, with every second arrow glancing off the edge of the target or plunging into the dust. He had grown strong in these last months, but not yet strong enough.

He and the others shot on, almost entranced by the practice. Despite his limbs becoming fatigued, he found a rhythm, and soon each set of four or five arrows were thwacking into the timber target. They even took to betting against one another, though few wanted to gamble against the hawk-faced Kisna, who was skilled from the outset.

When at last dusk claimed the remaining light, they were dismissed by Nuwanza. Hattu had always been scared of the generals whenever they had appeared in the acropolis grounds. Still, he considered Kurunta a living nightmare of sorts. But he realised he liked Nuwanza – warm, encouraging and approachable. A fine teacher. As they filed back from the archery school towards the infantry compound, he, Dagon, Tanku and Garin joked and chatted with the others. It seemed they had accepted him at last. Hattu, as usual, glanced up at the scowling warrior statue standing over the barrack gates. For a change, he returned the stone effigy's glower with a wry one of his own, then laughed to himself.

They returned to their barrack hut and combined rations to prepare a hearty stew of lamb boiled in yoghurt and a few loaves of bread, eating it outside the porch area around a fire. The veterans from the neighbouring dorm offered them a barrel of barley beer which they took gladly, and Raku, the flat-faced regimental chief brought them a vase of strong wine too. It seemed that it was not just the recruits who had thawed to the idea of having the *Cursed Son* in their midst. The warm meal filled Hattu's belly and the frothy beer washed it down perfectly, warming his blood and softening his thoughts. Garin started a tale about home life and the woman who lived next door. All the recruits listened, rapt, as he began to describe her, drawing her figure in the air with his hands.

'... and she had the most massive... and I mean *massive-*'

'What's this?' a stern voice cut the story short.

Hattu looked up to see Kurunta standing there. His face was fixed in its default state of apoplexy as he eyed the recruits and the fire. And he was a little gaunter than usual – probably thanks to his extended spell in the latrine pits.

'Sir,' Garin saluted with a croak. 'I was just telling my comrades about the woman that lives by our house in the temple ward.' He held out his hands again, squeezing invisible orbs, his face wide with a grin. 'You should see her t-'

'Ah,' Kurunta said, his good eye brightening, 'yes, I know her. Caya, isn't it?'

Garin's neck grew long. 'Yes,' he nodded in excitement.

Kurunta's face fell expressionless. 'She's my niece.'

With a whimper, Garin shrunk and stared intently at his feet.

Hattu watched as Kurunta strode around the sitting circle of recruits. When the general passed behind Garin, he did something entirely unexpected: he winked at the others, flicked his head towards the shamed Garin and mouthed: *she's not really.*

A few gasps and stifled laughs brought Garin's head up again, confused. 'Eh, what?'

But Kurunta threw down a small sack by the fire and crouched by it, his mien uplit by the flames. 'You can all talk about tits and arses again soon enough. First,' he said, opening the sack, 'you must make the Comrades' Oath. It signifies... ' he started, then sighed, a brief look of sadness crossing his lone eye, 'the end of infantry training.'

The recruits all looked at one another, owl-eyed.

He drew from the sack a handful of tallow, grey-white and gelatinous, smearing a dab on the back of Garin's hand, then on Tanku's, then passing the sack around. Hattu followed suit, smearing the cold sheep fat on the back of his hand. Finally, the sack came round to Kurunta again. The general took another scoop of fat and tossed it on the fire. It hissed and sparked and quickly melted away to nothing.

'As the fat melts away into the Dark Earth, so also will he who breaks the trust of his brothers.' As he said this, the general passed his fat-smeared hand across the fire, holding it at the highest point of the flames. The fat bubbled and spat and the hair on his arm shrivelled and vanished. Kurunta was like a rock, unflinching, until the molten fat had liquefied and rolled off his hand into the flames. He looked up, darkly. 'Next?'

Garin, on the end of Kurunta's glare, slumped, then steadied himself, meeting the eyes of each of the recruits. He passed his shaking hand through the inferno, stiffening, his face aghast at first. But Hattu saw a change in him and knew the hand would remain. 'Comrades, I will never abandon you,' he said as the fat dripped away.

As Garin furtively nursed his hand, Dagon went next. 'Kin, friends...' he looked up, catching Hattu's eye, 'I owe each of you my life. Comrades until I breathe my last.'

A low rumble of anxious, excited agreement broke out amongst the others.

Tanku was next. 'I will honour you as I honour the Gods, always,' he said, the flames licking at his thick arms. 'We are *one* spear.'

Sargis, Kisna and a handful of others took their turn. Next, Kurunta's good eye swivelled round to Hattu, narrowing to a crescent. It was time.

Hattu held his gaze as he passed his hand into the fire. The breath caught in his lungs as the flames licked around his flesh. The pain was instant and intense, but he knew it would take a team of six Lukkan horses to drag his hand away. 'All my life I have been alone,' he said. 'Now, I am a soldier, a soldier with ninety-nine brothers... I will give my life for the Mountain Wolves.'

The circle exploded into a cacophony of cheering. Tanku and Dagon threw their heads back and howled, the others joining in. Hattu kept his eyes on Kurunta. The gnarled general made a single grunting noise, then rose from his haunches. Maybe, just maybe, there was a glint of respect in the haggard demon's lone eye.

***

As the summer came to an end, the land cooled and the trees turned russet and gold, and the Fields of Bronze grew busy with men preparing for winter billet. The standing troops stationed here over summer would disperse to their homes or to workshops in the cities, leaving just a skeleton garrison of a few hundred to look after the snowbound academy over winter.

Soldiers paced from place to place, towing carts of arms and supplies. Many eyed the arzana house enviously, hearing the pipe music and the laughter of the off-duty men emanating from within. Those who passed the command building near the paddocks cast spellbound looks at the royal carriage drawn up there, watched over by two glittering Mesedi.

Inside the cool, shady command building, King Mursili sat across a table from Kurunta.

'The Mountain... *Wolves?*' the king repeated as if he had misheard.

Kurunta nodded reluctantly. 'I named them the Hill Pups. They decided to change it.'

Mursili sat back on his chair, cradling his chin between thumb and forefinger. 'And it was my boy who named them?'

Kurunta shrugged. 'Aye. He did. The rest of the hundred agreed readily to his suggestion. And then they sat together, painting blood-red streaks on their shields and on their skin: like the tear of a wolf's claws,' Kurunta said with a weary flick of his eyebrows.

'They hold him in some esteem, then?' Mursili asked. 'When I sent Hattu to you, I ordered you to-'

'He will not break,' Kurunta interrupted. 'Forgive me, My Sun,' he reprimanded himself. 'But I have put him through the grimmest trials. First it was the Water Ordeal, carrying to the hills a burden that no soldier could manage.' He snorted in incredulity. 'I even told him Prince Muwa had beaten the challenge, yet I have only ever subjected troublemakers to it.' He leaned forward to hold Mursili's attention. 'The point of the task is that it is impossible. It is designed to break the spirit and the body. Yet he found a way. *He* broke the damned *challenge*!' He shook his head. 'There was one night, before he managed it, when I could tell he was wavering, thinking of leaving. I opened the gates to the infantry compound before I turned in, thinking he would be gone in the morning. But he did not leave. The sentries told me he had risen and taken to scrambling up the hills in the darkness. For over a month I left the gates unlocked. He had ample chance to leave and refused it.'

'I've known you a long time,' Mursili said. 'You have many tricks to break a man.'

Kurunta shrugged. 'Indeed. Next, I took him to the Bridge of the Mountain God.'

'The jump?' Mursili said, leaning forward in interest.

Kurunta avoided the king's eyes. 'I, er... wrapped cloth around his eyes and... '

Mursili drew in a tight breath. 'You made him jump blindfolded? When I asked you to break my son, I did not mean physically... '

'Absolve me, My Sun, I did not expect him to actually attempt the jump, but he did – and he made it with room to spare. Then I subjected them all to the River Ordeal, up in the ice stream,' Kurunta's face crumpled, 'and I will admit I maybe only did that because I was angry... and a bit hungry... and I had a sore tooth. But I watched them and I saw that it was Hattu who worked it out – the key to minimising the pain of the ordeal. Next, he saved one of his comrades – probably his biggest detractor – who had fallen into the ravine.' He threw up his hands in exasperation. 'After that I took them on a full morning's run around the hottest valleys in the fells. I noticed Hattu falling back. I thought I had cracked it then, until I saw that he had merely slowed to help the lad at the rear – Garin, built like a date pudding.'

'Yet he has not excelled, has he?' Mursili mused. 'You say it was the big one named Tanku who they elected as their captain?'

Kurunta chapped the table in frustration. 'Half elected Tanku, half

Hattu. Hattu convinced them Tanku was the better choice: stronger, louder and fiercer.'

'Then his meekness remains?'

Kurunta flashed a dry, foul grin. 'Not meek… bright, selfless. Tanku selected Hattu as his chosen man. It was the moment I knew that the boy's place is in the army. Raku flat-face, the Chief of the Storm's First Regiment, did not want him in his thousand at first. Now he does. Hattu is the finest prospect I have trained in some time: bright of mind and fleet of foot. He is stronger even than Prince Muwa was at that age.'

Mursili felt Ishtar's invisible finger trace his spine. 'Aye, well, he will serve as a fine *assistant* when Muwa becomes king,' he said, more tersely than intended.

Kurunta searched the king's face, confused, then relaxed. 'There is not a hint of treachery in him, My Sun. Let Ishtar forgive me for this, but what she told you that night… is not true. He will not seek to harm you or his brother, I can assure you of that much.'

'Can you?' Mursili replied instantly.

'You have known me your entire life, you know that I don't fawn to you like others. I can only give you my honest opinion.' Kurunta sighed. 'But that aside, you asked me to break him. I am sorry, My Sun, for on that front I have failed you.'

Mursili's eyes drifted across the scars on the table. 'Alas, I fear you could never have succeeded. Fate, it seems, is a river that no man can divert.'

'What for Hattu now?' Kurunta asked. 'Will you take him with you, back to Hattusa? I have overheard him talking with the others. He has spoken with some fondness of returning to the acropolis over winter.'

Mursili's eyes brightened. 'He yearns for a soft bed?'

'No, he merely longs to show you how well he has done,' Kurunta replied. 'He itches to make you proud, My Sun.'

Mursili tapped his lips with his forefinger a few times, caught in some inner dilemma. 'He is to stay here over the snows,' he said at last, 'with the winter guard.'

Kurunta's eyes fell. 'Aye, I will tell him so,' he said sadly.

'His training is not complete,' Mursili grumbled. 'He may think he has beaten the rigours of the academy, but he has yet to be put through his paces by Colta.'

Kurunta's gaze lifted to meet the king's again. 'True. Many infantrymen, nobles… some princes even, have been reduced to white-faced wrecks by the old hurkeler and his damned horses.' His good eye glazed for a moment and he issued a short, reminiscent laugh.

Mursili drummed his fingers on the table. 'Then that is how it shall be. Hattu will stay here through the winter and next summer too. And it will be me he will stand before, at the end. The Chariot Ordeal separates the strong from the mighty. It will be me who grants him… or denies him… the status he covets,' he snapped, 'as a true prince.' A streak of hot, stinging pain shot down his left arm as he heard his own words ringing around the room. He clasped a hand to his armpit, feeling pins and needles in his left hand.

'My Sun?' Kurunta gasped, half-rising from his seat.

Mursili waved him back testily. Recapturing his breath, he dipped his head. 'Watch over my son: that he grows strong and skilled should fill me with pride and hope. Yet, still, all I can see when I look at him is what I gave up so he could live. And all I can hear when he speaks is Ishtar's pledge, of the dark future…'

'Hattu is a good lad, My Sun,' Kurunta said earnestly.

Mursili's bloodshot eyes flicked up, alight, his face sombre. 'No man is born wicked, old friend.'

***

Hattu sat by the window of the arzana house, oblivious to the skirling, pacy pipes and the raucous goings-on around him. His eyes were trained on the command house across the track: still and silent in the twilight, the ruts of King Mursili's recently departed carriage still fresh in the dust.

I understand now, Father. You wanted me to fail, to return to my old life and remain there, Hattu mused. He felt no anger, just a heavy sense of betrayal. In his short visit to the academy, the king had not even sought him out. Instead, Gorru the Mesedi had come in to the arzana house to tell him that he was to remain at the Fields of Bronze throughout the winter. *Why? Because you think I will finally break and cry for my soft bed in the palace? Or to keep me safely distant from Hattusa and the Grey Throne? The chair you think I am destined to seize for myself? You do not trust me. You believe Ishtar and think me a curse. But if there is anything I can swear by, it is that I will never break our oath, Father. If that confounds the Gods, then so be it.* He barely realised that one hand had curled into a shaking, white-knuckled fist. *I will show you.*

A sudden frantic clatter snapped him from his introspection. He swung round just as the two wrestlers in the sunken pit at the heart of the low, dark hall tumbled up onto the floor in a baleful embrace. The larger of the two hauled the smaller up by his loincloth and his club of hair, then hurled him towards the edge of the hall. The fellow flailed through tables and chairs, sending cups of barley beer fountaining in his wake. Hattu ducked back an instant before the fellow went plunging through the window with a strangled yelp. A great roar went up from the spectators and they exchanged trinkets and copper rings to settle bets. The victorious wrestler stood tall, beaming, his oiled skin glistening and his smile spoiled by the tooth that had been knocked out during the bout. 'Next?' he shouted with extreme confidence, leaping back into the pit.

The fellow who had exited hastily moments before made a commendable attempt at climbing back in the window. 'N-not finished,' he slurred, blood streaming from his broken nose and one eye swollen shut.

'I'd say you are,' Hattu suggested, helping him inside then resting him on his chair where he passed out at once, snoring. He turned away to find the rest of the Mountain Wolves. The interior of the arzana house was as big as a paddock, packed with men in military tunics or kilts, hugging the maze of niches and benches or craning over the wooden balcony of the mezzanine, beer cups sloshing as they drank in great, untasting gulps, belching and cheering the next wrestling bout. Bubbles of orange lamplight gave the place the appearance of a cave, and coils of fragrant smoke battled hard against the olfactory assault of stale drink and the rank odour of unwashed men.

'Hattu,' Garin called from the darkness of one niche. His fleshy features were ruddier than usual and beaded with sweat.

'Are you well?' Hattu asked.

Then the harlot sitting behind him in the darkness leaned forward, her sultry, dark lined eyes glued to Hattu as she nibbled on Garin's ear, then wrapped her legs around his waist and drew him back into an embrace.

'Dagon has something for you,' he said, before his words grew ecstatically muffled.

Hattu cocked an eyebrow and left them to it.

A hand with a fresh cup of foaming beer shot out in front of him. 'There you are,' Tanku said, pushing the cup into his hand. The big recruit was seated, wearing just a kilt and cradling his newly-awarded captain's helm – dark brown leather with a bronze browband like the others', but with a long, dark plume that trailed to the small of his back when wearing it. Behind him a bald masseur was rubbing oil into Tanku's back and grinding his elbows into the muscles. 'We've made it. Summer is over and we're unbroken. Drink. You should be enjoying this as much as the rest of us,' he insisted.

Hattu drew a mouthful of the bitter drink through the reed straw. Just months ago, he would never have felt such ease alongside the burly soldier. Now he did. Tanku was bold, stubborn and at times reckless, and all those things had surfaced thanks to Kurunta's brutal training. But underneath, Tanku was a good young man who sought simple pleasures for himself and his close ones.

'The women are quite beautiful,' Tanku said, eyes combing the niches where soldiers and harlots cavorted. Then he held up his cup with a grin. 'Especially after a few of these.'

Hattu smiled, taking another mouthful of beer. The drink was warming his blood already, loosening his stiff neck. He saw a few intent-laden and expertly-painted female faces peek out from the dark recesses. He had never lain with a woman and, for a moment, his loins stirred. Yet all he could think of was one girl, far from here.

'I'll let Garin and the others enjoy their company. For me, there is someone else,' he said.

Tanku's eyebrows arched. 'Aye?'

'Atiya. She lives at the Storm Temple. She is bright and beautiful like the dawn,' he said without effort.

'Ha! But she is in Hattusa, is she not. You are here, now. Some say it is the last rite of a prince to make him a man,' Tanku grinned.

When one of the harlots coiled and uncoiled a finger, beckoning him, flashing one up-tipped breast, he felt his throat drain of moisture. The truth was it seemed more daunting than the leap over the bridge of the Mountain God. 'I... I... '

A slurred voice and stale-beer breath ended his quandary. 'You don't talk to... *him*,' a hulking soldier growled, pushing in between Tanku and Hattu. He was from the Blaze Division, Hattu realised. 'They call him the *Cursed Son*.'

Tanku stood and elbowed the man away. 'Then they are fools,' he shouted.

The pipe music faded and the wrestling stopped.

'Tanku, it doesn't matter,' Hattu whispered.

'Aye, it does,' Tanku countered. 'We are the Mountain Wolves!' he cried. 'Prince Hattu is one of us.' He beat his fist against his chest.

From dark corners and tables dotted around the arzana house, ninety eight other young men suddenly shot to their feet and emitted the keening wolf howl. Raku flat-face and a handful of other Storm men also thumped their cups on their tables in agreement.

A tense silence passed. Hattu saw the many other veterans in the place cast chill looks upon his comrades – the kind of looks they had previously reserved for him alone. Soon though, the pipes struck up again, the raucous chatter continued and the two wrestlers resumed knocking lumps out of one another.

'How do you do it, Tanku?' Hattu asked as they both sat again. 'You have no notion of fear.'

He laughed once, then dropped his head a little and began knitting and un-knitting his fingers. 'One night, when I was a boy, I noticed a white, glossy orb on the ceiling above my bed,' he said, the fire in his voice now but an ember. 'I was fascinated by it: so sleek, so delicately woven in the finest threads. I went to sleep that night and I woke, hearing a terrible scratching noise. Near me, all around me… *on* me. I opened my eyes and saw the white orb on the ceiling had ruptured like a boil. Three dozen or more spiders were scurrying across my face, one in my ear, many in my hair. I had heard tales of venomous spiders and what their bites could do to a boy. My mother was asleep nearby, but I was too afraid to scream, lest they crawled into my mouth. So I lay there for the rest of the night, silent, alone… terrified. I understand fear well enough.'

Hattu felt an invisible itch on every part of his skin. He rose, clamping a hand to Tanku's shoulder. 'I don't know what lies ahead for us, but whatever it might be: spiders, brigands, Kaskans – you will not be alone.'

Tanku planted a hand over Hattu's, looking up. 'That's the greatest lesson I've learned during this summer,' he said with a smile.

Hattu wandered off, sat on a bench by the wall and took a long draw on his beer. He felt warm and weightless now. He barely noticed Dagon sitting down by his side. He pressed something into Hattu's hand. Hattu spread his palm: it was Atiya's teardrop beryl stone.

'This? How did you know?' Hattu gasped. The last he had seen of this was when he had traded it for three loaves of bread, months ago.

'I bought it back for you. I saw you, on those early nights – stroking the stone for comfort. Then I saw you barter it in exchange for food for the rest of us.' Dagon laughed and took a drink of his wine. 'Were we worth it?'

Hattu tied the stone back in his hair and looked around the smoky haze, the drunken chaos and the many soldiers. One face in ten was friendly now, at least. 'Aye, you were,' he smiled.

CHAPTER 10

SACRED RAIN
LATE WINTER 1301 BC

The winter was severe, the days short and perishing. The heartlands were blocked with deep snow, the countryside deserted, every sane person having retreated to the safety and shelter of the Hittite cities.

A bitter wind blew into Hattu's eyes as he plunged along the top of the snow-coated fells under an angry sky, his bare chest running with sweat, his now shoulder-length hair and linen kilt wet with it too. It had been a long, lonely winter, with just a few soldiers and Kurunta for company in the all-but-deserted Fields of Bronze. The Wolves were gone. Dagon, Tanku, Garin, Kisna and Sargis had all left in the days following the drunken night in the arzana house. In the distance he could see the white-coated mass of Hattusa off to the east. *Damn you, Father*, he growled, vaulting over a boulder, a shower of snow spraying in his wake.

His skin stung and his chest burned with every breath as he came to a red outcrop mottled with patches of clinging snow. He launched from the run and onto the lower face, feet and hands latching onto the holds he had spotted from a few strides away. A moment later, he was on his way up. The cold bit at his fingers but the holds were good, and soon, there was nothing in his mind but the climb. He hauled himself onto the top of the rocky tower and sat cross-legged, swiping the sweat from his face and tucking his hair behind his ears. He pulled a woollen cloak from his leather bag around his body. The keening wind picked up for a moment. This, he decided, was probably the definition of alone.

Then he heard something else – something familiar – high above.

He looked up into the sky – white and bruised with full storm clouds – to see a tiny shadow up there swooping down towards him. 'Arrow?' he gasped. He shot out his left arm, offering the dark-brown bracer to her. She landed on his wrist as if they had never been apart. 'You are far from your nest, girl, and a storm threatens,' he reprimanded her, stroking her back with one finger. Then he heard another shriek. A smaller falcon appeared – a male – swooping down to settle in the snow near Hattu. 'A mate?' he cooed. Arrow shrieked at him in reply, head tilting one way then the other. 'Ah, just friends, I see,' he said puckishly.

She beat her wings a few times and Hattu could tell she and her new partner were eager to fly again, so he pulled out a strip of dried pork and fed her a piece, tossing the other part to the male falcon. While they devoured the meal at frightening speed, he took the opportunity to draw from his purse the small animal bracelet he had won in a wrestling bet at the end of that heady evening in the arzana house – a bet that had resulted in an over-confident Sargis being turned nearly inside-out by the champion wrestler. The trinket wasn't a fine piece like the things Muwa often brought Atiya, but it meant just as much. 'Take this to her,' he said as he tied it to Arrow's leg and flicked his wrist, sending her skywards again – the male bird quickly taking flight in pursuit. He took a mouthful of icy water from his drinking skin, then climbed down from the outcrop and set off at a jog for the edge of the fells. As he descended the slope – the same slope that had nearly bested him the previous summer – he saw the Fields of Bronze down at the foot, veiled in white. He heard a guttural grunting from down there and saw a lone figure in the snowy training ground, loping up a small, artificial dirt hill. Up, then down, then back up again, over and over, the lone silver braid jostling.

Now try it with six buckets of water, Hattu chuckled. He had come to admire Kurunta One-eye – much in the way a runner might appreciate the calluses on his heels and toes. One night, in the depths of winter while thunder crackled above the academy and a blizzard howled, he had heard the so-called 'breaker of men' crooning. Soft, gentle tones: first, it was a sonnet of love, of his fondness for his wife; next he sang a quiet dirge – one that had Hattu rapt.

Tarhunda weeps and the rain pours,
His lightning blinds, his thunder roars,
Our fallen sing his ageless song,
And in our hearts they're never gone...

He smiled at the memory, then set off at a jog for the downhill track that would take him back to the academy. But something wasn't right. Something in the corner of his eye was not still. Something in the frozen, deserted countryside had moved. A grim shiver crept over him as he turned to see a figure loping along a high, snowy track. For just a moment, the horrors of the Kaskan raid came to him like a nightmare. But this was no Kaskan, he realised. Nor was it a raider. He fell to his haunches and peered at the stranger. A man, loping, wearing rags, his feet bare, leaving red blotches on the snow behind him. He cupped a hand to his ear and heard the fellow's distant, ragged breaths. This man was no threat, he realised. Within a moment he was up and running towards the poor wretch.

The man saw him, gawped at him with wide, bloodshot eyes, then fell to his knees, weeping. The fellow's hair was matted and his chin thick with stubble, his fingernails broken and packed with dirt. 'Who are you?' Hattu asked.

'A fallen man,' he wailed, sobbing deeply again. 'I have failed my family, my people.'

Hattu crouched by the man, pulling his water skin out and offering it. 'Where did you come from?' he asked, looking out across the man's red-tinged footprints in the snow – coming from the northwest. The countryside beyond had been blocked with snowdrifts for months.

'From the lands of Pala,' he gasped after nearly draining the skin. 'A land that now lies in ruin. Our cities had no walls, we could not hold them back,' he wept. 'They slaughtered everyone... *everyone*. And on they went, razing neighbouring Tummanna to the ground too. I ran from them... like a coward. I ran and I have been running all winter, through the white wastes, wading through the blocked valleys. I hid in caves, ate grubs and roots.'

Pala, Tummanna. Hattu thought of the northwestern vassals. Loyal, *vital* states. 'Who? *Who* did this?'

The man looked up, his eyes wet. 'Pitagga,' he wailed. 'The Lord of the Mountains has reduced my homeland to ashes. He roves in my lands, waving the head of Prince Sarpa on the end of his spear.'

***

Many in Hattusa looked on with wide eyes as a stablehand from the academy ushered the bleeding stranger up the main way, to the acropolis. They gossiped and whispered of troubles in nearby allied lands. But their curiosity vanished when the first burst of spring rain came just a few days later. The snow was washed away and the city exploded with song and colour as the Festival of the Earth began. A month of joyous praise to the Gods for the coming of the New Year.

By the eighth day of the downpour, the rains had grown tepid, falling in sheets. The swollen Ambar River was thick with people – children playing, pregnant women waist-deep, mouthing words of worship to the sky. Silvery-haired Wise Women stood midriver, pouring droplets of honey into the current, lips moving in muttered incantations as they launched hand-sized 'prayer boats' of kindling. The main way was even more crowded, the silvery cascade of rain drumming and leaping from its flagstones. People lined the broad avenue. Their robes were drenched as they cheered and chanted at dancers weaving down the road in a snaking line. The lead pair of dancers held up a fierce, fanged clay serpent's head with a lolling, forked tongue while those behind carried a patchwork trail of feathered yellow and orange linen. This was the feared Illuyanka, the demon serpent, nemesis of the Storm God. Warriors play-fought against the serpent as the dancers twisted around them, much to the crowd's delight.

Atiya clapped and sang as the procession wound past her. Her heart skipped to the rhythm and she felt wonderfully free of responsibilities and troubles – soaked to her skin and blithe. Women and men bumped into her as they passed but she didn't care, laughing like they were. Another fellow bumped into her and she turned her bright grin upon him.

Suddenly, she was seized with surprise.

The handsome, amber-haired man smiled, his freckled cheeks lifting. 'My apologies, Priestess,' he said, bowing to her. Since that first time she had seen him, over a year ago, she had been unable to stop meeting his eye – at the market, by the banks of the Ambar, around the outskirts of the Storm Temple. Whatever wares or business brought him to Hattusa, they certainly brought him here often. 'The wagons are ready – for the Tapikka pilgrimage?' he said, looking past her shoulder down to the Storm Temple's gates.

Atiya looked there too: a collection of ox-wagons were lined up. These would see the silver statue of Tarhunda taken from the innermost sanctuary of the Storm Temple and towed to the fort-city of Tapikka, to bring it before the city's High Altar where the supreme god could commune with the sky. Again, she had been overlooked and would not be part of the temple party that would ride with it. But next year, the Elder Priestess had told her that morning, she *would* be included. A shiver of pride ran through her. 'They are,' she said, 'the silver effigy needs only to be anointed and blessed and then the journey can begin.'

'A hard road though, is it not?' the fellow mused.

'The high road is hard but swift, but there is a low road too – lengthy but gentle,' she answered, echoing what the Elder Priestess had told her.

'I see,' the fellow nodded.

A man and a woman, drunk and giggling, barged between them. When they passed through, she returned her eyes to the spot the amber-haired man had been. But he was gone. She looked around for a moment, before returning her attentions to the procession, letting out a *whoop* and clapping.

Prince Muwa, his thick dark mane drenched and plastered to his face, could not relax. The festival had to be held lest the Gods be angered. But much more serious affairs were afoot. He looked beyond the Earth Festival celebrations and uphill: on the Noon Spur, regiments were already being drilled by the Great Barracks, readied to form the campaign army. The Kaskan invasion of Pala and Tummanna had to be countered. Sarpa's shame had to be ended. Soon, they would march and he would be gone from this place until autumn. He swirled his cup then took a swig of wine, casting his eye downhill a little, where the play-serpent was now approaching the banks of the River Ambar.

He saw her there, in the crowds by the stonemason's yard, her headscarf and robe wet through and locks of soaked hair spiralling across her cheeks. Every time she cheered and laughed his heart ached. Then he saw her talking with the amber-haired man. A spike of jealousy ran through him, until he laughed it off and the sadness returned. They were drifting apart, he realised. No, *she* was drifting away from him, no matter how frantically he paddled to stay with her. During last winter and this, the precious time he had planned to spend with her, she had been distant. *Why? I can give you everything.*

He eyed the tiny vial of petal oils. It wasn't quite as opulent as gifts he had given her before, but it would remind her how much he cared for her, and that was what mattered. He took a last swig from the cup of wine, then clasped the vial in his fist and made his way through the crowds to reach her. He stole up behind her and grabbed her by the waist with a playful 'raarrr!'

She squealed and swung round in his embrace. 'Muwa!' she cried, beating a light hand across his chest.

'You look sweet as honey when you are happy,' he said, unable to stop the thought tumbling from his lips.

She looked away, embarrassed. 'Who could not be joyous, on a day like this?'

Muwa thought of battles past and the struggle for the beset northwestern lands that was to come. Cleaved bodies. Screaming men. Blood. Vultures. A frenzy of flies. He blinked the thoughts away, trying to keep his face bright and his eyes on the serpent procession. 'Aye, it is a fine spectacle, is it not?'

'The Elder Priestess and I wove the tail section,' she pointed out proudly. 'It took us a month, but it was worth it. The textile trader was asking for fortunes to buy a length, so instead we bought flax and-'

'I'll be leaving soon, Atiya,' he said, cutting her off.

Her smile fell a little. 'I know.' She glanced up at the acropolis.

'You will look after your father, won't you?'

'Aye,' Muwa replied. 'His ailments are worsening, but his generals know this. He can still march and ride.'

'I will miss you,' she said, tilting her head a little.

He saw her full lips and the look of expectation on her face. He cupped a hand to her chin and made to kiss her. But she turned her head a little to the side, the kiss landing on her cheek, she kissing his.

Rejection, again. Another weight pulled at his heart. 'Atiya I, I will miss you terribly.' He gave her the petal oils, but she pushed it back into his palm.

'I should not take gifts from you, Muwa,' she said.

'Why not? Do you not see how much I delight in giving you things?'

'But it's not right,' she insisted.

'Of course it is. Why would-'

'Because there is another,' she interrupted. 'I think I am in love with... someone else.'

The words raked his heart. He felt like a fool, holding her like this. He let her go, stepping back. He noticed how she had on one wrist a cheap animal trinket – something from the trade wagons that passed the Fields of Bronze, he reckoned. She was toying with this as she stood there before him in unease. 'I'm sorry,' she said, turning to run off into the crowd.

Muwa's heart ached as if a smith's anvil hung there now.

***

'Muwa?' King Mursili called. His shout echoed through the corridors of the palace. 'Muwa,' he called out again. Silence. Angered and unsure why, Mursili slammed the leather bags down on the hearth room floor and stuck his head out of the door in search of a palace slave. None were nearby. '*Muw-*' he started then fell silent with a stifled croak, clutching a hand to his left armpit. His whole arm stung with invisible needles. He felt his chest tighten as if an unseen armourer was buckling a willow-thin man's bronze cuirass around his trunk. The pain seemed set to crush him.

It was stronger than ever before. But, as always, it passed after a few moments.

'My Sun,' a voice said, startling him. He swung round to see a horned apparition approaching him: Volca had entered the hearth room via the other door. He stalked across towards the king, silent in his bare feet, the red cloak that had once been Zida's floating in his wake. 'You need help?'

'Aye, Prince Muwa was supposed to be helping me choose what things we might need for the campaign. My arm, you see,' he said, wincing as he tried to lift one of the bags, 'it grows weaker.' He felt ashamed that he was even out of breath from that speck of effort.

'Sit, My Sun,' Volca gestured to the wooden chair by the circular hearth. He tapped the silver hawk cloakpin Mursili had given him earlier that moon. 'I am your Gal Mesedi now. That means I must protect you from others... and from yourself.'

Mursili was about to protest, but the fight left him and, with a sigh, he slumped onto the chair, rubbing his palms on the armrests and resting his head on the back. 'But damn, when I was twenty, I could have sworn I was a lion. Tall, proud, lean and brimming with energy. When I was thirty, I felt sluggish, a little slow thanks to the lack of daily drills with the army,' he clasped a pouch of loose skin near his waist as he said this. 'At forty, it was as if someone had taken out all my muscles and replaced them with straw – and then there are the aches and pains in the cold season: all those bumps and cuts from my younger days now haunt me when the winter comes. But now, approaching my forty-fourth summer, I feel a hundred times worse than that. I have never known frailty like it. The pains in my chest, the weakness of my limbs, the quickness with which I tire and the ease with which my mind wanders is... terrifying.'

'There was an old king on the Island of the Sherden who suffered a similar ailment to yours... ' Volca said, then added swiftly: 'not that *you* are old.'

'Not as old as I'll be tomorrow,' Mursili said, managing a weak chuckle. It still amused him how much Volca's jagged accent had softened and how well he had mastered the Hittite tongue. 'Tell me about him – this king.'

Volca crouched by the fire at the king's side. Mursili noticed how his pale blue eyes grew distant, the reflected flames dancing in them. 'He was a kind man. A good ruler. Every day he would invite families to dine with him: highborn, farmers, beggars, even. He did not keep vaults of silver for himself; indeed, he saw little value in shiny metals and gems.'

'And his illness, did... did it kill him?'

Volca shook his head ever so slowly. 'No. A young guard of his did. The old king was too trusting, you see. This young guardsman and a band of co-conspirators dragged him from his bed one night and up onto the keep roof. They slit open his belly, pulled out his gut ropes and tied him there, alive, and let crows and vultures descend to tear him apart from the inside. He lived for two days like that, tormented.'

Mursili recoiled in disgust. 'Why? Had they put a knife through his heart or tossed him from the roof they would have achieved their end all the same. Why the grim torture?'

'Some said the young guardsman enjoyed it.'

Mursili felt glad of the heat from the hearth. 'But why anyway? The king, as you say, stored no wealth – what had they to gain?'

Volca shrugged. 'The throne. The power to horde the wealth that the old king chose not to. Respect.'

'Respect?' Mursili said, arching one eyebrow. 'Respect is won by example.'

Volca nodded slowly. 'And that was the mistake the usurpers made: for all the Sherden people heard the old king's cries. They knew what had happened. They rejected the young guard.'

'Rejected him? Put him to death, surely?' Mursili laughed dryly.

A log snapped and hissed, then settled in the fire.

'They put him to an equally cruel torture,' Volca said. He turned his gaze to Mursili. 'Now can you see why I left such a place behind, My Sun?'

Mursili felt an odd chill for a moment, but put it down to the dying fire. 'Yes, yes I can. A brutal land.'

Volca sighed and smiled sadly, then rose. 'Let me carry the bags to the stables and the carriage. You rest here. And shall I bring you a cup of the root brew?'

Mursili's mood brightened. The tangy drink was pleasant – nothing like the vile muck the asu healer had been trying to ply him with. 'Aye, that would be good.'

As Volca made to leave, Mursili added: 'Tell me, Volca – and I have been itching to ask – why do you insist on wearing that brutish helm at all times?'

'I have my reasons,' Volca smiled, halting in the doorway.

'Very well,' Mursili shrugged. *Every man has his secrets.* 'But the horns – are they not a bane in battle? They merely give your foe something to grab hold of, do they not?'

Volca chuckled. 'They do, true enough.' Then he smiled, his pale face half-obscured in shadow. 'But don't they make me look damned terrifying?'

***

Volca made his way to the palace scullery: the place was empty and a picture of cleanliness and organisation: a spotless stone floor, ovens, rows of hanging, pristine white aprons and shelves stacked with pots and cooking implements. He came to a wooden bench lining the walls and selected a cup from the row of gleaming copper vessels resting upside down on a shelf there. He poured priest-anointed water from a vase to fill the cup halfway, then brought a small wooden box from his purse. It was no bigger than his hand. Opening it released a waft of decay. He took a knife from a trough of implements and scooped out just a speck of the green-brown purée within the wooden box. The mixture – sweet clover petals putrefied with fragments of funghi – was known only to him. He tapped the knife on the edge of the cup so the mixture dropped into the water, then stirred it in. The odour of decay was still strong, so he lifted a small clay pot of honey, popping the wooden lid off and tipping in a copious measure of the thick, sweet, nectar. That was why the root brew tasted so good, he smiled, the flavour of decay masked.

It reminded him of the venison he had once hung in his stony barn on the Isle of the Sherden. Some of the nobles had wanted to devour it on the day the deer had been caught, but he had dissuaded them, convinced them to let the meat rest over a period of two days. When they had protested, he had convinced them to wait by describing the process of 'controlled rot', to age the meat.

Controlled rot, he reaffirmed, a smile tugging at the edges of his mouth.

'Ah, Volca,' a voice spoke.

Volca swung round to see the king's favoured, weak-chinned asu approaching.

The healer held up a fistful of leeks and a leather bucket of wet red clay 'I have had a thought: the *Labarna* enjoys leeks, aye?'

Volca glowered at the asu.

'And the red clay of the Ambar is said to be sacred, healing, even. So perhaps if I was to cook him a broth of leeks and clay, it might prove to be enjoyable *and* beneficial.'

'Perhaps,' Volca said. *What next – bread and ox-shit?*

'Well, you don't seem too perturbed by the notion, so I'll give it a try. Thank you.' The asu turned to leave, but halted, looking back at the cup in Volca's hand. 'Ah, is this the famous root-brew the king talks of?'

'Yes. Now I'd best get it to the ki-'

'My, it does look thick indeed.' The asu's eyes widened, his head craning over the cup. 'May I ask what the ingredients are?'

'Maybe next time I can show you,' Volca said, brushing past the healer.

But the asu caught his arm. He stared down at the fragile man, knowing that his horned helm and a stiff look was enough to ward off most bothersome types. Yet the healer was insistent. 'I really ought to find out now. I wouldn't be doing my job if I did not thoroughly test the potion and have the ingredients catalogued by Ruba and his scribes.'

Volca laughed. 'You are dedicated to your duties, aren't you,' he said, slipping an arm around the asu's shoulder. 'Come, I will show you,' he said, walking the fellow back to the bench. He lifted the wooden box from his purse with one hand, placing it on the top of an upright barrel of wine next to the bench. 'This is the key ingredient,' he said. 'Take a look.'

The asu rested his hands on his knees and crouched a little to inspect the box. He reached out to lift it, then opened the lid. His nose wrinkled and he turned his head towards Volca. 'It smells revol-'

Volca shot one hand down to grip the back of the asu's neck and with the other, batted the lid from the wine barrel. The asu's strangled cry had barely begun when Volca then plunged the healer's head into the blood-red wine.

As the healer thrashed, Volca's arm shuddered to hold him there. Wine bubbled and leapt from the barrel. 'It does smell dreadful, doesn't it?' he said, catching the box as it slid away with the barrel lid. The asu's arms flailed now, his gurgling cries barely audible from deep within the barrel. 'And so will you, if and when they find you washed up on the Ambar's banks.'

As the healer's body convulsed and gradually weakened, Volca looked up at the scullery ceiling, imagining King Mursili on the floor above. 'Aye, controlled rot… '

CHAPTER 11

UNDER THE SHADOW OF PERUWA
SPRING 1301 BC

The distant pipes of the Festival of the Earth played for thirty eight days, the skirling song just audible at the Fields of Bronze. Every night, Hattu lay in his rough soldier's bed, the barrack dorm empty, imagining the goings-on back at Hattusa. The celebrations would begin with a procession to the north of the city through the ossuary fields known as the Meadow of the Fallen, and on to the Rock Shrine. He imagined the feasting, the strong beer, the song, the games and the laughter. Strangers would share each other's homes and exchange food and gifts. Nobody would be alone... nobody back in the city, at least.

He sighed and rolled over in his bed, now wondering if Arrow had made it back to Hattusa safely, and if Atiya had received the bracelet. For a moment, he mused jealously at the thought of Muwa giving her something finer.

His days were spent helping Kurunta and the small knot of veterans still stationed here to drag equipment to various spots on the training fields, to sweep out ox byres and to count and distribute weapons around the various armouries attached to the many dormitories. On the thirty-ninth day the rains stopped and so did the tantalising pipe music. The day after, as he chopped logs for firewood, the distant call of the campaign horn sounded. He stopped in his duties and shielded his eyes to peer to the east. He could see nothing at this distance but rising vapour from the drying rain pools, but he knew what was happening: the army was on its way to Pala and Tummanna, King Mursili and Prince Muwa at their head as always.

A momentary ire flared as he thought of Father, but it faded fast. 'Gods be with them. Let them take back Sarpa's dishonoured head,' he whispered, imagining his dead brother's wraith marching with them.

A few days later, the sky was cloudless and the sun warm on the skin. And so Hattu began his fourteenth summer knee-deep in a pit near the edge of the academy grounds, shovelling spadefuls of ox dung onto a heap at one side. It reminded him of something – about this time a year ago...

'Hattu?' a voice said. Hattu swung round to see Dagon standing there, clean and looking the better for a winter at home. Hattu, on the other hand, was smeared in filth. The pair gawped at one another for a moment, a mirror image of their meeting like this the previous year, then each buckled in two with laughter.

As that day and the next few wore on, companies of men trickled in from Hattusa – veteran hundreds who had been left behind by the king. Every so often some of the Mountain Wolves would arrive. The last to arrive were Tanku and Garin who sauntered in when Dagon and Hattu were still working together on the infinite dung-pile. 'Ah, it's as if we've never been away,' Garin teased.

Yet it turned out – as Tanku explained – that the two new arrivals had spent a winter of squalor, living and working at Kurunta's home in Hattusa's lower town, also slipping and sliding in animal filth whilst the general's favourite pig terrorised them, chasing them and sneaking up behind them before squealing shrilly. 'And Kurunta's wife was worse,' Garin said, quickly looking over his shoulder to check who was within earshot.

'At least Kurunta wasn't there for long,' Tanku said. 'After two nights on the receiving end of his wife's fiery tongue, he upped and left, back here – to torture you, no doubt,' he nodded to Hattu.

'Welcome back, hurkelers,' Kurunta barked, sneaking up behind them.

'Sir!' the four replied in panicked unison.

'My wife is a walking earache, isn't she?' he said dryly.

Tanku and Garin's faces drained of colour. 'If you were listening to us a moment ago then you must have misheard,' Tanku started.

'The rest of the *Mountain Wolves*,' Kurunta cut Tanku off, embellishing the appellation with a scoff, 'are in the barracks. You pair are the last to arrive.'

'I apologise, sir, it is my fault,' Tanku said. 'I'll have them kitted out at the muster area within the hour. Come,' he waved the other three towards the gates of the vast barrack compound.

But Kurunta held an arm out to bar Tanku's path. 'Oh no, not for you.'

'Sir?'

'This one is to be trained on the chariot,' Kurunta stabbed a disdainful finger at Hattu.

Tanku, Garin and Dagon all looked at Hattu. Hattu's mouth moved wordlessly as he tried to find some sort of explanation.

'And he needs others to train with him. Kisna will lead the Wolves while you're away.'

'Away?' Dagon said, bemused.

A frantic rumble and a crunch of gravel and stone split the air.

Hattu and the rest swung round to see an apparition coming for them, ploughing across the dust from the stables like a serpent: The tongue was a thrashing mass of hooves and dancing manes of a pair of yellow-dun stallions, laced with strips of bronze and dangling ropes. The head was a wooden, bronze-trimmed war chariot, the copper hobnails in the two wheels glittering as they blazed across the dirt. And the fat plume of dust spiralling up in the contraption's wake was the serpent's body and long tail. It sped for them, maybe three times faster than the quickest sprinter Hattu had ever seen. He saw, just behind the two stallions, an ebullient, leathery-skinned driver with wind-tousled brown hair, streaked white at the temples – white as his grinning teeth – and a brown, forked beard: he was a fair age but his eyes were wide and gleaming like a boy's at the first sight of lightning, mouth agape in his cajoling of the horses, the whip cracking high over the traces to urge them onwards. For that instant, it seemed certain that the chariot was about to trample straight over the group of four and Kurunta. Garin screamed in a fashion that would have embarrassed a girl.

But, with a sharp tug on the reins and a cry: '*Ho!*' the chariot horses leaned to one side, bending the path of the charge around the five in a wide arc. The chariot slowed and settled, having circled them once. The stallions' mouths and necks were laced with sweat and white froth as they panted through the bronze bits in their mouths, and the pungent smell of stableyard grew suddenly rife. The driver's wild expression settled, but only a little.

'Old Horse,' Kurunta enthused, pumping his clenched fist in the air in greeting.

Instantly, Hattu recognised the driver even though he had only seen him a few times in his life. Just as General Nuwanza was the army's Master Archer and Kurunta the Infantry Champion, Colta was the famed Master of Chariots. Colta was a Hurrian by birth, and as with all Hurrians he was an expert trainer of horses, he had come into the service of the Hittite King many years ago, schooling the army on the construction, repair and operation of war cars and raising the herds that would haul them.

The charioteer lashed the reins to a small hook on the bronze-lipped rim of the chariot then leapt down from the open back of the carriage, his bare feet slapping onto the dust. He wore an ornately etched brown leather cuirass with no under-tunic. His legs were like the trunks of an aged tree – knotted and bulging with muscle like Kurunta's upper body. He was not a big man but all the same, the vehicle slumped forward a little as soon as it was unburdened with his weight. As Kurunta and the Chariot Master embraced, dust puffing up from their garments, Hattu and the others shared suspicious looks.

'Come late summer, the *Labarna* will judge this shower in the Chariot Ordeal,' Kurunta said, sweeping a finger across Tanku, Dagon and Garin. 'Should they fail, then they will forever be infantrymen,' then he pointed at Hattu. 'And should this one fail, then he will fail as a warrior... leave the Fields of Bronze and return to his tablets. No prince can serve as a low-ranking foot soldier – it would be a bleak omen.'

Hattu's body clenched with fright and fire.

'Put them through their paces, Old Horse,' Kurunta said to Colta, then swivelled his good eye at the four – particularly Hattu – and grinned. 'Then tonight, when they've soiled their loincloths or fallen under a horse, send the whimpering curs – or their remains – back to me.'

Kurunta turned away, roaring with laughter at his own words, and stomped back towards the infantry barrack compound.

'Hilarious,' Dagon muttered. 'I think I might have laughed up my liver.'

A warm breeze swept around the four. Hattu beheld the chariot. His heart thundered at the closeness of the vehicle. His stomach melted at the thought of riding one.

***

Later that afternoon, Hattu, Tanku, Dagon and Garin stood under the hot sun on the chariot fields just north of the academy with no armour or weapons. The dusty grounds were hemmed by the red fells to the west. On a tall boulder there, the pale-stone statue of a prancing mount – an effigy of Peruwa the horse-god – watched as a group of veteran chariot riders sped across the training area in a blur of bronze, hooves, lashing hair and whips. They operated a good arrow shot away, leaving this edge of the chariot plain free.

The Lords of the Bridle, as they were called, counted nearly four hundred battle cars in their ranks. Some three hundred of the vehicles had been disassembled and packed onto the wagons that had gone northwest to Pala with King Mursili, and another fifty were distributed to the garrison towns and the frontier forts, leaving this handful of thirty or so in reserve. Each chariot bore a team of two men, one with a bow, tipless arrows and an equally tipless spear, the other grasping reins and whip, the long, flowing hair of each snapping in the wind like night-black banners. They sped to and fro, criss-crossing the plain like snakes in some ritual dance. All the time, the armed man on each car turned to face the nearest speeding vehicle, eyes tracking the movements of their 'foe'. One man hurled his spear pole across the void. It was like the lash of a lizard's tongue, striking the driver of another car square in the chest.

The driver fell from sight onto the car floor and the chariot rounded quickly and almost toppled over. A moment later, the coughing, spluttering driver rose with the aid of his warrior and the pair saluted the opposite chariot crew who had bested them. The victorious two saluted back then rode off with a whoop and a lash of the whip.

'Warrior and driver,' Colta said of the spectacle. 'Like the bee and the flower, each depends upon the other, and one has an almighty sting!'

Hattu glanced to the tutor, and noticed that a trio of stablehands had begun fussing around the resting chariot nearby.

'Yet men are but components of the whole. A chariot is not just a fine carriage,' he moved over to trace his hand over the blue-dyed poplar planks and bronze lip that formed the three sides of the chariot. 'Yes, it involves metallurgy, woodworking, tanning and more. Then he strode over to stoke the muzzle of one of the two sorrel-red stallions they had led here from the nearby byre that morning. 'Nor is a chariot the horse, nor is it the crew. Neither is a chariot the mere coupling of these things.' He held up one finger. 'A chariot is the result of these things becoming one in mind and body – when driver and warrior think the same thoughts, when the horses speed up even before the crack of the whip, when the carriage's timbers bend under the impact of a hard rock, saving the wheel.'

The stablehands beckoned the four over to assist in belting a thick, bronze-studded cloth around the stallions' heads to protect their heads and necks. The beasts began snorting and pawing at the ground, no doubt sensing the training schedule that was to come. Hattu smoothed one beast's mane and this seemed to calm it. Next, the stablehands lifted two bronze scale aprons from a storage hut. Hattu took the edge of one and gasped at the weight as they lifted it onto the leftmost stallion's back. Tying the straps, he now felt genuinely sorry for the creature – burdened with such weight in the hot afternoon. But even when the stablehands secured a breast harness around the stallion's necks, still they did not show any sign of complaint, standing firmly, their thick muscles bunched under their smooth dark-red hides.

'Don't pity the horses – they are arrogant creatures, eager to confound their drivers,' Colta said, while the stablehands took to grappling with and plaiting the horses' tails. Hattu almost laughed at the vain practice, then noticed the horses pulling the chariots sparring nearby all had their manes and tails neatly groomed likewise. The mesh of reins and gear lashing, tightening and slackening all around them illustrated the purpose: to stop the creatures' hair becoming entangled.

'This is Rage,' Colta said, patting the muscled shoulders of the leftmost mount, then did the same with the other, 'and this is Thunder. A lovely, peace-minded pair,' he grinned. The horses nickered as if in reply. 'They came to us from Troy as foals and enjoyed play and pasture when they were colts – thought they were in for an easy life,' he said with a chuckle. 'Then, last year while you were being broken on the red hills, this pair were put through seven months of galloping around the oval,' he pointed to the foot of the fells, where a well-worn racetrack was marked out with wooden posts. 'They rode alone, at first, then with light riders sitting on their croup – and, by Tarhunda, they were not easily pleased with those passengers. After that, we slit their nostrils,' he pointed at the dark, healed gashes either side of the beasts' noses. 'They near-enough kicked one of my grooms across the Red River, but we only did it so they could draw in deeper breaths and maintain longer charges. After that, we taught them to race with empty chariots in tow. Now... what could possibly be next?' he said, eyeing the four, drumming his fingers on his chin.

For Hattu, the answer was obvious. 'Next, you train them to tow chariots with men on board?'

Colta's eyes lit up and he shot a finger out at Hattu. 'Wrong! Next... *you* will train them to tow chariots with men on board,' he clarified, leaping where he stood, clapping his hands once and laughing.

Two stablehands were now securing an ox-horn shaped willow yoke across the shoulders of the two armoured red stallions, securing it to each beast's breast harness. 'Pay attention,' Colta said to the watching four. 'You will be doing this yourselves after today.' The third hand then lowered the hinged draught pole attached to the base of the chariot car so the free end came down across the centre of the yoke, where the other two stablehands clipped it in place with bronze rings. Lastly, they skilfully coaxed the horses to open their mouths with a handful of hay, then inserted a bronze snaffle bar in each duped mouth and threaded the four reins through the loops at either end of each snaffle, back and through loops on the yoke and then rested the free ends of the tethers on the bronze rim of the chariot car.

'Your vehicle awaits,' Colta beamed. He waited just long enough for each of them to stammer some half-word of doubt and confusion, before hopping up into the car himself. 'One at a time, with me. You first,' he summoned Hattu. 'Come on, don't stand there shaking with bravery.'

'We'll share your bread tonight in your memory,' Dagon whispered after him. Hattu cast him a sour look and nearly stumbled, then gingerly climbed up into the car to stand just left of Colta. The space was limited, with his and Colta's hips touching. He detected an odour of horse, sweat and leather and couldn't quite work out whether it was coming from the Chariot Master or the horses. The car only came up to his thigh, giving him the feeling that a sudden push in any direction and he would be pitched out. He righted his feet for balance and, to his surprise, the car floor flexed under his soles: it was made not of solid wood but of a thick lattice of rawhide strips.

'Better that than broken legs should you hit a rock,' Colta said. 'You'll get used to it.' He cleared his throat and shuffled his shoulders, handing Hattu a stiffened leather belt. 'You'd best put this on to support your sapling back.' Hattu was about to complain but noticed that wild look returning to Colta's face as the chariot master raised the whip. So instead he buckled the wide leather belt on as swiftly as he could with trembling fingers. 'Now,' Colta yelled, 'all you have to do... is hold on... *Ya!*'

The scream was enough to convince Hattu to grab the lip of the chariot car in the breath before the whip cracked and the stallions' bodies tensed. The chariot lurched forward. Stillness to a violent surge in a heartbeat. Faster, faster and faster. Hattu felt the fears in his belly shoot across his entire being like raindrops blown across a smooth surface. And the still day was banished as the wind of the ride grew into a shrieking whistle, warring with the thunder of hooves and the din of breaking stones under the wheels. The gust battered Hattu's face, casting his hair up in his wake, throwing his brow band off, stinging his eyes. He clung to the car lip with all his strength as the vehicle bucked and leapt as if determined to cast him out. Very quickly he understood how Colta had built up such strong, sinewy legs.

'You see?' Colta howled gleefully. 'Does not every man long to move fast and free like a horse? This is it. *This is it!*'

'I...' Hattu croaked, panic strangling his words.

'Scared? Ha, then all is well. Courage is like a muscle, it must be worked and strengthened, fuelled with fear time and again until the muscle is hard and strong,' Colta shouted over the rushing air.

Scarcely comprehending, let alone capable of replying, Hattu noticed the chariot master's arms tensing, the rightmost of each horse's two reins tightening and pulling on that side of their mouths. He sensed the violent turn before it happened, and just threw his weight towards Colta before the horses swung to the right. He felt every sinew of the muscles developed in the red hills groan and ache as the turn went on, around the shaded southern end of the oval, seemingly lasting forever. 'Good, *good.*' Colta shouted. 'Not many anticipate the turn.'

'Not many? What happens to them?' Hattu yelled.

Colta said nothing, drawing a shard of burnt gold rock from the pocket of his tunic and tossing it off past Hattu and out of the left side of the chariot. It shattered against a larger boulder with a puff of dust. 'They tend not to make it past the first session. They return to the barracks to serve in the infantry... if they can still walk.'

Colta released the tension in the reins and the horses straightened up again, now heading back towards Dagon, Tanku and Garin. Hattu felt the initial wave of terror pass. Now there was a crumb of certainty – just like that which he sought when climbing. A hint of smugness crept into his thoughts, knowing that his turn was almost over. They thundered on, then made another, gentler turn to slow and stop where they had started by the oval's northern end. Hattu leapt down from the car, his step shaky, his heart still racing.

'Let's get this over with,' Garin said, stepping forward, his face pale.

Colta laughed, leapt down and held up a hand to bar the lad. 'Not yet.' He pressed a hand onto Thunder's breast and invited the others to do the same. It was beating fiercely, Hattu realised, just like his own. 'Thunder indeed,' Colta said. 'And a good driver never rides his horse to exhaustion. The storm in their hearts must be harnessed and used wisely. A charge can win a battle, but if overused, it can also ensure defeat.'

'My father keeps horses on his farm,' Tanku interrupted. 'The stouter ones are strong but slow. Perhaps a more spry horse might be able to gallop longer?'

Colta grinned. 'Fast at the gallop, but hardy enough to trek to faraway Retenu should the Egyptians invade? No, you need balance,' he said, one wagging finger raised in example. He returned his hand to Thunder's heart then checked Rage's too. 'It is time,' he said, bidding Garin forward.

For the rest of the day, they took turns to ride with Colta. At times he made sharp turns and sudden stops, testing the new horses and potential crew in every aspect. Near sundown, he called over a pair of the chariots sparring nearby and had them ride just ahead of Thunder and Rage. On his command, the leading chariots would slow suddenly, allowing him to test the reactions of the four young soldiers and of Thunder and Rage. They were swift to veer around the chariots ahead. Soon, the four were vying to have another turn driving the vehicle.

At last light, the chariot field was laced with a mesh of scars from the many twists and turns. Hattu and his three fellow soldiers helped dismantle the chariot and Colta watched on, silent, stroking his forked beard in thought.

'What happens now, sir?' Dagon asked.

'You walk with me back to the stables. Then you return to the barracks.'

'And tomorrow?' Garin asked.

'Well, you have not soiled yourselves or died horribly under the wheels, so you have the makings of a chariot crew in you. Kurunta will be disappointed. Come back to the stables at first light.'

Hattu gazed up at the staring eyes of the Horse-God, Peruwa, an almighty shiver shooting down his spine.

***

Over the next month, Hattu lived for the thrill of the charge. Some days he would waken before the dawn horn, his blood already fired with excitement. These mornings he would glance around the barrack hut to see Tanku, Garin and Dagon's eyes glinting, awake, like him, while all others lay in a deep, exhausted slumber, snoring like boars… and some releasing inhuman quantities of gas. As soon as the morning muster was over, the four would race to the stables, help Colta and his hands load a wagon with fodder and equipment, then ride to the nearby chariot field. After a month with Colta, the chariot master chose Hattu and Dagon to ride together as a team.

They practiced like this for days on end, taking turns as driver and passenger. Soon, Colta brought up a second chariot and pair of horses and took to racing one team against the other: Tanku and Garin rode two silvery steeds against Hattu and Dagon with Thunder and Rage. Speed and swiftness of thought won Hattu and Dagon six of ten bouts. Hattu learned exactly when to lash his horses and when to slow them, allowing them to flow round the bends and storm along the straights. And when Dagon had the reins, Hattu learned how to apply his weight to add grace and momentum to the ride. Skilled as Hattu was with the reins, it soon became apparent that Dagon was the better driver.

The summer became a blur: racing, grooming, learning how to lead the horses across deep water – swimming with them when necessary – and then night riding, using the echo of their hooves and wheels to manoeuvre with only starlight overhead.

It was not until the hottest month that Colta had stablehands bring arms to them. They handed Hattu and Tanku each a leather cuirass and pointed helm, a headless spear, a bow and a quiver of snub arrows. The pair looked at one another then at Colta.

'Drivers,' he said, pointing to Garin and Dagon. 'Warriors,' he added, meeting Hattu and then Tanku's eyes. 'Battle is the test of horse, man and vehicle to see if they can stay true to all they have learned so far, while all around them men howl, horses charge and missiles fly through the air. Today, you will race around the track, but in opposite directions. When you pass one another, you must seek to strike the driver or warrior on the other vehicle. 'Victory can be won by any means, in a true battle, at least: spear and bow, sword or mace; you can even toss your weapon at the opponent's wheels; your horses can bite and kick like demons; the whip, even, can down a foe. Today, I'd suggest you limit yourself only to the blunted spears and tipless arrows – lest we end the day with a pile of shredded timber and mangled bodies.'

The four mounted their chariots.

'Ready?' Dagon asked, whip ready to lash.

'No,' Hattu replied.

'Excellent, neither am I,' Dagon agreed, then cracked the whip with gusto.

A moment later, the pair were crouched, feet wide apart for balance as they came shooting round the oval's northern bend. The chariot came onto the straight then spat forward with another snap of the whip over the yoke. Hattu's eyes locked onto the blurred shape hurtling round the southern bend and onto the same straight, coming for them in an inferno of cast-up red dust. He saw the thrashing hooves, the wild-eyed horses, Tanku and Garin's clenched teeth. Tanku had his spear hoisted like a javelin. Hattu knew he could get a shot off from his bow before the big soldier could come close enough to throw. He swung his bow from his back and plucked out an arrow, now at ease having no hands on the lip of the car. He fumbled and nocked the bow then raised and stretched it, his thumb vibrating by his ear. The vision of Tanku and the oncoming chariot juddered furiously before him, always avoiding the tip of his arrow as he tried to train it. Closer, closer... Tanku was about to throw his spear.

Thrum, the arrow flew off the string... then fouled on the leather bracer on his left wrist. He saw it squirming through the air like a fish. It whooshed past Tanku and plunged into the dirt track harmlessly. Before Hattu even had time to curse, Tanku's spear rushed through the air for him, the speed tripled by their opposing charge. He ducked down on his haunches and the shaft grazed the lip of the car with a loud *thwack*, splintering the wood.

'Gods!' Dagon yelped, glancing agog at Hattu and the scarred battle car.

On they went for another lap. Again they came at each other on the straight. Hattu held up his spear this time. Tanku, spearless, loosed a shot from his bow. Something told Hattu that he was safe, that there was no way Tanku's first attempt at shooting from a speeding chariot would be a success. And he was right. The arrow flew over his head... by the width of a gnat's wing. As the two chariots drew closer, Hattu hoisted his spear and threw it.

The lance thwacked into Tanku's breast, punching him back from view. As the chariots sped past one another, Hattu gawped backwards. From here he could only see the trail of dust. Dagon slowed the chariot, reading Hattu's concern. His eyes tortured him, making out dull outlines of a fallen, mangled body on the track. But the dust cleared and there was none. A violent bout of coughing sounded as the other chariot came round again at a canter. Tanku was pulling himself to his feet from the car's floor, clasping his breast, his eyes streaming with water and his face red.

'You bastard. You lucky, lucky bastard.'

For a moment, Hattu wondered if the burly lad was about to leap for him, but the big soldier grinned and nodded back to the starting point. 'Next time, you won't be so lucky.'

They sparred all day and for the next seven days, the victors emitting lasting, triumphant wolf-howls and the vanquished launching a chorus of blistering oaths. It came to a point where they even took to drawing swords and clashing them together as they passed one another. Soon, they left the oval track behind and moved onto the open field, where the veterans' chariots were mock-sparring under the statue of the prancing horse-god.

It was a mass of criss-crossing dust plumes, a riot of shouting, whinnying and crunching of wheels on dust. Hattu, with his comrades at the edge of the fray, eyed the maelstrom of speeding chariots like men viewing a violent blizzard from a doorway. Hattu looked to Colta in concern.

Colta grinned. 'Now go. And remember what my tutors told me: enter the fray with guts and grace. End the day with your guts in place.'

Dagon set Thunder and Rage in motion. 'Ya!'

'Take us in easy,' Hattu said, waving one hand towards the left edge of the contest. Garin and Tanku, nearby, veered away, preferring to take their chariot towards the right.

'Two kills, that's all we need,' Hattu encouraged Dagon, recalling Colta's instructions. Any two mock-kills for a chariot team meant they finished as 'winners', along with any other teams who achieved the same feat. Anyone 'killed' just once was listed as a loser for the day. Hattu saw the red dust before him swirl and pucker. With a growl of breaking scree, a chariot burst forth, the driver urging the horses onwards, the warrior a nobleman judging by his jewelled headband and long, emerald earrings... and his supercilious, hectoring screams directed at his driver.

'Ha – the Cursed Son rides!' the noble spat with a serpent's glare, then thrust his spear pole out like a snake's tongue. The strike was aimed well at Dagon's chest. Hattu threw his own spear out like a club, across Dagon's front, blocking the strike. The noble cursed and berated his driver, before vanishing into the dust cloud again. Now, Hattu realised, he and Dagon had been drawn into the midst of it all. Another chariot sped past behind them like a wraith and a snub arrow loosed from it thrummed between him and Dagon. By the time he had spun round to find the bowman who had loosed it, their attackers were already gone, consumed by the dust.

'Hattu,' Dagon yelled.

He swung back round to see the jewelled noble and his driver coming from behind at a gallop and at an angle, set to ride alongside and strike. 'Stop!' Hattu cried.

'Ho!' Dagon yanked on the reins. The horses obeyed and slid to a stop within a few paces. The noble's chariot spat past in front of them and the noble twisted round, lifting his spear to throw. Hattu raised his bow, nocked in a heartbeat, trained the tip on the noble's chest and loosed. With a dull thud, the snub arrow struck home and the noble's face fell, spear still unthrown. The chariot slowed and he turned to his driver and began beating him around the head.

At the side of the field, a watching academy scribe shielded his eyes from the sun and peered through the dust, then noted the successful strike on a tablet of soft clay.

'One kill,' Dagon said with a relieved but somewhat devilish grin. He snapped the whip again and the wheels ground to life. They cut in and out of the fray again. Most of the time, they saw just dark shapes speeding past. Hattu quickly learned there was no point in shooting hopefully at these. Only when he could see rider and warrior, and had a reasonably steady shot, was it worth loosing an arrow or a spear.

But then he saw one chariot moving at a trot, the driver and warrior crowing about a fresh kill, unaware of Hattu's proximity. 'Forward, steady,' he croaked to Dagon, but already his friend had read the opportunity. Hattu raised his spear, sure he could make it a true strike. He tensed his shoulder and clenched his teeth... when a dull, sideways blow took him by surprise, crunching into his ribs – below the raised arm – and sent him pitching out of the chariot car. The world turned upside down and the next sensation was a hard return to the earth. His shoulders crunched and every bone in his body jarred. Round and round he rolled. When at last he came to a halt on his back, he groaned and blinked, raising his head to see what had happened. Dagon had slowed the chariot a few strides away, his head hung in defeat. The vulnerable, crowing chariot team were gone. But who had struck him? Then a headless spear shaft poked into his chest. He looked up and, at once, relief washed through him.

Muwa gazed down the length of the spear from the side of his battle car, having stolen up on Hattu's flank unseen. Now seventeen summers, his handsome face, uplit by his polished silver scale vest, had lost the last traces of boyishness. The *Tuhkanti's* nostrils flared and shrank with a few snatched breaths. His ice-bright eyes were alight with mischief. 'Kill,' he grinned, holding a hand in the air to attract the attention of the nearest watching scribe.

'Brother?' he croaked, taking Muwa's offered arm to rise then clasping his other hand to his brother's muscular shoulder. 'I did not know you were here. The army is back? The Kaskans were repelled?'

'Pala and Tummanna have been liberated. The Kaskans were driven back,' Muwa replied, the mischief in his eyes fading.

'And Pitagga?'

Muwa's eyes grew glassy. 'He… he is dead. We found the mangled remains of a body under the wheels of one of our chariots – fiery-haired and clad in Pitagga's armour.' He hesitated, as if uncertain, but then shook his head to rid himself of doubt. 'It is done. Our brother is avenged,' he said with a barely-choked sob. 'We did not recover Sarpa's head, but his killer has been struck down.'

Hattu closed his eyes and held back the tears, seeing in the blackness Sarpa by the Spirit Bridge: at last the sadness was gone from his face. Within the memory, he faded and was gone. Avenged. 'Bless all the Gods,' he whispered.

Muwa averted his eyes as if ashamed of the reddening in them. 'Pitagga's armies fled – great numbers of them unharmed – but without that foul bastard to unite them, their threat is surely over.'

'And what of you?' he asked Muwa, looking him over: no signs of injury. 'You are well?'

'Well enough,' Muwa smiled. 'Perhaps when next the army marches, you will be there with me?'

A rousing shiver shot up Hattu's spine. 'Perhaps, Brother. If the Gods will it. The Chariot Ordeal will make me or break me, I am told.'

'The Ordeal is like no other,' Muwa said without a trace of play, then swung away and remounted his chariot. The driver lashed the whip and they moved off. 'Fare well, Brother, until next we speak.' And then he was gone, into the dust cloud.

Hattu and Dagon returned to the edge of the field where Colta, who had seen the incident, had summoned an asu. The young healer had with him a clay basin of water, some rags, roots and pastes.

'A charioteer needs a hunter's eye,' Colta said, pointing to where the incident had occurred. 'Never lose sight of what is coming at you from the side.'

'Aye,' Hattu agreed, wincing as the asu unbuckled his leather armour and raised his tunic, dabbing at the unbroken skin there. He made a few non-committal noises then shrugged. 'It'll bruise like a lettuce, but he'll live,' the healer joked.

'Good,' Colta said, 'because now the king has returned from war, the Chariot Ordeal can be arranged.'

***

'Now *breathe*,' Colta said, inhaling noisily and sweeping his arms out to the side within the shade of the byre as if to illustrate, before exhaling with a husky rumble. 'All four of you have proved yourselves to be skilled and able. You make strong chariot teams.'

'Pardon my rudeness, Old Hor-' Garin started, then coughed, 'er, sir, but you don't have to demonstrate your driving before the king, out there,' he said, pointing out of the tall timber byre to the sun-soaked parade track and the growing clamour around it.

'No,' Colta beamed. 'But when I first came to Hittite lands I did. Had I failed I would most probably have been sent back to Hurrian lands. Or worse – relegated to the infantry.'

'Is that what happened to Kurunta?' Hattu asked.

'Not quite,' Colta replied, averting his eyes. 'He took the Ordeal and proved to be a fine chariot warrior until,' he tapped under his eye. 'Well, a man needs both eyes to ride well – to judge depth and distance.'

'Easy with that thing, you pair,' Hattu whispered, pointing to his eyes then to the whips Dagon and Garin held.

Garin, Tanku and Dagon laughed, spiriting away a dash of tension.

'Is there anything you can tell us about what awaits us out there, Master Colta?' Hattu pried.

The Chariot Master merely smiled. 'Ten teams, sixteen circuits of the track. What could be simpler?'

All four of the riders looked at one another, certain they were being toyed with.

'It is a test of everything I have taught you, and that which Kurunta taught you last summer too,' Colta said in a whisper as if breaking some code. 'Speed, skill, teamwork, sharpness of mind... mastery of fear,' he added, his face stony.

The parade horn sounded. They each clasped arms with one another, then strode from the byre and into the sweltering midsummer heat. The red-dust oval track warped and writhed in front of them in the heat haze. The high statue of Peruwa flickered in and out of view, so hot was the air. A timber stage had been erected on the far side of the track, a cloth awning casting shadow over the jumble of faces within. More spectators stood in the full sun, either side of the stage. Three, maybe four thousand were in attendance – mainly nobles here to watch their sons, or rich men coming to enjoy the free wine. And there were strange wicker walls or barriers of sorts at either end of the oval – but no people there. They strode to the starting line where their chariots awaited along with eight other cars and crews. *Ten teams, sixteen circuits of the track. What could be simpler?* Hattu tried to reassure himself.

He climbed aboard his chariot with Dagon, reaching over to pat Thunder and Rage's croups. To his surprise, he found a snub spear and arrows inside the car, along with a bow. He cast a suspicious look back to the byre, but Colta was gone.

'A short, smooth ride, that's all we ask,' He whispered to Rage and Thunder, taking the leather thongs dangling from the cheek pieces of his helm, fastened them under his chin, then looked to the straight edge of the track. Now he could see the occupants of the shaded plinth: a collection of highborn from the Panku stood in there, as well as Orax, Gorru and eight more of the ever-present Mesedi. Old Ruba stood to one side, in the full sun, forfeiting the shade so he could stand by his beloved pony, Onyx. He saw the pale-skinned Volca too, but for once it wasn't the man's horned helm that caught the eye, but the Sherden's red cloak and the silver pin on it: in the shape of a silver hawk – the mark of the Gal Mesedi. It had once been Zida's. So now Volca was chief of Father's bodyguards, he realised. And where was Father, he thought? The Chariot Ordeal surely couldn't start without the king. He noticed another figure on the plinth: an odd, withered stranger with long, thin, patchy and entirely grey hair, seated and staring at him with sunken, dark-ringed eyes. A shiver of fright struck through him as he noticed the silver sun-circlet the fellow wore, and realised who it was.

Father? Hattu mouthed. It had been just over a year since last he had seen the king. Could any man age so much in such a short space of time? Father had never looked young to him, but today he seemed as old as the rock upon which Hattusa sat. The king's eyes met Hattu's with a weary, haunted look. Then he waved a finger listlessly and the horns blew.

Ten whips cracked and the chariots were off. Hattu, taken by surprise, nearly fell to one knee, shooting out his spear hand to the lip of the car to steady himself – the mark of a poor chariot warrior. A ripple of gentle laughter broke out at this. He saw some of the crowd nudge and mutter to one another, and felt sure he knew what they were saying.

The Cursed Son.

'To the pits with you all,' he whispered back at them, then stood strong and tall, his skin prickling with the heat of embarrassment. They circled the track in an easy trot, keeping time with the others. Hattu knew that as the warrior of the team he had little to do here other than to ensure he adjusted his weight shrewdly – it was Dagon's skill with the reins that would keep them right. They came round again to pass the start line. Now there was a ripple of polite applause from the crowd at the awning. Then a single, short blast of the horn sounded from Colta – now at the plinth – and his stablehands.

Hattu and Dagon glanced at one another, reading the signal. *Faster,* they mouthed in unison.

Ten shouts of 'ya' sounded and the chariots picked up into a canter, Hattu spreading his feet a little more for balance. It seemed incomprehensible that another fourteen laps would be any great challenge, but by the fourth circuit, the horses had been geed by Colta's signals into a gallop and Hattu was in full battle poise just to stay steady on his feet. Thunder and Rage were sweating – their red hides slick – and the sun was growing fiercer. Their stride was now ever-so-slightly less than perfect – Hattu watching with a tightening stomach as flailing hooves from the mounts either side wavered closer to Rage and Thunder, axles swerving to within hand-widths of one another. By the tenth lap, foam bubbled from the beasts' mouths and Hattu's thighs and lower back were on fire – sapped of energy.

Dagon snapped the whip above the traces. 'Six more laps to go and-'

His statement went unfinished as, from behind the wicker barrier on the north end of the oval, a row of archers rose up, bows nocked and drawn. Nuwanza, at the end of the line of bowmen, grinned then bawled:

'loose!'

Thrum! A storm of shafts shot towards the line of ten speeding cars.

'Down!' Hattu screamed, pulling Dagon by the shoulder as he sank to his haunches. The shafts rattled down. A shrill cry sounded and Hattu saw, from the corner of his eye, a warrior from another of the cars falling, barely harmed from the strike of a blunt arrow but lucky to escape broken bones as he tumbled over and over in the dust. The pair stood again, only just in time to turn around the oval's northern edge, seeing that the neat line of ten chariots was now staggered and down to nine. They came round to complete eleventh and twelfth laps, exhausted and tense – but nothing more could happen now, surely? The wicker barriers at the southern end of the track were too high to hide more crouching archers. But before Hattu could convince himself of this, he heard a scream from the right of the track, near the byre. Like a demon rising from the dust, Kurunta sprinted from the heat haze and into view, carrying two poles like swords. A thunderous roar echoed his as Raku and a hundred veteran Storm infantrymen appeared in his wake, washing towards the flanks of the chariots.

'Hattu,' Dagon howled as Kurunta leapt at their car. Kurunta's twin poles came whipping round towards Dagon's arms – a stiff whack there and he'd drop the reins. But Hattu shot out his spearpole to forfend the strike. The twin poles spun from Kurunta's hands and he fell back onto the track, roaring curses. Then Raku expertly bounded onto the chariot car. At once the extra weight sent the vehicle zigzagging across the track, cutting across the paths of others. Raku batted Hattu's spear from his hands then grappled with him – his hands were enormous, his fingers gripping and pinching like a wrestler's, then he wrapped his mighty arms around Hattu's arms and torso like a rope, drawing them face-to-face. Hattu felt Raku drawing back to the rear of the chariot, ready to drop off with him. He stared the big officer in the face and realised he had only one option. 'I'm sorry,' he croaked, then thrust his forehead into Raku's nose. With a crack and a splatter of warm blood, the officer moaned, releasing his grip and falling onto the track.

Hattu saw Raku land on his back then sit up, legs splayed, touching a hand to his bloodied nose before tossing his head back and roaring with laughter.

'Hattu, face front,' Dagon cried as the chariot swerved deliberately left then right to avoid the chaos around them. The sudden ambush by the infantry had been telling. Two cars bumped together, sagging and slowing to a halt as their shredded wheels became entangled. Another thumped into one of the track's posts as infantrymen pulled warrior and driver from the back, pinning them to the ground and marking them with a 'kill'.

Hattu and Dagon panted, unblinking despite the dust swirling around the track, on through the thirteenth, fourteenth and fifteenth laps, each time passing the ominous high screens at the southern end with doubting looks. The bright sky dulled as they went, surly clouds gathering. By the sixteenth lap, they were in fourth place of the six remaining chariots. They weaved around the now abandoned other four vehicles, seeing that just the southern bend and half of the straight lay between them and the end of the Chariot Ordeal.

'We've done it, Hattu, we've...' Dagon started and then faded off with a wail.

The southern screens toppled to the dust with a bang. Behind them, five bronze-strapped chariots waited, crewed by mean-eyed veterans. With a lash of whips, they jolted forward, coming head on for the now exhausted and beleaguered Ordeal racers. The car coming directly for him and Dagon shot out ahead. Hattu's eyes bulged as he saw the warrior. *Muwa!*

Muwa's face was taut with the wind of the ride, bent into a feral grimace, his thick hair leaping and dancing as he trained his tipless spear on Hattu's breast. Hattu had nothing but his bow, and found his hands working to swing it from his back, nock and draw. It was swifter than ever he had managed at the archery range. Muwa was but a car's length away. No time to sight, no time to think. *Loose!*

From the edge of his vision, Hattu saw King Mursili lurch forward in his chair, his eyes bulging at the sight of the two princes set to clash. The shaft flew true and straight at Muwa's heart. The tipless missile bounced away harmlessly off of his shining white cuirass. A great gasp rose up from the crowd. All around Hattu and Dagon, the crunch of wood and the yells of men rang out as the two onrushing chariot lines tangled. There was a trice of calm, before Thunder and Rage sped clear with three other cars – two having been brought to an abrupt halt by the veteran riders.

Hattu looked back, disbelieving, then forward, seeing the finishing line as they pelted round the southern bend for the last time. They raced across it to a chorus of acclaim, beating another car to finish second while Tanku and Garin came fourth. They came round on another lap to slow, panting, laughing hysterically, then came to a halt by the stage. They slid from the back of the chariot and embraced. Then, pacing over from their vehicle came Garin and Big Tanku, who emitted a wolf howl and punched the air, then drew the four into a huddle. After a blur of snatched breaths, guzzled water, more hugs and wolf howls, the four chariot teams who had passed the Ordeal were called before the plinth. The clouds above were now heavy and dark, the air spiced with the stink of an impending thunderstorm – and no wonder, given the heat.

'Brave charioteers, you have proven yourselves here today,' Mursili said, a clear tremor in his voice and his upraised hands quivering with weakness. 'I bless you in the name of the Storm God, Tarhunda. You will bring his thunder to the battlefield.' A series of gasps rang out as the sky grumbled, as if the Storm God was listening. 'And in the name of Peruwa the Horse-God. The Lords of the Bridle will be proud to call upon you when next they take to war.'

Each team was called up before the king one by one. King Mursili muttered some blessing to them, pouring driver and warrior a cup of wine each as they went. As it came to Hattu and Dagon's turn, Hattu felt his heart race. The moment would be seminal, with his father – the man who had sent him here to break his spirit – about to bless him and effectively confirm him as a soldier and a charioteer. As a true prince.

He came before the king, dropping to one knee with Dagon and dipping his head. His eyes rolled up and he caught a glimpse of Father's expression, so sad, mournful even. *Is this not a time to rejoice? Now you have not just one valourous, courageous son, but two.* And the king truly was unwell, he realised – his eyes were sunken and black lined and his lips were tinged with blue. The sky growled again, louder this time.

'By all the Gods, my boy,' Mursili whispered while all others cooed at the divine thunder and the sheet of blinking light that flickered behind the clouds, 'you thrash and strive to liberate yourself from my tether. Well now you are free. Do not fail me... remember our oath.'

Hattu felt a cold shiver pass across him. 'Always,' he affirmed, his gaze unwavering.

'Drink, and go forth,' Mursili said aloud, addressing the crowd again, handing Hattu and Dagon each a cup of wine. 'Honour your family, your fellows and your country,'

Descending from the plinth onto the now overcast track, he supped on the wine, tart and strong but refreshing given the circumstances. The twelve crewmen of the six failed teams loitered at the foot of the plinth, heads hung in shame.

'I'd heard rumours,' Dagon said, 'but I really hoped they weren't true.' He nodded towards Kurunta, who was holding up an empty cup, grinning like a shark.

'Right, who's thirsty?' Kurunta beamed, eyeing the failed teams. 'All of you, I'd say. Yes, it's tradition, after all. Wine for the winners, and for the losers... '

Kurunta slipped behind the awning for a moment. The sound of a stream of liquid tinkling into bronze sounded. A moment later he returned to hold the cup out to the first of the losing teams. A coil of steam rose from the vessel as the driver beheld it with a weary face.

'Drink up,' Kurunta chortled. The poor fellow drank and gagged his way through the foul offering, stopping at one point to pick something from his teeth. Such was the fate of his warrior partner. But a short while later, the tables were turned: the third chariot crew awaited their punishment drink, but when Kurunta took leave behind the awning to fill the cup again, there was no tinkling of liquid. A painful silence ensued, then: 'Curse you. Six teams failing is unheard of!' he howled, his head poking round the edge of the awning, his good eye searing into the ashamed crew as the thunder boomed overhead. 'Did you fail just so you could humiliate me?'

A series of stifled laughs brought Kurunta's bald head swivelling further like that of a furious vulture. 'What are you laughing at?' he fumed at the king's entourage. 'I'll drink enough tonight to fill a cup for every one of you.'

His words were cut off with the rapid drumming of hooves. All heads looked to the east, in the direction of Hattusa. A messenger, perched awkwardly on a horse's croup, streaked across the sullen countryside, shouting out as he approached, but the words were unintelligible.

'Black news... My Sun.'

The crowd gasped and broke out in a babble of interest. Hattu's skin crept. King Mursili sat upright and alert in his chair. The messenger slid from the horse and came skidding onto his knees before the king.

'My Sun, the Lord of the Mountains lives.'

Mursili beheld the messenger as if he carried the plague.

'The man whose body we found, he was a mere mountain chieftain – an enemy of Pitagga. Pitagga dragged him into the battle, wrists roped, wearing a set of his own armour and had him cast under the wheels of our chariots, knowing that he could despatch a foe and deceive us at once. It was a wicked hoax.'

Mursili stood, swaying on his feet. 'Tell me this is a mistake or I will have you whipped!'

The messenger bowed his head, shaking. 'It is as I say, My Sun. Already, he seeks to gather a fresh army; already he plots a new invasion.'

Mursili took three unsteady steps towards the messenger. Hattu recognised the fierce ire that shone in the king's eyes. But then it happened.

Like a candle being snuffed out, the king's eyes grew dull, his face drooped, and he stumbled and crashed from the plinth and onto the dust where he lay, stock still.

Lightning lit up the grey land and thunder roared.

'Father?' Hattu and Muwa cried in unison.

Ruba, Nuwanza, Kurunta, Colta, Orax, Gorru and many others rushed to encircle him, Muwa fell to one knee, lifting the king's head. Hattu clasped his father's hand – limp and cold. He squeezed it. Mercifully, the king squeezed back – but with the strength of a child. His pupils were dilated and his breathing shallow. The right side of his face was trembling in a pained rictus, and the left side hung horribly, like that of a dead man.

Volca lifted Mursili's fallen cup, tucked it inside his cloak, then knelt by the fallen king too.

CHAPTER 12

SOLDIER PRINCE
AUTUMN 1301 BC

After King Mursili's collapse, the *Labarna* was carried back to Hattusa, while Hattu and his chariot-comrades were posted back to the infantry barracks. Three more months of advanced training under Kurunta passed before the autumn arrived and Hattu's time at the Fields of Bronze came to an end and he too returned to the capital after seventeen long moons.

As he walked the cropland tracks leading to the city's western walls, a biting wind moaned, casting golden brown leaves across his path. Hattusa itself glowed oddly in the low autumn sun. It was not how he had envisaged his homecoming.

Yes, he was taller, stronger, self-assured too, the rough itch of his white military tunic reminding him of the trials he had faced... and won. And with fourteen summers behind him nobody could call him a boy any longer. He wore his hair scraped back often now – the notion of disguising his odd eye and his identity repulsive – into a tight, high tail that had grown long, dangling between his shoulder blades and weighed down by the beryl stone and a few lions' teeth he had found on a patrol. But the city he had left last spring seemed... different.

He entered through the Tawinian Gates. The main way was sombre and quiet. All knew that their *Labarna* lay enfeebled up on the acropolis hill; a sign that the Gods were not happy with his rule or with his subjects. And a double watch stood on the walls, for rumours of

Pitagga's whereabouts were rife, and the system of northern watchtowers lay broken, many ungarrisoned. Grand Hattusa reeked of fear and doubt.

He held his chin high and made his way through the sparse crowds. A smith working a sickle over an anvil stopped hammering and scowled at him like a hawk. Hattu looked the fellow square on with a confident glare, the smoke-grey eye glinting in the pale light. The man bowed from the neck, respectfully.

He strode on up the main way, to the Noon Spur and then up the steep, narrow approach to the Ramp Gate. When a screech split the air, he looked up to see Arrow, circling high but spiralling towards him. 'Here, girl,' he whispered, his heart soaring, thrusting out his arm with the leather bracer. Arrow swooped down and landed on his forearm, then began pecking playfully at his face.

'Easy, girl,' he laughed. Then her neck lengthened and she keened shrilly over his shoulder. Hattu heard from behind a pair of stifled yelps from Orax and Gorru – the two Mesedi who were escorting him a few paces in his wake. 'She says she has missed you,' he threw back with a wry look. In truth he wished these two no harm. He had seen the pain in their eyes when Father had collapsed. Good soldiers, he realised.

The Ramp Gates groaned open as he ascended the slope towards the acropolis, the chill wind whistling at this exposed point. Hattu did not wait to let the Mesedi and Golden Spearman pairing atop the gatehouse decide how they would react to this new, hardened version of *the Cursed Son*, instead shooting up his clenched fist decisively.

'Prince Hattusili,' they barked in reply, returning the gesture. His self-assurance grew stronger with every such happening.

Once inside, the wrath of the wind ebbed. The open centre of the acropolis ward was an odd thing to behold: warming and familiar, yet cold and melancholy at once. Slaves busied themselves grooming the stallions in the royal stable and bringing water to the kitchens from the cistern. He noticed the spot near the stone pool where he had so often played, alone on the red slabs, fashioning toy boats and joking with invisible friends. So many days spent gladly away from Father's anger. His gaze swung up to the northwestern edge of the acropolis. Up there on the palace building's forgotten balcony, he saw himself with Father, on that snowy day when everything had changed.

'My pupil returns,' a familiar voice said.

Hattu turned to see Ruba, mounted on Onyx, ambling towards him. The Chief Scribe looked painfully old these days, and so small too. He helped Ruba down from the pony's croup. He was overcome with a desire to embrace his tutor. But he offered the scribe a clenched fist salute instead.

Ruba tilted his head a little to one side and eyed him shrewdly. 'Very good. They have made a soldier of you, then?'

'They tried to crush me first,' he said. 'It took me a long time to figure it out.' Another glance to the balcony. '*He* sent me there to fail.'

Ruba nodded once with tight lips, as if holding back his true response. '*He*... loves you, Hattu,' Ruba said. 'A man's fear for his loved ones can manifest itself in the most unexpected of ways.'

Hattu sighed through his nose. 'How is he?'

Ruba's eyes grew distant for a moment, and he seemed confused.

'Tutor?' Hattu asked again, placing both hands on the old man's shoulders in a tentative embrace. Ruba's eyes sharpened on Hattu, as if the gesture had drawn him back from the fog.

'The King? No better, I'm afraid,' Ruba said. 'His left side remains asleep from face to toes. His speech is still halting and slurred. It is a sad thing, for I can tell that the brightness remains within his mind... and how I envy him for that,' he finished with a dry laugh.

'Can he be healed?' Hattu asked.

Ruba's brow creased. 'Several asus have been living in the palace for this last moon. None of them are a patch on the one who vanished – not that he was particularly good, anyway. The Wise Women were here too: tying bells to the feet of mice and making tallow effigies. By the Gods, we all had to suffer their droning for two whole months. They had the clothes he was wearing on the day he fell taken by ox-cart to distant Kummani, hopeful that his affliction would travel away with the garments. They rubbed honey, meal and mud into the left side of his body, then took to laying the still-warm organs of a ram there too, thinking those bloody morsels might take on his illness. I was not sad to see them leave.'

'Then they have given up on him?' Hattu asked.

'Oh I'm sure they'll be back,' Ruba replied. 'But now another tends to him – Lady Danuhepa of Babylon. She was sent here recently by the Assyrian King with a dowry – a token of temporary truce.'

Hattu's sardonic expression was reply enough.

'She is not like the others,' Ruba smiled, looking towards the harem where a pair of scowling women glared out, faces streaked with so-called 'beauty-paint'. 'They crawl to the king when he is strong and beg him for fineries, she coddles him when he is weak and asks for nothing.'

Hattu gazed at the palace, suddenly reticent about facing his ailing father. The Fields of Bronze had taught him much, but nothing that would equip him for this.

'Go to him, Hattu,' Ruba said. 'He has asked for you more than once.'

***

He watched from the shadows of the hallway, yet to make his presence known. The king's bedchamber was thick with white spirals of incense vapour, the air warm from the sweet cedar logs on the crackling fire, defying the cold autumn afternoon beyond the closed, wind-trembling shutters. King Mursili lay prone, his sun-disc circlet resting on his sweating brow. A young lady sat by the edge of his bed. Danuhepa, Hattu surmised. She had seen perhaps twenty summers, he reckoned. She was a beauty indeed: high, sharp cheekbones and thick, glossy dark hair hanging to her waist in bold tresses. It was such an odd sight: Father and intimacy were strangers, yet this Danuhepa stroked at his hand like a doting mother. Hattu heard her gentle words to the king:

'Enkidu ate grass in the hills with the gazelle, ranged over the mountains with the goats, lurked with wild beasts at the water-holes... he filled in the pits of hunters...'

Hattu realised he was smiling. The words of the Epic came to him as if he had never been away from Ruba's classroom. '... he helped animals escape from their traps.'

The woman looked up, startled.

'Lady Danuhepa,' he said, stepping into the room.

Her eyes searched his face for a moment, switching between his odd eyes. 'Ah... Prince Hattusili?'

He bowed curtly in affirmation.

She clasped her fingers round the king's hand. 'The few times the *Labarna* has spoken since my arrival, it has been of you. He was certain you would not come to him.'

'Why?'

'Because it has been three moons since he fell ill and you have not come to him in that time.'

Hattu cocked his head to one side, looking at the king. Even in sleep, the lop-sidedness of his face was stark. 'He wished me to see out my two years at the Fields of Bronze. I want him to respect me, to trust me, and so I stayed there till the very last day before winter billet set in.'

Danuhepa smiled sadly. 'Three times he asked, today alone: has my son arrived home yet?'

Hattu sat on a stool at the opposite side of the bed and clasped his father's free hand. 'I am here, Father. My training is complete. I am your loyal servant, just like Muwa.'

The *Labarna* did not stir.

Hattu eyed Danuhepa from the corner of his eye. Noblewomen rarely travelled without purpose. Had she known the king was ailing so badly when she came here? 'Did you foresee this?' Hattu asked, thinking of Ruba's description of the world. 'When you journeyed all the way from Babylon, at the edge of the world?'

She laughed. 'As I see it, I have travelled from the heart of the world *to* its edge. Babylon is a wonder: a land of green rivers, swaying date palms and smooth, sunbaked plains.'

'One day I hope to see it with my own eyes,' Hattu said wistfully. He gestured towards the shutters as if to indicate the lands beyond, 'and you must have longed to see our legendary country?'

Danuhepa measured a smile. 'The Hittite realm is... different.' The wind moaned and the shutters chattered as if to chuckle at her subtlety.

'The Empire of the Hittites is as its soldiers: rugged, mettlesome, dauntless,' he said, recalling one of Kurunta's 'motivational' cries as he urged them on through a gruelling all-afternoon run headlong into a vicious dust-gale that swept through the red-fell valleys. 'Anyway, I fear I interrupted you just as your story was building. Enkidu soon faces Gilgamesh, does he not?'

Her face broadened with a warm grin. 'The king also mentioned you were a scribe. Ruba's protégé, no less.'

'Part of me always will be,' Hattu smiled.

'The Epic is one of the things that binds our world together, don't you think?' Danuhepa said. 'From one edge to the other, all know of the tale.'

Hattu smiled and looked at her hand, clasped around Father's. 'And now you and my father will form another bond. You are to wed him, no?'

Her eyes glinted in the firelight. 'I am an offering,' she said gently, 'from the Assyrian King. Tensions run high between the throne of Hattusa and that of Ashur. My part is to take your father's hand, to buy a few years of trust and truce.'

'You speak candidly for a woman of high station,' Hattu remarked. 'What will happen if,' he faltered, looking at King Mursili's sleeping form, his shallow breaths, 'if...' his words were choked off by a thickening in his throat.

'I *will* wed your father,' she said. 'War *will* be staved off.'

'How do you know it is right?' Hattu asked, thinking of Father's sullen nature and fiery moods. 'Not for the kings who arranged it, but for *you*?'

'I had opportunities to marry men before. Some I cared for, one I loved.'

'Why didn't you wed the one you loved?'

'Because he was poor and that meant it was forbidden,' she replied. 'And because my Father caught him stealing into my chambers and had him beheaded.' She said this flatly, in a well-practised way that seemed to act as a wooden stopper on her true feelings. 'I will always remember him. In my heart, we have lived this life together.' The stopper was coming loose. 'I feel a flutter in there when I think of him, and I know he's still with me.'

'There is a girl I know, she is the daughter of the Storm Temple,' Hattu said gingerly. 'I feel that same feeling.' He drew the lock of hair with the teardrop beryl stone from his shoulder as he said this, stroking it with a thumb.

Her face brightened. 'Then you are a lucky young man. She feels the same?'

Hattu felt a sudden pang of fright. 'Well, I haven't... '

'You haven't told her?' Danuhepa gasped.

Suddenly, he felt like a boy again. 'No, I couldn't. What if-'

'What if you didn't, and someone else did?' Danuhepa laughed. 'Would you want to forever look back and wonder, like me?'

Hattu felt his mouth grow dry. This was fear altogether different from that experienced at the Fields of Bronze. He imagined Atiya shrieking with laughter if he even tried to put into words just how she made him feel. 'Aye, but. Well, maybe I... I don't know.' He looked at Father once more, then made to leave, bowing again. 'I had best be going. Let Father know I was here when he wakes.'

With that, he left the bedchamber. The corridor was bitterly cold in comparison, and he passed Volca on his way – the Gal Mesedi was carrying a cup. 'Good to have you back, Prince Hattu,' the Gal Mesedi bowed with a convivial smile.

***

That night, Hattu entered his bedchamber and felt lost in the well of silence within. No snoring, no scratching, no sudden gastric outbursts. Just the plump bed in the centre of the room and an old oak chest by the window, set out with a copper wash bowl and white linen towels. He moved over to the window which looked down upon the square of the acropolis' upper ward. The wind had ebbed and the shutters lay open. He drew back the curtain hanging there and inhaled. The citadel grounds were inky-blue under the moonless night sky. A sharp, beaky poke to the wrist brought his attentions to the outer portion of the sill, and Arrow's nest. She glared up at him.

'Let me guess: food?'

Arrow cocked her head to one side, with a look Hattu read as outrage – for she already had a worm held captive on the sill.

'Then what?'

Arrow screeched quietly, then stepped from her nest. Shards of speckled eggshell and the down of fledglings lay in the swirl of twigs. A moment later, a trio of shrieking young falcons flapped down to bother Arrow, and she took to tearing up the worm and giving each a piece.

Hattu stared for a moment and then laughed aloud. 'So the mate you found was a good one?'

Arrow cocked her head one way then the other as if carefully evaluating her mate's pros and cons.

He noticed the young falcons had a full plumage and were almost ready to leave the nest. 'Tend to them well, girl. Keep them warm.'

Arrow waddled back to her nest and settled down, back turned to him, her attentions fully on her three worm-munching progenies.

Laughing at the typically abrupt snub, Hattu leaned back in, drew the curtain, closed the shutters then stepped over to the bed. He swept the pristine white linen sheets and grey woollen blankets back. A large copper flask full of hot water lay there, warming the bed. It was an odd sight after seventeen months on an uncovered mattress of hay. He didn't even hear the barefooted slave boy scuttle in to take the flask away, bowing as he went. Hattu tried to thank the boy but this caused the slave to hurry away all the faster. Suddenly, being a prince again felt odd.

He slipped off his clothes and slid into bed. The soft comfort soothed his hardened limbs and should have cajoled any man to sleep, but his thoughts would not settle. For most of his early months at the Fields of Bronze, he had eagerly anticipated this return home. Now that he was here, he realised that part of him was impatient to return to the academy and the enjoyable balance of shared hardships and camaraderie that went with that life. He thought of Atiya, and this lured him into a half-slumber, until he remembered Lady Danuhepa's words.

Would you want to forever look back and wonder?

This wrenched him awake. 'I should go to her and tell her how I feel. Tomorrow, I will,' he asserted, then rolled over to lie on his other side. But time passed and still he could not switch off. When the scuffing of a guard's boot outside cut through another spell of drowsiness, he sat up with a frustrated sigh. He rose and moved to the shutter to peer between the cracks, and saw Gorru and Orax down there in muffled hysterics, Gorru performing some crude mime, mock-thrusting into a make-believe animal and mouthing the word *hurkeler*.

Hattu's annoyance evaporated as in his mind's eye he saw Dagon, Tanku and Garin back at the barracks, acting up just like that. He wondered what the other lads were doing right now in their homes and winter billets. *Sleeping, probably*, he mused, returning to bed. The entire city was no doubt asleep. But when he heard more footsteps outside, he rose again. Through the cracks in the shutters he saw... Kurunta. Nuwanza too. And Colta was with them, entering the palace in the dead of night. What was this?

'Is this a soldier I see before me?' a voice said from behind, startling him.

Hattu swung to see Muwa in the chamber doorway, clad in black robe and cape. 'Brother,' he cried, the pair embracing. It was the first time they had seen each other since the day of Father's collapse. They pulled back, and Muwa clapped both hands on Hattu's shoulders as if measuring their width. 'The warrior-prince – as I always knew you could be,' he beamed.

'Not if you had knocked me from my chariot at the Ordeal,' Hattu replied with an arch look.

'Ah, yes. Fortunate I let you loose your bow on me then, isn't it?' Muwa grinned.

'*Let* me... of course,' Hattu said, then the pair erupted in laughter and hugged again.

The burst of jubilation faded then as Hattu thought of the king. 'Father is no better,' he said. 'I sat with him today.'

'He is weakened, but he is not beaten,' Muwa gave him a reassuring shake.

The sound of boots on the polished stone floor downstairs sounded.

'The generals are here. What's happening?' Hattu asked.

'Father called upon them and me too. He woke a short while ago and despite the hour, he feels strong enough to begin planning for spring

– how to set up our armies against the threat of Pitagga. It will be a long night,' Muwa said, striding away towards the top of the stairs.

Hattu watched him go and felt that old, sinking feeling of isolation. Talks between the king, the *Tuhkanti* and the generals, with no place for the *Cursed Son*. Old habits crept into his mind, and he glanced out of the window to the night-bathed cistern and the spot he was so used to playing, alone.

But a squeak of halting boots on the floor turned his attentions back to the top of the stairs. Muwa had stopped and turned to him.

'Hattu? Are you coming or not?'

Hattu cocked his head to one side.

'Father waited to hold these talks,' Muwa explained with a smile. 'He waited for *you* to return to the city. It was your visit to his bedside that roused him, Danuhepa reckons. Now come, there is much to discuss.'

***

Hattu followed Muwa along the corridor towards the tall oak door. He had rarely been allowed into the planning room at the rear of the palace, and certainly never when Father was holding council. Muwa entered first, Hattu sucking in a deep breath before he entered too. Pale moonlight glowed through the high windows, shining weakly on the polished floor, and the torches in the copper sconces lent a fine lustre to the emerald-green relief of a hunting scene on the other three walls. A smell of polished bronze and old leather hung in the air, as if to underline that it was a room for military matters. He felt his anxiety swell and his stride grow clumsy as he realised the company he was in: already seated at the hexagonal map table in the centre of the room were General Kurunta, General Nuwanza, Chariot Master Colta and the Sherden, Volca.

Muwa drew a stool to sit and Hattu followed suit. Kurunta gave him that lone-eye copper rod glower, accompanied by a tiny upturn at one side of his mouth that might just have been a crumb of cordiality. Nuwanza and Colta gave the princes curt welcomes. Volca, on the other hand, smiled a welcoming smile that was at odds with his wintry eyes. The head of the table, by the high windows, was unoccupied.

Hattu, ill-at-ease with the company, dropped his gaze to the surface of the table: ancient, scarred in places and worn smooth in others. It was a bewitching thing, carefully crafted from different types of wood to present a map of the world – one of the few in existence. Light ash for land, dark oak for the distant, strange seas. The land regions were marked with ink and dyes, outlining mountain ranges, forests, passes, pastures and wastes. Hattusa was marked boldly near the centre. The strange lay of the world beyond sent shivers across his skin.

Then, the side door creaked open: Orax and Gorru shuffled in, carrying a cedar litter upon which King Mursili sat. They set him down at the empty space at the table's head.

Mursili's eyes rolled round to meet his council, hanging for a moment on those of his two sons. It was with great effort that he gave the pair a nod. The left side of his mouth gaped, the lips hanging open and wet with drool. Likewise his left eye was dilated, gazing into infinity. His right eye, in contrast, was bright, his lips on that side taut. 'My council… ' he said, taking breaths between words, '…is complete.'

A moment later Ruba shuffled in, his eyes heavy with unfinished sleep, bearing a blank, soft clay tablet. He looked lost and confused for a painful moment, before the light came back to his eyes. He came to stand by Mursili, then held a reed stylus over the clay to indicate that he was ready. All eyes fell on the King.

'The summer scout… was correct. Pitagga… is amassing… a new army…' Mursili said. No preamble, no ceremony.

The king gestured to Kurunta, who took over.

'Pitagga frames his failed attack on Hattusa like the corpse of a martyr. He preaches to his people about our recapture of Wahina in the northeast and Pala and Tummanna in the northwest as if those lands had been stolen from *them*. His bards, oracles and champions have travelled all across the mountains of the Upper Country to tell tales of his 'glory' and the glory yet to be had. The twelve Kaskan tribes venerate Pitagga as a demigod. Even the tribes of the dark northern woods of Hatenzuwa have answered his call. And one of our spies in the distant northeast, in the lands of the Azzi, told us of Kaskans there, trading Hittite captives in their hundreds.'

'Trading captives with the Azzi,' Nuwanza said. 'For *what?*'

Kurunta's dark expression seemed to pervade the room. 'We do not know. And that is a concern.' He took a swig of well-watered wine before continuing. 'We have oft talked of one day recovering the Lost North; of rebuilding the long-ruined cities of Hakmis, Zalpa and Nerik – the shame of the Grey Throne. Yet it is Pitagga who holds those lands still, and aims to extend them…' Kurunta traced a finger over the ancient map table top, drawing attention to the strip of highland territory lining the north of the Hittite heartlands, squashed up against the foot of the Soaring Mountains, '… most recently, he has been probing the lands of Galasma.'

'Why Galasma?' Muwa said, leaning forward on his elbows to get a better view of the Kaskan territory and the Galasman realm.

Unconsciously, Hattu mimicked his brother's actions. The Galasman people manned a large stretch of the Hittite border forts and watchtowers designed to rebuff any Kaskan attacks that might spill from the mountains. Galasma – the mere mention of the place in Hattusa's streets usually conjured pulled faces and groans: *Gruff, rugged men. Not true Hittites. Fierce bastards, though.* Then he thought of Darizu, the meek Galasman Lord of the Northern Watchtowers he had watched quail and mumble through a confession of cowardice before the king. After his disgrace, Darizu had been given another chance – posted to Galasma, his homeland, to marshal that vital frontier.

Muwa's eyes darted then widened. 'Pitagga wants the lead mines,' he gasped, answering his own question.

'Exactly.' Kurunta's good eye swivelled to meet those of the others in turn. 'Those lead mines are vital. Without the dark ingots we bring from the rocky depths, we can barter for ever-less tin in the eastern markets of Ugarit. Without tin, there can be no bronze… ' he stopped and sighed heavily. 'Suffice to say I shattered three swords this year at the academy – three swords worked thin as reeds, such is the scarcity of tin. Axes too – now fashioned with gaping holes in the middle of the blade to spare as much of the precious metal as we can – are breaking like clay.'

A handful of low grumbles sounded around the table.

'Those mines must be protected – fiercely,' Muwa insisted. 'The Galasmans mustered a few thousand men the last time we levied them. How many has Pitagga rallied to his cause?'

'My two kinsmen rode north and sighted them. Ten thousand spears, they counted,' Volca claimed.

Every man around the table bristled at this.

'Ten thousand?' Kurunta stroked at his bottom lip. 'Then put the Galasman forces to one side. With all four of *our* divisions fully mustered – farmers and freemen included – we can field nearly twenty thousand spears.'

'Aye, enough to end the Lord of the Mountains,' Volca cooed enthusiastically.

'While we could muster twenty thousand,' Nuwanza countered, hands raised to slow things down, 'we would have to leave at least a division behind to protect the heartlands. That leaves us with fifteen thousand. And what if Pitagga has mustered more since Volca's men scouted north? The margin shrinks.'

Volca laughed mockingly. 'We can tarry and play with numbers all winter, Bowman.' Nuwanza's nose wrinkled in annoyance. 'But, come spring, Galasma is set to be assailed – *heavily*. Without action, the lead mines will fall into Pitagga's hands.'

'Aye,' Kurunta agreed grudgingly, shooting Nuwanza a semi-apologetic look at the same time. 'If Pitagga seeks to take the mines, then there is only one way he will be approaching.' He traced a finger along a narrow line in the map that bisected the Soaring Mountains, north to south. 'The Carrion Gorge.'

The Carrion Gorge? Hattu's eyes grew wide. He imagined a corridor of rock, teeming with the wild-eyed, shaggy-haired brutes, pouring south right now as they spoke, axes honed and intent on splitting Galasman heads then forging south to Hattusa once again.

Kurunta held up a pacifying finger, as if reading the same troubled thoughts from the others. 'Early snow in the north has blocked the gorge *and* the passes that would take us there, so neither Hittite nor Kaskan will be able to approach Galasma during the cold season. But come the spring the snows will be gone… and it will be the swiftest who claims Galasma as their prize.'

Nuwanza stroked his jaw in thought. 'At the least we should right now despatch winter scouts – men who could pick their way round the snowdrifts – to take word to Darizu.'

Kurunta shook his head. 'My thoughts too, old friend, but the northern snows are deep – no man or horse could get there. Galasma will winter alone.'

Mursili nodded weakly. Mute and still throughout it all, the king had been listening intently, taking everything in. 'It will be… so. Come the first thaw, the Wrath Division will stay here to garrison Hattusa and the heartland cities.' He sighed heavily. 'The other three divisions… will be… levied in full. The standing regiments will be joined by the shepherds and the farmers. Fifteen thousand spears will set for the north. Prince Muwa will… lead the Fury, Nuwanza the Blaze, Kurunta the Storm. Colta will lead… the Lords of the Bridle.' His eyes swung to Hattu. 'Prince Hattu, you… will march… with the infantry under Kurunta.'

Hattu considered this for a moment. Father's tone was cold. The words were intended to put him in his place. Was that why he had been summoned to these talks? He glanced to Kurunta, remembering the one-eyed general's words:

No prince can serve as a low-ranking foot soldier – it would be a bleak omen.

Kurunta watched him carefully. Father too. They were expecting a reaction – a boyish response of petulance.

'You wish me to march with my comrades in the Wolves? Happily. I would march with the ox train if you asked me to.'

Kurunta's appraising eye creased at one side, lifted by a hint of a smile. King Mursili's sagging face darkened.

'My Sun,' Colta interrupted, pausing a moment to consider his words, 'Hattu is also a fine charioteer. We have a shortfall of riding teams at the moment following the losses at the battle in Pala – less than two hundred pairs are fit and able to man our battle cars. Hattu and his driver, Dagon, could-'

'The *Labarna* has spoken,' Volca snapped.

Colta's nose wrinkled in ire and Nuwanza opened his mouth to argue the Chariot Master's case.

'Enough,' Mursili said with a wet rasp, slapping his good hand on the table.

All settled down, discontent caged.

Mursili continued: 'I will journey with the army too.' A few nascent protests were swiped away by another raised hand from the king. 'I will ride in my carriage. Prince Muwa will lead the expedition in consultation with me. I must be there. I *must* see it done.'

Volca stared at him for a moment, his copper earrings jangling. '*It?*'

Hattu saw a tear brimming in the king's good eye. 'It. This,' he gestured to the map with a shaking hand across the lost north. '*This* must... end. Pitagga has flattened my towns... slaughtered my garrisons... broken the walls of my home...' he looked at Hattu and Muwa. '... slain Prince Sarpa. Yet still, every year he marches into my lands... with my boy's skull on his lance,' a weak sound that might have been a sob escaped the king's drooping lips. 'We must secure Galasma and its mines. But then we must end the Kaskan threat forever, before they destroy us, before our enemies in Egypt, Assyria and Ahhiyawa realise we are paralysed by the mountain men.'

'Respectfully, My Sun, the Kaskans cannot be beaten,' Nuwanza said. 'They are too numerous, and always angry sons will grow and form new armies that will emerge from the mountains to avenge defeated fathers.'

'Their armies, we must face,' Mursili replied. 'But to end the Kaskan threat... we must throw down only one man... Pitagga.'

Hattu felt a wave of fire and pride rush across his skin and saw the other generals roused by it too.

'Aye!' Kurunta, Nuwanza and Colta called out gruffly.

'We will hunt him like the pig-herd he is,' Volca agreed, his wintry eyes gleaming.

***

The snows came and went, and the tail end of winter saw the New Year rains fall and the Hittite army entire gather around Hattusa. Wagonloads of weapons came from the armouries of the outlying cities to the east. The smiths' workshops glowed night and day as scarce tin ingots were forged with copper and new bronze arms were added to the stockpiles. Soldiers came in from far and wide. Many hundred-strong companies filtered in from the southern river towns and villages. A full regiment of one thousand Blaze soldiers arrived from the city of Ankuwa. Farmers from the western pastures were called up to serve their country – freemen, bringing with them the weapons they had not used in several years. And more men still would be picked up along the route of the Galasma expedition. For the first time since the chaos of the Arzawan War, the divisions of the Grey Throne would swell to their capacity. They camped on the bare hills around Hattusa in a sea of off-white bivouacs, ready for the king to lead them to war.

On the first day after the rains ended, Hattu stood on the Noon Spur, tapping one foot nervously like a man wishing he could conjure a twin to be in two places at once. He looked towards the Great Barrack gates, appraising every soldier who emerged then sighing, before every now and then turning to look downhill towards the Storm Temple and the trappings of the imminent Tapikka pilgrimage: a line of ox wagons, crates and mules. So much effort he had poured into helping Atiya prepare to leave Hattusa... and all the while the words had gone unsaid. *Fool!* Every day since his return from the academy, he had visited her. Every single day. They had walked together in the gardens of the temple. They had watched from the Dawn Bridge as Arrow hunted along the Ambar ravine. He had even taken to standing behind her, hugging her, linking his hands on her stomach, mouthing the words he longed to say to her. But not once had he mustered the courage to say it aloud as Danuhepa had urged him to. *Idiot!*

Then another soldier emerged from the shadow of the Great Barrack gates, drawing his attentions back to the other matter. A handsome, beaming young man, his eyes and skin bright, his black hair cut short above the ears but growing long over the nape of his neck.

'Kol?' Hattu said.

'Captain of the Eagle Kin, my Prince,' the warrior replied with a clench-fisted salute.

It was still a welcome surprise when soldiers greeted him positively. The Eagle Kin was a company in the Third Regiment of the Wrath Division, and it seemed some men of the Wrath, like the Storm ranks, were warming to him. 'Comrade,' Hattu replied, reflecting his ebullient smile.

'What brings you here?' Kol said, looking past his shoulders at the campaign preparations across the lower town and in the countryside around the city. 'I thought you would be camped outside for tomorrow – for the march?' The soldier's eyes betrayed his disappointment. As part of the Wrath, he and his unit would be bound to Hattusa while the rest of the army journeyed north.

'I'll be heading outside soon, but first I have something vital to arrange. Something I need you for.'

Kol's eyes brightened again. 'Anything.'

'The yearly Tapikka pilgrimage is due to set off tomorrow after the army has departed. The king cannot lead it as he normally would for he will be at the head of the march. But the Gods must not be neglected,' Hattu explained, being sure to recount the brief as Muwa had given it to him.

'Lest we bring their anger upon us,' Kol nodded.

'The procession will go ahead, leaving at noon tomorrow. The templefolk will ride in the wagons with the sacred effigy. The *Tuhkanti* has tasked me to select a strong escort for the procession – for the wagons will be taking the low road to Tapikka, a safe route but a long one. I have been asking around and the Eagle Kin has a fine reputation. I want your men to see the procession safely to Tapikka.'

Kol's face lifted with a wave of pride and he stood a little taller. 'I will protect them with my life.'

Hattu knew he had made the right choice. He gestured up the slope to the Ramp Gate. 'I have arranged for a few horse scouts from the king's stables to go with you.' He held up two small parcels, offering the one in his left hand first, 'these silver shekels should pay for new boots for your men. And these,' he said holding out his right hand, 'should keep your comrades strong and spirited on the march – honey cakes, cooked by the palace staff.'

Kol laughed and took the parcels. 'Unnecessary but welcome, my prince... comrade.'

'Fare well, Captain,' Hattu said with a smile.

The pair saluted one another then parted.

Hattu broke into a jog, off down the main way, his eyes fixed on the Storm Temple again. He burst into a run, knowing he only had this one last day to do what he should have done long before now. *What I should have done the moment I returned from the Fields of Bronze.*

He dived through a gap in the drawn-up pilgrimage wagons and charged in through the ceremonial gateway leading into the temple complex, startling a pack of priests and workers on a lawn there in mid-chant. He halted at a washing font, hurriedly throwing water over his face and hair and scrubbing his hands swiftly with the brush as custom demanded. He pelted down one loam-flagstoned cloister, then emerged onto the small meadow near the heart of the temple grounds. It was freckled with snowdrops, edged by a pale, sandy colonnade, veined with budding jasmine, all overlooked by the great shrine of Tarhunda. And there she was, puffing and groaning, hauling two large buckets of oil across the meadow towards a row of foreign statues – a tin-coated griffin, a silver dog, a man with an eagle's head and lapis lazuli eyes and a rising bronze serpent with wings.

Atiya noticed him at last. 'Ah, Hattu. Temple workers... ill, so I need to clean this lot before tomorrow,' she panted, wiping the sweat from her forehead with the back of her hand.

Wordlessly, he went to her and took the burden. 'You should have summoned more workers from the acropolis to help. You should have called me down. I would haul pots of oil to the horizon for you, you know that.'

I'd do anything for you.

Atiya looked to her feet, a little embarrassed, but smiling too. She walked across to the end of the meadow, Hattu huffing and puffing with the oil buckets in her wake.

'Atiya, come tomorrow, I'll be gone and so will you,' he started. But an oaf of a priest staggered between them, belching loudly and drowning out his words.

'What was that?' she said.

'We won't see each other again until autumn at least. I need to tell you something before we part. I-'

Hsssss yeeeooowl! A calico cat scampered across the meadow beside him, hotly pursued by an eager temple hound. Again, his words went unheard. 'Atiya, I-'

'I can't hear a word you're saying,' she laughed, then she began walking backwards, beckoning him with a finger. 'Come on, not far to go now. There's a good mule,' she said, eyes laden with mischief and her tongue peeking out between a small gap in her teeth.

'Gods, Atiya, even Kurunta was less cruel than this,' he gasped as the oil in the buckets sloshed and fought against him. They reached the statues at last, but before he could rest the buckets down, Atiya produced a chunk of carrot and held it up to his lips.

'What the-' he started, the sentence ending when the carrot was pressed into his mouth.

'Good mule,' she said as he bit off a chunk.

He stood tall, crunching through the root then holding his hands to his head like ears and attempting a braying *ee-aw* noise.

She stared at him, then shook her head. 'Do remember that you are a prince,' she said with a cheeky tut and a sigh, then dipped a clean pad of linen in one of the buckets and took to polishing the eagle-headed statue. He watched her work, feeling his throat closing up and his tongue tying itself in knots... and his loins growing warm. She was nearly two summers older than his fifteen, as the curves of her hips and chest attested. And there was a single coil of dark hair trailing from her headscarf, resting on the nape of her neck. The sepia skin there was flawless. The sight of it evoked a sweet, almost tortuous feeling across his breast, like the stroke of a feather. For a moment, he allowed himself to imagine what it might be like to kiss her there, gently. Of course, she chose that moment to shoot a coy look over her shoulder. He averted his eyes. He then set about convincing himself that he was a fool for thinking more of their relationship than was real. *You are but a boy to her,* he told himself.

When the statues were bright as stars, she vanished inside the temple's kitchen hall and brought out a bowl of honeyed porridge each for them and they sat and ate together. It was easier now, Hattu realised, without his foolish imaginings stilting his words and tangling his movements. He took to combing his hands through the grass as they chatted about old times, then noticed a caterpillar crawling along his finger.

'One day it will fly – like Arrow,' Hattu mused, lifting his hand, gazing down his nose and examining the caterpillar. 'It has no comprehension of what lies ahead. Of what it will become.'

'Nor do any of us,' Atiya added, holding up a fingertip to meet the end of Hattu's. The caterpillar then wriggled across, oblivious to the smiling pair beholding it.

A short while later, she walked him to the temple's main gates. He looked out across the lower town, seeing the sea of tents and soldiers in the countryside beyond the walls. Perhaps it was time to focus on the campaign ahead, he affirmed. Notions of anything else would be but a distraction – a silly, boyish distraction.

'So it is time? The mule must become a soldier again?' Atiya said, sidling up next to him.

'I love you, Atiya,' he said.

Silence.

Hattu felt the whole of the city and the sprawl of the mustering army outside writhing, buzzing, no doubt turning to point and mock him. Even the chanting, singing troupe of priests seemed to fall quiet. *What have I done? I've ruined everything, I...* 'I... I... '

He fell silent as she stretched up on her toes and kissed him. Her lips were wet, warm and sweet with honey from the porridge, and a trace of her floral perfume danced in his nostrils. A gentle breeze picked up. Her headscarf fell to her neck, her braid tumbling loose. A few locks that had escaped Hattu's tight, high tail of hair coiled around them to meet it, like curtains drawn for privacy. Pure instinct took hold and he wrapped his arms around her waist and drew her close, she clasping hers around his back.

When they parted, he felt a surge of elation, a desire to cry out so all could hear.

'I've always loved you Hattu. First, as a brother. Then, from the moment you came back for me – saved me from the Kaskans – as so much more.'

He made to reply, but she lifted and pressed a finger to his lips. 'I must prepare to travel to Tapikka. And you? Go to war, Prince Hattu. I ask only that you do not break my heart.'

At that moment, Hattu realised all in his life was right. The girl he loved was in his arms, he had become a warrior, and the wicked prediction that he would grow to fight his kin had been proven wrong. Tomorrow, he would march forth *with* his kin, to fight *beside* them. And he would return... to be with Atiya, always.

***

Muwa halted dead in his stride. What was this he saw before him? Atiya in an embrace with... *Hattu?*

Atiya's coldness. The soldier-trinket. It all made sense now.

Then, when they kissed, he felt an invisible dagger of ice sink into his breast. He swung away, pressing his back to the gatepost opposite the temple gates. His breath came galloping back to him like a wild steed. All his days he had been told that the *Tuhkanti* wanted for nothing. The heir to the Grey Throne could have any woman in the land. And it was true: the greatest beauties in Hattusa, noblemen's daughters and vassal princesses had been mooted as potential spouses. But he wanted none of them. He had long ago known that the priestess who lent colour to his dreams would one day be his wife.

It has to be her! he screamed inside.

When he looked back he saw them kissing again. Ever so slightly, his top lip twitched and his ice-bright eyes blackened under the shadow of his brow. The sour pool of rejection curdled within him, darkening and boiling like pitch.

CHAPTER 13

TO WAR
SPRING 1300 BC

Pipers played a stirring song as the sun rose from the horizon. Golden light spilled through the pillars of the Dawn Bridge, flooding Hattusa and setting the waters of the Ambar ablaze with its reflection. The city streets and the roofs of every house were packed with crowds, who cheered and chanted as the royal carriage ambled down from the acropolis, its bronze straps polished to catch the sun, the ring of one hundred Mesedi escorting it glittering likewise.

'*Missa! Kasmessa!*' – the crowds cried the cultic words in adulation of the king and their Gods.

The carriage stopped by the Storm Temple to allow the ailing King Mursili to make a libation of wine and an offering of wheat before trundling on out of the Tawinian Gate. A gentle breeze combed the land as the wagon rolled towards the three ordered bronze divisions awaiting it on the flatland outside, side by side and facing the city.

Within the ranks of the Storm, Hattu stood alongside the Mountain Wolves, stock still despite the grass tickling his bare legs above the collar of his soldier boots. He hoped the whole of Hattusa could see him like this: clad in his linen tunic and kilt, encased in his glistening, well-oiled leather corselet and helm, armed with spear, bow, mace, sword and shield. The weighty hide pack tied near the head of his spear was crammed with soldier bread, sheep's cheese, salted hare, barley and a small flask of wine. Fresh pangs of fear and excitement curdled in his belly. He rolled his eyes left and right, seeing Tanku, Garin, Dagon, Sargis, Kisna and the rest of the Wolves doing likewise. Dagon shuffled his weight from one foot to the other, chewing nervously on a stalk of already overchewed grass. Garin's belly groaned and protested like an angry man trapped in an urn. Tanku stood a little taller than the rest, expression granite-hard, the sides of his head freshly shaved and his bulky shoulders draped in a dark green cloak. Hattu could not help but look again at the garment – was it just his memory toying with him... or had that strange apparition of a warrior not been wearing that very cloak? Tanku claimed he had been gifted it by the tailors in the academy workhouse, but the others had jibed that his mother had made it for him, so proud was she at his attainment of the rank of captain. Regardless, it was a fine cloak, and it marked him out well as leader of the Mountain Wolves.

Hattu looked forward again, across Hattusa, seeing the acropolis silhouetted in the dawn sun. His smoke-grey eye ached as he caught sight of something: it was surely a trick of the light, but for a moment he thought he saw that round-shouldered, humble scribe, watching them from those lofty turrets. He shielded his eyes from the sun to see better and the vision disappeared. The scribe was gone, and Hattu knew that this time it was for good.

You're going to war, he realised. Suddenly, the weight of his armour doubled and the thought of facing Kaskans seemed like a cruel trick. He felt his heart race as fear began to conquer the excitement within. An old habit came to him then: he reached up to his long tail of hair, as if to draw a strand round to cover the odd eye. But his fingers found the beryl stone tied there. He stroked its smooth surface. For a precious moment, the panic vanished and the burden of the armour and equipment was gone. His eyes drifted to the lower town and the cluster of wagons waiting by the Storm Temple. The Tapikka pilgrimage. Already the templefolk were busy loading the supplies and soon the silver statue of Tarhunda would be brought out and loaded too. He could not discern any of the tiny figures from this distance but he knew she was there.

Atiya. Sweet Atiya: her name enough to kindle warmth in his breast. *I will return... and we will be joined before the Gods.* It seemed so simple, so clear. He had yet to tell Muwa. His brother stood some distance away at the head of the Fury. From here, Hattu could only see his black robes, silver scale armour and his mass of thick, loose hair obscuring his face. *We will rejoice later, Brother,* he smiled.

Volca ushered the king's wagon and the Mesedi into place, sandwiched between the Fury and Storm ranks, then strode over to stand with Muwa, his red cloak and the small red rag knotted near the head of his trident spear snapping in the gentle wind.

'Warriors of the Grey Throne, the day is young and the skies are fine,' Muwa proclaimed, his voice oddly hoarse. 'Pitagga of the Kaskan northlands roams yonder... his hands stained with Hittite blood.' Muwa stabbed a finger towards the hazy outline of the Soaring Mountains. 'Now he seeks to slay our allies, the Galasmans, and take from them and us the precious lead mines. Let us march with haste. Let us meet this cur with fire in our hearts and unleash upon him the wrath of the Gods!'

Close to fifteen thousand voices exploded in a guttural roar, clenched fists punching the air. The bronze campaign horn sounded in a low, ominous note that filled the countryside.

'Riders,' Volca howled, stepping out from behind Muwa.

A smattering of twelve lightly-laden, lean men on horseback broke northwards at a canter, scouting ahead. As soon as they had departed, Volca hoisted his trident and swished it down and to the north.

'Ad-vance,' he cried.

'For-waaaaard!' the many commanders howled. Then, with a rock-shaking chorus of myriad boots grinding on earth, every man in the Hittite army swung on their heel away from Hattusa to face the north, the gold-topped staffs of each division were hefted high to catch the sun, then the Hittite Army marched to war.

They moved like a bronze chain drawn across the countryside by an invisible hand: the Fury, the Storm and the Blaze. The noble warrior-driver teams of the Lords of the Bridle rode on ox-wagons, rumbling along astride the marching divisions, and one long wagon carried a knot of priests and augurs. Behind them came a mass of solid-wheeled ox-carts carrying arms, supplies and two hundred of the precious chariots – which would be assembled if and when needed. Thousands of pack mules and unburdened chariot steeds trailed behind this wagon train under Colta's guidance.

For Hattu, marching in the front rank of the Mountain Wolves, those first few steps felt like massive strides. A storm of emotions raged inside. An urge to laugh, to weep and to shout aloud. Just when it almost boiled over, a gentle braying noise off to the left of the column drew his eye to the comical sight of old Ruba astride Onyx the pony. It was the first time Ruba had been summoned on campaign by the king for many years. While Onyx was struggling somewhat to carry his master, it would surely have been crueller to leave the pony behind and separate the doting pair. His old teacher cast him a warm smile, and Hattu replied in kind.

They skirted the alder woods, and Hattu shot a look to his left over the dawn-lit canopy of green, seeing the fin-like ridge he had often climbed poking out, suddenly so small in comparison to the heights he had scaled in his training and his night-scrambles. Then many thousands turned their heads right and threw up clenched fists and cried fond words of affection towards the Meadow of the Fallen and the jagged Rock Shrine on that side of the track. Hattu's eyes hung on the Rock Shrine. Memories of highborn joinings within surfaced. Imaginings came to him – of him and Atiya stepping onto the bedrock dais within, to drink sacred wine before the gods, to become one...

With a barking of many voices and bumping of shoulders, the reverie was scattered and he turned his attentions to the road ahead. The divisions were narrowing to file through a tight pass that led up and into the northern hills. Soon, Hattusa was but a blotch behind them, slowly slipping into the horizon.

Hattu had never been any further north than this. Thoughts of his home dragged on his heart like an anchor. At that moment he could recall only the few happy moments that had threaded his bleak boyhood in the great city. He felt a keen urge to look back one more time, but did not. He noticed many of the other young soldiers do so. He looked to Tanku, who seemed somewhat uncertain what to do about their misgivings. 'Talk to them,' he urged quietly, thinking of the times he had seen Father quell disquiet in the Panku sessions. 'A few words will settle their nerves.'

'Aye – and mine,' Tanku flashed him a nervous grin. 'This is but a stroll,' the big captain called back to them, rolling his neck one way and then the other. 'We'll be back with our families in no time... as heroes.'

Garin whooped, and others laughed and chattered in agreement.

But a slit-eyed captain ahead at the rear of the Fury ranks did not share their enthusiasm. He was leading a hundred known as the Leopard Clan who wore paw-prints on their shields. He turned his age-lined face to them and shot each of them a derisive scowl, the look hanging on Hattu longest. 'You'll be lucky to keep your head with that one in your midst.'

Hattu bristled. While many within the ranks had come to accept him, most still had not.

'That's Hattusili, my chosen man!' Tanku shouted at the captain. 'Do you have a problem with him?'

'Many have died when close to him,' the captain snapped back.

'I would have died – plummeted into a ravine – were it *not* for him,' Tanku snarled.

'And I would have burned to ash in the Kaskan raid,' Dagon added.

'But he carries a curse,' the Fury captain argued.

'I carry a spear and a sword like you,' Hattu shot back.

'Enough,' Chief Raku snapped.

The Fury captain obeyed the superior's demand, but turned away in disgust.

But Dagon did not let it drop – instead he threw his head back and took to howling like a wolf. A moment later, the rest of the hundred joined in before breaking down in laughter.

'I said *enough*,' Raku barked – but only after letting the howl resonate long enough to make its point.

The sun rose and the land was soon hot and dry. They followed the ancient northern route across high, windswept plateaus studded with boulders and tussocks of grass, across rope-bridges that crossed churning rivers, down steep, treacherous slopes and up energy-sapping hills. Dust thrown up by the many boots ahead clung to Hattu's face, coating his nostrils and the back of his throat and buzzing flies harangued the column in swarms. His tunic was soaked with sweat under his cuirass. By mid-morning, the leather vest was chewing at his shoulders and his boots gnawed at his heels, his spear shaft and shield handle were grating at his palms, but all those places were well toughened and callused. Now the excited chatter of the early march had fallen away to be replaced by panting and coughing.

Kurunta's bare scalp was a shade of pink and slick with sweat, his brow lined like a freshly-ploughed field. Hattu noticed how he was glaring ahead at the royal wagon, where Colta had jogged forward and taken a seat on the bench attached to the rear of the vehicle, facing backwards, arms folded and his face decidedly smug. 'Who does that pointy-bearded bastard think he is, sitting on a march?'

General Nuwanza, jogging forward from the Blaze ranks, laughed, nudging an elbow into Kurunta's side. 'That you are marching means you are strong and fit, Kurunta, as fresh as your latest young recruits. You should take it as a tribute.'

'Young? I'm at least three times the age-' he stopped and looked around him, then feigned a coughing fit to avoid finishing his sentence.

So would you rather sit in the wagon, like an old man?' Nuwanza asked with a playful edge.

'Eh?' Kurunta said, disgusted. 'What nonsense are you talking now? Have you been drinking the foul glue from your fletching workshop?' he scoffed, marching with a little more spring in each step, almost prancing, the silver braid by his temple swishing like a prize pony's tail. 'Nothing like a stiff march. And, what is age anyway?' Kurunta waved a dismissive hand. 'My wife has a polished bronze mirror, but I tell her,' he said to Nuwanza, but loud enough so all would hear, 'throw it away. If you don't have a mirror, then you don't grow old. *I* certainly don't have a mirror.'

Silence, then a voice from the ranks behind chirped...

'Sir, you don't have a mirror because you're an ugly bastard!'

Several hundred soldiers exploded with laughter until Kurunta swung to seek out the anonymous voice. He jogged backwards in time with the march, casting an evil glare across the marching ranks of the Storm that seemed to last forever, then his face bent in a demonic grin.

'Aye, and don't you forget it.'

Another chorus of laughter.

They marched onwards to the rhythm of boots. Fatigue crept up on them swiftly as the afternoon wore on. After a while – at Kurunta's signal – the pipers near the head of each regiment struck up a skirling tune that seemed to fill the land, and set the hairs on the back of Hattu's neck standing proud. When they played, the going seemed much easier. When they took a break, the men sang choruses of well-practiced songs, some to praise the Gods, others to stoke hearts:

'They say we're born on the crags and raised by bears,
That we've got knife-sharp fangs and flow-ing dark hair,
We can march from dawn till dusk and all night too,
Need no water or bread, just some bones to chew,
So while the Pharaoh thinks he's so widely feared,
While the King of Ashur combs his curly beard,
While the Kaskan bastards take their pigs as brides...'
'In their hearts they all wish they were brave Hit-tites!'

And some songs spawned bouts of thick laughter:

I was tired of my ever-nagging spouse, Chief Raku began, eyes rolling left and right, hopeful he would not be left to recite this one alone.

So I fled to the arzana house, many more immediately joined in.

I sat down for a drink,
A whore gave me a wink,
Then laughed for I was hung like a mouse!

Hattu cackled despite having heard that one a dozen times. Shielded like this in the centre of the thirty-wide marching column, the sense of danger seemed distant, unreal. Each terracotta slope or scree-lined vale rolled onto another empty, still landscape – brush, rock and dust in every direction. They heard tinkling goat bells and saw the odd herdsman sheltering from the punishing sun under small thickets of pink myrtle. The faraway mating yowl of a lynx caught the ear too, but all was sedate, so unlike the march to war Hattu had always imagined. And the Soaring Mountains were still but a jagged mirage on the northern horizon.

'That is how it is, Prince Hattu,' Kurunta grunted, noticing his curiosity. 'All those days you lingered in the Scribal School, you might have thought you were missing out on high adventure. Alas, no, a campaign is one hundred days marching and a mere trice trying to stop an evil hurkeler from cutting your heart out.' He roared with laughter at his own maxim then took to offering similar words of 'advice' to others.

Eventually, they rounded a low hill to see before them a jungle of stone and pale clay in the centre of a large tract of golden grassland. It was a city, like Hattusa but on level ground, not quite as large as the Hittite capital and shaped like a teardrop. A small palace stood on an artificial mound near the centre of the settlement.

'Arinna,' Hattu realised, looking over to old Ruba, who now walked alongside Onyx. The Chief Scribe nodded once in praise then mouthed back to him. *City of the Sun-Goddess.*

His eyes combed the place, seeing Hittite sentries on the walls, singing and punching the air in salute. More, on the high roof of the city's Sun Temple, a line of dark-robed priestesses sang a lilting melody that sailed across the plain – a song of silver and sacrifice, of gods and glory.

'They say that place takes the brunt of the Kaskan raids,' Dagon whispered. 'They see days like the one Hattusa suffered every few seasons.'

A thick clunk sounded from the city gates – an ornate arched entrance flanked by two giant stone sphinxes and watched over by a carving of the Haga, the mythical eagle's two crying heads and fierce claws outstretched. Three companies of one hundred men and a cloth-covered pair of wagons emerged from the gates to join the campaign army, the most senior captain announcing one wagon held numerous skins of wine to a great cheer from the marching divisions.

As they marched through the early afternoon, Hattu had a strange sensation that he was being watched. He looked behind him and saw, of course, myriad eyes of many soldiers. But it wasn't them. It was odd, he felt it on the back of his neck, as if someone was looking down upon him.

By evening, Hattu noticed how the hazy Soaring Mountains had changed: now they loomed larger, less chimeral, veined in places with the deep gold light of the setting sun. He could now see features on the range – smaller peaks, overhangs and sheer rises.

The order to halt and set up camp was given when they reached a defensible, dusty banking just as the sun was slipping away. The Fury men began to mark out the perimeter with torches while the other divisions caught up, each staking their golden divisional staff in the ground like conquerors.

Hattu and the Mountain Wolves unbuckled their armour and helmets then took up a place on the flat ground atop the banking. Hattu helped Dagon to set up one of the open bivouac tents consisting of a sheet of hide and two poles – light to carry and providing ample shelter for the warm season. As he drove a pole into the dry earth, he felt that odd sensation again – the burning of eyes upon him. He looked up and around: just the usual doubtful looks from the many veteran soldiers. Then something dark sped across the dusk sky. *What the?* But it was gone as swiftly as it had appeared.

As darkness fell, each hundred kindled and settled around a fire, using a little flour to thicken water and flaking some hare meat into the mixture to create a stew. Hattu prised off his boots and sat with his comrades under a full, coppery moon. Kisna and Sargis swigged at their water skins – spiced with a dose of wine, as they stirred the bubbling copper pot of stew then ladeled out a clay bowlful to each of the Wolves. The stew was thick and hearty and Hattu ate ravenously, mopping up the juices with a hunk of bread.

Replete, they sat back against rocks or made pillows of their bags, gazing into the fire or up at the night sky. All were relaxed. Except Dagon, who seemed to have a bellyache of some sort.

Garin, whetting his sword meticulously, hummed a low tune. Dagon shot him a sour look.

Tanku crouched by the fire and belched near Dagon's face, offering only a pale apology. Dagon's eyes were alive with murder now.

Zing! Garin's whetstone sang for the millionth time.

'I think your blade will be keen enough,' Dagon grumbled, wincing and clasping his belly tenderly.

Garin halted in drawing the whetstone along the edge for a moment, the croaking cricket song taking its place. He smiled, then returned to making long, slow, extra-grating strokes. Dagon flipped over onto his other side, grumbled and lay down fussily, shuffling and sighing. 'This ground is as rough as the Dark Earth,' Dagon moaned, wincing again and clutching his belly. We'll never get a moment's sleep.

As if to mock him, a clicking, drawn-out snore sounded from nearby – like a woodcutter drawing his saw slowly across a giant bough. There lay Kurunta, in the open without a tent, as if he had been knocked on his back by a punch, still dressed in his leather kilt and cross-bands, mouth open. He had been attentive enough to take off his boots, however, and a pungent stench of goats' cheese wafted from them.

'That one could sleep soundly on a bed of nettles,' Dagon groused, wincing at the stink.

'Someone put sand in your loincloth?' Tanku smirked.

Dagon, lying back turned to the big captain, looked over his shoulder, eyes blazing, then raised one leg and let loose a long, mighty, rasping bellyful of wind that sounded a little like a furious goose. Hattu was sure he saw big Tanku's hair rise, such was the force of the gust. Tanku gagged and spat, traumatised. Bellyache gone, Dagon settled back down again with a contented smile.

Hattu chuckled, then turned his gaze away from the fireside. He scanned the circular camp. The sentries on the edge of the rise were spaced every twenty paces or so with a tall torch guttering in between each pair. On a wart-like outcrop of limestone, Volca sat enshrouded in his red cloak, shunning conversation and company, merely carving at a pear with a short knife, lifting each slice to his lips, slowly, carefully chewing. His eyes were fixed on the north and the looming mountains. Slowly, the Sherden's head turned, his gaze falling upon and pinning Hattu.

With a jolt, Hattu looked away.

'What will we find up there at the frontier towers?' Tanku mused, linking his hands behind his head, looking northwards.

'The lead mines and a thousand Galasman allies,' Sargis cooed, his gaze combing the dark horizon.

'Glory!' Sargis grinned.

'Galasman women?' Kisna mused. 'I hear they do this thing with their tongues…'

'What, talk?' Dagon added wryly.

Hattu chuckled guiltily, knowing he would right now give everything to hear Atiya's voice. He licked his spoon and pointed it at the dark mountain range. 'When Gilgamesh went in search of a cure for death, he wandered the earth far and wide. He once ventured into the Mountains of Mashu, a range as big as the Soaring Mountains, no doubt.'

All heads turned to Hattu now. Around a night fire, the words of the Epic were all the more enchanting. 'There, he braved raging storms of rain and snow. At nights he huddled in caves with the sparest of scraps to eat and no fire to cook them upon. Then there were days of blistering heat that almost peeled the skin from his back and left him parched and half-mad. Up there, some say, he even faced mighty creatures, long gone now.' He looked up, seeing the men hanging on his every word. 'Great scorpion-men.' When they sucked in a collective breath, he took up a twig and drew the figure of a man's torso joined to a segmented lower body with many legs, a wicked-looking tail and a lethal sting.

A log in the fire snapped, hissed and settled. All were rapt.

'Brave bastard,' Tanku remarked, pulling his green cloak over himself like a blanket. 'Did he find what he was looking for: this cure for death?'

Hattu smiled sadly. 'He is no longer among the living, so we can only surmise that he did not.' He brushed the sole of one foot over the scorpion drawing. 'But what is death? Are we not here, eons after his time, talking of him, seeing his adventures in our minds, feeling the thrill of his quest, the chill of the snow, the sting of the heat? He lives on.' Hattu remembered Ruba speaking these same words in the scribal school. 'His name rings eternal because of his deeds.' He set down his spoon and pointed a firm finger towards the mountains again. 'In Galasma, *we* will carve our names into eternity.'

The faces of the reclined Wolves brightened and a few grinned and wiped fond tears from their eyes. Hattu felt a surge of elation. For that brief moment, he sensed their enchantment. Was this a vein of that golden aura the king possessed – the ability to inspire and enrapture others?

'But if I have dreams of scorpion men tonight, you'll pay for it tomorrow,' Tanku concluded.

As the men drifted off to sleep, Hattu glanced up at the clear night sky, seeing that – as Ruba had insisted they would – the stars had shifted; only a little, but the Hunter constellation was maybe a finger's width more southerly. Suddenly, the stars blinked – gone for a heartbeat as something dark and fast cut across them. Was this the watcher above? Hattu sat up, confused, alarmed. A shadow descended for him at pace... then the shriek of a falcon pierced the night air.

'Halki's balls!' Garin yelped, waking with a line of drool hanging from his chin.

'What the?' Tanku choked, leaping to his haunches, the green cloak falling from him, taking up his spoon as if it was his sword.

'Hmm?' Kurunta sat upright for a moment, swept his head around and uttered something in gibberish, then lay back down and resumed snoring as if nothing had happened.

Arrow descended from the night sky to land on Hattu's shoulder. Another shriek.

'In the name of-' Tanku panted in relief. 'Your hunting bird?'

Hattu laughed, reaching up to stroke her tail feathers. 'Aye. Followed me all the way here, watched our every step,' he said. He heard the familiar braying of a pony nearby – perhaps in response to Arrow's calls – and looked up to see old Ruba feeding Onyx near the king's tent. He rose, taking Arrow with him.

As he cut through the many rings and groups of tents, he spotted the eyes of those still awake glint like an army of fireflies, watching him. Some spared him only a moment's attention, before returning to their ribald camp-games: one lot were taking turns in holding their genitals in the flames of their campfires in some absurd twist on the Comrades' Oath. The stench of burning hair near this group was rife, and one lay on his side, clutching his crotch, groaning.

He noticed from the corner of his eye a ring of Fury soldiers on their haunches. With them was that slit-eyed captain of the Leopard Clan who had voiced his disgust at Hattu earlier that day. They were clustered around the glistening innards of some poor bird. Hattu shot a protective hand up to stroke Arrow's wing. They were asking low-voiced questions, pulling the entrails out bit by bit for answers. He had seen oracles do this often in Hattusa, by the banks of the Ambar. A lesion on the gut ropes could mean ill-fortune… or good fortune, if the oracle chose to answer that way. He heard their murmuring dialogue.

'Will his curse blacken our march?' Slit-eyes asked.

A gangly Fury soldier pulled a strand of sinew, considered it for a moment then replied: 'Surely.'

'Will he bring death upon us?' Slit-eyes said.

Hattu's heart sank as he realised that he was the subject. The gangly Fury soldier was about to pull another part from inside the bird to answer when he realised they were being watched. He looked up, eyes wide with shock on seeing Hattu, his lips moving soundlessly as if afraid to give an answer.

'Tell them,' Hattu said, exasperated. 'Tell them what you have already decided.'

Slit-eyes and the rest looked up as well now. The gangly one who was supposed to answer remained silent.

'This sparrow flew three times over our fire at dusk,' Slit-eyes said coldly. 'Each time coming from the direction of your company.'

'So you swatted it from the sky?'

'To look ahead, to see what our eyes cannot,' Slit-eyes said.

Hattu sighed. 'I'll tell you what I see here: a sparrow dead needlessly; a company of soldiers gossiping like old wives.'

They grumbled and turned away. Hattu sighed and walked on, all sense of relaxation gone.

He came to Ruba, who was now brushing Onyx, but in brisk, irritable strokes. 'Teacher, what is wrong?'

Ruba looked up. For a moment, the old teacher's eyes were vacant. Hattu took up a spare brush and began grooming Onyx too. After a few moments, the light returned to Ruba's eyes. 'Hattu? I didn't realise you were on the march?'

Hattu winced. The old man's forgetfulness was worsening. He tried again: 'You look troubled, Tutor?'

'Ah, yes. The king,' Ruba started then lowered his voice, 'the king made a mistake in coming with us. He is ailing badly, merely from sitting in the carriage.'

Hattu stepped forward towards the two Mesedi by the tent entrance, but Ruba put up a hand to halt him. 'He is asleep. Best we do not rouse him.'

Hattu slumped. 'Very well,' he agreed. He noticed a slave slipping inside the tent, taking a cup of something to the king.

'Volca's root brew. It is the only thing the *Labarna* asks for these days. He merely picks at bread or meat we put before him.'

'I'm glad you're here for him,' Hattu said. 'And when this is all over Danuhepa will see that he eats well.'

Arrow cawed. Ruba started, as if only just noticing her. Onyx nickered. 'Ah, feathery reinforcements? Understandable; I could not bear to leave Onyx behind.'

'Well,' Hattu said, stroking Arrow's head, 'at least Onyx was invited.'

Ruba chuckled, then his eyes grew distant again. After a painful silence, he said: 'Have you heard? The king is unwell.'

Hattu's heart ached. He squeezed Ruba's arm. 'I know, Tutor, I know.'

Leaving the old teacher to it, he turned to one tall bivouac by the Fury quarter. Muwa sat on a log there, shaving the end of a stick with his dirk, his eyes fixed intently on the point.

'Brother,' Hattu said, sitting on the small rock across from him.

Muwa stopped shaving at the wood. For a moment, his eyes remained on the point, as if he wasn't sure whether to look up. When he did and his lion's mane of hair toppled back from his face, he looked weary and irritable.

'Ruba tells me Father's health is deteriorating,' Hattu said. 'Perhaps we should have brought another few healers with us.'

Muwa snorted and shrugged, gesturing with his knife to the nearby knot of blue-robed, sleeping priests and asus who had accompanied the king in his wagon. 'I doubt there would be room for them. When we pass the city of Sapinuwa tomorrow, we will see what the chief asu there can do for him.'

His words seemed blunt, designed to end conversation rather than encourage it. Back to sharpening the twig he went. It had been a long march, Hattu reasoned, and the best of men were weary from it. He sought something to say that might cheer his brother, then remembered: 'I have bright news,' he said.

Muwa slowed in honing his stick again. An unconvincing grin lifted one side of his mouth. 'Aye?'

'Of Atiya and me. I will need to speak to her when I return to Hattusa and I need to discuss it with Father, to see if it can be arranged, but I want to donate a bride price to the Storm Temple.'

Muwa stopped sharpening the stick now. It was an awkward silence.

'I... I want to ask Atiya for her hand. I love her, Brother,' he felt his cheeks flushing, his hand reaching up to the beryl stone in his hair for reassurance. Muwa was the first he had told since that precious moment when he had confessed all to Atiya at the temple gates.

More silence.

As if to demand a response from Muwa, Arrow flapped down from Hattu's shoulder and hopped across the short space between them, tilting her head up to stare at Muwa.

Muwa sat upright, discarding dirk and twig. 'You should empty your head of such thoughts, Hattu,' he said sternly. 'Out there,' he glanced to the north and the dark outline of the Soaring Mountains, 'await warriors. Not training comrades with blunted poles but killers who will have your head. Think of the struggles that lie ahead, not of mist-like fancies.'

Hattu felt the words like a stinging slap. 'I... I thought you would be happy for me, and her.'

'This is war, Hattu,' he said, standing, 'and you are new to it. So listen to me when I tell you: forget Atiya – think only of your spear, your sword, and victory for us all.' With that, he stomped from the bivouac, only to trip over Arrow. Arrow shrieked and flapped in a flurry of feathers, Muwa stumbled and righted himself. The moonlight betrayed a feral twitch of Muwa's lip and clenched teeth. 'And that bird should not be here either,' he snapped, then turned to stalk off deeper into the sea of Fury tents.

Hattu helped Arrow onto his bracer, backing away, confused. He heard a collection of uncharitable laughs from nearby Fury soldiers, wakened and having heard it all. 'Even Muwa rejects his shadow now,' one whispered to another.

***

Volca sliced a thin disc from his pear soundlessly, lifting it to his lips slowly, chewing on it carefully. Perched on the perimeter boulder, he had watched the Cursed Son speak with the king's heir, heard almost every word too. Spite like that could be extremely useful, if nurtured carefully…

***

Sixteen temple-wagons rolled along the low ridge track, heading east. Two palace scout riders led the way, three or four Hittite soldiers sat on each vehicle's roof and Captain Kol and the rest of the Eagle Kin jogged alongside the convoy.

Inside the third carriage, Atiya sat, one hand on her belly, the other on her mouth. It had been an unpleasant ride. The motion of the vehicle combined with the heat and the dust of the ride had proved a nauseous mixture. And the constant wittering of the Elder Priestess sitting opposite helped little. At least this was the second day and nearly the end of the journey – a few more hours and they'd be in the high city of Tapikka. Its pleasant pools and cool temple quarters would soon soothe her.

In the meantime, she began to thumb the crude wooden beads on the bracelet Hattu had given her. There was a stag's head, a wolf's, a lion's, an elephant's… the distraction was working wonders for her nausea. Even better, the prattling priestess fell silent at last… only to draw a clay pot out of her hide bag, prizing the lid off to unleash the most horrific stink. 'Sturgeon paste,' she smiled to the others – everyone else now clutching hands to their mouths, 'mixed with egg. Don't worry, I won't hog it all to myself, you can have some too,' she said.

Another young priestess seemed set to throw up first, grabbing the edge of one curtain, when the whole wagon jolted forwards. 'Ya!' they heard the driver yell with the snap of a whip.

'What's going on?' the Elder Priestess with the disgusting food squawked.

Atiya rose from the bench to pull aside the linen flap that separated the rear of the carriage from the driver's berth. She looked over the driver's shoulder and across the dusty, noonday countryside: the larger, open-backed wagon ahead rocked under the weight of the silver effigy of the Storm God – covered under a hide sheet – and a trio of other vehicles rode in front of this. The city of Tapikka lay on the horizon – a small, fortified place set on a shard of bedrock that stood proud of the land like a battle helm.

'Driver, why have we sped up?'

'Sit tight, my lady,' he snapped in reply, cracking the whip again. This sent Atiya stumbling back onto the bench. The wagon jounced along, and Atiya was sure she could hear snatched, anxious calls outside from the now-running soldiers. A dull thud and a grunt sounded from the roof, then something heavy crashed onto the road.

'What was that?' the Elder Priestess screeched, dropping her urn of fish paste.

Atiya stood, throwing her hands to the carriage walls to balance. She yanked the curtain back again. 'Driver, what... ' her words tailed off as she saw no driver at the reins. The maddened oxen were trotting as best they could. Then she poked her head through the gap and saw the erstwhile driver lying slumped on the berth floor, an arrow in his breast, blood boiling from the wound. Then she looked up and saw something very odd up ahead: a lone rider, still and watching from horseback on the roadside, smiling, his amber hair framing his freckled face, one hand raised.

You?

His smile faded and he chopped his hand down like an axe.

Up ahead, the ridge track darkened and a poplar came crashing down across the road, between the wagons and the amber-haired man. The oxen bellowed in fright and pulled in opposite directions. She reached out towards the reins in the dead driver's hands to try to calm or slow them, but it was too late.

The leftmost ox tripped and fell with a pained groan, the wagon bucked across the poor creature and pitched over onto its side, rolling down the ditch at the side of the road. Roof and ceiling changed places. Atiya's shoulder crashed against the bench, then the ceiling, then another priestess was catapulted into her midriff, winding her. Next, her head thumped against the back wall of the wagon, and all was black.

She heard screaming and a frantic clashing of bronze, but saw nothing and felt nothing, other than brutish hands hoisting her from the wreck, carrying her like plunder.

CHAPTER 14

THE LOYAL WATCHMEN OF GALASMA
SPRING 1300 BC

On the fourth day of the march, the army came to a standstill by the edge of the Green River, all eyes on the pair of sorry-looking timber posts and dangling lengths of rope on the opposite banks. The bridge was but a memory.

'This is a cruel joke. I can almost spit into Galasma from here,' Kurunta growled, kicking a foot into the shingle by the river's shallows. The track resumed on the river's far banks and wound north like the waterway through a range of golden hills. The peaks of the Soaring Mountains stood proudly in the distance, but the low country of Galasma between the hills and the mountain range was obscured. 'But the waters are shallow,' he said, eyeing the shiny, wet and smooth rocks that poked from the river's surface, 'thigh-deep, I'd say.'

General Nuwanza cast his eye over the breadth of the waterway then back along the halted army column and the sea of soldiers squinting into the sun to see what was happening ahead. 'It'll take us the rest of the morning at least to move the divisions across. The wagons and mules will be the slowest part.'

'This was always a contest of swiftness. Can we spare a morning?' Kurunta asked.

Nuwanza bit his lip, the gesture answer enough.

'The sky darkens,' a soldier muttered nearby. Kurunta shot him a look then followed his gaze. Above the obscured flatlands of Galasma, a single, stark wisp of black smoke spiralled and twisted across the sky.

'Are the lead mines already under assault?' Nuwanza said, stepping closer to him so the men wouldn't hear. But already the murmur was spreading back along the column. 'Galasma burns,' they whispered.

Kurunta shrugged. 'A Galasman has left his bread in the oven too long while he sees to his wife,' he grunted, feigning good humour.

'Still, we had best be on our way across the ford,' Volca said, appearing between Kurunta and Nuwanza.

Nuwanza railed at the man's intrusion. 'Aye? Well maybe, if that is what the *Tuhkanti* decides.'

The trio strode back to the royal carriage, where Prince Muwa stood.

'We need direction, *Tuhkanti*,' Kurunta replied. 'You are the king's voice. The bridge is down. The river will hamper our progress but, he lowered his voice, flicking his head towards the black pall in the north, 'we cannot afford to tarry here.'

'Send me on ahead,' old Ruba said, ambling towards the carriage with Onyx the pony in tow. His bald head was burnt from the sun and his gait shambling, but he was insistent. 'I know the Galasmans well. I taught the sons of their nobles – I taught Darizu… well, I tried anyway. And if there are Kaskans up ahead, they will ignore me – what threat would they see in an old man and his pony?'

A fair plan, Kurunta thought. But Prince Muwa seemed deeply agitated. The young man had been on a number of campaigns already and Kurunta had never seen him like this. 'I can advise you on what *I'd* do if you wish, *Tuhkanti*.'

'Take a detachment ahead while the rest of the column crosses the ford,' Muwa replied swiftly and tersely, flicking a finger at Kurunta and Nuwanza. 'Nuwanza, you will lead.'

'Aye, well, he must be bored of following me,' Kurunta muttered with a salty half-grin to his fellow general.

'True, being downwind of you is not a pleasant affair,' the bowman shot back with an arch look.

'*Tuhkanti*,' Volca interjected, 'Is it wise to stumble into the lands ahead in pieces. Keep the army as one. Cross the river and march into Galasma in unison.'

'The army will not advance in *pieces*,' Muwa sighed. 'The detachment will be small – insignificant even.'

Volca made to persist, but Muwa raised a hand.

'I have made my choice,' Muwa said. 'Old Tutor, you will go too with a pair of scout riders,' he said to Ruba. Then he looked at Kurunta and Nuwanza and flicked his head down the line of the halted column. 'Summon two companies – one from each of your divisions.'

'Pitiless Ravens,' Nuwanza beckoned to a company of one hundred from the Blaze.

Kurunta looked down the line to the Storm Division. He saw the many companies of veterans, and the one with his most recent recruits. They would have to be stretched at some point, he thought, and perhaps this sortie would give them a first taste of true danger. 'If enemy soldiers lie beyond, we are not to engage, are we, *Tuhkanti*?'

Muwa shook his head. 'You are scouts, no more. See what lies ahead, then return to us. If something happens – if danger looms or you fall into trouble and cannot bring word back – send a single fire arrow into the sky to warn us.'

Kurunta nodded, then bawled: 'Mountain Wolves, with me!'

***

The two hundred splashed across the ford and moved at a gentle run on up the northern track, hugging the Green River's eastern banks. They moved with a rapid *crunch-crunch* of boots, rasping breaths, clinking bronze axes, swords and maces swinging in their belts. It was reminiscent of the red-fell training – moving at a pace that had Hattu's lungs burning as if there were hot stones sitting in each.

'Your falcon, if only she could talk,' Tanku panted, running by Hattu's side, his eyes glancing skywards where Arrow soared. 'She will see what lies ahead before the old scribe and the horsemen do.'

'The smoke is waning,' Dagon whispered. Indeed, that menacing, single wisp of black had vanished.

'But that doesn't mean the trouble has faded with it,' Kisna added.

Hattu saw the flinty look in the pair's eyes. The Kaskan raid on

Hattusa had robbed both of much: Dagon his home, his father crippled; Kisna his entire family.

The folds of the river valley seemed never-ending until, at last, they saw a broad V of azure sky ahead. They slowed at Kurunta and Nuwanza's command, moving half-crouched, breaths held captive.

'Whatever is beyond,' Hattu said, 'remember who we are.'

'Aye, we trained together, we bested every challenge of the academy,' Tanku agreed.

'The Wolves,' Dagon said in a strong whisper.

'*The Wolves,*' the rest agreed in throaty rasps.

The scarred veterans of the Pitiless Ravens seemed compelled by this to make a whispered oath amongst themselves.

They spilled from the end of the river valley to see not a waiting enemy, but a sun-soaked and broad stretch of alluvial flatland: a patchwork of gold crop, green meadow and brown fallow, dotted with farmsteads. The Green River separated into myriad brooks that meandered across this plain.

'Galasma,' the Captain of the Ravens muttered in a muted tone.

'Land of the loyal watchmen,' Nuwanza said.

A pleasant-enough country, Hattu reckoned, were it not for the proximity of the snow-capped Soaring Mountains, now a clear and crisp jagged wall, impossibly high, lining the north edge of Galasma like an army of watching giants. This was the northern edge of Hittite lands, hard and ever-so real. Now he understood the Galasmans' lot: gifted fine farmlands by the Grey Throne in return for helping man the northern watchtowers, accepting their lot as a buffer state, and enduring the lofty realm of the Kaskans hovering on their shoulder. On the foothills before the Soaring Mountains, Hattu saw the many dark pockmark-like holes of the famed lead mines of this region. On top of these low hills he spotted two stone and red-clay watchtowers. Broad, square turrets, three storeys high, but smothered in the morning shadows of the mountains. Against the backdrop of the imposing peaks and the Kaskan threat that lay within, these frontier towers looked like children gazing up at an oncoming tidal wave of stone.

Kurunta said nothing, his good eye fixed on the mountains. Then, at last, his gaze dropped to the Galasman flatlands immediately ahead and he said to Ruba: 'Lead the way, Old Goose. We have your back.'

Ruba led them down a gentle grassy slope into the Galasman flatlands, rich with the scent of woodsmoke, barley and ox-dung and the gentle sounds of nature.

'All seems well?' Hattu mused.

When they approached a cluster of mud-brick huts lining one brook, he saw the workers in the fields. And as they drew closer, Hattu saw many don nervous looks, gulping, some turning their backs.

'They fear us?' Hattu muttered. 'Why – we are allies?'

'The mighty Galasmans,' Tanku said mockingly, 'the hardy fighters that will join us and tilt the balance against Pitagga.'

'Hold on, where are all the men?' Garin said.

Hattu looked around. Women, children and old men. Not a man of fighting age to be seen. Only a few men of any age remained in open view, the nearest, a short-haired old fellow resting his weight on a crook who watched their approach with bagged, tired eyes.

The army halted when General Nuwanza threw up a hand. The Master Archer then whispered to Ruba, by his side. 'Old Goose? What is this?'

Ruba shrugged, smiled an unconvincing smile then heeled Onyx into a trot over to a man with the crook. 'Greetings, comrade,' Ruba said.

'Welcome,' the lame man muttered in reply. 'It has been some time since the King of the Grey Throne visited these parts.'

Tanku and Dagon exchanged a look.

'A warm welcome, eh?' Garin said.

Something irked Hattu about the man's words, but he couldn't work out what.

Ruba maintained his bright manner. 'Your people are well, I trust?'

'Aye... aye,' the old fellow sighed.

'We saw smoke. Black smoke, coming from these parts. We feared the worst.'

The lame fellow's eyes widened, unblinking. 'We... we had an infestation of locusts on one of our barley fields,' he said. 'A blight of black spots. We had to put it to the torch.'

Hattu saw beyond the small village a patchwork of fallow fields. One was darker than the others and might have been burnt, but he couldn't tell from this distance.

'Where is Darizu, Chief of the Watch in these parts?' Ruba asked.

The old fellow shook his head. 'All the menfolk have upped and left.'

A confused chatter broke out around Hattu from all the soldiers who heard this.

Nuwanza switched his head in every direction 'To where?'

'To the line of the northern watch,' he said, lifting his crook and pointing it towards the shadowy foot of the Soaring Mountains and the two towers visible from here, then dragging it along to the west a little, where woods and hills obscured the view.

Hattu saw just north of that area a narrow breach in the mountains, like an axe wound.

'Where *exactly?*' Kurunta pressed, growing impatient.

'To the high fortress at Baka,' the old man said after a pause, 'overlooking the throat of the Carrion Gorge. They left in a great hurry, you see, after an outlying goatherd came in from the Soaring Mountains and told of a Kaskan approach from the north. Darizu hopes to bed in at Baka and block any southwards incursions.'

'Then it is true: Pitagga comes to take our lead mines?' Nuwanza asked.

The lame fellow shrugged. 'We can only assume so. The only other thing he will get by coming this way is a damned hard fight.' He swung a fist as he said this and some of the Ravens and a few of the Wolves laughed. Hattu had never felt less humoured.

'Is there not a single man of the weapon who can take us there?' Kurunta asked, his good eye shooting across the houses and seeing just frightened children and women peering from the windows and roofs.

'Not one,' the old fellow answered.

Ruba, Kurunta and Nuwanza gathered to convene. Hattu strained to listen in. 'This is not what I expected,' Ruba said. 'I knew Darizu's father when he was chief of the Galasman Watch. He would never neglect to leave a small garrison of sorts to watch over this unwalled settlement.'

'But if a heavy Kaskan force is coming down the gorge, perhaps every man was needed?' Nuwanza countered as he looked to the north and that narrow break in the peaks.

Kurunta growled like a cornered dog and then spat into the dirt. 'I fear that picking over these bones for too long would be a mistake. We should hurry for Baka Fortress – find out what is going on there in good time before the *Labarna* and the rest of the divisions reach these parts.'

***

Noon came and went with few words spoken before the two hundred reached the northern end of the Galasman flats. The midday sun chased the last of the shadows from the land and the mountains shimmered like silver. The cicadas screamed now as they moved along the age-old track that took them into the foothills and along a rising path walled with pine woods. It was cool here at least, part-shaded from the sun by trees. As they marched, Hattu saw the shadow of a bird pass over him. He looked up and there was Arrow soaring overhead. She shrieked once, twice and again.

What's wrong, girl? he mouthed. She was a noisy bird at the best of times, but the way she beat her wings and tacked through the air in swift turns suggested this was no mere strop in search of food. Suddenly, the shade within the trees seemed to threaten. But nothing happened. As they approached the top of the path and emerged from the woods, Hattu could almost feel two hundred or so breaths being released as the landscape beyond rose into view. The Soaring Mountains towered over them, broken only by the wide Carrion Gorge which stretched off northwards, the silvery air within dancing in a heat haze. And not a sign of danger as far as the eye could see.

'The gateway to the Lost North,' he mused, peering into the mirage of the gorge.

'And its guardian,' Dagon added, nudging Hattu and looking up to his right.

Hattu and the rest turned to see it: atop a steep, dusty golden hill, speckled with knots of goat-thorn on the western side, stood Baka Fortress. The stronghold was founded on silvery stone blocks and topped with parapets of red clay.

'Only one approach,' Dagon mused, pointing up the western slope, almost blinding such was the reflected glare of the sun.

Indeed, Hattu thought, seeing that instead of a matching slope on the eastern side of the hill, it looked like there was only sheer, golden rock face. It was as if a giant had bitten away that far half of the hill – perhaps a scar of the earliest lead miners. The back wall of Baka Fortress was perched right on this precipice.

They came to the foot of the western approach. Nobody spoke as they halted at the base of the hill, yet every mind asked the same question as they looked up to the high fortress and the parapet in particular. Not a man was to be seen.

'Well the Galasman garrison here also appears to be shy,' Garin remarked wryly, then looked over his shoulder nervously, eyeing the shady pine woods behind them, then the Soaring Mountains and the deserted gorge just a stone's throw to the north.

Hattu eyed the broad dirt path leading up to the fort's main gate – that was the obvious approach, but he knew it could not be trusted until they sighted one of their own up there. He saw Arrow circling up above the fort. *What can you see?*

'Darizu of the Watch,' Kurunta called up the hill. The call died as a lonely echo. Silence. 'Galasman soldiers,' he tried again. Nothing.

Hattu eyed each rounded merlon on the battlements, the absence of life up there feeling more wrong with every passing breath. Then, at last – movement. A single head rose above the parapet. Darizu. His head of thick, curly hair hung to his brow, casting his pig-eyes in shade. 'Brothers!' he called down, punching a fist in the air.

'A garrison of one man?' Hattu heard Nuwanza say.

'Half a man, I'd say,' Kurunta replied saltily. Then filled his lungs to bellow again: 'I have been told that the Galasman Watch are here. Yet they are either very shy or afraid of the sun. Where are they?'

'Indeed, eighteen hundred men were mustered from the farms and came here. But it is just me and a few others who remain within these walls.'

Hattu recalled the grovelling Bel Madgalti's excuses that day at the Gathering. *Watching from the balcony while his soldiers went to war for him.*

'Where are the rest?' Nuwanza shouted up.

After a pause, Darizu replied: 'They went into the gorge, two days ago. To block the Kaskan advance from the north.'

Hattu looked north with every other. The empty, wide, silver-walled gorge stared back, the air swirling and the thin grass on the floor rippling in a hot breeze.

'And they left you, their leader, behind?' Nuwanza asked, shielding his eyes from the sun.

'I stayed behind with a skeleton watch of ten others... I thought it best to make sure the fort remained safe.'

'Did you now,' Nuwanza laughed without humour.

'He's shat himself again,' Tanku whispered to Hattu and the rest of the Wolves. Hattu had told them all about the Gathering and Darizu's blubbering excuses.

'Ten others? Then where are *they?*' Kurunta asked, his voice cracking in exasperation.

Again, Darizu hesitated. 'They have been stricken down with fever, I am afraid. They ate some bad bird meat – the worst of omens. But I have consigned them to a barrack hut at the corner of the fort.'

'You are trained as an asu?' Nuwanza asked.

'No, but I have seen how the healers work,' Darizu replied. 'Now where is the *Labarna?*' he said, craning his neck over the parapet to look back down the path the two hundred had approached from. 'I will slaughter ten sheep in his honour.'

'Each more courageous than you,' Hattu muttered.

'You should bring him here, bring him inside,' Darizu continued. 'He will have his pick of the storehouse and I can prepare him a comfortable bed in the command building. The sick-men's malady will not trouble him. I can ferry water down for the rest of you.'

'Generous bastard,' Kurunta grunted quietly, then squinted up at the sun before replying. 'The king is not with us, but aye, send water down.'

Hattu saw Arrow still circling up there, agitated.

'But the king is coming, isn't he?' Darizu persisted. 'I do not think I should be opening the gates unless it is for him.'

'Damn you, man,' Kurunta snapped. 'Either open the gates or come down here and speak to us.'

'Wait a moment,' an elderly voice croaked. Old Ruba hobbled into view on Onyx's back. He mopped his sweat-lashed brow with a rag. 'I know Darizu well. He is an awkward type, but I think I know how to deal with him. When he railed against my teachings, I used to tell him stories. He didn't realise that there were lessons in every tale. He would sit with me by the fire, eating bread and honey, learning obliviously, happily. Let me go up and speak with him.'

Nuwanza and Kurunta exchanged a look, then sighed and agreed.

Hattu stepped forward to help the shaking Ruba from Onyx's croup. 'Be careful, old tutor, I do not trust this Darizu.'

'Nor do I, lad,' Ruba said, eyeing the woods behind them and the empty gorge on their left, 'but I trust this silent land even less.'

They watched Ruba whisper fond words to his pony, stroking its muzzle, before the scribe slowly climbed the hill. Baka's narrow guard gate opened and the old fellow hobbled inside. Nuwanza and Kurunta gave the order to fall out, then the pair crouched to their haunches and muttered in discussion about their next move.

The men of the two companies sat, drawing off their helmets and setting down their shields and weapons. Some dug out bread and salty cheese from their leather bags, hungrily gulping down water from their skins to combat the lack of shelter from the sun. A few put up their bivouacs such was their discomfort at the heat.

'My loincloth smells like the academy latrine pits on a midsummer's day,' Dagon remarked as he sat cross-legged, hitching his crotch and sniffing the air to test his description.

Garin halted, mid-mouthful of a chunk of cheese wrapped in bread, his nose wrinkling. 'Dagon, I hope that one day a tiger pounces upon you when you're doing your business in the woods,' he said before returning to chewing, albeit more slowly and reluctantly.

Hattu chuckled. Other groups chatted likewise. But the light-hearted words were a veneer. He saw each man's eyes every so often shoot to the gorge. Could the few thousand Galasman warriors somewhere in there truly hold back Pitagga's Kaskans if they came in the numbers reported? Was that melting, rippling air in the gorge about to part and reveal a wall of bearded warriors, Galasman heads on their spears?

He shuddered and looked uphill at Baka fort to seek distraction. The blue sky above was now spoiled by a murder of seven crows, who flapped down to rest upon the parapet, looking inside. A moment later, a pair of vultures began to circle overhead. Something reminded Hattu of that lame Galasman back at the farming village by the Green River brooks.

It has been some time since the King of the Grey Throne visited these parts...

'No winter scouts came here – the snows were too deep. Nobody knew the king was coming...' he whispered into the ether.

'Hattu?' Tanku said.

'How did that old fellow know the king was coming?' Hattu said, a cruel shiver shaking him. 'And why does Darizu also expect the king?' The pair shared a silent look, trying to piece it all together, finding only that they could not.

Suddenly, a distant groan of timber echoed from within Baka's walls. All heads turned to look up.

The grunts of stressed timber grew as a great pillar swung up from within the fort, coming vertical and quivering to a halt. Across the top of the pillar was a shorter beam forming a crossbar, and upon it hung old Ruba, his arms outstretched, nailed to the crossbar through the wrists, his white robes torn into ribbons, streaked with crimson and fluttering in the gentle breeze. His skin was flayed and hanging in strips too. His head was lolling and trying to rise, and from the empty red pits where his eyes had been, runnels of blood poured like ghastly tears. His legs dangled, crooked and broken in many places. A weak, animal moan sounded from this misshapen remnant of life, the stub of his cut-out tongue glinting red from within his mouth.

Hattu's skin crawled and he staggered forwards up the first few steps of the golden slope then fell to his knees. Gasps rang out around him. Onyx brayed in fright. From the corner of his eye he saw Kurunta rise from his haunches, the water skin he was holding falling, splashing on the ground. Nuwanza rose with him. 'Old Goose?' Kurunta whispered, reaching out towards the hilltop with one trembling hand as if he did not believe his lone eye.

'Darizu?' Nuwanza cried uphill, his brow fiercely bent into a V. '*DARIZU!*'

The birds on the fort walls scattered across the sky, and an eerie silence followed.

Then, with a fierce, animal cry, a wall of bearded, snarling warriors rose up from behind the battlements, hefting and shaking spears, swords and axes. Twenty Kaskan noblemen. Central was Pitagga, atop the fort's gatehouse, his black armour shining, the lion-skull helm glaring, his double-headed axe gleaming.

Hattu staggered back, gawping. The heads of the others in the small Hittite reconnaissance party flicked this way and that.

'Men, come together,' Kurunta bawled, Nuwanza echoing the order.

Panicked shouts rang out as the men scrambled to and fro, tossing down half-eaten food, kicking over the few bivouac tents, roaring at comrades, taking up the nearest weapons. It was a ramshackle line, ten deep, twenty wide, facing the slope up to Baka Fortress. Hattu shared a glance with Garin, Tanku and Dagon, each panting on the shielded front line. The hot air seemed to crackle. Then Kisna cried out: 'The gorge – up on the gorge sides!'

Hattu swung his head to the north to see the tell-tale glints of copper and bronze up there on either side of the rocky passage. Kaskan soldiers – Pitagga's ten thousand, he realised – hidden moments ago, now rising to peer south at this paltry group of Hittite soldiers. He caught sight of spears, arrows, rocks – an arsenal designed to crush an unsuspecting army on the gorge floor. 'We've stepped into a hunter's pit. They were waiting for the king, for the divisions entire, to wander into that corridor,' he realised.

'Send up the signal!' Nuwanza demanded of one of the Ravens. An archer fumbled with his bow and dropped an arrow – already wrapped in a resin-soaked cloth. Nuwanza growled and snatched the weapon from the man, nocking the arrow and striking a pair of flint pieces to light the soaked rag. His powerful body bent as he tilted the weapon skywards and loosed. The arrow sped up, up and into the blue, slowing and hovering for a moment, ablaze, before streaking back down into the earth with a thud.

Pitagga laughed long and loud from the walls of Baka. 'Empty your quiver, famed Bowman,' he roared. 'None will see your flaming sticks.'

'The hills are too high,' Nuwanza said, his voice tight and his eyes bulging, shooting across the golden southerly hills hugging the banks of the Green River. 'The army will not see the signal – they will stumble on to this place unawares.'

'Today was the wrong day to volunteer for reconnaissance,' Pitagga cried. 'This,' he gestured to the gorge and the waiting snare, 'is not for you. This is for your *Labarna*. As was this,' he stabbed a finger towards the cross from which poor old Ruba sagged. 'For I will have his skull, and his *Tuhkanti's* too, when they come through. I will stride over the carpet of Hittite dead and pluck their heads from their necks… to add to my collection.' He swung up a spear to hold it aloft in the sky.

Hattu's eyes locked onto the spear tip. Affixed there was a gaunt, hairless, shrivelled human head. Its features were unmistakable. 'Sarpa?' he wailed.

'And now I must bid you farewell,' Pitagga said, 'to the Dark Earth with you, so I can prepare my snare once more before your king comes this way.'

Kurunta stepped back from the slope, head shooting to the meandering river valley through which they had come. 'Back… we've got to get back… we have to warn th-'

'Destroy them!' Pitagga roared.

As if a sudden breeze had struck up, the woods opposite Baka fort, behind the startled knot of Hittites, rustled and shook. Hattu twisted his head to look behind him, towards the disturbance. A shiver ran up his legs, across his back and over his scalp as he saw the shade within the pine woods writhe. With a shrill cry, a wall of men spat forth from the trees. Not Kaskans, but short-bearded, dark-skinned men in leather armour. The loyal watchmen of Galasma had appeared at last: over a thousand hardened fighters, armed with swords, spears, bows and brutish clubs. They ran at their erstwhile allies.

'Turn... face!' Kurunta shrieked.

The instincts honed in training bested the panic in every man's breast as they swung to face the Galasman charge. Hattu and the frontliners sifted back through the ranks to present their shield-front to the oncoming wall of warriors, a hundred paces distant and coming fast. Then, from behind, the creak of Kaskan bows and whirring of slings sounded from up on Baka's walls.

'Square!' Nuwanza howled. Another flurry of movement and the line of two hundred dissolved into a tight and tiny box of men, the Ravens presenting shields to the missile troops on the fort walls and the Wolves showing their wall of shields to the racing Galasman army.

Hattu's veins were suddenly drained of blood and instead pumped full of some horrible, icy, viscous soup as he saw the Galasman warriors now just thirty strides distant and bounding for him: screaming maws, wicked eyes and sharp metal honed to cut through necks and break bodies. He saw moments of his childhood, flashes of rare pleasant days and of momentous storms, tasted honey and brine, felt long past thrill and misery as if they were here and now. The day of the Kaskan raid staggered into his mind. There, he was a fleeing boy, and flee he did. Here, he was a soldier: trained to stand, to fight and to die. And each of those things felt equally certain. He heard the rain of bronze arrowheads and slingstones battering down on the fort-facing shields behind him, heard the gurgling scream of one man stricken. Poor Onyx brayed in agony and crumpled to the ground as a Kaskan arrow took the pony in the neck.

Twenty paces.

'Shoulder to shoulder, shield to shield,' Kurunta bawled, then brought his twin curved swords out from his back-sheaths with a *zing*. 'The Gods are with us!'

Another barrage from the walls of Baka saw the hot, stinking blood of a comrade shower the Wolves' backs.

Ten paces, nine, eight, seven...

Hattu's muscles quaked with a glacial chill and his belly and bladder demanded to release their contents. He sensed Dagon and Tanku – each pressed by his sides – shaking.

'Tarh... Tarhunda... c-coat my heart...' Garin tried to wrap his lips around the Storm Division's battle cry. 'Tarhunda, coat my heart in bronze!' Kurunta finished for him.

'Ishtar,' Hattu snarled through snatched breaths, thinking at the last of his guardian goddess who had so far offered him nothing but a life of bleak riddles. '*Hear* me... stand with us!'

Tanku repeated this with a roar as the Galasmans leapt across the last few paces. '*Ishtar stand with us!*'

Hattu discharged an animal cry as a fiend with bulging, red-veined eyes shrieked and loped towards him. Then came a blow like the kick of a horse and a din like the wildest storm as the flood of Galasmans crashed against the small Hittite party with a clatter of shields and screeching bronze. He and the red-eyed one were nose-to-nose for a moment, panting, gasping, growling. But the Galasman, far bulkier, drove Hattu back a pace then two. Blood puffed and sprayed across them as Hittite soldiers fell to Galasman blades, and Hattu was sure he was to be next when Red-eyes freed an arm and swung his axe down for Hattu's head.

Hattu ducked down and threw up his shield as the red-eyed one's axe struck. The blow was fiercer than anything he had experienced in mock-combat, tearing through the shield. Red-eyes hacked at him again and this time the act of deflecting the blow sent Hattu staggering back.

Indeed, the entire Hittite line was rocked, forced to walk backwards up the Baka slope. Hattu righted himself and surged back to the gap he had left between Tanku and Dagon. Red-eyes came at him again, his and Hattu's shoulders crashing together. Hattu dug his boots into the earth but only when the Mountain Wolves behind him added their weight to his back was Red-eyes matched. Hattu lashed out, elbowing the Galasman in the jaw, sending the foe back a pace or two. It was enough for Hattu to bring his spear level again. The fellow's neck was exposed. But the enormity of this moment cast a spell upon him: a first kill... a man's body would be rent. A life would be ended. The Galasman's red eyes changed then – into those of a frightened man – a son, a father?

Hattu's heart crashed twice before he noticed Red-eyes bringing up a mace, the fearful family man now a fiery killer again.

Hattu at last thrust his spear forward, the tip plunging through the man's neck, splitting it like thin cloth. A deep red weal bulged from within and then a torrent of blood spat with the man's every dying heartbeat. Hattu's heart thundered as he pulled his spear free and the man fell away. But, with a surge, the Galasmans drove the Hittites back pace by pace up the hill, Pitagga and his Kaskan nobles whooping with delight as they loosed arrows and slingstones on their ever-closer targets.

'For the Storm God!' Garin screamed to rally his comrades, only for a Galasman axe to rip away his shield, tearing it to pieces, then a fire-hardened club came down on his head, crumpling the leather helm and crushing his skull like an egg. His head fell away in pieces and his body slackened and pitched backwards. Hattu gawped at the mangled corpse. A friend, dead in a trice. Bone-shaking reality. Then the two Hittites either side of Garin's corpse were cut down in quick succession. Kisna and Sargis, in the rank behind, found themselves facing the gap where the three had been. The pair were agog, frozen.

Hattu barged over beside them, lurching into the gap. 'With me! Close the gap or we're all dead.' he howled. He leapt up, hurling his spear down and into the shoulder of one Galasman. The shaft punctured the bare strip of skin by the Galasman's collarbone and sank deep into his chest. A fountain of black blood jumped from the rim of the wound and the man fell, shaking violently, mouth agape. He drew his curved sword from his belt and drove it up into a tall Galasman's gut, wrenching it to one side as Kurunta had taught him. Hot, stinking guts flooded across his forearm, then pink-grey entrails squirmed clear like escaping worms as the Galasman folded over. He tore the blade free then shoved the dying man away.

But comrades fell either side of them, riven with spears, shoulders and heads cloven with axes or staved in with clubs. Hattu blocked a sword strike of one foe and stole a look across the battle line: the two hundred had lost sixty at least. *Thrum, thwack!* Another volley of missiles from the high fort landed in the flesh of the men at the hillfort-facing side of the tiny square.

Another two Hittite soldiers were cut down with gurgling cries.

'Set fire to the sky,' Kurunta rasped, twin-swords working in a blur, cutting down Galasmans like wheat, 'else our king and our comrades will die in that damned gorge.'

Another blazing arrow was loosed from within the beset Hittite square with a *snap* by one archer sitting on the shoulders of a spearman.

'Still not high enough,' Nuwanza cried. 'Gods hear us!'

Hattu dug his spear into the ribs of an attacker, then glanced over his shoulder and up at the lofty Baka Fortress. A fire arrow loosed from there would be seen for miles, but the fort was nigh-on impenetrable, its front wall lined with Pitagga and his nobles, its approaches a death trap. And in any case, the Galasman traitors had them pinned here at the foot of the golden slope in a maw of spears. Hattu heard the blood crash in his ears. Was this it? No hope of escape, no way of alerting the rest of the army as to what awaited them.

When a Galasman speared towards him, he flinched, caught his foot in a rock and fell back into the crushed Hittite square. He landed hard, right beside a small patch of ground where the dust was puckering, sinking, falling away from underneath. He scrambled away from it just before the ground vanished with a *whoosh*. A puff of dust shot up like the breath of a spirit, clouding the skirmish. He blinked and coughed, then saw the hole that had been revealed: as wide as a man and leading to a warren-like passageway. An old mining tunnel leading under the hill, Hattu realised. And there was light within. A dim glow of daylight… coming from the far side of the hill, to the eastern face? He leapt to his haunches, staring into the hole, trying to imagine the path of the shaft. If it indeed led to the sheer eastern face…

He looked up at Baka fort again. 'Sir,' he shouted over the battle-din to Kurunta. 'I can get up there, into Baka. I can send up the fire arrow.'

Kurunta glowered at him for a heartbeat, his good eye like a hot coal, his face streaked with runnels of blood. 'Have you taken a blow to the head?' But then his lone eye grew wide as he saw the burrow in the ground.

***

Muwa stood on a smooth rock, midriver, waving the ranks of the Blaze on over the Green River ford at a gentle, splashing march. The wagon train was still perched on the western banks and they would take the longest to cross. Every so often he shot a glance up to the northern sky. Sun-streaked and clear, still. Colta and Volca, by the royal wagon on the far side, were watching for the fire signal in any case, but Muwa felt an acute need to lend his eye to the matter also. For just a moment, he imagined that his brother had been assailed up ahead. For a trice, he even wanted it to be true. Then he was overcome with horror.

What have you become? he warred with himself. He felt a panic grip his breast as he imagined his younger brother in danger… then he saw the image of Atiya and Hattu again, by the temple gates. It was a lover's embrace. The guilt ebbed and he felt detached from the troubling thoughts. He looked back to the lazy Green River, gazing into its depths. *You knew how I felt about her,* he seethed, *yet you chose to betray me.*

A cry split the air and Muwa's head swung back to the north. There, a Hittite soldier was shielding his eyes and standing on his toes, peering into the sky… but the fellow slumped and waved a dismissive hand. 'Just a bird,' he said contritely.

***

They fell from the skirmish as if being snatched by some great underground creature. Hattu thudded down into the tunnel first, then Dagon, Kurunta and a pair from the Ravens: a reed-thin soldier and a small, muscly-limbed one. The din of battle suddenly became an odd, distant sound. The roughly-hewn tunnel was cold – mercifully so compared to the baking heat above – its walls veined with black and green, old timber props supporting the shaft every so often. The ceiling was low, forcing them to run at a crouch. Hattu kept his eyes on the dim orb of light ahead, praying to all the Gods he was not mistaken. Then… daylight!

They burst clear of the tunnel and onto a shelf of rock that ran like a belt around the foot of Baka hill's sheer eastern face. Hattu tilted his head back, staring up at the impossibly distant rear wall of Baka Fortress high above. This was higher than anything he had ever attempted before – at least twice the height of any of the crags around Hattusa. Hattu felt the splash of moisture left in his mouth drain away.

'Dispense with everything: boots, helms, armour,' he said, throwing off his battle gear as he spoke until he was barefoot, wearing just his linen kilt, carrying his bow and quiver and his curved sword. He eyed the climb: blank. Where to start? Now his eagerness stalled.

'Prince Hattu!' Kurunta said urgently. The muffled din of their comrades dying on the opposite slope came in waves.

Hattu looked around the three with him and Kurunta. They were pale, still shaking with battle-vigour, eyes wide and on him, demanding. He turned back to the rock face.

Every climb looks blank on the first read, Sarpa's words came back to him like a welcome hand on his shoulder. *Read the rock once, then read it again – like one of old Ruba's tales... always, you will find new meaning, new possibilities.*

It was like the scrape of a whetstone on a blade, honing his thoughts. Now he saw the faint ribbons of shade and tiny dots of darkness here and there. 'We start here,' he said, stooping to gather dry dust from the ground in both hands, before patting his palms together – they now felt dry and smooth, the moisture of sweat absorbed.

He moved to the cliff face. 'Follow my every handhold and foothold,' he offered over his shoulder, but saw the doubt on their faces. Over winter, Dagon had climbed with him, but on the smallest slopes near Hattusa and no more. The troubled looks on the faces of the two Ravens suggested equally patchy experience.

He turned to them. 'It is always worst at the outset, when the rock face is looking down on you like your master. Climb, and watch it shrink. Become the master of the rock.'

Dagon managed a half-smile. The two Ravens filled their lungs and nodded.

Hattu and Kurunta led the way, the powerful general scaling the cliff-face by Hattu's side. The lower surface was rich with handholds, Hattu found, and it soon became a rhythmic ascent, shifting his weight from one side to the other, gripping crimps with his fingertips and sliding his hand into cracks – making fists to anchor himself. But after a while he began to appreciate just how much higher this face was than any he had attempted before. He became annoyed at the sound of his ever-quickening breaths echoing from the close rock. The hot, still air grew a little breezy, and he felt the strength ebb from his battle-weakened limbs. Worse, the hot sun had caused the granite to sweat – the moisture within seeping out to form a fine film on the surface of the rock. A sloping hand-grip – near vertical and reliant on the friction of his palm – felt like it was smeared in tallow thanks to this. *Climb with your feet, balance with your hands,* he retold himself one of Sarpa's old mantras, pushing up with his right leg to find another scant and clammy-feeling impression.

A weak groan from one of the soldiers below drew his eye downwards. The drop was enormous. A lock of hair escaped his tight ponytail and whipped round to stick to his sweat and blood-spotted face. As he lifted a hand to sweep it away, a shard of rock in the other handhold shifted and his entire body locked up in fear. He shot the free hand back to the rock just in time to stabilise himself.

'Take heart, Prince Hattu. We are nearly there,' Kurunta panted, flicking his eyes up.

Hattu looked up to see the chunky stone and red clay wall of Baka Fortress looming just a short stretch above, flush with the cliff face. But over the muffled din of the battle on the far side of the hill, he heard two low, gruff voices on the near parapet. *Kaskan sentries,* he realised. Old Ruba had taught him parts of the mountain men's tongue. He whistled like a swallow to halt Kurunta. The three men below them halted too. But then one slipped, losing his grip, dangling by one hand and barely catching a stifled yelp.

'Did you hear that?' one of the voices said. 'Have a look.'

Hattu's heart galloped as a set of fingers wrapped around the parapet, knowing a staring head was about to follow. He imagined a thousand deaths: being poked from the cliff face by long poles, shot with slingstones or having boiling water poured down on them. Instead, a falcon's shriek was enough to spare them. Arrow swept down and Hattu saw the hands up there flap and swat. 'Damned bird. I'll wring its neck,' the Kaskan snarled.

Hattu's breath stayed captive in his lungs until he was sure the sentry would not return for another look, then he whistled again and mouthed silently to the climbers. *Onwards.*

When they scaled right up to the fort's foundations, the stonework offered easy handholds. The mud brick of the upper section, however, proved tricky – smooth and crumbling whenever he tried to work a handhold. But up they went, carefully, until he and Kurunta clung just below the battlements like spiders. They waited a moment for Dagon and the two Ravens to ascend to the same spot. The din of the clash on the far side of the slope was a little sharper now: screaming, grunting, and a smashing of bronze. He thought of Tanku, Kisna, Sargis and the rest of the Wolves. Of poor Garin. Only a short time had passed since they had stolen away from the fray, but it felt like an eternity.

When we go over, Kurunta mouthed, signalling up and over with one hand, *we must despatch the sentries up there silently.*

They checked for agreement. Hattu noticed the Raven soldier beside Dagon freeing a hand to repeat and affirm Kurunta's 'up and over' gesture. As he did so, the mud brick securing his other hand wrenched loose. It was a horrific sight: the soldier suddenly peeling back, arms flailing, legs kicking out as he plummeted.

Hattu and Kurunta could only watch, horrified, seeing the soldier's face agape and moon-white, knowing death was unavoidable. But the man was heroic, uttering not a sound as he fell. He was cruelly dashed from a jutting wart of rock, a blow that ruptured his head and sent him spinning crazily on towards the ground. But then, at the last moment when his lifeless body thumped into the hard dirt below, a loud animal grunt leapt from his bursting lungs. The grunt echoed around the Baka hillside.

Gods, no, Hattu mouthed.

'That was no falcon!' the gruff Kaskan voice on the battlements exclaimed. Footsteps padded over rapidly to the parapet again. A bearded warrior poked his head over, angered, then suddenly flooded with alarm when he saw the four Hittites clinging to the precipice like limpets.

Quick as a striking snake, Kurunta lurched up to chop his hand into the sentry's throat, winding him, then tugged at the man's collar, hauling him over the edge. The sentry flailed to the ground far below, a jagged star of blood exploding from under him.

Hattu saw a second sentry, the one the first had been talking to, glance over the parapet then back away. The man's mouth peeled open, ready to alert the rest of the Kaskans in the fort, when Arrow swooped down again, thrashing past the fellow's face. It gave Hattu time enough to lever himself up and over, onto the walkway, then throw a right hook at the Kaskan. It connected sweetly, sending the warrior into a spin and toppling to the parapet, dazed. In a flash, Dagon leapt over too and, as the sentry tried to rise, whacked him hard on the nose, breaking bone and knocking him out cold.

Instantly, Hattu ducked down behind a pair of barrels on the eastern battlement walkway, only now seeing the interior of the fort: the stronghold floor was all but empty: Pitagga and his knot of nobles lined the western wall, backs turned obliviously and still hurling all they could down the golden slope at the beset Hittite scouting party. All eyes were on that clash. Just the two now-despatched men had been spared to watch the seemingly impossible approach on this sheer side.

Bows, Kurunta mouthed as the reed-thin Raven leapt over to join them on the parapet.

The general struck his flint pieces to light his lone fire arrow, then knelt – like the great effigy at the archery range, and loosed. The flaming missile tore high into the sky, silent and surely high enough to be seen from many danna away.

'What now, sir?' Hattu breathed. Only now he realised the magnitude of that fire arrow: the Hittite column would spot it and halt at once, knowing it meant danger lay ahead. The scouting party were alone like thieves in this fort and on the hillside, forsaken and beset.

'And now, we die with honour,' Kurunta whispered, nocking his bow again with a normal arrow and looking across at the Kaskan nobles on the far wall.

Hattu realised it was the only option. 'Pitagga is mine,' he hissed to the others as they each unhitched the bows from their backs and lifted an arrow from their quivers, kneeling on the eastern parapet and aiming across to the western one.

'Make your shot count,' Kurunta whispered, encouraging him and the others. 'For once we have loosed we will have to face with swords all of those we do not strike down.'

Hattu exhaled the last of the air in his lungs. Normally, this would see his body fall still for a perfect shot – but his forearms still trembled from the strain of the climb. He drew the string back to his ear, winked, training his right eye on the arrow tip and sighting it on the back of Pitagga's neck. This was it: with the slaying of the Lord of the Mountains, the twelve tribes would break apart and the Kaskan threat would disintegrate. The war would be over.

Like a breath of wind soughing through the trees, Kurunta said: 'loose...'

For Sarpa, for Ruba... Hattu mouthed as his fingers peeled away from the bowstring.

***

Muwa's head craned back with nearly fifteen thousand others, his eyes following the tiny orange streak that shot past the sun, hovered, then fell towards the earth, somewhere beyond the hills of the river valley. A clamour broke out around him.

All he could think about was his choice. And it would be an easy one to make. Hittite generals for generations had heeded such a warning signal in one way and one way only: by halting the march of their column, by not striding on into the hazards ahead. And the scouts who braved those dangers to send the fire arrows skywards?

To the Dark Earth with those brave souls.

***

The bowstring whipped past Hattu's face. His arrow and the three others flew. They spat across the fort interior, the targets unawares... until the fire arrow whacked down into a wooden hay cart by the fort gates with a thud.

Pitagga and his noblemen swung round at the noise. Three of the finely armoured mountain men could only gawp before the shafts aimed at them punched into their chests and bellies, but Pitagga shifted his weight onto one foot, Hattu's arrow grazing past his neck. The Kaskan lord gawked at the four figures on the eastern wall. The seventeen unharmed guards with him did likewise. There was a stunned hiatus, ended only when the wooden hay wagon roared with a sudden eruption of flame.

'Defend your lord,' Pitagga howled, shoving his men towards the parapet stairs, urging them onto the fort floor before him like a shield.

Kurunta and Dagon drew and hurled their maces into the bunched group, staving in one's head and shattering the shoulder of another. The surviving Raven soldier picked up the felled Kaskan sentry's spear and launched it down, lancing one man through the belly, the tip shooting on through to skewer the thigh of the man behind. The cluster of noble guards broke apart, panicked, despite Pitagga's hectoring demands.

'Swords!' Kurunta cried, drawing his twin blades and leaping down onto the fort floor.

Hattu leapt down with Dagon and the Raven soldier, swords drawn. The smoke now billowed across the fort floor as the wagon fire spread to the timber beams jutting from the armoury walls. The thirteen Kaskan guards fanned out to encircle them, now grinning and confident seeing there were just these four Hittites to deal with. With a cry, they pounced. Hattu dashed the spear from one fat noble's grasp before throwing a leg out to trip another. Spinning, he brought his blade across the thighs of a third. A thrown spear cut through the air before him, nicking his shoulder as he dipped to avoid a fatal blow before lunging forward to clash swords with the black-toothed thrower: Hattu's curved dirk slid along the Kaskan's straight-edged blade, all the way to the hilt until the enemy blade bit deep into his knuckles. Hattu cried out then threw Black-teeth off with a kick, then ducked as an axe from another tried to take his head off.

He sprung up to defend himself against these two, who circled him, certain they had picked an easy kill – each of them a head taller than Hattu. He flicked his dirk up and caught it to hold it blade down, watching each man's eyes and step. The axe-man scythed down for him and Hattu staggered back, almost losing his footing, and when he threw up his dirk to block the sword-strike of Black-teeth, it was feeble, the curved blade sailing out of his hand. Weaponless, he backed away from the two. He saw a dropped Kaskan straightsword and made to squat and snatch it up, but the axe-man's blade chopped into the ground, almost slicing his fingers off. He felt sun-warmed stone behind him and realised he had backed against the fort wall.

'Down!' Dagon cried.

Hattu fell into a squat as Dagon's thrown mace met the axe-man's temple with a boom like a bursting bag. The foe's skull crumpled with a spray of foul matter and he wilted like a flower. Hattu pounced on the moment of shock to snatch up a burning faggot of hay, ramming it into Black-teeth's face. The fellow screamed, his beard-hair and flesh melding with a stinking sizzle. Dagon rushed forward to plunge his sword into the man's flank with a crack of sinew and bone. Black-teeth fell to his knees, face ruined with fire, then collapsed completely, legs kicking in death-spasms. Hattu and Dagon swung one way then the other in the scudding smoke and licking flames, back to back, certain another foe would be rushing for him, but there was none: each of the Kaskan nobles lay dead or groaning, bodies riven.

All but one... Pitagga's body was absent.

No! he mouthed, then almost leapt from his skin when a small door at the edge of the fort clicked shut. His head snapped round, his smoke-grey eye focused on the door. Without a second thought, he snatched up a dropped sword and lunged for the door, kicking it open, sword levelled. Inside, he found not a room, but a dark-walled stairwell, hollowed out of the rock, winding down into the mount. Another part of the honeycomb-like lead mines, he realised.

In the meagre light before the door swung closed behind him, he saw Pitagga further down the stairs, fleeing but pausing to look up, eyes wide. Then off he set again, descending out of sight. If the Kaskan leader escaped then this would all have been for nothing. Hattu stumbled down the stairs after him, shoulders scraping from the jagged stairwell walls, tripping and rolling down one stretch of steps and skidding down others. It felt like an endless descent, then suddenly he spilled into broad daylight again, stumbling through golden grass at the southern edge of Baka hill. Hattu shot a look one way then another around the deserted space, before a shape shot up from the grass and a flash of bronze came for his face. He leapt to one side and rolled across the ground just as Pitagga's double-headed axe cut through the air where he had been. The Kaskan Lord stalked over, ready to raise the axe again. 'This time, *Cursed Son,* I don't think I will let you live.'

Hattu leapt to his feet, levelled his sword and crouched like a warrior. 'The last time I faced you I was a boy. Now, I am a warrior. You will pay dearly for what you did to my brother and my teacher.'

Pitagga's eyes came alight with menace as he laughed darkly, and both raised their weapons.

'Lord,' a voice cried from the trees nearby. A Kaskan warrior in the shade there was pointing in panic to a cloud of dust coming along the Green River valley. Hattu peered at it too, until he saw the screaming, snarling wall of men... soldiers... *Hittites!* The Fury Division, alert to the danger, weapons drawn. At their head... *Muwa!*

Suddenly, the air was alive with skirling pipes singing a bold song of war as the Hittite ranks came to conquer Baka hill.

'Your ruse has failed,' Hattu spat.

Pitagga backed away, his confidence draining. As he went, he held up and shook a dark bag. 'But your brother's head will stay with me, and your own will join it in good time, as will your father's and the *Tuhkanti's.*' Then he pulled something from his cloak – a rag of sorts. 'Your silver god is already mine.'

Hattu frowned, confused, catching the thrown rag as Pitagga vanished into the trees.

A strip of dark cloth. Then he held it up, saw it for what it really was, and his heart fell into his boots.

Dagon staggered out from the stairway passage and saw his friend's face turn paler than snow. 'Hattu, what's wrong?'

***

The Battle of Baka Fortress ended as soon as the Galasmans saw the Fury Division surging from the Green River valley. Most of the Galasmans melted away before the Fury could reach them, but those too slow were cut to pieces. The well-placed Kaskan forces positioned along the high sides of the Carrion Gorge just to the north vanished too, retreating deeper into the mountains now that their ambush had been exposed.

Hattu staggered breathlessly round the foot of the hill, coming to the western slope, he and Dagon supporting each other as they went. From the corner of his eye, he saw the smoking mess that was the fort – the fires only now being tended to. He saw a hundred or more Hittite warriors strewn on the lower slope of the golden hill, entangled with the brutish corpses of many more Galasmans. Shards of white bone jutted, sinews stretched and dangled, red and black blood and foul grey innards coated this macabre undergrowth. The stink of death was powerful and unremitting. Flies droned in thick, black clouds over the mess. His face wrinkled like a hissing cat's and he spat in the ground by one staring Galasman corpse. 'The *loyal* watchmen...' he said with a bitter growl, then saw in the dead man's hand a small wooden pig. A child's toy. The dying fellow's last thought had been of his little ones. A great sadness swept across him.

Then he looked at the rag of cloth Pitagga had given him, and nothing else mattered.

Amongst the bloodied living, he saw Tanku with the rest of the Mountain Wolves. They were stained red with smoke, dust and blood, and the hundred were now only sixty or so. Big Tanku seemed to be holding back tears as he held up a clenched fist and let loose a forlorn wolf howl. As Hattu and Dagon walked amongst them, many hands clasped their shoulders and shook them warmly.

But still Hattu saw only the rag in his hand.

Stumbling on through the masses of the Fury ranks, he felt many eyes upon him. Something was different. Their hard looks had changed, softened. And then he heard the whispers from the Ravens to the Fury men. 'He saved us, saved us all. It was he who led the climb to send up the signal, to take the fort. Is this truly the Cursed Son?'

But a Raven corrected this one. 'Did you not hear him before battle? Did you not see him fight? He called upon Ishtar and she heard his call. He is no Cursed Son... he is the Son of *Ishtar*.'

The title was innocently voiced, but of all appellations, this was the darkest they could have chosen. Yet still there was only the rag in his hand.

'Son of Ishtar!' many others echoed, laughing, panting, oblivious to his thoughts.

An hour or more passed, with Hattu sitting, head between his knees, the frantic events of the day shooting before his eyes, the rag clutched in his fingers.

By mid-afternoon, the Blaze and the Storm had arrived, Volca and the Mesedi leading the royal wagon up the stained hill and into Baka fort – the fires doused now but the bastion blackened and still smoking. Hattu followed, almost in a trance. Up there he saw the generals of the day were inside. Kurunta and Nuwanza, lashed with dirt, sweat and blood. Volca, unsullied.

A noise behind him caught him unawares: a weak moan. He twisted to see the now-lowered timber crossbar and the gruesome pennant of poor Ruba's body – almost forgotten in the mayhem of the battle – still twitching, his lips still quivering as if trying to talk. A pair of royal healers were crouched by the old teacher, but their sagging shoulders and sad faces said it all. 'There is nothing we can do to save him,' the nearest said. 'He is in great pain.'

Hattu's throat thickened fiercely as he knelt by the old fellow's side, clasping his hand – the fingers already cold.

Kurunta knelt with him, clutching a short dagger. 'Old Goose,' the general said, his voice hoarse. A short, sharp nick across Ruba's neck and his torment was over. Silence reined. A warm, late afternoon breeze lifted Kurunta's silvery braid of hair, and Hattu was sure he saw a single, crystal-like teardrop fall from the grizzled general's bowed head and blot the dirt.

Farewell, old tutor, Hattu mouthed, tears openly streaking his dirt-stained cheeks. Arrow settled lightly on his shoulder, emitting one long, elegiac cry.

The sombre moment ended with an eruption of scuffling and shouting. From behind the armoury in one corner of the fort, two Hittite soldiers dragged the thrashing Darizu from some rat hole he had been hiding in. The Galasman was kicked to his knees before King Mursili's wagon. A weak, white hand peeled the veil back and Mursili looked out, his lopsided face like a wraith's.

Darizu's pig-eyes widened and his features paled. 'The Kaskans arrived here first and they came in great number,' he stammered, the words falling over one another. 'They said they would burn our families alive unless we sided with them. Those who resisted their demands fought fiercely but were overcome, then Pitagga burnt them in high, awful pyres made purely of bodies – fires that only this morning breathed their last.'

Hattu thought of the smoke pall that had drawn them here and let his eyes close to rid himself of the image. But in its place he saw the strip of cloth and all it meant. *It cannot be true...*

'They threatened to gut me and let hawks pick at my innards if I didn't deceive you from the fort walls. What were we to do?' he pleaded. His thick, silver necklace – a Kaskan piece – jangled with his every gesticulation, undermining his every word.

'You could have stayed loyal to... your *Labarna*,' Mursili said flatly, 'donned the armour and spears... I had sent for your... fighting men and stood alongside the few who resisted. Together, the Galasmans might well have fended off the Kaskan advance until we arrived. You had that choice, Darizu, but you chose instead to betray me... and to betray your ancestors.'

Darizu's head turned, eyes searching the merciless faces. There was a moment where his pig eyes widened with some inner realisation. 'Spare me, My Sun,' he said, turning back to the king, 'and I can tell you everything... '

A shiver shot up Hattu's back. Darizu had known the king was coming. How?

Mursili sat up too, quivering and pale within the carriage.

Darizu nodded hurriedly. 'Everyth-'

Suddenly, three points burst from the man's breast with a shower of dark blood, his head shooting back and his face contorting like that of a stunned fish. Volca placed one foot on the Galasman leader's shoulder and wrenched his trident free, kicking the corpse onto its face.

'Have you lost your mind?' Kurunta said, rising from beside Ruba's body. 'A dead traitor won't tell us much, will he?'

'His voice was boring me,' the Sherden said with a smirk. 'And he was armed,' he added, pulling a small skinning knife from Darizu's belt.

Hattu gazed at the dead traitor, pink froth bubbling from the three grim holes in his back, at Ruba, his oldest mentor, at the scores of bodies lying riven, mangled and mutilated all around the fort, at the swarms of flies and buzzing and birds picking at the cadavers. And the rag in his hand felt like an ingot of lead.

'And what of Pitagga?' King Mursili croaked.

'Pitagga lives,' Hattu said flatly. He felt his father's scornful eyes on him.

'Then we cannot return home,' the king tremored, the effort clearly sapping what little strength he had. 'We may have foiled Pitagga's trap today, but the Lord of the Mountains has succeeded in destroying our generations-old alliance with Galasma. This frontier is broken. We must continue to the Lost North. We must hunt Pitagga down.'

'My Sun,' Nuwanza, standing by the carriage, protested in a whisper that was inadvertently loud, 'the north is unknown, treacherous. Those mountains…'

Volca sidled over to the carriage, much to Nuwanza's annoyance, addressing the king but speaking loud enough for all to hear. 'On the Isle of the Sherden, we used to suffer bandits. Swift and spry, they would fall upon our trade wagons like wildcats then melt back into the rugged slopes of the Fire Mountain. Gone,' he flashed the fingers of both hands before him, 'like shadows. One of my greatest mistakes was in thinking that by driving them back, we had beaten them. Because they, like these mountain men, always come back stronger, like weeds. Heed your king. Outright victory is the only kind we should seek.'

'We will regroup and tend to our wounded,' Mursili wheezed, 'then we *will* cross the mountains... we will find Pitagga.' He shook a weak left fist. 'Into the Lost North.'

A muted cheer met this proclamation, amplified by a short, whistling breeze.

Hattu swung to the north, to the Carrion Gorge and its rising path through the Soaring Mountains. The notion of marching there seemed like nothing... the rag was everything. He eyed the strip of cloth once more, then heard approaching footsteps.

He looked up to see his brother. Muwa's face was like a quarry, his frown lines like deep cuts, his gaze stonier than any of the whisperers' had ever been.

'Brother, you are hurt,' Hattu said, seeing a thin red slash on his face from the edge of an axe.

'The wound is a decoration, nothing more,' Muwa snapped.

'You and the Fury saved us,' Hattu said.

'We did. Yet the men speak of you as the champion of the day,' Muwa muttered darkly, his tone a war of jealousy and grudging respect.

'There was no victory today, Brother,' Hattu said softly, handing Muwa the piece of cloth.

'What is this?' Muwa scowled.

'It is a strip torn from a priestess' robe,' Hattu replied, his throat thickening. 'Pitagga had it. Pitagga... has *her*.'

'What?' Muwa gasped, his face crumpling.

'They must have ambushed the wagons of the templefolk on the way to Tapikka. The divine statue. The Eagle Kin. The priestesses... *Atiya...* '

Muwa took a step back from Hattu. 'I put her wellbeing in your hands, Hattu,' he croaked.

Hattu felt a fire creep across his skin. All around him, he heard whispers and then laments as the men of the army realised what had happened. The silver effigy of Tarhunda, the holiest of holies, had fallen into Kaskan hands. Their beloved priestesses had been carried off too. 'Tarhunda, forgive us,' one soldier cried out, falling to his knees.

'I trusted you to choose an able escort,' Muwa continued.

'I did,' Hattu insisted. 'The Eagle Kin are a strong company and-'

'*Were* a strong company,' Muwa interrupted.

'*And* I raised horse scouts from Father's stable too,' Hattu snarled, anger rising in his breast. 'What more could I have done?'

'You should have chosen a second company, you should have sent them on the high road – shorter and swifter,' Muwa snarled.

'Brother, I did as I thought right. A single company is the normal escort. And the high road? Are there not bandits on its stretches too?'

But Muwa's lips grew thin and his nostrils flared. He backed away from Hattu, shaking his head. 'You claim to love her, yet you let her fall into the hands of the vilest of creatures.' He took another step back, stabbing a finger at Hattu. 'This… is *your* doing.'

'Enough,' a frail voice called from nearby. Hattu and Muwa looked to the royal wagon, seeing the trembling king, eyes wide, face pale.

With a snort, Muwa turned his back and strode away. Hattu's heart rapped with dread, his mind screamed a thousand different words of justification and curses, and his eyes blazed with fury.

CHAPTER 15

INTO THE LOST NORTH
EARLY SUMMER 1300 BC

The army remained at Baka Fortress for eleven days, tending to the stricken, digging graves and building pyres. Old Ruba was cremated with Onyx by his side. Priests' incantations were unrelenting as the dead were consigned to the Dark Earth, and the weak and sometimes blood-curdling cries of the wounded grew gradually fewer as the mortally injured faded and the rest grew strong again. At the end of it all, one hundred and seven Hittite warriors had fallen in the fray – thirty nine of them from the Mountain Wolves. A tiny fraction of the army, but each of them grieved for like fallen brothers. They spent another day replenishing the baggage wagons with game caught in and berries foraged from the woods and water from the Green River. On the twelfth day, they left Hittite lands behind, setting forth into the Carrion Gorge, cutting deep into the Soaring Mountains – realm of the Kaskans.

The gorge was like the throat of a giant. Wide, spacious and carpeted in soft moss at first, then after the first day of marching it became tight, twisting and rocky underfoot. And despite the illusion of freshness lent by the snowy mountain peaks that loomed high above, these lower parts were uncomfortably hot, with the air in the gorge still and arid, the silvery sides of the corridor reflecting and multiplying the early summer heat. A vanguard of Nuwanza's champion archers moved like spiders along the high sides of the passageway in case Pitagga had merely moved his gorge snare a few danna further northwards. They went barefoot, scuttling along in just kilts, scouting the caves, niches and ambush points along those heights and signalling back to the column.

Hattu and the Wolves marched in their place within the chain of the three great divisions, but there was less chatter than there had been in the march through Hittite lands. He felt acutely aware of the shrunken pack around him. Thirty nine young men – mere boys just a summer ago, boys who had trained with him in the red fells, who had resented him once, but had grown to love him as one of their own – were gone. Looking across the soldiers on this front rank with him, he saw Tanku and Dagon... but no Garin. Just as Hattu had beaten Kurunta's challenges and become accepted in the ranks, so too Garin had shed his extra weight, turning from a chubby recruit into a lean, confident warrior. He remembered Garin's tales about his beloved mother and pet cats, and felt the urge to weep for her, alone in Hattusa, unaware of her son's death. He noticed Kurunta, just ahead. The one-eyed general seemed to be marching with invisible weights tied to his shoulders, his head uncharacteristically down. Ruba's death and the fallen at Baka had hit him hard, it seemed. It stoked in Hattu something he never thought he would feel for Kurunta: pity. Pity and a memory, of something from that cold winter he had spent at the Fields of Bronze: a chorus he had heard Kurunta singing alone in the barracks.

'Tarhunda weeps and the rain pours,' he began nervously.

A few paces ahead, he saw Kurunta's ears prick up.

'His lightning blinds, his thunder roars,' he continued, a few others joined in.

'Our fallen sing his ageless song,' more were roused to sing along. The gorge trembled such was the strength of the baritone doggerel.

'And in our hearts they're never gone...' Kurunta sang louder than any other, his head twisting to look back, his lone eye narrowing to a crescent as it settled upon Hattu.

Two more days passed, with the Hittite column making slow progress through the gorge. Tanku muttered an oath as he slipped and nearly turned an ankle on a loose rock for the third time that day. Hattu looked over his shoulder across the ranks of the Storm. Back there he saw the mules and ox wagons labouring over this torturous ground. The army could only move as fast as this vital sumpter train.

Dagon pulled the collar of his linen vest to try to usher in a breath of air. His face was streaked with sweat and his thin hair was matted to the sides of his face. 'Too damned hot,' he panted. Hattu tried to reply, but his throat was coated in dust and it came out as a cough. He envied Arrow, gliding in a breeze near the front of the column as an aerial vanguard of sorts. There was some commotion in the front ranks of the Fury when she evacuated her bowels over one hulking, red-faced soldier.

The drowsy, hot march seemed to lose its sense of danger until a sudden, urgent call from up ahead echoed sharply from the gorge sides. 'Halt!'

Angry curses split the air as nervous soldiers, surprised by the sudden stop, marched into the back of the men ahead. They quickly righted themselves, each division bringing their spears level, ready to react. But after a short silence, the order was given to continue. Hattu saw the cause of concern as the Storm Division marched past a stretch of flat ground where the gorge swelled: a large Kaskan 'settlement' – or at least one of the seasonal camps they built in and around these mountains. It consisted of several hundred timber shacks and domes of mud and twigs – each a home for a dozen or so. These mud huts were dried out and broken, shards of the domes having fallen in like holes in smashed skulls, and the many black stains of campfires dotting the ground had grass growing through them – a sure sign the place had been abandoned some time ago.

'My father used to talk of these mountains as the home of the Kaskans,' Dagon said, eyeing the deserted settlement, 'and I always imagined the peaks to be crawling with them – like ants on a nest.' He shrugged. 'Where are they?'

'Retreating,' Tanku said confidently, eyeing the north. 'Ten thousand strong, I heard. They don't have the numbers to beat us.'

'Drawing us further from familiar ground,' Hattu said, his face stony. 'Where our greater numbers might mean little. Where many more tribes of uncertain fealty roam.'

They passed three more Kaskan settlements – broken, derelict shells like the first one – during the following day. The heat continued to rob the marching men of their vigour. But things slowly changed as the path rose with the surrounding mountains – the route becoming more of a high pass than a gorge, studded with dark green conifer thickets and alive with the chirping of sparrowhawks. When they rose into the smaller peaks, the air became decidedly fresh. Some men even took to pulling their woollen cloaks from their bags and throwing them over their shoulders. The cool, dry winds up here moaned through the crags and caused men's lips to crack and throats to grow hoarse. They climbed into the upper peaks and were soon so high that goats in the gullies below resembled tiny insects. They even marched over patches of rock that were veined with frost, so cold it was – with one nearby peak clad in snow, a white streak of ice crystals being whipped from its summit by the winds. Vultures and eagles cried out overhead, and Arrow got caught up in a tussle with one angry raptor.

They marched until twilight obscured the precarious path and they could go forwards no more. Strewn along the high pass, they camped that night in the chilly heights, wind moaning around them and causing their bivouac tents to rap fiercely. Hattu helped Tanku, Dagon and a clutch of the Wolves to set up their tents, then threw himself down on the rocky ground in Kurunta-esque fashion, sure that a deep, exhausted and dreamless sleep was soon to follow.

***

Muwa sat by the royal carriage, hearing from within his Father's weak breaths, each digging into him like a spade. The chill wind rocked the wagon with every gust, and the shutters and curtains – supposedly sealing the carriage's interior off from the elements – rattled and creaked.

'The *Labarna* should not be up here,' Muwa said. 'The mountain air is for the young and the strong.'

Across the small fire, Nuwanza washed the last bite of his bread down with a mouthful of water, his three tight tails of hair billowing in the latest gust of cold wind. 'There is a fire in his eyes yet, Tuhkanti.'

A scuff of boots brought both men's heads round to the figure approaching the carriage. A horned helm, a billowing red cloak, a fierce trident.

'Watch out, arsehole approaching,' Nuwanza muttered under his breath.

'The *Labarna* is asleep?' Volca asked, halting by the small fire, his pale features and copper accoutrements ablaze in the reflected light.

'Aye, it would seem so,' Muwa replied absently.

Volca nodded a few times as if in some inner dialogue. 'The men have not seen their king on his feet once during this march. It is not ideal for morale.'

'If he is ill, he is ill,' Muwa snapped. 'Why fret over that which we cannot change?'

'True, true,' Volca replied. 'In any case, I've been talking with the men of the ranks. It seems they have a new hero of sorts – one whose presence is partly making up for the king's continued malaise.'

Muwa's ears pricked up.

'Your young brother,' Volca beamed, crouching to warm his hands by the flames, 'they talk in fulsome tones about Hattu. They laud him as they do you, *Tuhkanti*,' He squared his shoulders and rested his trident butt on the ground, staring off into the night with a mock-heroic gaze. 'Son... of Ishtar! That's what they call him.'

Muwa felt the words sting his skin like a nettle. 'The men are fickle. Let them praise who they wish, as long as they are loyal to the *Labarna*,' he said, annoyed that his tone sounded terser than he had intended.

'Hmm, the way some speak, it's as if they'd rather see the 'Son of Ishtar' as their *Labarna*. Ha! Can you imagine?' Volca's shoulders rocked with laughter. 'But then again, like you he has all the attributes...'

Muwa shot to his feet and swept by the Gal Mesedi. 'I'll check on the sentries.'

***

'Was it something I said?' Volca asked, wide eyed.

Nuwanza stoked at the embers of the fire with a twig, his eyes narrow and his lips thin. 'Every word to the *Labarna* or his issue should be measured and worthy. Keep idle chatter for the arzana houses.'

'You've never liked me, have you, Bowman?' Volca chuckled.

'I don't make friends easily,' Nuwanza shrugged. 'My trust is hard won.'

Volca stood, stretching. 'Aye, perhaps. You are the king's longest-serving general, are you not? I can see why he values you so.' His playful expression faded and he bowed from the neck. 'I have some way to go to even deserve a place in your shadow.'

Nuwanza's eyes narrowed further.

'I will do all I can to prove myself. That's what I came to tell you: I cannot sleep, so I'm taking a few scout riders out to look around while it's dark – up onto the mountain spine. Perhaps we'll be able to spot the Kaskan camp beyond? Their night fires will be like beacons.'

Nuwanza looked up, his high forehead wrinkling. 'Night scouts? I think the *Tuhkanti* should be the one to sanction the idea.'

Volca sighed and looked off into the night in the direction Muwa had gone. 'The *Tuhkanti* is in no mood for conversation, it would seem. I will be back not long after daybreak.'

***

King Mursili heard taunting voices in his fitful sleep, his sons exchange of fiery words at Baka Fortress echoing over and over. He saw a ring of bulls standing in a circle, pushing his two boys towards one another. Hattu and Muwa fought back at first, batting the animals on the nose with the flats of their swords. But try as they might they could not break free of the pen of beasts. Suddenly, Muwa asked for help from Hattu, but Hattu snapped at him in reply – too busy trying to batter back one of the bulls to come to Muwa's aid. Muwa snarled some curse in response. They fought the bulls valiantly, and slew them. But a moment later the pair swung to face one another, their heated words exploding into shouts.

Beyond the ring of bulls, he saw a tall, curvaceous, winged woman watching on from a veil of shadow. In her palm, she held a silver chair. Blood dripped down its back and the armrests. 'And so it begins,' Ishtar whispered.

King Mursili sat up with a start, his right arm propping up his useless left side. Despite the perishing mountain wind that searched and shook the carriage, his skin was drenched with cold sweat and his grey locks were plastered to his face and neck. The noise of trotting hooves sounded, fading into the north. He pulled the curtain and shutter there open. Fading into the darkness of night, he saw three scouts riding off along the pass, up and over the mountain spine, into the Lost North. Confused, he fell back, panting, groaning.

***

Despite aching shoulders, burning calves and throbbing feet, Hattu found sleep hard to come by. His body longed for rest but his mind sought answers. *Atiya, where are you?* Silence, bar the bivouac cloth flapping in the stiff wind. He opened one eye. The five other Wolves under the shelter with him were sound asleep, using their woollen cloaks as blankets, comically hugging one another like nested bowls for extra warmth.

Hattu rose, drawing his cloak around his shoulders, tossing his leather bag over one arm, thinking a light snack might help him feel drowsy. As he walked to the edge of the irregular camp, the pale light of a low moon portrayed the Soaring Mountains like a frozen sea of sharp, white crests and grey, plunging troughs. Clouds scudded across the moon from time to time, their shadows creeping across the mountains. 'Arma, God of the Moon, watch over us... watch over Atiya,' he muttered, placing a hand over his heart.

'The Gods are cruel,' a voice said, a few paces away from him. Unnoticed, Kurunta had settled down on a rock nearby. Dressed inexplicably in just the same leather kilt and crossed-leather chest bands that he had been wearing in the boiling lower stretches of the gorge, the bald general was peeling a strip from a piece of goat-meat, munching and dragging stringy parts from his teeth, good eye fixed on the moon. 'So how does it feel? This is always what you wished for, is it not?' he flicked his head back over the camp. 'To be a soldier?'

Hattu felt the chill stiffen around him. He looked back across the mountain camp and saw the bronze ring of Mesedi guardsmen around the king's wagon. 'He wanted you to break me, didn't he?'

Silence.

'That's my job,' Kurunta said in a low, expressionless voice.

'And I realise that now. I don't begrudge you for any of it.' Hattu flexed one arm straight out before him, seeing the ribbons of shadow and moonlight that marked out his hard-won muscles. 'I longed to be a soldier because that is what my father was... is. Before my time at the Fields of Bronze I spent long summers left back in Hattusa, dreaming of making him proud, of being a shield for him as Muwa is. To stand alongside the Great King Mursili – that was the dream. And now I have passed through the military academy and find myself here on campaign, yet he is barely able to speak. When he does, his words to me are still curt, frosted. He will never truly trust me, will he? Even as he gave me the cup of wine at the victory ceremony after the Chariot Ordeal, or when he consigned me to march with the ranks, I could see it in his eyes. He fears me still.'

'He fears the Gods,' Kurunta corrected him, 'and what they show him.'

'You believe Ishtar's song?' Hattu asked.

Kurunta shuffled awkwardly. 'The king was a different man from that moment onwards.'

'Do you believe it?' Hattu repeated.

'I don't want to,' Kurunta replied, shooting a nervous look at the sky as if worried that the Moon God might hear and tell his kin.

Hattu sighed, looking over towards the royal wagon. 'What does it matter? Now I fear it is my father who is broken.'

Kurunta's pitted features creased a little. 'When I was a young soldier – a mere spear-stand, like you,' he said, deadpan, 'I fought in the Mitannian wars – out in the hot east.'

'I know where Mitanni was,' Hattu said.

'Aye, of course you do. Old Ruba may be gone, but his wisdom is not,' Kurunta's face bent into something akin to a sad smile. 'Once a great power in the world, the people of Mitanni made the mistake of plotting against the Hittite Empire. Now, they are no more than a fable.'

He looked up at the stars, his silver braid coiled across his neck like a scarf. 'Out there, I served under a beast of a general. Lurma was his name. Imagine you could catch a lion's roar and mould it into a man… *that* was Lurma. His mind was keen as a blade: when his fellow generals were planning for the day after tomorrow, he was already setting in place his designs for the next moon. He marched with us, broke bread with us, took his share of marching burden and endured our every hardship. I would have died for him, gladly.' He patted the crossed sword belts on his chest. 'Yet it was not to be. He is gone and I wear his war-garb in witness to his legend.'

'What happened to him?' Hattu asked.

'He routed the Mitannian chariot elite with half their number of vehicles and only a small party of infantry. Won us the battle and the war. On the way home, he went to his stallions who had served him so well the previous day, to feed and water them. One of them had taken a cut to the eye and it was agitated, nervous. I saw how it nickered and snorted, but the more he tried to calm it, the more anxious the stallion became. It reared up and thrashed its forelegs in the air.' Kurunta paused to spit into the dust. 'A hoof caught Lurma on the temple. He was fine, or so it seemed – he waved away his closest comrades who rushed to aid him. Later that night he fell asleep by the fireside before he had even eaten. Most thought he was merely tired after the exertions of the war. But the next day, men noticed how distant he seemed. He became weak – easy to tire and shambling in his gait. I was sure then that he was a spent force. But I noticed something: every day he took to drawing out in the dirt the routes and the supply strategies for the division. Wily and careful in every aspect. While the horse's hoof had robbed him of his strength, his mind was as sharp as ever. The fire still burned brightly within,' he said, tapping his temple. 'The healers insisted Lurma could not ride or march any longer. Yet we soldiers did as soldiers do: we formed a shell around him, refused to heed the advice of the healers and others. It was for the good of the division and the good of Lurma. Every day we carried him from his bed and helped him onto his chariot, strapping his weakened legs to a frame within that allowed him to stand, to ride and to see the battlefields – to direct us with his expert eye. We were the division's legs and arms, he was its mind. We won another six clashes like that, and Lurma embraced us all like brothers after each, weeping, thanking us for our support. After a few years, the king of the time – your grandfather – forced Lurma to retire to his estate, thinking the offer of a life of comfort would be a gift.' Kurunta shook his head slowly. 'He died within a few days. The crack to his skull damaged him, but it was the loss of his most trusted comrades that killed him.' The general looked Hattu hard in the eye. 'The king needs strong men around him now. Nuwanza, Colta and I will do what we can, but it is you and Muwa that matter so much to him. You and your brother are the only things that can keep the fire burning within him. He... he heard your crossed words at Baka Hill.'

'It was because of Atiya,' Hattu said.

'The young priestess on the Tapikka pilgrimage?'

'Aye. Now she is in Pitagga's hands,' Hattu threw a cold look northwards, 'somewhere, out there. She means a lot to both of us and... it was a misunderstanding,' Hattu insisted, but the anger still stung at his breast even as the words came out. *A misunderstanding on Muwa's part!*

'Aye, I truly hope so,' Kurunta said, rising. 'You and Muwa will make strong leaders one day, when...' he left the rest of the sentence unsaid, looking away awkwardly. 'And I... I have grown to tolerate you both,' now he really was struggling, 'and your bothersome ways,' he added with a cough. 'Now don't stay out here too long. Turn in, get some rest.' He flicked his head in the rough direction of the Mountain Wolves. 'You and your men will need to be sharp, fresh.'

'Tanku's men,' Hattu corrected him.

Kurunta made a short grunting noise and arched one eyebrow, then rose and left.

As Kurunta stalked away, Hattu noticed another figure standing some way away dressed all in black, one foot mounted on a boulder, watching him, *staring*. Muwa. His thick mane of hair danced in the mountain wind, the moonlight setting his bright eyes aflame. A moment later he turned away and was gone.

***

Atiya saw blackness and tasted a coppery bile in the back of her throat. The gloom of the rough sack they had pulled over her head seemed to have lasted for an eternity. Voices moaned and mumbled as if speaking in another room. Strange words, yet familiar all the same. Kaskan, she realised with a shiver of horror. Her mind's eye flooded with images of the severed heads on spears the day they had raided Hattusa. Rough hands carried her here and there, through cold and warmth, through winds and calm, day after day. She smelt clean, high air, then the rich aroma of damp earth and then the stink of horses and pigs. The sack was torn off and she was dumped, exhausted, onto her side on a bed of sorts. It was here that she lay still for some time, barely conscious and unable to open her eyes. She felt a healer's hands upon her, but there was something missing from the healer's touch: it was cold, methodical. Whoever it was pressed chill swabs against the back of her head roughly, carelessly. After one session of prodding and dabbing, Atiya fell asleep. When the blackness receded and she woke again, her head ached as if it had been struck by a hammer. Voices, angry and loud, pealed nearby, though she could not understand the mountain men's native tongue. Then another voice spoke, and at once she understood.

'You risked much by seizing the silver god,' a voice said in the Hittite tongue, 'too much. Had word of this reached King Mursili sooner than it did, he might have ordered his divisions to turn away from the mountains and towards Tapikka to intercept your bandits.'

Atiya's head swam: *that voice...*

'Nonsense,' another voice said in Hittite but with a Kaskan twang. 'Mursili is obsessed with tracking me. In any case, my man infiltrated Hattusa, planned the ambush well and brought me the prize I asked for. We always needed silver to fund this war. It was an unexpected prize to steal their holy women too – all the more bait to draw the Hittites through the mountains to these parts. And are the divisions of the Grey Throne not right now marching to this land?'

'They are right now halted at the spine of the mountains, awaiting my word,' the hauntingly familiar voice corrected the other speaker.

She began to prize open an eye, seeing the interior of what looked like a dome of dried mud and twigs – like an oversized bird nest turned on its head. The light from a pig-fat lamp nearly blinded her, but after a few moments her eyes adapted and she could see the gloomy home she was in. She was lying on her side upon a bed of bracken and ferns. The lamp sat on a low, crude table on the dirt floor. Nothing else? Then she rolled onto her back and saw, at the foot of the bed, an arc of dim pre-dawn light; a doorway. A cane grating covered the doorway like a cage, but beyond, she could see the edge of a colourful forest and a few other such mud-dome huts dotted around. She blinked and rubbed her eyes, seeing the wagon with the silver statue of Tarhunda resting there, uncovered, shamed, bedecked with Kaskan trinkets and painted in their gaudy dyes. Her heart wept at the sight. Bearded, tousle-haired Kaskan men sat around dung-fires, naked to the waist, tearing at joints of roasting meat like wolves as blue smoke billowed from the burning manure. Kaskan women, bare-breasted, danced around the men and the stolen wagons to the buzzing tune of a flute, drunk, faces painted in streaks of red. And then she saw him: the handsome amber-haired fellow, bare-chested like the other men, his chin now sprouting with the beginnings of a shaggy beard. He tore at meat with the rest, some slapping his back and offering him congratulatory beer.

'Fine work, Bagrat,' one barked gruffly.

Shame crept over her as she realised it had been her fault. She had talked loosely with the man, told him of the high road and the low road. Her wretched thoughts were scattered when two figures stepped over the cane grating like jailers. The two she had heard talking. Pitagga, crowned with a lion's skull, eyed her like a lecherous drunk, a greasy, half-chewed pork steak in one hand, his red beard stained with pig fat. The one with him, however, beheld her like a treasure.

'Volca?' she croaked.

He peered through her as if she wasn't there.

'The silver effigy will buy us many mercenaries,' Pitagga enthused, looking over to the wagon and the statue of Tarhunda. 'Already, more tribes of different blood come to my side simply because they have heard that the great Storm God of Hattusa lies in my camp. And I have sent word again to the distant Azzi, telling them that I can pay them what they seek.'

Volca looked around with a doubtful eye. 'Talk of great numbers is all very well. But all I see here are your twelve Kaskan tribes. Ten thousand, I told the *Labarna*, yet you probably only have eight thousand here.'

Pitagga threw his head back and laughed. 'I will tell you all... in good time.'

Volca's nose wrinkled in disapproval at this. 'Be sure that you do, and remember how important I am to your ambitions.'

'No one man will make or break me,' Pitagga said stonily with an ill-fitting smile.

'Don't be so sure,' Volca said, returning his cold gaze to Atiya, 'for I may well have found the key. The Azzi and the many tribes will be crucial, and the statue is a fine prize... but this priestess is the most valuable of them all,' he said in little more than a whisper.

'Volca?' she whimpered, backing up against the back wall of the hut, drawing her knees up to her chest. She saw two Hittite Eagle Kin being carried on poles across the clearing behind Volca and Pitagga, trussed by their arms and legs like animals, their necks opened and their lifeless faces sheeted with dried blood.

'*She* will bring you what you wish, Lord Pitagga,' Volca continued as if Atiya had not spoken. 'If my potions do not suck the life from King Mursili, if the snares you have laid out in these lands do not crush his army, then this priestess will break them from within... the two princes – the king's last hopes – yearn for her... and grow resentful of one another.'

'What have you done?' she croaked.

They ignored her, Volca turning to the fires then looking out over the surrounding forest. 'But first, the snares. Be sure to stock your fires high and let them burn brightly at full light. If all goes to plan, then come the next dawn this clearing will be heaped high with Hittite dead... '

CHAPTER 16

THE DARK WOODS OF HATENZUWA
EARLY SUMMER 1300 BC

Morning came and the Soaring Mountains, cadaver-grey in the twilight of the night before, now shone like coral. The Hittite army struck camp and climbed the last stretch towards the spine of the range – the highest point of the pass. By noon, they came to the jagged ridge, bare apart from an ancient stone stela erected by some long-forgotten king, all framed by the pure blue sky. The chill zephyrs whistled and sang. The Fury Division at the head of the column crested then poured over the ridge first. Next came the Storm.

Hattu crested the ridge and drank in the sight of the land below and beyond: the mountains descended into a low land, emerald and gold, with rounded hills and river valleys, teeming woods and squat cliffs draped in lush greenery.

'The Lost North?' Dagon cooed as they at last began their descent.

'Aye,' one grey-haired veteran of the Storm nearby whispered in reply, then pointed to the tract of dense forests hugging the foot of the mountains. 'And first we must make our way through Hatenzuwa.'

'A dark maze of woods and necromancers,' a comrade replied.

Kurunta's head switched round at this, his lone eye wide. 'Hatenzuwa… a land that was once ours,' he corrected them. He held his spear out like an extension of his arm, swiping it across the northern horizon. 'As all this once was. All the way to the Upper Sea. The Mother of the Rivers. The edge of the world.'

'And that?' Dagon asked, pointing to an odd rock formation in the distance, near a river, incongruous with the surroundings. Splinters of grey stone rising from the Hatenzuwa forest and largely coated in moss and vines, almost completely swallowed by the vegetation.

'That is… *was*, Hakmis,' Kurunta said wistfully.

Hakmis, Hattu mouthed.

Many of the soldiers gasped and repeated the name. They had only heard tales of the place. The nearest of the three fallen holy cities, lost many generations ago to the Kaskans who razed it and drove the Hittites from this strange land. Hattu struggled to tear his eyes from the sight as they marched on down the mountainside. He could not help but think of Ruba and the teacher's tales of these lost lands – stories of imagined adventures and the elusive glory of reclaiming them. 'Old tutor, you should have been here to see this with me,' he said quietly.

'He is, lad,' Kurunta said in an uncharacteristic whisper so no other would hear, 'he is.'

Hattu stretched a fraction taller. 'Wherever Pitagga is, we will find him. All this… all of it… can be ours again.'

Kurunta's lips bent a little in a wry smile. 'There was a boy I knew who once spoke like that – as if victory was a certainty.'

'What happened to him?'

'He lost an eye and realised he was mortal,' Kurunta grinned then jogged on ahead. 'For-waaard!'

The army crunched down the mountains, descending from the cold heights into warmer, humid air. They eventually halted on a broad, grassy spur that overlooked the forest. The generals drew together around the royal carriage, pointing this way and that. There was talk of the missing Gal Mesedi, and confusion about where he had gone the night before.

Hattu, Tanku and Dagon crouched around a small fire, chewing on flatbreads freshly-baked in the flames, eyeing the land ahead. The Hatenzuwan woodlands just below seemed impossibly dense and impenetrable. Hattu noticed his comrades' eyes combing over the roof of leaves nervously, gulping, dry tongues darting over dry lips.

'No army can move through such a maze,' Kisna whispered.

'We may have to. It'll be just like the forest drills we did at the Fields of Bronze,' Hattu said, belying his own doubts. 'We move carefully, stay in sight of one another, keep our eyes sharp.'

'Slowly, steadily,' Tanku replied, encouraged.

'But which direction do we take?' Dagon mused.

Hattu dragged his gaze over the jumbled roof of green. Dagon was right – no tracks, no tell-tale dust clouds from enemy boots or scatterings of disturbed birds. His eyes did snag on large break in the trees – a huge oval shaped clearing, about three danna in the distance. His grey eye ached and he saw the small, dark brown shape sweeping across the sky above the clearing. *Arrow!*

'There's something in there,' he said. Only when he became aware of the many heads nearby turning to him did he realise he had spoken.

'How so?' the slit-eyed Captain of the Leopard Clan grunted. Hattu recalled the fellow's efforts in dissecting the poor sparrow at the camp on the first night of the march. Now his demeanour was awkward, like milk and wine curdling: the old, fading mistrust mixing – ever since the events at Baka Hill – with a droplet or two of respect.

Hattu pointed to his falcon. 'Bird signs...' he said. *The kind I trust*, he added inwardly.

The men muttered, craning necks and shading eyes to see Arrow.

'How can you be sure?' one soldier grumbled.

Suddenly, a riot of breaking twigs and snapping branches sounded, form the foot of the spur, from within the trees. 'Archers!' Nuwanza rasped. A score of bowmen were on one knee, bows nocked and trained on the spot. Hattu's heart thundered.

Like a brawler being tossed out of a tavern, Volca emerged, panting, coughing, dishevelled. He scrambled up the steep path leading onto the spur, one foot bare, blood spattered on his horned helm and his cheek bearing a gash as crimson as his cloak – and he was sopping wet, streaked with marsh slime. 'They're in the woods,' he panted. 'In the northern clearing. We saw them, but the two riders with me were shot through with arrows before they could even turn to run.'

'By the Gods,' Slit-eyes whispered, staring at the clearing then glancing back at Hattu. The big man rose and joined the chatter with his comrades. Amongst their words he heard a few that sent a chill across his shoulders. *The Son of Ishtar saw it first.*

'Be quick and we can catch them – they assume we are still in the middle of the mountains,' Volca urged.

'Hold on. If they saw you and know you escaped then they will also know we will soon be coming for them,' Nuwanza argued.

Volca gestured to his bloodied robes. 'They shot me too – or they thought they did: the arrow skimmed by my arm and I fell from my horse and into a bog. I hid there in the reeds as they hunted for my body. I heard them laugh when they found my boot, and they seemed to think I had been sucked down into the morass. They gave me up for dead, taking my horse and wandering back towards the clearing. I waited in the mud hours, then ran back. No Kaskan knows I live. They think they are safe, their location unknown.'

The generals mutedly called their divisions into order, as if fearful that whoever or whatever lurked in that strange forest might hear. 'Can we be sure?' Hattu heard them muttering.

Just then, a series of wispy grey columns rose from the clearing, growing dark blue. The army babbled in interest.

'See?' Volca exclaimed. 'They cook and celebrate around dung fires, unawares that the mighty army of the Grey Throne watches on.'

Arrow swept across the top of the forest, arcing round to land on Hattu's shoulder, screeching in Volca's direction over and over. 'Is it true, girl?' he asked her. She was agitated, that much was certain, stamping her feet on his shoulder. Eventually, Muwa stood on a rock and announced that they were to enter the woods and converge upon the clearing in a bull horn formation. 'For the silver effigy, for the captured priestesses... for the Gods!' he growled. The army responded with a gruff chorus of agreement.

They set off, crunching down the scree path that led from the plateau to the edge of the Hatenzuwan woods. The scouts dismounted and went barefoot into the trees, spreading out like the fingers of a hand searching through thick hair. The three divisions spread from a thirty-man wide column into three fronts, five-hundred men wide, ten ranks deep, poised on the edge of the treeline. Whispered prayers to the Spirits of the Woods sailed up into the air, before they plunged forwards into the green maze in the direction of the clearing.

Hattu set Arrow off in flight, and stepped into the trees. At once, the air became muggier, hot, still as a tomb and tinged with the odour of musty foliage. They moved at a slow walk, most men half-crouched, spears twitching at every quivering branch or falling leaf. The woods were not so thick at first, with elm, lime, chestnut and beech spaced well enough to allow them to make decent headway across the bracken floor. It was not too dissimilar to the alder woods near Hattusa, Hattu thought. He took to glancing across the advancing men either side of him to be sure they were moving in line. The Wolves and the veterans wore owl-eyed expressions, faces beaded with sweat. From somewhere above the trees, Arrow did her bit by keening every so often as if to keep them in touch with reality. At one point, Hattu looked up and was overcome with fright as he saw a cluster of dark shapes up in the branches. For that heartbeat, he was certain it was a band of Kaskan warriors, poised and ready to leap down upon them. But in the next, he realised it was just a set of large, abandoned nests.

The deeper into the trees they penetrated, the thicker the woods grew, and the fewer the shafts of sunlight became. Strange bird calls trilled and sang from the shade. After what Hattu reckoned was a two danna trek, they entered a dark labyrinth of tall, sprawling rhododendrons. A sea of pink, purple and dark green, along with night-black shadows where the canopy of leaves blocked out the sun entirely, and pools of swirling grey vapour where the dampness and the stifling heat mixed – surely a lair of dark and vengeful forest spirits? And Hattu noticed how he couldn't even hear Arrow's calls any more. Myriad strange insects croaked and chirped as they ventured deeper. Wet bracken, leaves and twigs crackled and snapped as they walked, now no longer in tight formation – men spreading out to take the clearest route forward. Hattu looked either side of him, seeing Tanku and Dagon who had been right next to him for the whole march now ten paces distant. They slipped in and out of view thanks to the vapour – now thick and heavy like wet linen. Tanku cursed as time and again his green cloak caught on branches, and Dagon groaned as creepers snagged on his spear tip every few paces. Sweat traced a hundred paths down Hattu's skin in never-ending rivulets, so humid it was, and the faster he drank from his water skin, the more copious the sweat became. Before long, his water was gone and his head throbbed, demanding more. And it was only mid-afternoon, he reckoned. At one point, Tanku had strayed in front of him and Hattu saw shapes writhing on his shoulders. To his horror, he saw that it was a scurrying clutter of spiders – the white, wool-like traces of spider eggs still stuck to Tanku's cloak where he must have brushed against and ruptured them. Tanku hadn't noticed, so carefully, Hattu reached forward, lifting one hand and skilfully brushing the eight-legged denizens of the forest off with one stroke.

'Hattu?' Tanku said, jolting.

'You had a vine on your back,' Hattu lied.

On they went until the forest floor before them was freckled with livid crimson toadstools and stumps of bedrock coated in a silver lichen that seemed to glow from within. In the occasional spots where oaks had managed to sprout up amongst the horde of rhododendrons, they were draped in weightless, pale streamers of the same lichen, which wafted as they passed like an old woman's hair. Creepers and vines hung like nooses, sometimes so thickly Hattu had to part them like curtains or slice them with his spear to progress. Likewise he had to bend back clawing branches and scramble over knotted roots where trees had grown too close together. His skin itched with what felt like a hundred bites, cuts, grazes and scurrying insects. He heard the groan of a bending branch and then a thwack and Tanku, several paces away to one side, yelping, followed by a hushed – if not entirely genuine – apology from Dagon. They saw pale, waxy orbs dangling from branches and clinging to the wrinkles on tree trunks. Beehives, Hattu realised. The sight stirred some memory – something Ruba had told him, something he was infuriatingly unable to recollect.

On they went until at last they saw a golden glow ahead. *The clearing.*

'Slow,' Kurunta's voice hissed from somewhere in the arboreal gloom.

At once, each of them fell into a warrior's crouch, spear levelled. Hattu glanced left and right, seeing the maw of spear tips nearest him. He looked ahead, thinking of what lay in the clearing: Pitagga and his mountain men. His heart pounded fiercely and his mouth grew as dry as the ashes of a pyre as he recalled the clash on Baka Hill. Then he thought of the taken priestesses, of the great silver effigy of Tarhunda, of poor Sarpa's head, of Ruba, of Garin... of Atiya. He reaffirmed his grip on his spear and his fears backed down like an obedient dog.

'We are the Mountain Wolves,' Hattu growled in a low drawl.

'We will have vengeance for our fallen,' Sargis replied from nearby.

'With the Son of Ishtar and Tanku the giant, we are unshakable,' Dagon said, his voice quivering with pent-up ferment.

Their careful pace picked up from a slow stalk to a walk, to a quick walk. Then they broke into a jog and a run. The light grew stronger, brighter at last, the air cleaner, more plentiful – it was as if they were about to surface from a dark pool. Hattu filled his lungs, ready to cry out with the others as they poured towards the clearing.

The front ranks of the bullhorn of soldiers burst into glade, the air shaking with their cries.

Emptiness greeted them. No Kaskans. Nothing.

The war cries faded and they slowed, looking around the deserted space. Hattu squinted in the late afternoon sunshine and saw the abandoned dome huts, the spent dung-fires, now just embers. Recent prints of boots, wheels and hooves marked the flattened grass. A small brook ran across the space. Not a soul to be seen.

'They were here but they've left,' a scout said, kneeling by the remains of one fire.

No Atiya...

But there was a stake rising from the largest ash-pit. Tied to it were four bodies, lashed there by their wrists. They were merely shapes of men, black as pitch, their flesh and bone burnt through. Hattu scrambled forward, sliding to his knees, hands raking the ashes. In it he found a sliver of hide – a piece of a Hittite helm, blackened but etched with the wing of a bird. 'These are men of the Eagle Kin,' he said. He looked up, seeing Muwa emerging from the trees, eyes wide on the burnt corpses.

Hattu ran his fingers through the ashes again – still warm. He stood and looked at the direction of the prints in the earth, all leading into the northern treeline. He glanced up to the sky, seeing that the sun was dropping and dusk would soon be upon them. An interminable itch stabbed at him, a fiery desire to be on the move again. *Atiya: find Atiya!* He clambered up a moss-covered rock near the centre of the clearing and craned his neck, giving himself just enough height to see across the forest roof. The woods ran for another danna and then a green haze of open countryside followed. Such a short way. In his mind's eye he saw the Kaskans just beyond the woods, Atiya bound and helpless. A fire of pride and anger flooded his mind and he felt an urge to rush through the trees himself. If there was just a patch of a chance... a chance to stuff Muwa's unjust words of blame back down his throat.

'A good soldier chooses the right time to march and the right time to wait,' Kurunta muttered, just behind him. 'That will be the hardest danna we've ever trod: roots, vines, uneven ground – we'd still be fighting our way through it when darkness came.'

'Does that make it the wrong choice?' Hattu asked.

'I didn't say that,' Kurunta replied, rising up the rock to look across the forest roof himself.

'They might be just beyond?' he pressed. 'What if Pitagga lingers there with just a small guard, the priestesses and the stolen statue? This could be over within hours.'

Kurunta's lone eye seemed narrowed at the prospect, but he shook his head. 'It will be the *Tuhkanti's* choice,' he surmised, turning to the treeline where the royal wagon was emerging – covered in foliage, Muwa directing the driver with waving hands and shouts.

Soon, the three divisions entire had poured into the clearing, near-enough filling the space. They stood in their groups, awaiting orders. Muwa, Nuwanza, Volca, Colta and Kurunta gathered by the royal wagon. Hattu, standing with the Wolves, saw how Colta, Kurunta and Nuwanza weighed the virtues of staying and making camp here against moving on and trying to escape the last stretch of forest in the final hour or so of daylight. Volca, on the other hand, seemed certain that it would be folly to leave with darkness so close. Muwa seemed swayed by the

Sherden's convictions.

Hattu felt his mind and his heart swing one way then the other. His head said stay and his heart said go – still imagining himself ploughing headlong through the undergrowth, alone. He wandered from the Wolves, towards the generals.

'Perhaps we should do both,' he said.

The generals swung round at the unexpected interruption.

'Forgive me, for I know my voice holds no weight in such company, but I feel we could camp here, but also send a knot of men ahead, to sight and track the Kaskans… maybe even to take back the things of ours which they hold.' He looked at Muwa as he said this.

'You're right,' Muwa said, 'you have no place in this discussion.'

The words were like a stinging slap. His brother then turned his back, closing the circle of generals, his black cloak swishing out like a drawn veil.

'There is still an hour of light left,' Kurunta said to Muwa, firmly but respectfully. 'Maybe an advance party would be viable?'

'Like at Baka?' Muwa snapped. 'Disaster almost had us there, General. More than a hundred good men fell thanks to that calamity. And for what?'

'A bigger disaster would have been certain had the advance group not stumbled upon Pitagga's trap,' Kurunta countered. 'Thousands would now lie dead had the army entire wandered on into the Carrion Gorge unawares. The king himself. You, *Tuhkanti*. All of us.'

As Muwa stifled an angry reply, Volca looked to the skies, then across to the treeline. At last the Sherden shook his head, pointing to the branches of the nearest elm: a long-eared owl sat there, watching them pensively. 'A night bird watches us. It is an omen we should heed. It is night and thus we should make camp – all of us.'

'It is a day-hunter,' Hattu said.

Muwa swung to him again. The troops nearby were watching on now.

'His eyes are amber,' Hattu continued, hearing Ruba's voice from the classroom, 'like the sun. This means he hunts by day. Only black-eyed owls are night-predators. There is no omen here.'

Volca sneered dismissively.

Muwa's face twisted. 'Return to your ranks... *soldier*,' he spat.

'Perhaps there is merit in sending a troop of archers ahead, *Tuhkanti*,' Nuwanza now argued. 'They could move silently and with mud and dark garb so as not to be seen.'

Colta stroked his forked beard and added: 'We still don't know exactly how many warriors Pitagga has with him. Any knowledge would be a boost to our hopes.'

Muwa swung to the pair. Hattu could see the signs: the few times in years past when his brother's temper had exploded – all reason and wisdom cast aside. By now, most of the soldiers had heard the terse words of their leaders and had turned to watch.

'Camp here and send a troop forward as Prince Hattu suggests,' one group of Wrath soldiers muttered. 'The Son of Ishtar has been a good omen so far, has he not?'

'The *Tuhkanti* has chosen,' Volca cut in, stepping over to stand beside Muwa. 'Prepare camp. We remain here for the night,' Volca concluded. 'There will be no advance party.'

Muwa seemed to draw in a sharp breath, his dark and taut, eyes fixed on Hattu. Hattu imagined a hundred whispered, acid words travelling upon his brother's fiery gaze.

***

As the three divisions set about fortifying the clearing with a strong watch around the edge and a rough, circular palisade of spears, Volca sat on the driver's berth of the king's wagon, watching the men at work on the defences then settling down to cook their evening meals. Darkness seemed to descend swiftly and the rhododendron forest penning them in was now pure black, illuminated only by the occasional set of staring gemstone eyes of curious, watching animals. Then there was another set of eyes: different, narrowed... narrowed on him.

Slowly, ever so slowly, he gave the slightest of nods.

***

Hattu felt his eyelids grow heavy as he sat by the fire, watching the horses and mules cropping at grass, listening to Dagon's gentle, wistful song:

'The wind howls like a hound, yet none flinch at the sound,'
'As rain lashes the fields, in calm prayer we kneel,'
'When snow blankets the walls, our proud sentries stand tall,'
'Thunder rolls through the sky, yet the children don't cry,'
'For they were born in might-ty Hat-tusaaa...'

The song conjured an image in Hattu's mind: of him and Atiya standing on the acropolis walls, hugging each other for warmth, watching Arrow bank and dart through the sky. He pulled the tight leather string holding his hair in a tail, the locks falling around his face. He found the lock with the beryl stone on it, held it to his lips and kissed it. *Tomorrow, I will find you.*

He saw Muwa across the camp, sitting cross-legged, head bowed, chin resting on steepled fingers. *Tomorrow, Brother, I pray for her sake... and yours... that she has not come to any harm because of our delay here.*

Another spoonful of his half-eaten bowl of rabbit broth, another mouthful of watered wine, and Hattu felt drowsiness creep across his mind. He gazed out into the blackness of the forest. Darkness. Sleep... and, right at the perimeter by the Wolves' fire... eyes. *Human eyes?*

'What the?' he gasped, suddenly alert and shooting to his feet, sparks rising from the fire with him. The Wolves rose too, startled. Tanku's sword screeched as he drew it. Dagon hoisted a spear.

A figure emerged from the trees, hobbling.

'Slowly,' the nearest sentry demanded, keeping his spear tip trained on the newcomer.

It was an old woman, her back hunched and her hair hanging in tousled clumps like the lichen of the forest. 'My, never have I seen so many faces in one place,' she croaked – in the Hatenzuwan tongue – eyeing the fifteen thousand men in the clearing. 'Hittites,' she mused, noticing their garb and features.

'Who are you?' Muwa barked, striding over from the royal tent area to see what was happening, adding his sword point to Tanku's.

'A villager,' she snapped, now in the Hittite tongue, flicking her head back towards the north from whence she had come, her nose shrivelling, 'and you ought to show a little more respect, boy.'

Muwa seemed disarmed by her motherly rebuke.

'She is alone,' Hattu confirmed, eyes searching the darkness within the trees.

Muwa's top lip twitched. 'I can see that,' he growled, tucking his sword back into his belt. 'Why are you here?'

'I walk these woods, and I stop here every evening to fetch water,' the old woman pointed to the brook then the rickety old hand cart she was towing – an empty bucket sitting on it. Nuwanza, Colta and Kurunta had gathered now too, along with a crowd of soldiers.

Muwa eyed the woods once more then narrowed his eyes. 'And have you come across the Kaskan tribes tonight?'

She frowned. 'By the Gods, no. And may every day forth be the same.'

He waved a hand as if to clear a path for her to the brook. She hobbled forwards with a sigh, then stopped to sniff the air like a hound, curling her bottom lip in disappointment. 'If you tire of that grim broth you all seem to be cooking,' she said loud enough for many nearby units to hear, 'then you will find plenty of nourishment in these honeycombs.' She gestured to the handcart. Piled in there were pale yellow waxy shards – broken chunks of hives.

Kurunta blew air through his lips, impressed by the hag's impertinence. 'Don't mind if I do,' he said, reaching over and taking one of the shards, dipping his finger into the waxy lattice and sucking the thick, runny liquid from the tip. 'Lovely... and interesting,' he said. Soldiers from each division harvested chunks of the nectar too.

A voice nagged insistently in Hattu's mind, stirred by the sight of the honeycomb. What *was* it Ruba had told him?

But Volca appeared at that moment. 'We'll lighten your burden,' he grinned, tossing the old woman a small bag of copper rings. 'Let's spare most for the watchmen, eh? It will keep them alert. Pass it round,' he said, taking one entire disc of comb and passing it on to the nearest perimeter sentry, who gladly broke off a piece and passed it round to the next guardsman.

Hattu noticed the old woman's face had drooped. She looked up at him, one half of her mouth raised in a sad smile. 'I had best be on my way,' she muttered.

Hattu saw that the leather bucket in her cart was empty. 'But your water?'

'Ah,' she sighed. 'Yes…' She hobbled over to the brook and awkwardly crouched to try to fill the bucket. Hattu pitied the sight. He walked over, taking the bucket and bending to fill it for her.

'You are a kind young man,' she said. More words seemed to be stuck behind her lips, but she said nothing.

'Thank you for the honey,' Hattu said. 'It will invigorate us for tomorrow, when I will free my love from Kaskan hands.'

'Hmm,' she replied.

'You *have* seen them, haven't you?' he asked.

'You build fine houses in Hittite lands, I hear?' she mused.

Hattu frowned. 'There are fine palaces. Shacks and shanty houses too though.'

'Your love,' she said, 'if she was in a burning room and a family were in another. If the house was about to collapse and you could save only one, which would it be?'

'That is a cruel choice,' Hattu replied.

'Aye, it is,' she muttered.

And off she went. Hattu watched her melt back into the woods. Dagon shoved a triangle of waxy comb into his hand and patted his back. 'It is wondrous,' he mumbled through a mouthful of the stuff.

They sat around the fire once more and he sucked out a good helping of honey, smacking his lips in satisfaction and drawing some soldier bread from his bag to dip into the comb. It was sweet and energising. Kurunta sat near him, and for the first time, Hattu realised he was glad of the one-eyed leader's nearness. He gazed at Kurunta's eyepatch as he ate. The 'vengeful general' was a myth. Kurunta was a steadfast warrior, a pillar upon which the king stood. Why, he wondered, had Father taken his eye?

'You'll never work it out,' Kurunta said quietly without looking up from his shard of honeycomb.

'Sir?' Hattu said, startled.

'Many a story has been conjured about this,' he said, tapping a finger on his eyepatch. 'Aye, they whisper about me just as much as they whisper about you, lad.'

'Tell me,' Hattu said gently.

Kurunta sighed deeply and examined the ground before him, gazing through the earth as if it was a window to a past era. 'Some say I lost it in a brawl with the king's guards. One hurkeler spread the tale that I was caught in the king's chambers at night with a knife. Others claim the king himself pinned me down and scooped it out with a spoon, wrenching with his bare hands at the sinew and tendons that dangled from the socket until they snapped away too.'

Hattu stopped chewing on his sweetened bread, mildly disgusted but also wondering who else was listening. Nobody – the rest of the Wolves were busy chatting amongst themselves.

'I don't believe any of those tales,' Hattu said.

Kurunta flicked his head to one side as if uncomfortable with the intimate words. 'And I believe you are no Cursed Son.'

Hattu frowned, chewing his bread slowly now. He was sure the general would say no more.

'It happened many years ago,' Kurunta added after a silence, 'Two hundred and seventy one men patrol the Dark Earth because... because of me.'

Hattu felt a shiver across his back.

'It wasn't long after the Mitannian Wars had ended. I was a regimental chief then, posted to the dry flats of Nuhashi. The king had given the order for all patrols and garrisons to withdraw from the area, as we expected a strong uprising from the loyalist locals. But a sand-storm kicked up, you see. The king's word was *withdraw*, but I knew my men would suffer were we to march on in that stinging tempest, so I led them into a small, abandoned mud-fort. The fort was bleak but sheltered enough for us to at least draw breath and wait the storm out.'

Hattu shrugged. The logic was sound.

'Then come morning, the storm had faded... but the local tribes had gathered around the fort in their thousands. They had barred the gates from the outside. Expert bowmen in those lands,' he smiled without a crumb of humour. 'They shot us down like pigs in a pen. Every last one of us... except me.'

Hattu felt a stone settle in his belly at the bleak tale. 'So an arrow took your eye?'

Kurunta shook his head. 'Somehow I was unhurt. The locals left. I clambered from the fort, over the rampart of heaped corpses. I staggered back through the baked wastes until I reached Aleppo's walls where the king and his various forces had retreated to. I had disobeyed my superior's orders, the *king's* orders. The punishment is clear enough – blinding, as has always been the way.'

'My father did not hear your story?' Hattu asked, looking once to the royal wagon then back to Kurunta.

'Aye, he listened,' Kurunta nodded. 'And he spared me.' Then he turned to Hattu, his face bent in disgust. 'But is the cruellest punisher not the one within?' He tapped his temple. 'I could not live with the memory of their deaths, the reality that they had died while I did not. I needed to feel *something*, something other than guilt.'

A horrible sense of understanding settled on Hattu's shoulders. 'You asked for the eye to be taken... '

'I begged the king,' Kurunta said quietly. 'I begged him as others might beg to keep their lives. And when it was done I found that it helped... a little.'

They ate more in silence, sharing a skin of watered wine. Eventually, Hattu asked Kurunta of the better times in the Mitannian Wars and of simple things, like his life outside the army, with his wife and his beloved pigs in Hattusa. The general struggled to speak of these things, but Hattu could see he was eager to try.

After a while, he noticed the watered wine flooding to his head even more swiftly than before. His blood felt warm and he noticed that despite the air growing cool with the darkness of night, a layer of balmy sweat had spread across his skin. He held up his water skin and the small wine flask, both blurry and outlined by the moon and its silver halo.

'Gods, this wine is strong,' Kurunta remarked, shaking his head like a wet dog.

Dagon, nearby, turned to Hattu and Kurunta. 'Are you feeling it too? It's as if I've drunk the lot,' he said, blinking hard.

Giddiness seemed to take hold within moments, and he heard many of the other soldiers laughing, some uproariously. Tanku rocked on his haunches, hooting with laughter at some weak joke Sargis had aired. Then he fell onto his back as if hit by a stiff wind, looked dazed for a moment then exploded with more laughter. Then, suddenly, he seemed to fall prey to a sudden fright, clutching out at the ground around him, kicking, his face agog. 'Spiders,' he yelped, booting at a bare patch of dust, then sweeping nothing from his shoulders and swinging round, eyeing every patch of ground with terror. 'They're everywhere!'

Hattu realised the enjoyable warmth of the wine and honey had changed within him too. He felt his head begin to swim and saw the faces all around him blur and contort like melting wax. Even the trees seemed to writhe and sway in the still night air like spirits. The vapour from the forest seemed to crawl out from the shadows and pour around him, enshrouding him.

And now – *now* of all the cursed moments – he recalled Ruba's words:

A trader friend of mine used to go months on the road with few supplies. He would gather water from streams, shoot hare and geese, raid beehives for their nectar. One year he didn't stop by Hattusa as usual. Turns out he had eaten honey from a bad hive. Somewhere in the north – a bitch of a forest, he said...

Nausea swirled deep in Hattu's stomach, rising and boiling in his chest. Nearby, he heard the sounds of retching and spitting. The laughter had faded. He heard thick thuds of men crumpling to the ground and saw the sentries around the spear palisade sinking to their knees.

'It's poisonous,' he groaned weakly. The memory of the dead bees on the forest floor stung him. *Of course...* 'Stop!' he cried with all the air in his lungs, seeing his comrades still greedily eating. 'The honey is bad!' he yelled, batting the shards of comb from the hands of the nearest.

Around him, other men rose, tossing down the shards of comb before they had eaten too much, gawping at the state of their comrades.

He retched, spilling the contents of his belly onto the earth. When he lifted his head again he saw the writhing woods... this was no illusion – they *were* moving. He spun round... moving in every direction. Coming through the trees like a silent noose drawing tight. Men... a ring of armed men! Kaskans?

'It's a trap. A ploy!' He rasped.

'*Kaskans!*' Dagon yelled, seeing it now too.

The cry spilled from the lips of a few others then exploded in one almighty chorus.

A thunder of boots sounded all around him. Those who were able raced to cover the perimeter where the sentries had fallen. They coughed and spat, taking up their shields, swords and spears.

'More men... *more*,' Kurunta howled, swaying alone at an unguarded stretch of the perimeter. Hattu, Dagon and Sargis and a knot of fifteen other Wolves were fit to go to his aid. They clattered into place with him, forming a wall of shields behind the spear palisade. Hattu gazed into the blackness, seeing the fiery, eager eyes of the mountain men, coming to within a handful of paces of the clearing's edge. But the *boom-boom-boom* of Hittite shields and *clack-clack* of spears being levelled multiplied. Hattu shot a look over his shoulder. The perimeter was covered. Thinly, but covered all the same.

'Tarhunda... coat my... ' Kurunta gasped, struggling.

'Coat my heart in bronze!' Dagon and Hattu finished for him. Another chorus followed, rich, full, defiant. The cry fell away. The Kaskan noose slowed to a halt, deathly silent. It was a moment in which men considered their very lives, a battle of wills. Then, with a muted rumble of boots and gruff voices, the Kaskan watchers receded, the cruel eyes and sharp weapons melting back into the blackness.

Hattu stared at the spot they had been for what felt like an eternity.

'They're gone. The woods are clear,' cried Gorru the Mesedi from the far side of the perimeter.

'Clear this side too,' Orax replied a moment later.

'Damned hag! A moment later and we would have been like... '

Kurunta started, 'pigs in a pen.'

Hattu rested his spear on its haft, panting. His head ached, feeling as though he was wearing a red-hot and way-too-tight bronze helm.

Muwa staggered over, head switching this way and that, eyes alive with fear that the danger was still keen. 'Up, *up,*' he demanded of the prone, retching men. Nearly half of the army lay like this.

'We have the perimeter covered, *Tuhkanti,*' Kurunta reassured him.

Volca leapt down from the driver's berth of the royal wagon and strode over. Hattu noticed how he wore an odd look on his face – like that of a man denied the company of a woman. But as he approached, his face changed: handsome, bright and smiling. 'Give worship to the Gods,' he bawled so all could hear. Then he took one of Hattu's hands and raised it in the air. 'Give thanks to Prince Hattu – the brightest mind amongst us tonight – for raising the alarm before we fell prey to the Kaskans. Ishtar truly has blessed him with her gifts.'

Many heads had turned to the address now. Most rose clenched fists in support. 'Son of Ishtar!' they cried in a baritone chorus.

Muwa's maddened eyes darted all around at the men lauding Hattu.

***

King Mursili held the wagon curtain open, seeing this strange glade they were in. He felt a horrible sense of puzzlement at his whereabouts. The air smelt odd, the trees looked wrong. Then he saw an old hag give out honey to the men. He heard their cheery talk, especially the perimeter sentries, as they ate. Oddly, he felt no appetite for the fare. Tired by the small effort of observation, he made to lie back down again, when the wagon rocked a little. Volca had leapt up to sit on the driver's bench with a shard of the waxy nectar. But while other men ate, Volca merely watched. Odder still, the Sherden then dropped his piece of honeycomb and didn't bother picking it up again.

Mursili fell back into a deep sleep. When he woke, it was to terrible sounds, sounds of wounded men. He tried to prop himself up on his right elbow, but even those muscles were failing him. He managed only to lift his trembling right hand to the curtain and draw it back a fraction.

By Tarhunda's grace, what is this?

Men staggered and fell, vomited, pitched over as if shot. Befuddled, he poked his head from the wagon windows and looked around for Lady Danuhepa. She could help them, just as she had helped him. But she was absent, far away back in Hattusa, he realised, feeling foolish. Instead, he saw Volca. The red-cloaked Sherden sat there on the driver's berth of the wagon, watching while his comrades fell.

'Hel... help them,' Mursili said in a half-whisper.

But the Gal Mesedi continued to watch, motionless, as they fell. He was like a sober man in an arzana house.

'Stop: the honey is bad!' a cry sounded.

Hattu? Mursili mouthed.

He heard muffled exchanges, then a brash cry: 'Son of Ishtar!'

The moniker crept across his skin like wriggling insects. 'Hattu?' he whispered.

Then another shout: 'Laud your King and your Chosen Prince... not mere foot soldiers.'

'Muwa?' he croaked, hearing his older son's words clash with the cries of acclaim like a sword. He tried to twist his head, to look round and locate his sons.

Then Volca filled the squared window and cupped a hand behind Mursili's head to lift it a little, then held a skin to his lips.

'All is in hand, My Sun. Now drink. Drink it all. It will help things along...' he said in a soothing voice.

The root brew flooded into Mursili's mouth, washing away the confused thoughts. He drank every last drop, then fell back into a deep, exhausted slumber.

CHAPTER 17

ISLAND OF THE DEAD
SUMMER 1300 BC

With a cacophony of snapping twigs and branches, the Hittite army surged through the northern half of the rhododendron forest the following day. Men bore fiery looks and marched doggedly, despite many sporting sore heads and foul bellies. Hattu looked ahead, to the King's carriage, making its way through the woods with great difficulty, and behind, to Muwa, leading the Fury with a face that did justice to the name.

A hand clasped onto Hattu's shoulder. It was the slit-eyed, aged captain from the Leopard Clan. His face was stony still, but his words were very different now.

'My granddaughter was born the day we left Hattusa. I was fearful I might never return to see her, to hold her. Last night in the woods I thought we were done for, but you saved us, Prince Hattusili. I will never again speak ill of you.'

Hattu tilted his head a little to one side, unsure how to respond, then saluted.

At last they broke clear of the muggy, dark woods and found before them a broad, verdant heath, bathed in noonday sunshine. Just ahead lay another carcass of a Kaskan camp. A sea of mud domes and rough timber shacks, pig bones, broken clay pots, uncovered cesspits. And as they approached, they saw something else.

Three spears, hafts fixed in the earth, long-haired human heads impaled upon the tips. Around the two spears at the sides lay torn white Hittite soldier-garb. By the base of the central one was a black garment. A priestess robe. Even from here, Hattu could see the ragged section where a strip had been torn off. His hand moved to the rag in his purse, his eyes fixed on the impaled head.

'No... ' he whispered, feeling his body tremble.

'Stay back,' Kurunta cried across the lines, he and Nuwanza at once scouring the seemingly empty landscape for further threat.

But Hattu broke ranks and staggered forward, sliding to his knees before the three heads. He barely noticed Muwa do likewise by his side. Laments rang out from the men behind. Tendrils of bloody sinew and skin trailed from the leftmost head, the flesh blackened and the poor guard's face unrecognisable. The cheeks and forehead of the rightmost guard's head pulsed and writhed for a moment in a grim parody of life, before a set of black, shiny pincers cut through the skin from within and a flood of insects and maggots spilled over his face. The last head – that of the priestess – was veiled by hair, just the gawping mouth visible. Muwa and Hattu looked at one another, pale, then reached up, together, to sweep the hair back. The Elder Priestess' lifeless face was twisted in the pain of her final moments.

'Bury them,' Muwa snapped, rising and turning away.

'We should have sent a force ahead. You should have listened to me,' Hattu called after him. 'They were here, last night. Atiya was here. We could have freed her.'

Muwa swung to cast a scourge-like glower on him. He shot a fiery look of his own back. A murmur broke out amongst the men as they watched their two princes quarrel like this. Arrow flew down from above the woods to join them just then, settling before Hattu's feet as if to mediate.

'Had you done the job I asked of you – prepared the Tapikka escort properly – then she would never have been taken captive.' Muwa raked his fingers through his hair then, with a snarl, kicked out at Arrow, who hopped back and screeched at him. 'Damned bird. I'll cook it if it gets in my way again!'

The many watching ranks gasped in shock and dismay as Hattu fell to one knee to scoop Arrow up.

'They say death follows you, Brother… well, look,' Muwa towered over him, gesturing at the heads, '*look!*'

Hattu's limbs shook with fury. Muwa swung away and stalked back to the army lines. Had he not, Hattu wondered just what anger might have driven him to do.

***

The Hittite army marched on through the sultry north, following the Kaskan tracks like hounds. They trekked through marshy flats, over low bluffs and winding hill tracks. Only dusk halted them, and they set up camp on a green saddle of land between two brown, earthy hills – each peak serving as a natural lookout post.

Hattu woke in the middle of the night, his thoughts nagging him, the argument with Muwa echoing over and over in his head. And any time he did start to dose off, the grim image of the spiked heads stained the brief beginnings of innocent dreams. When he heard the urgent chatter of sentries atop one of the lookout hills he woke fully. Many of the Wolves were already awake, chatting mutedly or polishing their armour. He nodded to a few as he rose and dressed, then made his way to the brown earth slope and climbed to the hilltop. The night air was cool up here and he could see for many danna in every direction. The lookout sentries were in deep discussion with Raku flat-face, pointing and gesticulating towards a kidney shaped lake a few danna away, its surface reflecting the crescent of the waning moon like a highly-polished sickle blade.

'Trouble?' Hattu said.

Raku turned to him. 'On that islet,' he said.

Hattu followed his outstretched finger. He noticed how a section of the lake's surface moved and roiled, ever so slowly. It was not quite black, he realised as his eyes adjusted, but grey. Mist crawled across the water, and he could just make out a crooked neck of land, stretching out into the lake, a causeway leading to a small isle.

'One of the horse scouts reckons it's an old sacrificial isle – sacred to the Kaskans,' Raku said.

'We saw torchlight on it,' one of the lookout sentries said.

'And up here we heard a distant noise carrying on the night breeze,' the other sentry added. 'A terrible noise.'

Hattu's smoke-grey eye ached as he scoured the misty islet. For just the briefest of moments he thought he saw a dull orb of orange. The flicker of a fire or a torch right enough? *What if she is there?* he fretted. He felt a pang in his breast, an urgent need to find out, to right the wrong, to shove Muwa's cruel and unjust accusations down his throat. He felt his emotions run high, and took a moment to think, rubbing his temples, trying to let his mind make sense of it and not his heart – just as Nuwanza had taught him and the Wolves at the academy: *A good soldier knows when to become deaf to his heart.*

He eyed the scene again. Bare countryside lay around the lake's near shore. The approach was free of ambush points, as best as he could tell from the pale moonlight. The darkness would aid any covert investigation. More, the causeway offered an excellent means by which to pin down whoever was on that islet. The cold, clear pieces of his thinking clicked together, his head and heart in accord.

'We should send a scouting party,' he said, flatly.

'Aye,' Raku agreed.

'Does the *Tuhkanti* know?' Hattu said, the words sticking in his throat.

Raku shook his head. 'The *Tuhkanti* sleeps. He placed me in charge of night scouting.'

Now Hattu's heart took over. 'Then send the Wolves,' he said, gesturing to the restless company down on the saddle between the hills.

Raku looked doubtful. 'I don't know, Prince Hattu. I-'

Hattu clasped a hand to Raku's bicep and held his gaze – in the way he had seen Father regard men. 'We hesitated in the woods. Let us not make the same mistake here.'

***

Kol of the Eagle Kin had always been a selfless type – the kind of fellow who enjoyed a tasty meal most of all if he gave it to another more in need. And he had spent much of his life giving what little he had: his wheat, wine, bread and meat rations often went straight to the House of the Wounded, a wing in Hattusa's Great Barracks where the stricken veterans lived out their days: blind men, one-legged men and poor wretches confined to their beds. He would cook hearty stews for them and listen to their stories.

In his boyhood, tasty meals were few and far between; indeed, food of any sort was a luxury. Living in Hattusa's slums, he had often given what meagre fare he could buy to his sickly young sister. They owned a ramshackle hut, left to them by their plague-claimed parents, and they would huddle there at night, eating scraps of bread or the thinnest of soups, hearing the night calls of the wretched in the slum streets staggering between taverns. He would cradle her in his arms and tell her tall tales of adventure and good deeds to drown out the sorry din.

One summer a nobleman, low on slaves, had hired him. The rich man had put him to work on a sprawling villa up on Tarhunda's Shoulder. He spent many days there, mending the roof under a cruel sun, wearing his fingers to the nub in the process. By dusk on the last day, the roof was mended and Kol could barely stand. He almost fell down the last few rungs of the ladder. The nobleman had thrown two thin copper rings across the dust towards him in the way a man might toss a scrap of meat to ward off a mangy dog.

Kol did not dwell on the chasm between the rich man's lot and his. What good would it do to moan over that which he did not have? Instead, he loped down the hill into the Ambar valley market to trade one ring for four eggs and a sweet loaf, then to the Storm Temple, to place the other ring before the votive altar by the gates, whispering a few words of prayer for his sister's wellbeing. Someone claimed they later saw the noble taking the offered ring back for himself, but Kol chose not to believe the story. A man was little more than his thoughts, he had always said, and if you chose to dwell on the darker thoughts, then they would become you and you them. Instead, he cooked the eggs, broke and buttered the sweet loaf, fed his sister and told her a new story, where she was the heroine at the heart of the adventure. He noticed that her smile was broader than ever... and that her breaths seemed shallower. When she fell asleep in his arms that night, it was forever. It had been the saddest moment of his life... but he did not cry, for he knew, beyond doubt, that he had done everything in his power to make her short life as pleasant as possible. 'Sleep well,' he had whispered, kissing her cold forehead.

For those precious few moments of introspection, Kol could see nothing, hear nothing. He was a boy again, his sister alive once more. He could feel nothing of the grazes and bruises on his skin from the ambush on the approach to Tapikka, recall none of the horrors his Kaskan captors had subjected him and his comrades to since. It was akin to being underwater.

Then, like a diver being hauled from the depths, the sound of all going on around him returned: sharp, brutal sounds of metal ripping skin, of harrowing cries and of foreign tongues barking out dark oaths to strange gods. 'A good fisherman knows how to fillet a carp!' a Kaskan laughed as the sawing continued. Kol's eyes slid open to see a veil of coiling mist. He could smell the coppery stink of blood and the stench of loosened bowels, mixed in with wet earth and the incongruously calm lapping of gentle waves on a shore.

From the corner of his eye he saw one of his fellow soldiers. He was positioned just like Kol, naked and spread-eagled to an upright, X-shaped timber frame. The blurry form shuddered violently, drenched in red wetness. There was something terribly wrong about the shape of the man's body...

'And now it is your turn,' the Kaskan voice whispered in his ear from behind. Kol leapt with fright, his restraints biting into his flesh. A crow-faced man stepped into view, right by Kol's side. His bearded face was spattered with blood, and his teeth shone in an ill-fitting grin. He held a long and savagely-toothed, two-handled copper saw. Kol tried not to look as the fellow mopped at the saw with a filthy rag, wiping the remnants of the last victim away.

Crow-face flexed his fingers and took hold of the handle at one end of the long saw, a second warrior stepping over to hold the other end. Like men pulling a piece of furniture into place, they passed the saw between Kol's spread legs and carefully lifted it, so the ragged teeth lightly touched his crotch and genitals. So delicate, so expert in their movements. Kol shivered violently. Crow-face nodded once to his comrade, behind Kol, then yanked up and back, hard.

The copper saw rasped like a hoarse lion. Kol's blood and tatters of his skin showered Crow-face. Pain. White, maddening, agony. The noise that lurched from Kol's lungs was inhuman, like an animal mangled in a trap, his face agape and his neck cracking back to look skywards. There was a moment of quiet, just enough for the fire of the wound to flare in full, then…

Rasp! The saw was pulled back by the fellow behind Kol.

Kol closed his eyes tight, feeling the numb sensation of his tongue coming free in his mouth, chewed off in the blindness of agony.

Rasp… Rasp… Rasp! Over and over. Blood, innards and organs splatted to the ground. Skin and cartilage groaned and stretched as his body was hewn apart from below.

'Be quick,' another Kaskan hissed through the night. 'For someone approaches!'

Crow-face glanced over his shoulder into the mist, peering, uncertain, then turned back to the other sawman. The pair resumed their vicious work with great haste.

Rasp-rasp-rasp-rasp!

Lost in hideous torment, Kol's mind leapt in every direction that his bound limbs could not. Then, blessedly, the sound of the rasping saw faded away into insignificance and his screams seemed to be coming from another as, gradually, he returned to the vaults of the past. His sister was in his arms once more, hugging him, smiling, laughing at his tales. 'I have missed this,' she said, looking up at him.

He kissed her head. 'As have I.'

***

A ragged cry rang out across the blackness then faded away to nothing. The sixty one Wolves moving across the causeway halted.

'What was that?' they whispered.

Hattu looked along the front – eight abreast. Their eyes were wide, glinting in the starlight. Either side of them, the tranquil waters of the lake twinkling likewise, and up ahead, the small fog-shrouded islet churned and cast impossible shapes. He imagined in the mist swirling serpents, great birds, warrior wraiths.

'We have to be swift,' he said softly to Tanku. 'Order them onwards.'

But big Tanku seemed – for once – paralysed with fear. Uncomprehending, Hattu followed his gaze, seeing something hanging from the branches of two skeletal trees up ahead: webs, hanging across their path like delicate veils, dark, eight-legged shapes upon them.

'I... I can't,' Tanku said in a tremulous whisper.

Hattu looked down, seeing the big captain's feet anchored to the earth with fear. He lowered his voice so only Tanku could hear. 'Walk behind me, I will see you safe, just as I did in the barracks, remember?' Then he turned to the rest of the Wolves: 'Together,' he whispered, taking the lead. The others clacked their shields together like a mini wall and edged along behind him. As they crept between the trees and into the roiling fog, Hattu flicked his spear tip up, silently cutting away the veil of webs. The way was clear. He shot a furtive glance at Tanku, whose tense features eased in relief.

'Now, be ready,' Hattu hissed over his shoulder to the sixteen Wolves at the rear who went with their bows nocked and part-drawn. 'But be careful to identify your target before you shoot. We don't know what lies on this island. The priestesses may be here.'

On they went in breathless silence, Hattu at their head. A toad croaked somewhere within the mist, and more than sixty yelps were stifled. Then they saw curtains of fog part... to reveal shapes. The Wolves halted, crouching, breaths stilled.

Hattu peered through the drifting fog. *Men?* he wondered. *Sentries!* he was sure, seeing how they stood, feet wide apart, arms raised to their sides. But when a light wind parted the fog, he saw that they were not men but *creatures* – for they glistened like halved pomegranates, dripping red from the grievous openings that stretched, groin to chest. He now saw the frames upon which the pair were fastened, the nails that had been hammered through their shins and palms so they could 'stand'.

Underneath each lay heaps of steaming, purged, blue-veined innards. The leftmost wretch was dead. The rightmost one, however, was not.

Hattu took a step forward, cautiously, the whispered fears of his men sounding behind him. The rightmost wretch's head rose, shaking like that of a new-born fawn. His face, grey as a storm, gazed through Hattu.

'Kol?' Hattu croaked, his heart plummeting.

Kol's bloody lips moved silently as if he was telling a tale to an absent other.

'I'm sorry,' Hattu said, his throat closing up as he thought of the strong, handsome warrior of the Eagle Kin he had asked to escort the temple procession. Now he was but a butcher's scrap. Without a further heartbeat passing, Hattu drew his sword and pressed the curved tip quickly into Kol's ribs, splitting his heart. In a trice and with a wet sigh, the life was gone from him. Hattu withdrew his blade, his shoulders slumping.

But something deeper in the mist moved, and he realised it was not over. A figure moved in the grey ether. This time, it was like a dream… for she was a priestess, a Hittite priestess. And it was…

'Atiya?' he stammered.

It was her. This was no dream.

But when a muscled arm wrapped around her throat, holding a dagger there, it became a nightmare. The mist parted and a lion's skull appeared just above Atiya's head, Pitagga's face snarling between the long fangs.

'The *Cursed Son*?' he hissed, his dagger-arm tensing.

Tears spilled down Atiya's cheeks as the Lord of the Mountains drew her back a step, then another. Hattu found himself unconsciously being drawn with them, pace by pace, towards the far shore of the islet.

'Hattu, stop!' Tanku cried.

Hattu swung round to see the mist either side of him swirl violently. An instant later, small knots of Kaskans shot into view, ten coming from either side. Hattu swung up his shield in one direction and sword in the other, but knew at that moment he was dead or captured, certain the former was preferable.

But with a *thrum* the bowmen in the Wolves loosed their arrows, and a clutch of Kaskans fell. Hattu struck his spear tip at the axe of one who kept coming, deflecting a blow, then rolled clear of another. An instant later, a clatter of bodies and bronze sounded as the Wolves leapt into the fray. The fighting was swift and brutal. Tanku hacked clean through the shin of one Kaskan then drove his sword down into the man's heart. When another mountain man sliced the top of a Hittite soldier's skull off with his axe, Hattu lunged forward to pierce the Kaskan's belly with his spear, forcing the foe to his knees then kicking at the man's face to release the weapon. He swung round just as Dagon plunged his mace into another warrior's chest. The fellow went down, wheezing a mizzle of blood. And a moment later, it was over. Hattu looked this way and that for the next opponent, but the few left were melting into the mist towards the back of the islet.

'Atiya!' he cried, throwing down his spear and shield and drawing his curved blade as he staggered down the shingle bank, reaching the water's edge, splashing in shin-deep, the Wolves coming with him. Pitagga was already out on the waters aboard a raft, his surviving warriors clambering aboard with him. Atiya knelt by the Kaskan Lord, on a rope leash, weeping.

'Hattu!' she wailed. 'Hattu, don't come for me, do-' Pitagga's fist cracked across her cheek, ending her words. She slumped to her side on the raft deck.

'You'll die for this, you cur!' Hattu roared.

Pitagga laughed long and loud. 'Will I, *Cursed Son*? It looks to me like it is you and your kith and kin who stumble further and further from home, ever in my wake. The earth you tread is mine, and every tree, hill and river will conspire against you. Soon, you will be joining your brother,' he smiled, gesturing to the top of the raft mast, where a spear was affixed. The sight of Sarpa's black, hairless, desiccated head atop it stuck like an invisible lance into his heart.

Hattu fell to his knees in the water.

'Go back to your ailing *Labarna* and your cub of a *Tuhkanti*, weak prince. Tell them and all your generals how I mocked you tonight, how I mount a princely head on my raft, how I plan to melt the silver storm god into trinkets for my whores… how I will defile the last of your stolen priestesses.'

The blood thundered in Hattu's ears as Pitagga faded into the blackness hanging over the lake.

CHAPTER 18

THE BOWMAN AND THE BULL
SUMMER 1300 BC

On returning to the camp, Hattu was intercepted by Muwa and a knot of advisors. Hattu gave his report as flatly and factually as he could, trying to ignore what had gone between them before, trying to stick by Nuwanza's Maxim of calm. But Muwa exploded with ire, tugging at his own hair, calling out to all nearby and highlighting Hattu's failure to apprehend Pitagga, rescue Atiya or recover the likeness of Tarhunda. It was Nuwanza and Colta who led the Chosen Prince away, leaving Hattu standing alone, enraged.

So Hattu returned to the Wolves' camp area, mind aflame. Until he saw the lone bed roll that would go unused tonight and forevermore: the Wolf who had been struck in the head at the Islet. Suddenly he felt a terrible sense of guilt at having volunteered the Wolves for the sortie.

He curled up and closed his eyes to escape his thoughts, to get what sleep he could. But when he collapsed in his bed roll and his blood finally cooled, he suffered a night of terrible dreams. In one, he was walking gaily with his comrades into a cave whose mouth was rimmed with sharp stalactites and stalagmites, and from within which came a hot, fetid wind. On they went, none of them noticing how the ceiling of the cave became a series of ordered ridges like ribs. Next they came to a boiling, dark red pit. He realised at last that they had wandered into the belly of a beast, and swung back to the cave mouth only to see the upper and lower fangs of stone gnash shut. The hot boiling pit rose to burn them all in the darkness, sucking the air from their lungs and melting the skin from their bones... all to the sound of Pitagga's laughter.

The next day, he rose at dawn and the army set off at haste in the direction of the lake, picking up the Kaskan spoor once more. The far shores were pocked with the debris of a large enemy camp, and the tracks leading on from it took them in a wide northwesterly arc, through wooded tracks and wide, grassy plains, the hot sun baking them as they went. By late afternoon, the country grew a little less green, a little dryer and dustier, and they reached a forked valley with three tines. All three bore the markings of boots and hooves. Muwa drew up a hand and the column came to a halt, then sent one scout down each route.

'Three routes, three chances to be ambushed,' Hattu mused to the Wolves. His words were overheard by the nearby ranks, and he sensed many eyes upon him: not like days past, when their glowers would be accompanied by mutterings about the *Cursed Son* – now their eyes were bright with esteem, but also shadowed with a new concern: what would happen next between Hattu and the *Tuhkanti* – their newfound talisman and their beloved Chosen Prince?

'Fill the routes with rock and dust, block the Kaskans beyond,' big Tanku mused with a mirthless laugh.

'To what end? Pitagga would dig his way out like a worm. This isn't going to end until we confront him,' Dagon argued. 'And to confront him we must catch him.'

'You think he flees?' Hattu asked.

Dagon and Tanku gave him a puzzled look.

'That night on the islet... he was not afraid.' Hattu's eyes darted in thought. 'Think of his ploys so far: not the hasty ruses of a panicked mind – the Carrion Gorge was well prepared, wasn't it? Nuwanza's archers found rich stocks of spears and rocks up there atop the gorge sides, gathered over a period of months, ready to hurl down had our army passed through there unawares. And the woods, the honey: that was deftly done.'

Dagon, resting on his haunches, bit into an apple and looked down the three tines. 'And then there is the bait that draws us on in his wake,' he said. He looked up, meeting Hattu's eye. 'The last priestess and the silver likeness of Tarhunda. There is no more shameful loss he could have inflicted upon us.'

'She's not lost,' Hattu said immediately.

'Atiya? By the Gods, no she isn't,' Dagon agreed, standing, clasping Hattu's shoulder.

The dust of a rider rose from the northernmost tine. The scout returned to the generals and pointed down the path whence he had come. 'The Kaskan tracks continue on through that route,' he said, loud enough so many could hear. 'More, there is a Hatenzuwan village along the way. I saw… I saw her there – the hag who gave us the honey.'

Volca bristled, as if he had heard his own name. 'Then she and the rest of them should be arrested,' he said immediately. 'Let me take a force ahead at haste and the rest of the column can follow.'

Muwa gazed down the route, considering this. 'Take a pair of companies and apprehend the hag.' He pointed to Slit-eyes and his hundred. 'Take the Leopard Clan,' he said, then continued to look along the halted column, eventually meeting Hattu's eyes, 'and the Mountain Wolves.'

'*Tuhkanti*?' Kurunta interrupted. 'The Wolves are depleted – from Baka and from their sortie to the islet last night.'

'The fiasco at the islet?' Muwa said. 'I'd have thought the Wolves would be eager to make up for that – their *second* failure to apprehend Pitagga – as soon as possible.'

Hattu, eyes shaded by the browband of his helm, was unblinking, Muwa's gaze and his clashing like spears.

'But surely a veteran company would be better suited?' Kurunta persisted.

'You trained the Wolves, General?' Muwa barked.

Kurunta's eyebrows shot up. 'I took them to the edge, *Tuhkanti*, and none moreso than Prince Hattu.'

'Then they are ready for this.' He twisted back to Volca. 'Take them.'

'But, *Tuhkanti*…' Kurunta protested further.

'Do the men not acclaim the Wolves and this… Son of Ishtar?' Muwa snapped, throwing out a scathing hand towards Hattu. 'Well?'

Kurunta said nothing, though his stance suggested a few fierce thoughts swirled in his head.

'Wolves!' Muwa cried like a drillmaster.

Hattu and the Wolves jogged forward, their boots crunching, shields jostling. As they moved along the column, many they passed gave them firm nods and some dared to throw clench-fisted salutes too. They reached the front then waited as the Leopard Clan formed up alongside. Hattu avoided Muwa's gaze now, but his lips quivered with anger, on the cusp of shouting the darkest oath ever uttered.

Kurunta strode over, grabbed Hattu's bicep and shook it. 'Your brother's head is in disarray,' he whispered, 'but due to the king's malaise, he is our leader. We cannot turn upon each other out here in this strange land, so put his anger from your mind. Think only of what lies ahead. If you run into Kaskans along that route, get your shield up, get your head down and fend off everything they throw at you. You hear me? The men of this army believe in you now. Live, let them continue to believe.'

Hattu looked across the Wolves, each of the young men he had trained with wore hard looks, their faces bearing cuts and scrapes and their hair tousled and ragged. 'We'll do as you trained us to, sir.'

Volca waved the group ahead. 'March!'

***

The small party trooped on ahead at speed, the rest of the column following on at normal pace in their wake. Soon, the advance group lost visual contact with the rest, and they jogged alone along the dusty vale. After an hour, they slowed at a low hummock. Volca climbed up, crouched and looked ahead like an eagle. Further west the vale widened. By a still, brook-fed pond lay a small village, hemmed on three sides by a sea of yellow gorse bushes.

Hattu spat the dust from his lips, eyeing the place: a simple collection of timber shacks and animal corrals, a well, a small row of market stalls heaped with bright fruits and a few workshops where smiths worked copper and men milled wheat. And a small wooden handcart resting by the gates. 'Hatenzuwans,' he whispered, then saw the old hag shuffling over from the well outside the village with a bucket of water, towards the handcart.

'The hag!' Tanku said with a tremor of ire in his voice.

'She nearly killed us all,' Kisna growled.

'She gave us the poisonous honey,' Hattu reasoned, 'because someone forced her to.'

'You don't know that,' Sargis argued.

'I saw it in her eyes. She knew what she was doing was wrong,' Hattu countered.

'Yet she still did it,' Tanku said.

'Hattu is right,' Dagon reasoned. 'Why would an old woman in an unwalled town want to make an enemy of an army like ours?'

'For the same reason as the Galasmans,' Kisna conceded. 'Pitagga has threatened them.'

'Of course he has,' Hattu agreed. 'But unlike the Galasmans, these people have no army, no choice.'

'Then what do we do?' Tanku asked.

'As we were ordered: we question them,' Hattu explained. 'If they see we mean them no harm – that Pitagga's threat is removed by our being here – then they will perhaps tell us what they know.'

Volca stood. 'The approach is clear. With me,' he said.

The tall Sherden hoisted his trident and broke into a quick step. The Leopard Clan and the Wolves fell into place behind him. Hattu saw the faces of the village folk turn to the approaching troops.

'Faster,' Volca said as they drew closer. The party broke into a light run. Now the village folk froze. Some of the men snatched up poles and hoes – farming tools, none of them true weapons.

'Sir,' Hattu said over the rumble of their boots, 'they're frightened. We should approach carefully, so they know-'

'At a run,' Volca bawled over him, then sped forward. With a cry, the Leopard Clan went with him, hoisting their spears when Volca pumped his trident aloft.

'They think we're attacking them,' Hattu yelled over the din, but none listened. On the Wolves ran in the wake of the rest, glancing at one another, confused.

Now the Hatenzuwans scrambled in fright, women and children running, men throwing down their crude implements. But there were a few who stood their ground. One fellow tossed a pole at them with a terrified scream. The pole thwacked against the shield of one of the Leopard Clan.

'The treacherous Hatenzuwans attack us,' Volca yelled.

'Slay them!' Slit-eyes bawled. He rapped his weapon against his small shield and waved his hundred into a charge. Swept along in the anger of what had happened in the clearing, they surged forward with a guttural roar.

'This isn't right, Tanku,' Hattu bawled over the din of their charge, slowing. The other Wolves slowed with him and finally Tanku did too. The big captain's face was dark with frustration at first, shooting looks to the recalcitrant Wolves then the rest, but his annoyance quickly faded when he heard the first piercing screams of women and children. They watched as, just ahead, the old hag fell to her knees before Volca and the Leopard Clan, dropping her water, hands up in fright. 'Pitagga said they would spare our village only if we fed you the hon-,' she stammered, before Volca's trident lanced into her eye. With a spurt of white, milky matter and black blood she crumpled onto her side like a dropped rag.

Volca and the Leopard Clan spilled across the village grounds. The horn-helmed Sherden was ferocious, leaping to and fro, his red cloak swishing like a counterweight to his trident. He struck down millers, smiths, weavers, herdsmen. The hundred men of the Leopard Clan went with him in a fervent spree, chopping out at everything that moved. Pigs and sheep squealed and bleated in terror as corral fences were booted over. One young woman ran for the cover of a mud hut when the tip of a thrust Hittite spear punched through her breastbone and hauled her back. Arrows spat across the small space, shooting down dogs and elderly men who were clustered in one corner, quivering.

'Not a soul raises their weapon to these people,' Hattu demanded flatly as the Wolves jogged into the village in the wake of the slaughter. Not one did. Tanku did not challenge him. 'Enough... *enough,*' he screamed as they came to the well where Slit-eyes had cornered an unarmed man and run him through with his spear.

Slit-eyes took heed, blinking and shaking his head as if breaking free from a spell. He saw nearby the tiny, swaddled crying baby the fellow had been trying to protect. 'What have I done?' he quailed, stepping back from the body of the man and the screaming babe. He had but a trice to consider his own question, before a young boy ran into him, shouldering him in the stomach. Slit-eyes' arms flailed as he toppled into the stony ring of the well. His cry was shrill and short, ended with a thick, bony crunch.

The cry of the slain captain only spurred Volca and the Leopard Clan men on more. They slew with fervour, kicking over carts, wagons and stalls and even butchering pets. When one Leopard Clan man came for the boy who had despatched their captain into the well, Hattu stepped forward and thrust out his spear, blocking the soldier's sword-strike. The veteran soldier swung to face Hattu with a snarl. 'What do you think you're doing?' he roared.

'Serving the Grey Throne… with honour. Slaying farmers is not what we were trained to do.'

The soldier's face creased in anger. 'Wait till the *Tuhkanti* hears of thi-'

'Nor is it what the *Tuhkanti* asked us to do,' Hattu cut him off.

The soldier took a step towards Hattu at first, but when Dagon, Tanku and the rest of the Wolves closed up around him, the man backed off.

'Run,' Hattu hissed at the little boy they had saved. The lad scampered away, snatching up the swaddled baby and sprinting off into the brush behind the village. By now, torches were being tossed at houses and the village was ablaze. Black smoke scudded across the land, and the simple dust streets were stained with blood. All within lay dead. Hattu eyed Volca with disgust.

The sun was casting long shadows by the time the rest of the army arrived at the village. 'We saw the smoke,' Nuwanza said, arriving first at a run.

'What happened?' Kurunta panted, close behind. 'Where are the Kaskans?'

'There were no Kaskans, sir,' Hattu replied. 'Just this village of simple men.'

Kurunta and Nuwanza's faces fell aghast. 'How... who...why?' Kurunta stammered.

'The Wolves played no part in this... ' he started, then saw the royal carriage drawing up alongside the wrecked village. The curtain was drawn back. Father lay inside, feeble but propped up to sitting. His eyes cut through everything, glaring at Hattu, blood and smoke-stained, standing amongst the bodies of men, women and children.

Muwa arrived next. 'What is this?' he gasped, eyes bulging at the horror of the slaughter. 'What happened?'

***

Later that evening, the army camped on a broad, dry heath at the far end of the forked valley. The ringed spear palisade was lined with a triple watch, so sure were they of Pitagga's closeness. The sun was dropping towards the horizon when Volca entered his bivouac tent, slid off his boots and red cloak and had an attendant unbuckle his green scale corselet.

'Clean it,' he snapped.

'Your helm too?' the slave offered.

'I'll clean it myself,' he growled. The slave scuttled off.

Volca waited a few moments, then checked nobody was looking before unbuckling his chinstrap and lifting off his horned helm. For a moment, he caught a glimpse of the strange creature in the dull, blood-spattered reflection of the helm. As he wiped and buffed it with a rag, the visage became clearer: a handsome man with a fiery, scabrous red cap of gristle, veins and ragged sinew clinging to a white dome of skull. The angry Sherden people who called him a king slayer had meant to skin him whole, but they had only got as far as peeling off his scalp and cutting away his genitals before he had broken free. He carefully wrapped a headscarf around the old, ugly wound, the rim of the linen overlapping the peeled skin, and knotted it at the back. Now he could see only a handsome fellow.

'Those ingrates should have hailed you as new King of the Sherden,' he smiled, his copper earrings shivering with each word. 'But you will not be denied. You will have a throne of your own one day soon.'

'Who are you talking to?' a voice interrupted his thoughts.

He swung round to see Nuwanza, his jutting, triple tails of hair almost scraping the tent ceiling. The bowman had always eyed him askance, but now his gaze seemed more prying than usual.

'My closest friend,' Volca grinned, then turned to the small table that bore a jug of watered wine and a few cups. 'Time to wash the dust from our throats?' he offered.

Nuwanza eyed the relative fineries with a slight wrinkle of the nose. 'No. I prefer to drink my wine from a skin, sitting by the fire with my men. I find they respect me more for it.'

'Ha! The asceticism of the Hittites,' Volca mocked. 'If not wine, then bread?'

'No. First, we scout the countryside.'

'Isn't that the job of... *scouts*?' Volca chuckled.

'Normally. But the Lord of the Mountains is close. Too close. I want to put my own eyes on the land, to see every hill, meadow and river for myself. You're coming with me.'

'Am I?' Volca said straightening up to express his height advantage.

Nuwanza was utterly unphased. 'The *Labarna's* orders,' he said with a smirk.

Alarmed, Volca looked past Nuwanza, towards the royal pavilion. 'The *Labarna* is well? Well enough to communicate?'

'Far from it. He's managed only a few words since we made camp: the order I've just passed on to you.'

Just then, the slave came back, presenting Volca with his now-gleaming armour.

'Very well,' Volca shrugged and slid on his boots again. He had bargained on having this time to think, to plan. Pitagga's last messenger bird had come in at dusk the previous evening. A white raven. A rare bird. It meant one thing, as they had agreed when last they met. *If a white bird comes, lead them to Nerik, the land of the waning moon. A* challenge indeed. He would think on the ride, he decided.

'The horses are being readied by the camp's western entrance and my servant is bringing water there – and Prince Muwa has gifted me a quiver of his goose-feather arrows too. Go there and meet my servant, then wait for me.' Nuwanza gave him another of those dry looks then left.

A short while later, the pair rode on horseback along a dry stream bed veining a rocky gully, two danna west of the camp, each man's head swinging steadily back and forth along the horizon. The echo of their horses' hooves played tricks on the mind, conjuring images of many hundreds of steeds in pursuit. But they were alone.

'Pitagga has drawn southwest, heading for the hill routes,' Volca sighed, removing his helm to stroke the linen headscarf underneath. 'All the tracks we have found say it is so.'

'Southwest,' Nuwanza mused. 'That would take him to the basin of old Nerik.'

Volca tried to hold back the grin that was tugging at his lips.

'But that's probably what he wants us to think,' Nuwanza concluded flatly. 'We keep scouting until the sun is down.' With that, he returned to scouring his edge of the gully.

Volca scowled at the back of the general's head. If he was to bring down the Royal House of Hattusa and take the Grey Throne, he would have to think carefully about who – if any – he would allow to live. He would have to begin a dynasty of his own. He thought of the mangled and useless lump of scar tissue the angry Sherden people had left him with between his legs. *Well, perhaps not a dynasty entirely of my own*, he mused. His two fellow Sherden would be needed to spread their seed amongst the highborn women of Hattusa in his stead.

It would be a challenging time. In any case, he mused, when that time came, there would be little need for irritating men like Nuwanza. *And here we are, out in the wilds, just the two of us...*

A shadow scudded across them. Both men looked up.

'A vulture?' Volca cooed. 'We're not corpses yet.'

'No, that's a falcon,' Nuwanza said with a chuckle. 'It's been following us all the way from the camp. Prince Hattu's hunting bird.'

'Preying on men?'

'Watching over us, Hattu would claim. She has had her moments, to be fair,' Nuwanza chuckled.

They rode on in silence. Volca shot Nuwanza sideways glances and he sensed the Master Archer do the same in return. The balmy heat and rhythmic cicada song lulled them into a sense that only they existed in this empty land, until the sound of crumbling rock brought both their heads switching round to the gully-side. For an instant, a face was up there, on the ledge, and then it was gone. Volca hoisted his trident like a javelin, but Nuwanza threw up a hand to catch his arm. 'Easy, it's just a boy,' he said. 'I'll deal with this.'

Nuwanza rode on ahead to the end of the gully, then wheeled round to ride back along the low side. Volca watched, his eyes tapering, as the bowman slowed and slid from his steed, then approached the spot where the boy had been, speaking soft, soothing words. 'At ease, lad. Nobody will harm you.' The boy rose timidly from his hiding place, and Volca saw how he held a swaddled baby, which began to cry. Nuwanza fell to one knee, handing the boy a strip of soldier bread and a tiny vial of honey for the baby. Nuwanza seemed to be winning the lad over. Volca sighed and slid his horned helm back on. As soon as he did so, the boy froze, eyes falling upon him. His face fell at once and he backed away from Nuwanza, who whispered at him, tried to calm him. After a hurried exchange of words, the lad turned and ran, off along the ledge and then scrambled up a snaking track into the hills. Nuwanza stood, watching him go, then turned and re-mounted his horse.

Shortly, Nuwanza cantered back along the gully floor to join up with Volca again.

'Strange, a boy and a babe on their own, out here?' Volca remarked.

'Aye, strange indeed,' was all Nuwanza said.

They rode in silence. It was some time before Nuwanza spoke again. 'That town you churned into the dirt earlier today. Tell me about it.'

'Ah. Now that was Prince Hattu's victory,' Volca corrected him.

Nuwanza smiled wryly. 'Only because you reported it as such. The prince's sword and spear were clean. Yet somehow he and the Mountain Wolves were the ones to suffer Prince Muwa's anger over the whole affair – condemned to half-rations when they played no part in the slaughter.'

'They will eat properly again soon. The victory was more important: don't you want Hattu to breed a strong reputation? Victory means little to me, but to the prince...'

'That was no victory, and no man would want a reputation for such an act,' Nuwanza said. 'Why did you spur the Leopard Clan men to behave like that?'

'You are a general too,' Volca reasoned. 'You understand that once inside an enemy town, soldiers cannot be restrained.'

'Aye, that is true,' Nuwanza conceded. 'But they did not slay soldiers in there. Just families. They cut down everyone. *Everyone.*'

Volca felt a streak of warmth at the completeness of the job. Too many within the Hatenzuwan village had seen his face in the past.

'Well, almost everyone,' Nuwanza added.

Volca gripped the horse's reins a little more tightly, his steed slowing just a fraction. 'Hmm?'

'That boy and the baby escaped the town and have been hiding in these hills in the hours since,' Nuwanza replied. 'It took a long time to reassure him I meant him no harm. I told him we could feed and tend to him and the babe in camp. He seemed to trust me, for a moment.'

Volca felt Nuwanza's gaze on the side of his face, unblinking.

'Then he said he froze with fright,' Nuwanza continued. 'Stammered something about *the bull-man*.'

'My helm,' Volca laughed.

Nuwanza did not laugh. '*The bull-man*, I asked? Do you know what he said?'

'Enlighten me,' Volca said.

'*The bull-man, the one who killed my parents today...* ' Nuwanza continued, '*the one who roamed with Lord Pitagga, four summers past.*'

Volca continued to laugh, long and loud while his mind flashed with a thousand replies.

'Tell me, Volca, why would a boy say something like that? Three summers ago we found you bound by an ants' nest. We saved you. You told us you had sailed east that year from distant lands.'

Volca's laughter tapered off, but his smile remained. 'As I say, Nuwanza, we may never have seen eye to eye, but you and I are generals. And a good general *should* be suspicious,' he lifted his water skin from his belt to take a sip from it, 'should think of this day but the next too, and most of all... *expect* the unexpected.'

He dropped the water skin, revealing the small copper knife he had drawn unseen, then hammered the blade towards Nuwanza's broad, unarmoured chest.

But the Master Archer, fast as a lion, threw up a forearm, deflecting the blow, then thrust an elbow into Volca's face. Volca felt sky and earth switch places as he toppled from his mount, his red cloak blinding and entangling him. With a crunch, he landed, then scrambled back, swinging his trident from his back and instinctively dropping into a warrior's crouch.

With a thud, Nuwanza dismounted, tearing his sword from his belt.

'And traitors like you,' Nuwanza snarled through gritted teeth, 'should be strung up by their balls. Throw down your trident and I might let you live, but only so you may kneel before the king's wagon and confess to him all you and Pitagga have planned.'

'The king will find out all we have in store for him and his army... in good time,' Volca replied, flexing his fingers on the trident shaft, his eyes tapering to crescents. 'However you, my friend, are done for.'

'Am I?' Nuwanza said stonily.

Volca's eyes widened as Nuwanza sprang for him like a bolt of lightning, curved blade coming round for his neck. He ducked, feeling the sword scuff across the tip of his helm, ripping helm and headscarf off. He felt the heat of the sun on his grotesque dome of skull, scar tissue and wiry strips of vein.

Nuwanza laughed once, without a grain of mirth. 'You are a web of lies and deception,' he scoffed.

Alight with indignation, Volca rushed for Nuwanza, trident trained on his belly. Nuwanza's face fell and he let one leg buckle to roll left, before leaping back to his feet, twirling his sword in one hand. 'I knew there was something odd about you. Kurunta said you were just an arsehole – and you are – but I knew there was more to it. You were behind Zida's death. You've been behind every misfortune we have encountered so far. The king will decide your fate, and I can assure you it will be grim. Perhaps an ants' nest? It would seem right.'

Volca felt his heart rap madly as Nuwanza stalked towards him, fearless of his hovering trident points. Panic almost consumed him before he spotted a root growing along the gully floor, running under his feet and Nuwanza's. He dropped to his haunches to grasp the root, hauling it up with all his strength. In a cloud of dirt and debris, the rope-like vine whipped up, hooking Nuwanza's ankle and throwing him onto his back. The impact sent the Hittite general's sword spinning from his hand and across the dirt, past Volca.

Volca brought his trident tip swinging round, sure it was certain to pierce the general's heart. But Nuwanza sprung up like a cat, unhitching the bow from his back in a flash. 'Never force an archer onto his bow,' Nuwanza growled, taking two steps back from the stunned Volca and reaching up to his back quiver, flicking the leather lid open. Then his face fell as he clutched at thin air.

Volca grinned like a shark. 'And never leave a Sherden alone with your weapons,' he purred. 'Your arrows lie in the dirt, back at the camp gate.' Then he lunged forward, plunging the central tip of the trident into Nuwanza's breast. With a gasp, the Master Archer dropped his bow. Volca rammed the trident in fully. Three thick runnels of blood poured from the wounds and General Nuwanza sank to his knees, mouth agape. 'And it is to the dirt with you, Bowman.'

He drew the trident back and Nuwanza thumped forward, dead. Volca panted, his mind already picking over the detail of how he might falsify his report when, from a pace away, the most unholy shriek sounded.

He swung round to see Arrow, that damned falcon, flying in a tight circle around him. Like a lizard's tongue, he swept out a hand to swat it away, but the falcon was too quick, banking clear.

The falcon settled a safe distance away on the gully edge, looking down at Nuwanza's corpse and keening. Volca thought then of the two brother princes, so hateful now. He smiled, closed one eye and lifted his trident like a javelin.

CHAPTER 19

BROTHERS ASUNDER
SUMMER 1300 BC

As the last vestiges of light slipped from the land, the Wolves sat around their campfire. Hattu poked and prodded at the single pot cooking over the fire. After a hard day marching, the meagre half-ration of spelt to make porridge would barely feed the sixty men. But Muwa had been insistent on the punishment ration. Hattu had challenged him to punish Volca too, but his brother had refused to even listen to him. He stirred the thin porridge and scooped a 'helping' out with a spoon, passing it to Dagon.

'You stood up for us, that's what matters,' Dagon said, sensing Hattu's mood.

'You spoke well,' Tanku agreed, taking the next bowl offered.

Hattu's teeth ground together behind closed lips as he sat down with his porridge. It had taken all his reserves of willpower not to scream at Muwa, to demand apology for the unjust blame the Chosen Prince had yoked him with. Even now the sight of his brother across the camp, the sound of his voice or of others saluting him grated like salt on broken skin. He barely realised he was holding his bowl with a throttle-like grip until the clay vessel broke with a think *clunk*, the paltry porridge ration seeping away into the earth.

'Not hungry?' Kisna remarked cautiously, one eyebrow arching.

'Not even slightly,' Hattu replied.

When a commotion erupted at the western entrance to the camp,

Hattu rose, Tanku and Dagon standing with him. At the entrance – a short and heavily patrolled gap in the spear palisade – many hundreds of soldiers had clustered around an arriving horseman.

'Volca,' Dagon said.

'Did he not set out with Nuwanza?' Tanku said, speaking for them all.

Hattu set down his porridge and pushed into the crowd, the Wolves gathering in his wake. 'Where is the Master Bowman?'

The Sherden warrior's gaze found him and the Wolves amongst the crowd. His forlorn eyes answered the question. 'A knot of Pitagga's hillmen fell upon us, just west. He fought like a lion but... ' he stopped and shook his head once.

As Volca ranged past them towards the royal pavilion, many others clustered around him, the questions coming thick and fast. Hattu, Tanku and Dagon watched the space the Gal Mesedi had ridden through, mute, disbelieving. Nuwanza had been there, always, at Father's side. Now he was gone.

'The Bowman is dead?' Dagon said, his words laced with disbelief. The men of the camp cried out in lament as word spread through the camp.

Hattu saw Kurunta, nearby, staring, his craggy face suddenly like a lost boy's upon hearing the news. It was doubtful whether the haggard general had any true friends, but in Ruba and now Nuwanza, he had lost two age-old comrades on this wretched march. The laments soon turned to angry chatter and arguments. The leader of the Blaze had been slain, some snapped. Pitagga's forces must be just a short way west, others argued – vulnerable and within striking distance at last.

Soon, the generals gathered by a large fire near the royal pavilion, with an audience of thousands of soldiers, Hattu and the Wolves included. Muwa stood before the flames, his broad face uplit by the fire. Using a stick, he traced a crude crescent like a waning moon in the dirt, the open end facing east. He then made a dot, just northeast of this crescent.

'We are here,' Muwa said, gesturing to the dot. 'Going by the location at which Volca and Nuwanza were ambushed, Pitagga has swung towards the southwest. I fear he now retreats across the nearby hills,' he said, tracing the stick across the upper arm of the crescent and into the circle of space within, 'and towards the basin of Nerik. If he crosses that basin and once again melts into the Soaring Mountains,' he concluded, indicating towards the lower arm of the crescent, 'then we cannot hope to continue the pursuit.'

'Do not dismay, *Tuhkanti*,' Volca interrupted. 'The basin of Nerik will be Pitagga's grave.'

All stared at him, rapt.

The Gal Mesedi sank to his haunches to gesture to the interior of the crescent. 'I have heard many tales of the place: flat, broad plains. Fine terrain for Hittite forces, for *chariots!* Not so good for mountain men...'

A regimental chief of the now leaderless Blaze division stroked his jaw, his eyes brightening. 'If we can get there first...'

Volca grinned, nodding.

Another chief beat a fist against his knee. 'Block the southerly routes into the mountains... trap him on those plains.'

'We can fall upon him as he tries to escape... he will be wandering into a pen,' agreed a third.

A chorus of cheer and pride rippled around the fire.

Colta gazed into the flames, tugging at his forked beard. 'A pen for whom? When does the fox become the hound?'

Volca glared at him for a moment then swiped a hand through the air and scoffed. 'Now is *not* the time for procrastination, Old Horse. With every passing heartbeat, Pitagga slides closer to his high mountains. Do you really want him to vanish into those heights? Do you really want another fruitless campaign?' He took to drawing more in the dirt, outlining a meandering line that entered the crescent from the north. 'Going by what I saw on my scouting sortie, Pitagga and his tribesmen are headed to Nerik via this awkward hill route. It looked slow and winding. But here,' he marked out a more direct route that cut straight for the open end of the crescent, 'is a good path that bridges a ravine and will get us to the plains in less time. It *can* be done.'

General Kurunta strode along the edge of the flames, his silver braid swishing, torso glinting in the firelight. 'In my youth I fought alongside

General Nuwanza in the eastern deserts, in these forsaken hills, in the western riverlands. The handsome bastard always drew the eyes of the local women.' The thick ring of gathered soldiers laughed fondly at this. 'Yet he was just as cautious with them as he was with foes on the field of battle. *Never hasten to battle, lest you trip upon your hubris.*' Kurunta shook his head bitterly. 'Now I rarely heeded his advice: one wink from a Lukkan maid, or the glint of raiders' armour across a desert wadi and I was off and running, weapon in hand – if you take my meaning.' More laughter. 'And right now, if I was alone against Pitagga and all his spears, I would most likely bound straight towards him just for the chance to avenge Nuwanza's death. But I do *not* see the Lord of the Mountains. We catch glimpses only of the scorpion's tail of his rearguard. Perhaps, Bowman,' he tilted his head to speak into the night sky, 'I will agree with you at last. Let us be cautious – has Pitagga not already shown what an asp he is?'

The gathered soldiers seemed deflated at this.

'But the wind is in our sails, the prey has been scented,' Volca argued. 'From what I saw, Pitagga has only two spears for our every three.' He gestured towards the wagons which held the disassembled chariots. 'And the Hittite chariots will cut across Nerik's plains like harvesters. Hasten for Nerik, I say!'

The soldiers erupted in a cry of support. Kurunta's face crumpled.

Hattu watched his brother's brow knit tighter and tighter, locked in indecision.

'Prince Muwa, this is your chance – to lead this great army to victory!' Volca persisted. 'To secure your reputation as their young general-prince.'

This seemed to strike a chord. Muwa's eyes rolled up to meet Hattu's. A dark look.

'Return to your tents,' Muwa said. 'Come dawn, we take the swift road to old Nerik.'

***

King Mursili heard the clamour outside his wagon. When it faded, he heard his breaths come and go with a weak rattle. He felt like a helpless babe in a cot, with his minders craning their heads in the wagon windows every so often to check on him. Only Volca's root brew gave him nourishment of sorts – but it was an empty nourishment that lifted him for mere moments before giving him a gnawing, fierce need for more. And what was this news that Orax, one of his long-serving Mesedi, had brought him? After he had asked Nuwanza to take Volca out on patrol – and the effort in issuing the command had near enough knocked him out – he had sent Orax to look inside the Sherden warrior's tent. Orax had returned a short while later.

'I found nothing of note, My Sun,' he shook his head and chuckled wryly, 'but something strange happened when I left the tent. A sentry from the camp perimeter – near the western gate – bumped into me. He was carrying these.' Orax had held up a clutch of arrows. 'A gift from Prince Muwa to Nuwanza earlier today. The sentry had found in the ditch near the gate. They had been discarded there... loosely buried under the dirt.'

And now Nuwanza was dead, starved of his arrows and slain on the scouting sortie. Mursili's head began to ache as he tried to piece it together, to try to find a conclusion that was not as dark as the one which seemed unavoidable. He recalled the dying Zida's eyes, swivelling to pin Volca. His illness and pains had started not long after the Sherden had joined his entourage. The Sherden had urged the Hittite army to hasten to the Carrion Gorge, had seemingly known the honey in the Hatenzuwan forests was bad, had robbed Nuwanza of his arrows...

A horn-helmed head poked in from the wagon window as if hearing Mursili's thoughts, gazing down upon him, the root brew flask in one hand.

Mursili's gummy lips peeled apart and his tongue lolled. 'Tell me... tell me I... am wrong.'

Volca's smile faded. 'Ah, I can see your troubled mind needs soothing,' he said. With a furtive look around, the Sherden tipped not a flask of root brew but the contents of a small vial into his mouth. It tasted like fire – one hundred times stronger than the root brew. 'This will soon bring an end to your suffering, My Sun. Drink swiftly. With any luck you will be numb for what is to come tomorrow. Your divisions will be marching to the plains of old Nerik, you see… to the land of the waning moon.'

Mursili shifted his head from side to side, weakly, trying to protest. Quickly, blackness filled his mind and he slipped into unconsciousness.

***

Hattu returned to his tent, his heart roused by the sounds and sights of so many warriors eager to finish this. 'The Wolves and the Storm will fight like gods,' Tanku said to the soldiers nearby as they went. 'Pitagga will cower on his knees by dusk tomorrow. The silver likeness will be recovered.'

'And we will free the templefolk… save your woman,' Dagon added privately to Hattu, squeezing his shoulder. Hattu patted Dagon's hand in a tacit acknowledgement, just as they rounded a circle of tents to come to their own.

There, Sargis and Kisna took hold of each other's shoulders, growling, slapping one another in the face as if battle was but moments away. 'Save your ire and excitement for tomorrow,' Hattu advised them, 'If we let our blood grow too fiery now, we will be spent by the time we come to face Pitagga,' he said as he ducked to enter his tent, drawing back the woollen blankets of his bed. 'And be sure to drink a good share of wat-' But the sentence was never finished as he froze. A mass of dark brown and white feathers lay inside his bed, stained red, shiny and wet. Fright, horror, then heart-rending realisation.

'Arrow?' he said, his voice suddenly like a boy's again. He reached down to lift her with trembling fingers. Her light body was cold and her head and wings hung limp. Her eyes – those magnificent eyes – gazed into infinity. He traced a thumb down her bloodied breast, finding the savage injury that had killed her. His eyes widened as he saw it was from a weapon wound of some sort. 'Who… who did this to you?'

Hot tears splashed on his hands and Arrow's body and he kissed her head. 'I'm sorry, my friend. I was not there to protect you. I'm so sorry… '

He barely heard the forlorn sigh behind him, but felt Dagon's hand rest on his shoulder again. 'Hattu? I'm so sorry... who did this? We'll find whoever it was.'

Hattu lifted one feather that did not belong to the falcon: a greylag goose fletching. His mind came alive with fire. He swung round, his face bent in a snarl. 'I *know* who did this,' he snapped, his eyes glowering past Dagon, across the night-cloaked camp and to Muwa, seated by the great fire. The *Tuhkanti's* quiver rested nearby, the matching fletchings jutting proud.

'Hattu, no, surely-' Dagon started, but Hattu shot up to standing, barged past him and stomped across to the great fire.

Muwa looked up, his sour face curdling further when he saw his younger brother. 'I don't have time for *you*, not now.'

Hattu felt his hand itch to pull his sword free. He did not, but his mind chewed over and over on the idea. 'Why? *Why?*'

Muwa looked up, eyes like slits, mouth twisted in an uncomprehending grimace. 'Go back to your tent, *soldier,*' he scoffed, waving a hand at Hattu. 'Eat your punishment rations.'

Many warriors nearby turned to look on.

'So that is it?' Hattu said, shaking with rage. 'When I was *the Cursed Son,* you were happy enough to endure me. Now some men call me the *Son of Ishtar*, you grow jealous?'

Muwa stood, nose-to-nose with Hattu albeit a hand's-width taller. 'The last I heard you were acclaimed amidst a heap of dead children and women at that village.'

'And so you felt justified in what you did?' Hattu roared, tossing the fletching feather at Muwa. 'You don't even care, do you?'

Muwa watched the greylag goose feather swirl and float between them, his brow creasing in confusion. 'I did nothing you did not deserve,' he said, glancing over to Hattu's tent where the Wolves' half rations bubbled away in the pot. 'Go back to your place with the ranks,' he added, then shoved him, hard.

Hattu stumbled back a few steps, then rushed for Muwa, shouldering him harder, knocking him onto his back. At once, a dozen or more flashes of bronze saw Mesedi blades circle the two. Orax and

Gorru, leading the guard party, looked at one another, unsure what to do.

Hattu stabbed a finger towards the rising Muwa. 'The shining silver vest of the *Tuhkanti* grows black on your chest, Brother, infected by the tendrils of your heart.'

Muwa shot his brother a wild-eyed look. 'And it would rest more easily on your shoulders, would it? That is what this is all about, isn't it?'

'I will never forgive you for this,' Hattu said then swung away, back to the tents.

CHAPTER 20

MASTER OF THE WOLVES
SUMMER 1300 BC

A white raven banked and arced through the cool, dry night air. It swooped down on the lone figure atop a dry bluff, landing on his outstretched arm, eyeing his lion-skull helm.

Pitagga beheld the odd bird fondly, and wondered how he might reward his Sherden accomplice for this. Perhaps with a swift death, once it was all over?

Then he turned his attentions to the flood of men pouring through the defile below. Men of strange blood, odd garb, different ways. All heeding his call. All draped in toughened armour and dripping with copper and bronze weapons, the Lost North was united in a way none would believe... until the time came. And that time was approaching. The coming dawn would herald the greatest of days...

***

Others within the Wolves offered to bury Arrow for Hattu, but he refused. Instead, while the rest turned in, he remained awake, cradling her in his hands, his throat thick with grief. Eventually, he buried her alone.

After that, he slept little and when he did, he suffered dreams more wicked than ever. In one, he and Muwa were young again, playing in the waters of the Ambar. All was well, Arrow soaring above them. It was a genuine memory and one he treasured like a gemstone. They laughed and joked, splashing each other, Arrow flying through the spray. But when Hattu looked down he saw that the Ambar's current had turned red around him. Aghast, he had staggered towards the banks, then looked to the midriver to see Muwa, laughing gaily, holding Arrow's broken body like a prize, wringing her corpse and causing her blood to stain the water. He woke and, for a moment, that warm blanket that so often follows a nightmare – the gradual realisation that it was not real – comforted him. Then he saw the small, freshly-dug mound near the tent. His heart cracked in two all over again.

Dawn had broken, he realised. All of the Wolves had risen – every other bed roll was empty. Sargis and Kisna were sitting cross-legged by a recently-kindled fire, eating a breakfast of scrambled eggs and soldier bread. He rose and sat with them, knotting his hair tightly at the top of his scalp, unplugging his water skin to drink a bellyful. 'Damn – no Dawn Call?' he asked the pair, hiding his grief by looking to the newly risen sun and then over the camp – cloaked in a veil of shade from the nearby hills and dotted with men roused and gathered around fires to eat and lay out their armour and weapons.

'Kurunta forbade it,' Sargis said through a mouthful of bread. 'For fear that the Kaskans might hear and guess our route.'

'A wise choice, I'd say.' Hattu chewed his lip as he looked west to the curved range of hills there, and the Soaring Mountains just south of them. This was the opening to the crescent from Muwa's dirt map. Cupped between the two ranges lay the plains of Nerik.

He saw that his two comrades were not enjoying their meals at all, Sargis tapping a foot and Kisna's belly gurgling and groaning. It set him thinking, and it was a welcome distraction from the sorrow pulsing in his breast.

'I used to fear every day at the Fields of Bronze,' he said, spooning some eggs into a bowl for himself even though eating was the last thing he wanted to do. 'I'd wake before the Dawn Call. You lot would still be sleeping, snoring… *farting*, louder than the thunder of the Gods,' he said with a gentle laugh, pointing an accusing spoon at the pair, 'while my guts would be turning over, my mind wide awake.' He took a spoonful of eggs – creamy and rich, more soothing and welcome than he had expected – and smiled. 'Fear absolutely had me, I admit.'

A few others had gathered nearby, listening. He felt an added weight of duty to make his words worthy, so he took a swig of water and continued:

'At one point I was ready to walk away, back to Hattusa and the acropolis' halls. I stayed though, because I sensed that there was something right about it all. True, we were put through torture every day, but we endured it together. Together, we saw it through. We are something special. Aye, we will face the Kaskans out there today. But, when the time comes, there is no other group of farting, snoring, daring and dogged bastards I'd rather stand with.'

Kisna snorted with laughter.

'Farting and snoring,' Sargis pointed at his comrade, then turned the finger on himself, 'daring and dogged,' he said, then rumbled with laughter too. Others close by chuckled and some lost that look of fear.

Hattu felt his own heart rise at the change in mood. His words had been as clumsy as they were worthy, he realised, but he had brought laughter and smiles to frightened men, shone brightness upon cold, black fear. Perhaps a vein of Father's aura ran in him after all.

But when the laughter faded, the small grave mound hovered once more in the corner of his eye. Hattu felt a renewed surge of sadness. *You should be up above, friend,* he said inwardly, *soaring high.*

When Kisna and Sargis shared a look, then set down their bowls and stood, Hattu frowned. 'Not hungry?'

'We'll finish eating in a moment, sir,' Kisna said.

Hattu was confused at the formal address, then realised they were looking over his shoulder at something, eager glints in their eyes. He twisted round to see Tanku, Dagon and the rest of the Wolves with them. With them also were eight other captains of the Storm, and Raku the flat-faced regimental chief. Each of them wore roguish looks that might have terrified him in his early days with the army.

'Tanku?' he asked his captain, who led the gathering.

Tanku handed him a folded bundle of green cloth.

'What is this?' he said, confused.

'A change of the watch,' Tanku said.

Hattu eyed the cloth. It was the captain's cloak. 'This is yours, Tanku,' he said, confused.

'Not anymore,' Tanku said, taking off his own helm and placing it on Hattu's head, the long, trailing black plume dangling to the small of his back. 'You are the true leader of the Wolves. I noticed it first at Baka when you led the climb to warn the rest of the army. Then in the woods, you were sharper than any other and spotted the Kaskan honey-ruse. And at that Hatenzuwan village, it was *you* who gave the order to refrain from Volca's slaughter... when I was set to rush blindly into the village and do Volca's bidding.' He leaned close so only Hattu could hear. 'And at that foul islet, I froze. You led us when I could not. You didn't do so to garnish your reputation – you did it to protect the Wolves.'

'Any one of us would have done that, Tanku. I was the closest to you, that is all.'

Tanku patted his shoulder and smiled. There was not a trace of sadness in his voice or his demeanour. 'See? You do not yearn for the power of the captaincy; that is what makes you the right man.'

Hattu looked across the sea of faces. Dagon, Kisna, Sargis, all smiling fondly.

'I've spoken with the men in the last days. They agree,' Tanku said, taking the green cloak from Hattu's hands and draping it over his shoulder. 'It is the way of the Hittite army. A hundred elect their captain from within.'

'Tanku, I can't... you earned this. The academy tailors made this cloak for you.'

Tanku shrugged and grinned weakly. 'Ach, in truth my mother made it for me. She also made me a matching loincloth, but you won't want that, I'm sure.'

A low chorus of chuckling rose from the gathered men.

'But still-' Hattu protested.

'It's yours.' Then he added with a cocked eyebrow. 'Though I'll be honoured to accept the post of Chosen Man.'

Then, in the silence of indecision, he heard the *scrape, scrape* of someone sharpening wood. He looked up to see Kurunta, sitting on a high boulder, hewing at a stake with his knife. 'Will you just take the damned cloak and be quick about it?' the one-eyed general grunted without a hint of a smile. 'We've got a Kaskan Lord's arse to kick today.'

Hattu smiled in his place. 'Aye, sir,' he said, sweeping the cloak over his shoulders, then taking hold of two corners of the cloak and tying them together on the right of his breast in lieu of a pin. The significance of the green cloak on his warrior's shoulders was just creeping up on him, when Dagon approached.

'And this is a gift, from all of us,' his friend said, stepping forward to hand Hattu a bronze cloakpin... a single white feather fastened to it. The sight brought a tear to his eye and a stab of pain to his heart. *Arrow*, he thought. 'It's... hers?' he said, his voice thick with emotion.

'Aye, one of the Fury men caught it falling from the sky as she watched over us on the march. He kept it for good luck. *'From the Son of Ishtar and his hunting bird – a fine omen*, he said.'

Hattu pinned the cloak in place, smoothing the feather fondly.

'Son of Ishtar... Master of the Wolves!' the group said in a low chorus. Other regiments eating and preparing nearby stood to see and echoed the call. At once, the mood in the camp was lifted. But across the sea of tents, fires and faces, Hattu saw one, dark as a thunderstorm.

Prince Muwa stole through to the Wolves' area, arms wide. 'What is this?' he spat.

Hattu's elation faded, replaced by a hardening of his heart and a stiffening of his shoulders.

'*Tuhkanti!*' one of the Fury captains said with a salute. 'Prince Hattusili is now Captain of the Mountain Wolves.'

Muwa glowered as he looked over the green cloak. Hattu felt his brother's gaze like the flames of a close-held torch. 'Has his captain died?'

'No, *Tuhkanti*,' Tanku said, 'but as is the way of the army, we elected within our group to-'

'Then this is a nonsense,' Muwa growled. 'We are out here in the Lost North – now is *not* the time to be swapping ranks ... on a *whim.*'

Tanku tried to interrupt: 'General Kuru-'

But before he could explain, Muwa barged past him and snatched out at the pinned right shoulder of Hattu's new cloak as if to tear it off. Instinctively, Hattu shot up a hand to catch his brother's wrist. It was a shaping moment. Tall, powerful Muwa's arm shook as did Hattu's. A battle of will and strength.

'Take. Off. The. Damned. Cloak!' Muwa groaned as a thousand gawping soldiers looked on.

Hattu felt his arm grow numb, Muwa's grasp hovering over the cloakpin and Arrow's feather. 'By Tarhunda… by Ishtar…' he said, 'if you touch that, I will… '

Muwa pulled his hand free and squared his shoulders. 'You will what? Remember who I am, Hattu. Remember who *you* are.'

Hattu saw how his brother's hand had moved to toss back his own black cloak and hang over the haft of his curved sword. Only then did he realise he had reflected the movement… or had he been the one to make the move first?

He thought of Ishtar's cruel words. He thought of his oath with Father.

But the charging horses in his heart defied that vow, and his hand trembled, tensed and ready to tear his sword free.

'Stop!' Kurunta barked, sliding down from the high boulder and rushing between them, casting aside decorum and pushing both princes away from each other. The general's face was bent with distress.

***

Mursili could barely keep his eyes open. The vial of fiery poison had sent him into an oblivion that he was only now waking from. It was raised voices and a close-by rummaging of busy hands that brought him round, shuffling to push pillows under his neck and lift his head a little so he could see from the carriage window. It allowed him to see Hattu and Muwa by a nearby ring of tents, leaning in towards one another, faces feral, hands hovering over their sword hilts. Only Kurunta's arrival put a halt to what might have happened next.

'You see?' Volca said, straightening the pillows. 'You see how hard

I have worked?'

Mursili rolled his eyes up to the smiling Sherden warrior.

'Soon, you,' he pressed a finger to the king's chest like a playful mother to a child, 'will be but a living corpse. The root brew has seen to that. Nobody knows how toxic it is... except you, of course.'

Mursili's wasted body convulsed once, yet not even a whimper escaped his lips.

'All those who found out about it along the way have been carefully dealt with,' Volca continued. 'Your physicians, your courtiers, your overly-suspicious generals.'

Mursili's mind flashed with memories of past glories and he conjured a new one: seeing himself leap up from the bed, grasp the Sherden warrior by the throat and then draw and dig his dagger hard and fast into the cur's guts over and over and over again. The fantasy faded and he felt a stinging, hot shame overcome him. *I took you in. Me...*

'I cut quite the wretch did I not? Staked by the anthills in Wahina,' Volca cooed, his eyes seemingly reading Mursili's thoughts. 'Pitagga did not believe you would offer me shelter. Yet he lacks my skills of persuasion.'

Mursili's breaths escaped in weak half-coughs now.

'Yes, the Kaskan lord thinks he is my master. True, he employed me to draw your grand divisions onto the plains of Nerik.' Volca smiled and cocked his head to one side. 'And Nerik *will* be the scene of your army's demise. I will see to it that you and I alone survive, however. Pitagga will then sweep south and plunder all of your lands. And a plunderer is all he is – he would rather topple your cities than secure them as his own. So when it is over... when the fires have died, when the pillaging is complete, when the Kaskans withdraw into their highland homes again and the remnant Hittite people return to their fallen cities and try to rebuild them, leaderless, they will stare agog as their corpse king emerges from the wilderness, aided by his loyal Gal Mesedi.'

Mursili saw tears of unbridled ambition in Volca's eyes. Madness unharnessed.

'And when you pass, *soon* after, the heirless Grey Throne will be mine.'

Mursili's eyes swept back to the two princes, now being shoved apart by a forceful Kurunta, while Colta did his best to disperse the watching crowds, urging them to prepare to march for Nerik imminently.

'Your boys? Aye, they are rightful heirs. But look at them. They will both fall at Nerik… if they don't kill each other before then!' he said with a laugh as if making a light-hearted remark.

Mursili closed his eyes, seeing Ishtar's writhing, curvaceous form in the blackness. He summoned all his remaining strength to cry out, but it amounted in only enough strength to open his lips a fraction, soundlessly. Instantly, the neck of a vial was pressed there.

'There, there, Great King; drink long and deeply,' Volca said, a fresh dose of the poison flooding into King Mursili's mouth.

CHAPTER 21

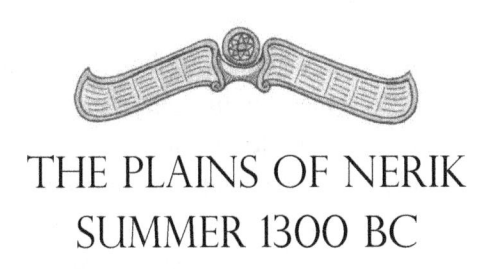

THE PLAINS OF NERIK
SUMMER 1300 BC

The dry, shallow ravine echoed with the clatter of boots, hooves and cartwheels. Russet dust spiralled up as thick as morning mist. Nearly fifteen thousand men moved in full armour. Knots of archers scuttled along the ravine-sides – wary once more that Pitagga might have lined up a pinch-point ambush as he had back at the Carrion Gorge.

Muwa and the Fury Division led the way. The royal carriage and the small pocket of Mesedi came next, Volca at their head. Then came the Storm and the Blaze – Kurunta leading both in Nuwanza's absence. The war horses and the men of the chariot teams straddled the flank of the Storm. Behind them, the massive train of ox-carts and mules sprawled. The hundred men of the Cruel Spears had been assigned to march to the rear of these animals to keep them in check, and the Mountain Wolves had been posted at the head, to guide them.

Hattu brushed dried dung from his leather cuirass as best he could then tried to grab the harness of a mean-eyed mule once again. But it slipped from his grasp and the recalcitrant beast continued to nip at his hands. He had often pitied the poor sumpter beasts when seeing them driven and lashed by heartless handlers, but now he understood. The supply train was the lifeblood of the column. If the supply train could not move, then the column could not move. If the column could not move, then the campaign would be broken.

'Come,' Tanku called just behind Hattu, stamping his spear butt into the ground. The ox he was leading shook its head from side to side but did not move a muscle – apart from its bowels. 'Dirty bastard,' Tanku sighed.

When the mean-eyed mule took to biting at Hattu's cloak, his patience snapped. He lifted the herding cane, ready to thrash the beast, but softened at the last, lowering the stick and instead rubbing the beast's muzzle. Finally its tantrums stopped and it moved obediently.

And in truth, Hattu's fury was not with the mule. He shrugged his right shoulder to toss back the forest-green cape and push the cane into his belt beside his sword, then glowered ahead to Muwa.

Not once did Muwa look back. No remorse. Not for any of it, Hattu realised. This was surely the *Tuhkanti's* most brazen affront: selecting the Wolves to help herd the animals, just moments after he and Hattu had almost drawn their swords upon each other, just a handful of hours after slaughtering poor Arrow.

Perhaps it would be best if I fell today, Brother... for I fear what will happen if we are to stand before each other again.

It was a shout from ahead that scattered his baleful thoughts.

The army slowed instinctively – even before the division leaders and many captains gave the order. Hattu saw the end of the low ravine about an arrow shot away to the south. Beyond it was a sea of hazy morning air filling a huge basin of grassy flatland cupped to the south by the Soaring Mountains and on the west and north by these high hills and valleys. The plains of Nerik. A place of legend.

But the army remained halted, and he saw why: separating the ravine end from the plains of Nerik was a dark, jagged chasm. Across it lay a single bridge laid with timber planks and edged with a rope rail.

Muwa, at the head of the column, raised and flicked a hand. A scout went forward, riding his horse up to the bridge, checking its timbers and the soundness of the ropes, then walking his mount out onto the mid-section. 'The bridge is good,' he called back. Next, he rode on to the far side, shielded his eyes and cantered around in a wide circle. 'The countryside is deserted,' he shouted. 'The heat blurs the air but as best as I can tell the land is empty.'

A murmur of excitement and triumph broke out along the column. They had done it – reached the old place before the Kaskans.

'Let us hurry,' Volca said. 'The sooner we cross, the sooner we can set up a line of bronze for Pitagga to run onto.'

'Forward,' Muwa barked.

The army rolled onwards again. The Fury thinned into a column two men wide, spilling across the bridge and reforming on the other side. Next went the royal wagon and the Mesedi, the Storm, then the Blaze. Left back with the baggage train, Hattu waited until Kurunta waved them across. 'Bring the pack animals first, then the chariots.'

The cluster of charioteers grumbled at having to wait.

Hattu jogged forward to head up the sumpter train. 'Now you will behave?' he asked the mean-eyed mule as they approached the bridge. The creature's ears flicked at buzzing flies and that appeared to be the closest thing to an answer he would get. As he stepped out onto the bridge slats, he saw that the chasm was indeed a deep, grim cleft, its floor cloaked in shade, somewhere far below. The bridge rocked a little with each footstep and clattering hoof, more and more as he moved towards the central, lowest point, his hand running across one of the rope-railings. Behind him, he heard worried lowing, braying and nickering from the animals and a few curses and moans of fear from the Wolves. The weight of the sumpter animals was certainly causing more motion on the bridge than when it had just been soldiers. 'Keep your eyes on the far end,' he called back. 'No point looking down unless you want to go there.' Indeed, Hattu could not tear his eyes from the silvery-green meadows that waited on the far side. The breeze gently combing the empty plain caused the stalks to sway like gentle waves.

A captain of the Blaze Division stood at the far bridgehead, holding out a hand to take the mule's ropes from Hattu. 'Come,' he said.

Hattu urged the mean-eyed mule on with a muted '*ya*', but it became suddenly agitated once again, straightening its legs and digging its hooves into the planks, looking back.

Colta, watching from the bridgehead behind, cried: 'Gah! Once they stop, it is like drawing the teeth from a serpent to get them moving again. Use your cane if you must.'

'Come on,' Hattu said, anger rising once more. But the mule tossed its head from side to side, its teeth snapping again, going for Hattu's buttocks this time. 'Curse you to the pits!' he snarled, turning his back on the destination bridgehead to face the sumpter train and drag at the ropes like a strongman, as most of his comrades and the other animals passed him. Just as he was tiring and ready to bring out the cane, his smoke-grey eye ached and he saw something – something very, very wrong: the briefest blur of motion near the northern bridgehead from which they had stepped onto the bridge – the twines of the rope curling, spiralling, shredding.

Lightning slashed across his heart and he cried out with a half breath: 'Get off the bridge.'

And before the words had fully left his lips, he heard the thick, reverberating twang of ropes giving way. The fifty or so beasts on the bridge and the Wolves entire erupted in a chorus of panic. At once they thundered forward. Hattu swung round too, bounding for the southern bridgehead.

Snap, twang! The bridge juddered violently and sagged to the left. He heard a scream as one of the Wolves pitched, flailing, off into the chasm, three braying mules going with him. Hattu slid to the left also, but grabbed the right-hand rope rail.

Twang!

Now the rail slackened in his grasp and the bridge sagged even more. He leapt for the bridgehead, clasping the Blaze captain's hand and stumbling gratefully onto solid earth. He spun round to usher the last few Wolves and as many animals as he could from the bridge.

Snap! Again. Now the bridge groaned, the sound amplified and deepened by the chasm. He saw the two Wolves stuck in the mid-section and the twelve oxen and two mules with them. Their eyes were wide with terror, looking to him for salvation.

I'm sorry, he mouthed, just as the bridge plummeted, breaking apart completely at the northern bridgehead. The roar filled the land as the men and beasts fell to their deaths, then the bridge slapped against the chasm's southern wall side with a shower of splinters and dust, dangling like a ribbon. For a moment there was silence. Even the cicadas had stopped singing. Hattu saw, across the way, Colta, gawping, the chariot teams agog, the Cruel Spears, mouthing panicked prayers, and then the many thousands of pack beasts stranded there too braying and lowing wildly.

'Chariot Master?' Kurunta called across the chasm. 'You are well? The animals are well?'

'Well enough – though I might need a fresh loincloth,' Colta grumbled, eyeing the flailing ribbon of the bridge.

'Can you see another way across?' Kurunta called.

Even as the general said this, all heads were already combing the chasm in both directions, looking for another bridge to no avail.

A shushing of armour and footsteps sounded behind Hattu. Muwa, Volca by his side. The Chosen Prince scowled at the frayed bridgehead and at the baggage train and chariot wing trapped on the far side.

'You said the bridge was sound!' Muwa cried at the nearby scout rider.

'I… it… it was,' the fellow stammered, quaking.

'I'll have your belly slit and your guts pulled free, you-'

'The bridge *was* sound,' Hattu interrupted. 'Those ropes were thick and new. They must have broken apart under the weight of the sumpter animals,' he finished, unconvinced by his own argument.

Muwa turned a white-hot look on Hattu. 'Damn you, mule-handler… what did you say?' Muwa growled.

Hattu felt his breast quivering again, remembering poor Arrow dead in his hands. 'I told you what I saw. If you choose to ignore me then so be it: an ignorant leader you will be.'

As at the camp, both men's hands reached towards their sword hilts… this time each part-drew their blades with a screech.

As at the camp, Kurunta stepped between them before either could do so, shooting each a maddened glance. 'Water,' he cried as if to break the spell. 'The wagons on the far side hold our water bags and barrels. We each carry just a skin,' he said. 'Skins that were full this morning, but I wager are now hanging nearly flat.'

Hattu let his sword slide back into his belt, as did Muwa. Both looked at one another with fire in their eyes and in their veins. *This is not over*, Hattu growled inwardly.

'Water is our priority,' Kurunta continued. 'We must find a way to bring the baggage train over.'

Volca issued a short, barking laugh. 'The sun is high – we might spend the rest of the afternoon searching in vain for another crossing, and thirsty soldiers will not last for long. And all the while Pitagga and his forces will be drawing closer. It is paramount that we take up position across the plain, to block the way to the Soaring Mountains,' he said.

'But we need those chariots,' Kurunta insisted, pointing over at Colta, with the stranded wagons and horses.

'I agree. But let a small team look for a crossing. The rest of the army should proceed at once onto the plain.' The Sherden warrior turned away from the chasm and pointed across the plains of Nerik. Muwa and Kurunta followed his outstretched hand, gesturing across the circular basin of silvery grassland, maybe five or six danna in diameter. 'Look: a stream, surely?' Volca cried, pointing out the slight furrow in the land, running east to west. 'Is that not one problem solved?'

Hattu, blood cooling a fraction, could not disagree: it looked like a brook of sorts. The only other feature in the basin was a high and sizeable tumulus, abutting the hills near the northwestern edge. He noticed a remnant crescent of tumbledown grey walls cupping the far edge of the mound. It could be only one thing. *Nerik?* But the haze on the basin floor was like a silvery sea. What else might it be masking?

'Sir,' Hattu said quietly to Kurunta. 'This land is veiled with heat. What if-'

'Silence, mule-handler,' Muwa raged.

Curse you, Brother, Hattu mouthed through tight lips.

'Chariot Master,' Muwa called across the chasm, 'take the mules and the chariot teams east, search for a route across. Rendezvous with us at the stream.' He then waved the quivering scout rider and two others off to the east along this side of the rift.

Turning to face the rest of the army, Muwa gave the order to move west across the plains of Nerik, towards the brook. As the Fury peeled away first like the head of an uncoiling asp, Hattu and the Wolves took up their places in the Storm ranks. Before they set off, Hattu glanced eastwards in the direction Colta was to travel: no crossing point as far as the eye could see.

'There are no other bridges,' Dagon said, reading his thoughts.

'And this one *was* sound,' Hattu agreed.

'Stay for a moment, Chariot Master,' he shouted across the void to Colta, shooting a glance to be sure Muwa was out of earshot.

The Hurrian, about to set off eastwards, cocked his head to one side and halted his wagons and animal-handlers.

Then Hattu called to one of Raku's men for a few coils of rope. 'Help me,' he said, beckoning the Wolves to the bridgehead. 'This bridge can be restored far sooner than another one can be found.' They tied the ropes to the dangling ribbon of bridge, part hoisting it, then lifted the free ends of the ropes and tossed them across the chasm. Colta's men caught them, then began looking over the herds for the sturdiest oxen who might manage to raise the broken bridge.

Just then, the rest of the Storm ranks began to peel away from the southern side of the void, trailing the Fury and the Blaze.

'Go!' Colta hissed, waving him away. 'We will do what we can here.' He then lifted and examined the short ends of the broken ropes on the northern side, frowning.

As Hattu and the Wolves fell into place with the Storm and set off across the plains of Nerik, he heard the Chariot Master once again, talking to others over there. 'These ropes. They look like they've been… part-cut.'

***

'Stay in line,' Muwa roared at one flagging Fury soldier as they marched alongside the northern edge of the shallow stream under the noonday heat. Instantly, he hated himself for it. He had never been one to drive men with a yoke of fear. But damn, Hattu had made a monster of him in these last days. *You claimed Atiya as yours. What right had you? She and I were destined to be. And now you seek to make a fool of me before my men, questioning my judgement, making bold calls before me as if to show you are stronger, wiser. You are a blight, Hattu. A blight! And you* were correct. *When you were the Cursed Son, things were easier. You knew your place and I mine. Now? Now you had best hope we do not cross paths again for some time. And when Pitagga spills from the northern hills and blunders onto these fields... if his axe falls for you... then, then...* he knew what the next thought was, but could not put shape to it.

'*Tuhkanti,*' Kurunta said, having marched forward to draw level with him.

Muwa looked at him, unaware how twisted his mien was.

'We should take great care as we progress across these lands,' Kurunta said. 'The shady passes in the Soaring Mountains,' he said, pointing to the southern edge of the basin, on their left flank, 'and the mound of Nerik,' he added, pointing to the still largely shapeless, undulating mirage lying ahead at the northwestern end. 'Both make me uneasy. And as Prince Hattu said, what if?'

Muwa felt the latest mention of his younger brother's astuteness like a lash on his back. 'Scouts,' he barked. The team of a dozen unarmoured men on spry steeds, riding wide of the column, six on each flank, cantered to his side. 'To the mountains and to the mound. See that nothing awaits us in either location.'

'Yes, *Tuhkanti,*' the lead scout said.

Volca fell back then, just before the riders set off. 'And if all is clear, signal.'

'Indeed,' the lead scout agreed, digging a polished disc of bronze from his purse. It fitted snugly in his palm and caught the light like a torch.

'Three flashes,' Volca said. 'If it's all clear... three flashes, aye?'

'It will be so,' the lead scout said before heeling his mount round. The dozen sped off ahead, long dark locks dancing in their wake, before splitting into two groups of six, one heading to the mountains, the other speeding on ahead to the mound of Nerik.

Muwa dispersed his generals back to their divisions, then scowled into the hot ether. Sweat gathered on his top lip and time and again he swiped buzzing black flies away. Volca was a strange creature, but a loyal one, he thought. Kurunta was a legend, but perhaps too set in his ways. Still though, a loyal Hittite. *And Hattu is but a flea,* he thought with a gurn.

A short while later, the swirling heat haze lit up, three times, from the mountains then again, from beyond the Nerik mound. Muwa saw it as some sort of vindication. The long-range scouting had been diligent, but unnecessary. On they rode for another half hour through the deserted basin. Hattu's prattling complaints had been proved flawed. Pitagga was nowhere near. *And you should be thankful for that, Brother, for if he came for us right now, I would throw you and your damned Wolves into the front ranks and...*

'*Tuhkanti*, what is that?' one regimental chief said.

Muwa, nudged from his baleful inner dialogue, looked up, following the chief's pointing finger. The mound of Nerik was a blur no more. He was close enough now to see the crumbled arch of stone that once marked the western gate of the city.

The three-flash signal came again and again. A knot of figures stood on the near brim of the mound of Nerik. 'Is that our riders?' Muwa said, shading his eyes.

The chief was mute for a moment, then his eyes bulged. 'No! By all the Gods, he's here! He's already here!'

Pitagga, festooned in the black breastplate and crowned with the skull of a lion, stood atop the ancient mount, holding aloft a long spear with Sarpa's desiccated head.

Then, the source of the flickering came into view. Not the scouts' discs but a tall, silver form: the great silver statue of Tarhunda, on the back of a crude wagon and draped with Kaskan trinkets and furs. The wagon rolled across the top of the mound and drew up beside a thick, round crucible, a fire raging below it and the air above warping and bending violently from the heat. The statue was hastily lifted onto a timber winch of sorts. A chorus of murmuring and dry-throated shouts of confusion broke out from the Hittite ranks before and behind as they saw their holiest of holies being lifted by mountain men and swung to dangle over the crucible. A lone Kaskan mounted a set of timber steps, braving the heat, an axe resting on his shoulder, just waiting for the order to cut the ropes and send the sacred icon to a fiery end. But Muwa cared little for the shamed effigy. He could do nothing other than stare at the next wagon that rumbled up to the mound's edge, at the X-shaped frame mounted upon it and the form tied to it. *Atiya?*

His heart fell into his boots as he recalled the rumours of what Hattu had found on that foggy island. Men half-sawn on frames just like this one. He thought of Volca's words last night as he polished the shining white silver vest in Muwa's tent. *Brother or not, Hattu has failed you,* Volca had insisted.

This is your fault, Hattu. You did this. You!

'*Tuhkanti?*' a regimental chief gasped in a panic. 'Give the order. We will rush the mound and free them.'

But Muwa felt his legs trembling. No... not his legs... the soil underfoot.

'Earth tremors?' one of his captains said.

But Muwa had felt earth tremors before. This was different, the soil shivering as he had felt it do in the Arzawan War...

His head swung to the south and his eyes widened on the agitated warm air there before the Soaring Mountains. The silvery grass there seemed to jostle and change like oil in water and then he heard a baritone roar of countless foreign mouths.

'The scouts flashed three times...' he said weakly. *The scouts are dead,* he realised. Pitagga and his horde had got here well before them. With enough time to spare to set up the most wicked of ambuscades.

'*Tuhkanti*, guide us,' another voice cried from the panicking ranks.

'Turn the men to the south,' he croaked, then repeated it, this time with a hoarse cry. '*Turn!*'

***

The earth shook. Hattu's gaze seemed to be detached from his body. He could feel nothing, smell, hear and taste nothing. Only the dark vision atop the Nerik hill existed at that moment. Atiya, bound there, was everything. The men on the wagon flexed their long, two-handled saw. His mind flashed with the grim memory of the torn Kol on the foggy island. He wished for nothing other than to shapeshift into a falcon and speed for the mound. But even a raptor would not be swift enough to get there in time. Pitagga, holding Sarpa's black, leathery head like a banner up there, knew this.

'*Turn! To the south!*' Muwa's cry echoed across the grassy basin.

Hattu and every man in the Storm Division swung in that direction, seeing the air bend and twist there. Fright seized every one of them. Then, like a nightmare escaped from a tear in the ether, a flood of fierce warriors spilled into view, just over a slingshot's range away. Not a raiding party of hundreds, nor an army of a few thousand, way more than the ten thousand or so they had pursued through the Lost North, their bounding ranks widening and deepening. There were bearded curs from every one of the twelve Kaskan tribes. And not just Kaskans: many fierce and strange others ran with them, faces painted, small bones piercing lips, hair dyed, spiked or shaven, backs clad in armour, skins and fleeces. All in the Lost North, it seemed, festooned with sharpened bronze and copper. In a trice, their front was as broad as the Hittite Column was long, easily outnumbering the army of the Grey Throne. The odds had been turned on their head: now at least three spears for every Hittite pair.

'The stream is our line! Don't let them cross the stream!' General Kurunta bawled across the hastily forming ranks of the Storm and Blaze soldiers. A few companies here and from the Fury had already moved to face south and hold the near edge of the stream but many were still in shock, panicked, confused.

The Kaskan war horns blared low and then piercingly high. Hattu felt his mouth turn to sand and his guts to water at the sight of what was coming for them. A storm that no soldier could weather, surely? But he had to live… or she would die.

'Take your positions,' Hattu cried to the Wolves. He lurched forward, his trailing plume, tail of hair and forest-green cloak lifting in his wake as he splashed into the shockingly cool waters of the stream, wading in until he was shin-deep. Tanku and Dagon came with him as he knew they would.

'Come together!'

Their shields amassed as the Wolves pressed up either side of him.

Ten men wide and just six deep. More Storm companies arrived on their left and more again on their right, along with the men of the other divisions. He spread his feet and levelled his spear through the small, eye-shaped gap between his shield and Tanku's.

On the far side of the stream, the Kaskans had closed to fifty paces. They came like rabid hounds, mouths agape in their war cries, eyes unblinking. One hurled a copper axe as if it was a pebble. It hurtled through the air then plunged through the browband of a Storm captain's helm, breaking the helm, skull and ruining the brain within. His eyes rolled up in his head and blood came in gouts from his nostrils. He sank to his knees like a puppet whose strings had been cut then toppled face first into the brook – the waters too shallow to carry him away. A shower of slingstones came rattling down too, ripping holes through men's helms, shields, faces and torsos. A thick, strangled scream sounded from one of the Wolves as a stone smashed through his cheek and exploded from the back of his neck in a mizzle of blood. The scream was short lived.

With another blare of the foreign horns, the Kaskans erupted in a chorus of inhuman shrieking and broke into a sprint.

'Archers,' Kurunta howled.

Hattu sensed the disorder behind this long, thin front. He shot a look over his shoulder: right enough, the archers within the Hittite ranks were fumbling, bows not even strung. He saw others notice this too, casting looks at the Kaskans now just twenty paces distant, then taking tentative steps back from the hasty line at the stream. Hattu recalled the utter terror of the raid on Hattusa. That moment where the city had seemed all but lost, until he heard the boots marching down from the Great Barracks.

'Storm Divisiooon,' Kurunta bawled, bashing his spear upon his shield. 'Raise your *weapons!*'

A hiatus of a breath was followed by a stiffening, a resolve along the line. The steps back halted. Then the Kaskan cries were almost drowned out by the almighty cry in return from the five regiments of the Storm.

'Tarhunda, God of the Storm, *coat my heart in bronze!*' Hattu roared with the rest.

At the same time, the pipers amongst the ranks found their lungs and blew hard – the fierce skirls quickly falling into the frantic song of war. And it seemed to instil a bronze spine through the other divisions also.

'Arinniti's fire rages in our *blood!*' the officers of the Blaze pitched in.

'Let Aplu's Fury *rise!*' Muwa screamed, his maddened, torn gaze shooting along the line of his division and all the way to Hattu.

'Protect the *Labarna*, Appointee of the Gods!' Volca shrieked, the horned one taking up a position behind the front lines, near the royal carriage with the ring of Mesedi.

Now the Hittites were like a bronze, hide and leather redoubt holding the line of the stream, bristling with sharp spear points. The Kaskans splashed across the stream, water churning up in their wake, the veins in their bulging eyes and the red wetness at the back of their throats visible, axes and spears raised like demons' talons.

'The Wolves,' Dagon snarled through gritted, chattering teeth in the final moments.

'The Wolves!' Hattu growled, his body pulsing with emotion.

'*The Wolves!*' Tanku bawled as the enemy bounded over the last few paces.

At the last moment, the Mountain Wolves erupted as one in an animal wolf howl.

The endless horde smashed against the Hittite line in a serrated, shuddering boom of colliding shields, metal and men. Heads were cleaved, faces scored, necks opened and limbs severed, sent spinning through the air, hands still clutching weapons. Water and shingle spat and sprayed, mixed with blood and spit. Swords, spears, maces and axes swung, ruining bodies as the two long lines tussled, surged and sagged like giant, entangled millipedes.

A bull of a fighter tried to barge Hattu over, but he stayed on his feet, shoving back as a mass of axes and spears bit, hacked, prodded and hammered at his shield. Hattu sliced his spear downwards into the foe's thigh so deep the blood that pumped out was black and he was dead in a few heartbeats. A mace slammed down on the top of his shield, gripping the edge, the bronze fangs of the weapon's gem-eyed lion head biting as the holder tried to haul away the shield. Hattu slid his arm from the loophole to the rear and let the foe take the shield. The rugged fellow's eyes brightened in a moment of triumph, only to see the small bronze axe Hattu held in his shield hand. A fire raged inside Hattu and his hair and plume swung like whips as he swept the weapon up and into the foe's temple. The Kaskan's skull broke, his eye burst and a soup of grey-red filth spurted from the ruined head.

Snarling, panting, enraged, disgusted, Hattu twisted to the flashing movement on his left. He ducked back from the Kaskan spear then cast the axe out with a backswing of his arm. The three fang-like spikes on the back edge of the weapon sank into the attacker's neck like the bite of a predator. He drew the weapon back and the Kaskan seemed frozen for a moment, touching the three black holes in his neck. The warrior grinned and started laughing, thinking he was unharmed; then three dark red springs spouted from the holes. The man's laughter vanished, his face sagged and turned grey and he crumpled from sight.

Men fell from either side, Kaskans run through with Hittite spears and Hittites cleaved with Kaskan axes. Tanku and Dagon fought like wolves, butting, punching and kicking. Sargis took an axe blow to the side of his head that tore his ear off before he drove his spear up and hard into his foe's guts. Chief Raku flat-face struck down three Kaskan warriors, before his arm was cleaved off by an axe, then a sword punched through his face and another plunged into his chest.

Vultures began to gather above, screeching and swooping as if they were part of the battle. The water of the stream had grown hot, Hattu realised, knowing from the stink rising up that it was blood and floating entrails that had stolen the chill from it. When a Kaskan spear ripped through the leather armour on his shoulder, scoring deep across the flesh there, he let out a fierce cry. The Kaskan drove forward, forcing Hattu back from the water and onto his knees, knocking his helm off with a swat of his free hand then bringing a mace out and raising it, ready to crush Hattu's skull.

Hattu, pinned, gazed up, not at the warrior, but at the mound of Nerik, off past the right of the Hittite line. 'I'm sorry,' he mouthed to the tiny figure of Atiya up there.

The Kaskan's hand swept down, but another clean, snapping noise sounded, and the man brought down not the mace, but a stump where his forearm had been a breath ago. The warrior made an animal grunting noise, gawping at the angry red oval with a white bone core at the stump-end, before Tanku finished what Dagon had started, driving his spear through the Kaskan's neck from the side. The fellow tried to rasp some killer final line, but died with only a weak hiss.

Dagon and Tanku, soaked with sweat, streamwater and blood, dragged Hattu back as the Wolves' front shrank a little to close the gap Hattu had left.

'Let me up,' Hattu snarled, thrashing to be free of them.

'Hattu, *Captain*,' Dagon bellowed. 'We need to defend the rear… look!'

Hattu saw it before Dagon had even pointed it out: a golden cloud of dust shooting up from behind the mound of Nerik, like a fast moving serpent racing through shallow soil. But Hattu realised what it was – far more deadly than a serpent. He saw the glint of bronze, heard the pained whinny of horses, the snap of whips. Chariots. *Kaskan* Chariots? Hattu knew the Kaskans fought on foot – never on battle cars.

'No… how?' Tanku gasped.

At first he saw just a single vehicle, the sides daubed with streaks of black dye and with the face of a fanged demon painted on the front. It was led by two white stallions, rumbling towards the Hittite right, set to strike along the rear of the three divisions. Then, with some high-pitched horn signal, many more fanned out from behind this one, left and right. The now wide, staggered line of some two hundred chariots sped into a gallop. The men on board wore their hair in a curious fashion: shaved bald on top, long and flowing at the back and sides. They wore hide armour, some with bronze vests instead.

'Azzi,' Hattu stammered, recalling the talks in the palace planning room. 'The Kaskans sold those they captured from our lands to the Azzi… in return for a wing of charioteers.'

The Azzi drew bows and hoisted javelins, emitting a shrill, foreign cry.

'Back ranks, about face,' Hattu rasped. '*About face!*' he screamed as the Azzi cars sped to within one hundred paces of the Hittite rear, then loosed a cloud of arrows and spears. Only a fraction of the rearmost men turned in time.

'Shields!' Kurunta cried.

Hattu knelt and snatched up a dead Kaskan's shield just an instant before a pair of arrows whacked against it at throat height. The hail was thin, but most of the missiles struck unshielded flesh. Hittites went down in a swathe across the back of all three divisions. Now panic set in. Some turned, while those still facing the stream didn't understand what was happening and thought they had been routed.

'Stay in line!' Muwa's cry to the Fury men sailed across the plains of Nerik.

Hattu was sure the Azzi – being mercenaries – would now wheel away and come back for another volley, staying at a safe distance. But on they came, hurtling towards the Hittite rear, the warriors now drawing out sickle-like swords, the drivers bending the chariots' paths to sweep along the rear of the Hittite lines like harvesters. One vehicle arced like this just by Hattu, Tanku and Dagon. A scar-faced Azzi warrior leant from the side of the carriage and swung his sickle out. Dagon ducked, Tanku fell back and Hattu threw up his spear to block. The chariot sped on towards Kurunta's men, the sickle taking the heads from two warriors and tearing the jaw from another – Scarface shrieking in delight, his tongue extended as he snatched one of the spinning Hittite heads from mid-air and roped it by the side of his chariot where it danced like a gory bauble. The rest of the speeding vehicles wreaked similar havoc. And when the Azzi chariots finally pulled away, Hattu saw that they were being driven into a tight loop, set to come again: for a hail of arrows then another harvesting strike. The rear-facing line was in some order now, but still no match for marauding chariots.

As the Azzi war cars came round again, Hattu tossed his spear at the spokes of Scarface's chariot with what strength remained in his numb arms. The lance was shredded into kindling and the chariot went on, unharmed. A comrade fell by his side, and others barged against him, back-to-back. The Hittite line was bending out of shape, disintegrating, compromised by the fangs of Kaskan pressure pushing across from the southern bank and the constant scourge of the Azzi chariots circling unimpeded on the northern side. He heard men of the Wolves trying to hold the stream crying out as they were run through with spears and battered with cudgels. The stirring pipe song faltered too. One glance back and he saw the nearest piper being lifted up on the ends of Kaskan spears in a grim repeat of poor Sarpa's end.

'We're being cut to pieces,' Dagon cried as a hurling mace skimmed past his ear from behind and a charioteer's arrow spat into the earth between his feet.

The Hittite line, besieged on both sides, was shortening and thinning, falling into a disarray of man-on-man melee combat – a spitting, writhing trough of boiling bronze. Hattu saw the jaws of Pitagga's trap for what it was, just like the maw-cave of his dream: cut the bridge to deny the Hittites their supplies and chariots, bring war wagons of their own to the field, hit them from the back and the front. He looked along the Hittite lines, seeing guts being torn out, heads staved in, limbs hacked off.

All was lost.

CHAPTER 22

THUNDER OF THE GODS
SUMMER 1300 BC

Volca leapt up onto the roof of the royal carriage and crouched on one knee. Axes, stones and arrows hummed past him from every direction. He looked over the sea of fighting men all around him. There were no lines now – just chaos: a mass of snarling faces, flashing blades and spurting blood. The Hittite army was doomed. He cast his eye up to Nerik's mound, seeing Pitagga and his small retinue of guards up there. A pair of men waited by the frame, holding a long, two-handled saw. The young priestess tied there writhed in vain to be free.

'Aye, Lord of the Mountains, today is our day,' he muttered. 'Tomorrow, and every day thereafter… will be mine.'

A scrabbling, clawing sound came from the edge of the wagon. A filthy, bloody hand slapped onto the roof's edge, then another, clutching a straightsword. Then came the bald, sneering head of a Kaskan warrior. The cur scrambled up onto the roof and leapt at Volca, halting only when he recognised the Sherden.

'Forgive me, Master Volca,' he said. 'I did not realise it was you.'

Volca's skin prickled with horror. He was sure some of the Mesedi defending the wagon had heard. Without a moment's hesitation, he lunged forward and drove his trident up, under the Kaskan's chin. The central spike burst from the top of the warrior's skull, his eyes flooded with blood and rolled in his head and his face half-collapsed as Volca yanked the trident free and kicked the corpse from the wagon roof.

'Fool,' he spat.

And sure enough, down on the ground where the Mesedi were locked in frantic battle to protect their king, Gorru, the hirsute guardsman, was alternating between keeping Kaskans back with his spear and glancing up at the wagon roof, his eyes dark with suspicion.

'Time for a distraction,' Volca mused, glancing up at the Nerik mound again and drawing the polished bronze disc from his purse, angling his hand so it caught the sun. This conjured a throaty tirade from up there.

'Dying men of the Hittite ranks,' Pitagga cried, his voice carrying across the basin. 'Turn your eyes, if you still have them, to me.' The fighting carried on unabated: screaming, gurgling cries, groans, smashing bronze, clacking spears and whizzing arrows; but more than a few Hittite heads glanced to the mound. 'You will all die here, in the shadow of your long lost city. And on the ancient rubble of its temples, I will melt down your greatest god and I will split the last of your priestesses in two.'

Volca's lips curled up in a ghoulish smile. He imagined Atiya to be two of the bastard Sherden people who had peeled off his scalp and mutilated his genitals. He heard laments from some of the Hittite warriors, saw some visibly slow in their fighting, exhausted and now robbed of hope. One was speared through the neck, another finally let his arms drop to his sides, strength gone, the clamour of Kaskan axes he had been fending off now sinking into his chest at all angles.

Volca stood tall, glorying in the sound of slaughter, seeing the two warriors up on the mound flex their long copper saw. He tilted his head skywards and spoke to the cloudless azure ether – now thick with circling vultures – in a spiteful whisper.

'Tarhunda, God of the Storm, when I first landed on these foreign shores as a starving outcast they told me that you were almighty... invincible. They were wrong. *I* am invincible. You are nothing. Where are you now? Where is your thunder?' He gloried at the god's silence, stepping round on the spot, goading the skies.

Then he heard it.

A low, reverberating grumble rolled across the plains of Nerik. His face fell and he swung round to look east. He scoured the chimeral heat.

Nothing. But the noise grew louder and louder, sharper and more frantic, invisible but coming right for the fray. He backed away towards the edge of the carriage. Many heads in the sea of battling men glanced to the east too, the fighting slowing just a fraction. Then the heat haze swirled and, with a clap of thundering hooves, an arrowhead line of speeding Hittite chariots exploded from the mirage.

Volca, eyes like full moons, gaped at the sight: charging steeds, gleaming chariots, howling, roaring scale-clad warriors crowned with high, bronze helms, spears and bows primed, speeding straight for the Azzi chariots. He saw the fork-bearded Hurrian bastard, Colta, expertly guiding his two yellow-dun horses, a brute of a fighter crammed into the car with him.

How? Volca mouthed in panic.

The Hittite war pipes struck up again, defiant and strident.

'The Lords of the Bridle are here – they found a way across!' Gorru yelled. A mighty cheer arose at this and the fighting recommenced in full. 'The Gods are with us!'

***

The Lords of the Bridle sped forth, one hundred and forty or so chariots crashing into the Azzi war cars like a storm wind. Arrows blazed out, striking down the fierce mercenaries and their horses. Spears plunged through Azzi hearts as Colta's finest joined the fray. But the Azzi were quick to react, turning their attentions away from the Hittite infantry and delving into swift and deadly manoeuvres of their own, speeding and striking like asps. Three Hittite chariots were cast on their sides and one noble warrior – a member of the Panku and one of Hattusa's richest men, was robbed of his head. The battle had swung, but only back to a precarious and deadly balance – the infantry locked in combat with the Kaskan horde and the Lords of the Bridle weaving and bending expertly in a deadly dance with the Azzi.

Amidst the infantry fray, Hattu readied to tackle a giant Kaskan running for him, when Colta – having pulled his battle car from the chariot tussle – ran the foe down with a wet crunch and struck down at three others, opening a narrow corridor of respite and drawing his vehicle close to the Wolves. 'Riders amongst you, take to your cars,' the fork-bearded Hurrian cried as he arced away again, waving towards an approaching, small secondary wave of Hittite chariots – sixty strong. Hattu saw that they were being ridden by servants and stablehands. 'We need every chariot active,' he screamed before plunging into action against the Azzi once more.

'Thunder,' Dagon gasped.

'Rage…' Hattu added.

'Tanku, the Wolves are yours,' Hattu rasped. 'Wolves, fight on!' he yelled, before lashing out with his spear and fighting clear of the battle, then bounding over to where the secondary chariot wave cantered, a few hundred paces away from the eastern edge of the fight. He and Dagon saw Rage and Thunder tethered to the pale blue war car they had trained in at the Fields of Bronze. They waved the stablehand over, running alongside then leaping aboard their vehicle as the stablehand leapt off. A few other teams serving amongst the infantry broke from the foot melee to do likewise. Within moments they sped into a gallop and arrowed towards the delicately-balanced chariot battle.

The wind of the gallop rapped and howled around Hattu, deafening him to all but the blood crashing in his ears. Balanced like a warrior by Dagon's side, his left hand on the bronze lip of their car.

'Nock your bows and choose your targets,' a commander's voice cried out from his right. The warriors on the reinforcement chariots left and right immediately complied, pulling bows from their backs and nocking arrows.

Hattu let go of the chariot lip, spreading his feet on the reverberating rawhide mesh of the carriage floor to balance – just as Colta had taught him. 'Keep her level,' he cried over the thunder of hooves.

'Aye,' Dagon replied, his sinewy arms flicking the reins a fraction this way and that. Rage and Thunder responded to the slight tweaks of the leather cords as if they were connected to Dagon's fingertips by sinew and flesh.

Hattu lifted his bow, pulled an arrow from his back quiver and nocked. Arrows spat forth from the other chariots along the speeding

Hittite reinforcement line, thudding into unsuspecting Azzi drivers' and warriors' backs. Nine chariots were stricken: some crashing into one another, some falling to a standstill with their arrow-riven drivers slumped over the reins and others speeding off across the plain, arrow-pricked horses panicked and fleeing. But Hattu's arrow remained strung as his eyes combed the fray madly to find the right target.

Nuwanza's wraith applauded. *An arrow loosed in haste is an arrow gone to waste.*

'The Wolves!' Dagon cried, flicking his head across Hattu, to the infantry clash on their left. There, Tanku and the Mountain Wolves had been hewn away from the Hittite line and corralled into a tight knot by two speeding Azzi chariots on this side of the stream and a band of Kaskans charging across from the far side. Tanku's mouth was agape in a constant roar of encouragement, despite the young soldiers with him falling in droves.

Hattu's chest broadened as he drew back the bowstring until the thumb of his draw hand touched his ear lobe. He almost heard General Nuwanza's coaxing words from back in the academy as he pulled his shoulder blades towards one another for a fuller draw until his arms trembled just a little, then winked and trained the point of his arrow on the foremost of the two Azzi chariots.

The warrior on that war car swung out his sickle like a snake's tongue towards Tanku's throat. Hattu's smoke-grey eye ached at once and he saw his friend and chosen man – the one who had raised him to captain of his own volition – on the edge of death.

When Hattu loosed, the arrow flew fast and true. It did not strike the Azzi charioteer on the chest as he had intended, but skewered the cur's hand instead. The Azzi warrior shrieked, dropping his sickle and falling from the chariot to tumble over and over across the earth. Then, with a thick *snap* of vertebrae, he came to a halt, twitching, a blade of white bone poking from the back of his neck.

Tanku staggered back from the expected sickle blow, not quite believing he had been saved.

The second Azzi chariot then ploughed over the top of the corpse, dragging it for a distance, leaving a streak of blood on the trampled grass, before some part of the body caught fast on the chariot's wheel – with a *bang!* the vehicle bucked forward over itself, tossing driver and warrior ahead and crashing upside down in a riot of splinters, upturned thrashing hooves and frantically whirling wheels. An almighty cheer erupted from the Hittites within the infantry fray.

'Son of Ishtar!' Tanku cried, pumping his fist in the air, the other Wolves joining in.

Hattu let loose a wolf howl in reply before Dagon yelped some monosyllabic noise that brought his eyes forward again: they had charged to within paces of the thick of the chariot fray. A wall of dust and speeding battle cars. Like the training sessions at the Fields of Bronze, but with a slim chance of life as a prize.

'Spears,' the commander of the chariot reinforcements howled. '*Smash them!*'

Hattu tossed his bow to the car floor and plucked one of his three spears from the small leather strap holding them to the chariot's side. He crouched a little, right foot extended backwards for purchase, bringing the lance to the level just as Dagon cracked the whip over Rage and Thunder, who exploded into a full gallop. Hattu saw the Azzi chariot directly ahead, flank presented mid-turn. He saw the strung, gawping Hittite heads dangling from the chariot's side. The warrior onboard – *Scarface!* – screamed at his driver to turn faster.

Scarface's chariot swung to face them and he raised a javelin, targeting Hattu but not soon enough. Hattu's whole body flexed as his spear flew from his hand and hammered into Scarface's chest. The tip tore out one half of the man's ribcage – bone, cartilage and half a lung remaining impaled on the tip as the warrior spun away and fell from sight. They streaked on through the fray, enemy drivers and riders falling like wheat, reins cut and spokes smashed with carefully tossed bronze staves. Horses thrashed and men were thrown. Within moments of the arrival of the reinforcement Hittite war cars, the Azzi threat was in pieces. A handful of enemy chariots sped away, some to the eastern passes that led away from this basin, but a few fled towards the Nerik mound.

'Turn,' Colta howled, swinging his chariot towards the Hittite right flank, rounding it then crossing the stream, throwing up a sparkling mist. An arrowhead of Hittite chariots followed his lead like a skein of geese, wheels roaring as they churned across the water, whips snapping, war cries and horns bellowing as they once again sped up, scything along the southern banks, across the rear of the Kaskan lines. Kaskan heads turned, eyes bulging, disbelieving. Their own snare had been turned upon them.

Hattu and every other chariot warrior loosed arrow after arrow into the massed mountain men. The surviving bowmen of the Hittite infantry, at last relieved from the Azzi threat to their rear, now took to loosing their arrows too. Back and forth across the Kaskan rear the Hittite charioteers went. As they turned for another sweep, Hattu's eyes shot to the Nerik mound. He saw Pitagga up there, crying out some tirade, hands shooting to the skies, to the mountains and then to the axeman over the crucible and the bound Atiya. He spotted a flash of copper... the two warriors were positioning the saw between the priestess' legs.

Atiya!

'Hattu!' Dagon cried.

Hattu swung round to see that a band of Kaskan infantry were surging against the Hittite chariot assault, hurling javelins. One plunged past Hattu, nicking his cheek. From the corner of his eye he saw comrade crews felled: horses staggering and plunging to their knees. Hittite war cries turned to screams of pain as a handful of cars were pulled over by a swell of defiant mountain men – warrior, driver and horse's heads staved in with bronze-spiked clubs. The balance was swinging again.

The chariot shuddered as a Kaskan leapt aboard. The man was a giant, and immediately grappled Hattu in a wrestler's embrace, squeezing the air from his lungs. Hattu saw spots and lights flash before his eyes. But just before darkness took him, the pressure eased. The giant staggered back, Dagon's knife jutting from his neck. The Kaskan fell from the back of the chariot and was sucked under the wheels of the chariot behind. Nearby, other Hittite chariots had repulsed the Kaskan surge too. It was somewhere in the midst of those few critical moments that the day turned for the final time. Trapped amongst the Hittite divisions on the stream's north bank and the Lords of the Bridle behind them on the south bank, the Kaskans' nerve shattered. Their swell became an ebb tide, masses of them surging not at the chariots but between them, flooding for the mountains, for the eastern and western passes.

Over the fading storm of battle, Hattu heard Colta shouting: 'The day is ours!'

A song of desperate triumph broke out.

But Hattu's blood felt like fire. His limbs were numb, his heart crashing relentlessly. He looked to the mound of Nerik once more. Then he saw the demonic apparition of Kurunta, plastered in strips of skin and dripping with blood as he splashed across the stream to drive back the last clutch of determined Kaskans like an angry hound, twin blades whirling. The one-eyed general slowed beside Hattu's chariot. 'Are you deaf?' Kurunta bellowed like an ox. 'We're done here. Now go to the mound... ' he rasped. 'Save the effigy. Save *her!* I will follow on.'

Dagon responded with a tug of the reins even before Hattu could reply. Rage and Thunder peeled away from the scene of the battle, speeding towards the Nerik mound like flames licking from a torch.

Hattu braced as the chariot sped up the mound's lower slopes, one bloodied hand on his last spear. He watched as the sawmen steadied themselves by Atiya. He recognised the crow-faced one from the foggy island, saw his fingers curl as he took a firm grip of the saw handle. Hattu's right eye ached and he saw it so clearly: the man's knuckles whitening, the saw rising, lifting with it the hem of Atiya's robe. Her scream was long and shrill. Without a moment of thought, he hefted his spear and hurled it with everything he had. The lance shot through the air, up, up, up, and straight into Crow-face's temple. The man collapsed in a puff of blood, his head bursting like a rotten olive, red-grey muck showering the other sawman who backed away in fright. Pitagga swore black oaths at the frightened man before realising how close danger was. 'Protect the hilltop!' he roared. At once, a squadron of forty chosen Kaskan axe-warriors burst from the within the ruins atop the mound, forming a wall, blocking Hattu's path to Atiya.

'Break them!' Hattu snarled, gripping the lip of the chariot, willing Thunder and Rage to plough through the wall of men.

But the chariot swung away at the last, speeding around the girth of the hill, parallel to the baying warriors just above. 'They're too densely packed – we'd break them and ourselves,' Dagon cried, just as a volley of hand-axes and stones rained down around them

'Then go round!' Hattu yelled, pointing to the back slopes of the mound. But there, another squadron had emerged to guard that approach. More spears rained down, one nicking Thunder's croup. Hattu, oblivious to the danger, craned his neck, trying desperately to keep sight of Atiya up there.

'We can't break through alone,' Dagon yelled as a Kaskan arrow zinged from his helm.

'By the grace of the Storm God, you are not alone!' a voice thundered from the foot of the slope. Hattu looked down there to see, charging up the mound in a pack, the forty young men who remained of the Mountain Wolves: big Tanku, Sargis, Kisna... and General Kurunta at their head, his face in an animal rictus, his silvery braid whipping in his wake as he raced uphill.

The Kaskans lining the edge of the mount bristled, then Kurunta sprung up the last stretch of the slope like a pouncing lion, legs pedalling through the air as he drew his twin swords mid-leap. 'Tarhunda, coat my heart in bronze!' he bawled as he brought the blades together like shears around the neck of the biggest Kaskan. The foe's head spun free. Then the Wolves erupted in a howl and fell upon the rest of the Kaskan defence. Blood and chaos reigned.

Hattu and Dagon shared a momentary look, then Dagon slowed the chariot near the fray and both leapt from the car and plunged up the hill on foot to join the melee. It was a visceral contest now, with gasping men, ripping flesh and screams all around them. Hattu's body was spent of energy yet on he fought with a fire summoned from deep within.

Through a tiny gap in the mass of thrashing soldiers, he saw Pitagga, face pale with fright, backing away towards the wagon and the frame holding Atiya. He saw her eyes, wide and wet with tears, wrists and ankles struggling against her bonds. Pitagga untied her and looped an arm around her neck, using her like a shield. He pointed to the dangling silver effigy and the boiling crucible.

'Your God will be cast into the flames,' he screamed. 'Cut the ropes,' he yelled to the axeman on the timber steps beside the crucible. 'Cut the damned ropes!'

Hattu knew there was nothing he could do. He was too late: the axeman was already swinging his weapon. The Kaskan axe chopped through one of the two ropes. But, like a heavy necklace suddenly snipped at one side, the statue swung away from the cut like a hammer, towards the wooden steps, crashing through the support pillars and sending kindling in every direction. The axeman atop the steps could only flail wildly as he fell, face-first, into the crucible and the boiling ore it held. Hattu heard an animal shriek from within, amplified by the vessel. A breath later, a skinless hand clawed at the cauldron's edge, blood vessels and sinew boiling and retracting to leave just a skeletal claw. For an instant, an inhuman face rose up too, riddled with swollen bubbles of skin and crowned with blazing, shrivelling hair, staring out in confused horror, before one eye burst from the heat and the axeman toppled back into his fiery grave. The statue of Tarhunda came to a rest safely, canted, the loose end finding purchase on the ground beside the boiling vat, the Storm God watching as his would-be executioner was reduced to ash.

The edge of a copper axe nearly brained Hattu, tearing his eyes from the sight. He blocked the warrior's next blow then saw through another gap: Pitagga, pressing a dagger against Atiya's throat. Hattu's veins filled with ice. He charged for the gap, squeezing through, only for the axe face of one of Pitagga's two bodyguards to smack him hard on the shoulder, casting him to the ground. He sensed the axe and the spear of the other rising to chop down on him, but he did not care, seeing only the red runnel of blood that shot down Atiya's neck as Pitagga pushed the dagger in. He heard himself cry out, one hand stretched uselessly out towards her, their eyes locked in her final moments.

What happened next was a blur. A spinning frenzy of twin blades. Kurunta stormed through the Kaskan defence, alone, rolling then bounding to his feet again, skewering one of the two bodyguards standing over Hattu with one sword, then ramming his second blade into the other's belly, before lurching at Pitagga and thrusting a palm against the Kaskan Lord's wrist. The dagger spun from Pitagga's hands, away from Atiya's throat at the last.

Hattu felt his heart surge and plummet at once: it was a reckless move, a fool's move, just as Kurunta himself had preached. *Never spend your last weapon.* The one-eyed general had neither sword, shield nor spear to block the counterstrike of Pitagga's swiftly-drawn axe. The cur's blade hammered into Kurunta's flank, cleaving deeply.

When Kurunta One-eye fell, the Wolves erupted in a pained roar and overran the Kaskan blockade, breaking onto the mound top, enraged at the felling of their battle-master. The remnant of the Kaskan guard pulled back, forming a ring around their lord, swallowing up Atiya too in their midst, shrinking back, deeper into the ruins of the Nerik mound.

Hattu and the Wolves surged forward in pursuit of the retreating Kaskan guards, then he slid to one knee as he came to the broken form of General Kurunta. No healer could treat the deep, dark axe-wound in his side. 'You gave your life to save me, to afford her another few moments,' Hattu tremored, unable to believe the teak-hard warrior had been beaten in combat. 'The silver effigy is safe too.'

Kurunta's good eye was growing distant. 'I have lived my life in worship of Tarhunda but... damn the effigy... save the priestess.'

Hattu nodded, grief entangled with the fire of battle. He made to rise and obey the general's last order, when Kurunta grabbed his wrist. 'Prove your father wrong, lad... prove Ishtar wrong... '

Hattu gazed down at him, hearing his breath rattle and seeing his pupil dilate. Like the passing of an uncontrollable storm, General Kurunta was gone. Hattu stood tall, his teeth grinding like rocks. 'Pitagga!' he roared, stalking forward, seeing the knot of Kaskans still backing away, vanishing into the shards of old Nerik's fallen buildings.

But before he could close upon them, a grinding of wheels and a puff of colour to his left snagged everyone's attention: there, three shapes spat forth from the ruins of an old stable and sped down the southern edge of the mound. Hattu's smoke-grey eye ached as he saw it: Pitagga, driving an Azzi chariot, racing down onto the plain and off to the south, the lance with Sarpa's head upon it standing proud. Flanking him were two more chariots, crewed by cruel-eyed Azzi men.

'He's headed for the Soaring Mountains,' Dagon cried. 'If he reaches them then he will melt away once again.'

Hattu heard him, but took none of it in. He glanced at the second, crumpled form on the floor of Pitagga's chariot. 'He has Atiya,' Hattu roared, backing towards his own battle car, where Thunder and Rage waited.

Dagon was onboard in a heartbeat.

'Ride... *Ride!*' Hattu screamed.

***

Volca, perched like a raven on the carriage roof, scowled at what he was seeing. The cursed armies of the Grey Throne had turned the day – Kaskan warriors were breaking away in packs, fleeing in every direction. And now... now Pitagga himself had abandoned Nerik.

He watched the three Azzi chariots speed away to the south. 'Aye, you pig-farming son of a whore, run. I should never have invested so much in you,' he growled. Then he saw Hattu's chariot in pursuit and realised something: it was over for the Lord of the Mountains and the Kaskans. The battle was lost. But *his* battle was still there for the taking. The sick king would soon fall into eternal languor. And the hateful brothers... were they not only hours before swearing death upon each other? His sulk lifted into a smile, and he leapt down from the carriage roof, landing with a wet crunch on fallen men. The carriage sides were spattered with blood and innards.

He leant in once to hover over the ailing king. 'Now, Great King, I must leave your side,' he said, uncorking and tipping his last vial of pungent root juices down the king's throat – the final dose, he reckoned. 'The princes need my help, it seems...'

King Mursili's eyes widened then the lids drooped and his whole face sagged.

Volca threw away the empty vial then swung away from the wagon, trod through the carpet of dead, inhaling the metallic stink of drying blood, hearing the rhapsody of buzzing flies and feasting vultures like a thunderous round of applause from a court full of sycophants. He came to Prince Muwa, whose black-armoured shoulders rose and fell in exhausted gasps as he directed his Fury ranks to refrain from chasing after the fleeing Kaskan infantry.

'Leave them to Colta's chariots,' he bawled.

'*Tuhkanti,*' Volca said. 'Pitagga escapes.'

Muwa swung round, following Volca's pointing finger.

'He makes for the mountains, and has the priestess in tow.'

Muwa instinctively stepped in that direction, then bristled in helplessness.

'Fear not, however, for the Son of Ishtar gives chase,' Volca said, then waited, watching, knowing what the prince would do next.

Muwa flinched angrily, then looked to one of Colta's chariots nearby, drawn up and driverless.

Yes, do it, Volca purred inwardly. 'Drive, *Tuhkanti,*' he said, leaping aboard. 'I will be your warrior.'

Muwa climbed aboard the near vehicle and fumbled with shaking hands to take up the reins. 'Ya!'

The chariot spat forward away from the remains of the battle. Men shouted after their *Tuhkanti* in confusion, but Muwa's face was hard, his eyes aflame with confusion and hatred.

The wind howled as they sped, tossing up Muwa's thick dark hair and Volca's red cloak. Volca caressed his trident and eyed the southern stretches of the basin and the mountain paths to which Pitagga was headed. It was foolish for one prince of the Grey Throne to give chase in there, detached from their army, but both? Anything could happen in there.

Anything.

CHAPTER 23

OF SPITEFUL KIN
SUMMER 1300 BC

The world around Hattu was a blur: the grassy plain speeding past in the whipping wind of the ride. The fleeing trio of chariots was but a distant blur, hurtling towards a shadowy pass that led into the Soaring Mountains.

'Their horses are no match for ours – they'll tire soon,' Dagon yelled. 'Colta's horses can run and run.'

Hattu willed it to be so. And a short way before the shadowy mountain pass, he saw that they were gaining on Pitagga's two flanking chariots.

'Look, they're slowing.'

'Aye, but not because they're tired,' Hattu said.

Indeed, the three Azzi war cars moved like ibises in flight, the two flankers falling back in perfect harmony until they were just a handful of paces from the left and right edges of Hattu's chariot. Hattu watched each, knowing that one would attack first and would need his full attention. The leftmost chariot warrior shrieked something and Hattu's mind flashed with Ruba's teachings once more, interpreting the words: *'Loose spears, as one!'*

'Ho!' Hattu cried, grabbing the lip of the chariot.

Dagon, Gods' blessing, did not hesitate. Colta's assiduous training kicked in and he yanked on the reins without delay. '*Ho!*' Rage and Thunder's blistering pace halved within a heartbeat – the same heartbeat that saw the spears of the two enemy chariots fly through the air where Hattu and Dagon might have been, ploughing harmlessly into the grass instead. The enemy pair gawped, then reached down to snatch up fresh spears as their drivers slowed a little to fall level once more. Hattu swung right, pulling his bow from his shoulder, nocking, drawing and aiming in one fluid motion. *Twang!* The arrow thrummed through the air and tore out the throat of the warrior, who slumped heavily forwards against the lip of the car, clawing at his neck. The sudden shift of weight result was calamitous, the front of the car tipping and knocking one horse from its stride, the forward end of the draught pole stabbing into the ground, bending then shooting upright, the car then bucking violently up and over the shredded end of the pole like a vaulter. It hurtled through the air, tossing both men out and dashing them on the ground, before crashing down in an explosion of bronze and timber.

'Hattu!' Dagon screamed, slapping a hand over his chest, pushing him back. A spear spat through the tiny corridor of space the action had created, and Hattu swung to the leftmost chariot. The warrior there did not attack again, instead shooting a look to the trail ahead then barking something at his driver. The Azzi war-car bucked and shuddered as it closed in, like a runner intent on shouldering a rival off the track.

Hattu soon understood: a wall of shadow enveloped them then as they entered the mountain pass. Instantly, the din of the chase intensified tenfold, echoing hooves, snapping whips, frantic whinnies and crunching wheels. As they sped side-by-side up the narrowing, winding mountain path – a wall of rock on the left side and a drop on Hattu and Dagon's right – the Azzi warrior lifted his spear two handed, preparing to thrust down towards Hattu's chest as if to poke him and his car off the edge of the swiftly-rising track.

Hattu's fingers flexed impulsively for the spear and shield he did not possess. The bow was no use at this closeness either. He snatched the curved sword from his belt. Against a lengthy spear, it was a poor match. The enemy warrior's lance lashed out. Hattu dodged it but lost his footing in doing so. Balance deserted him and he toppled from the back of the car.

He dropped the sword, head and feet changing places and dread seizing him. But his palms clasped the low lip at the back of the chariot. His knees and lower legs thwacked into the dust however, trailing behind the chariot, skin being flayed off as if by shaving blades. He cried out, dust and pebbles scattering under him, spitting out over the now precipitous drop on the right-hand edge of the path. He clawed at the mesh of the rawhide floor in an attempt to haul himself back into the car, when a crude thump knocked the chariot towards the edge of the high track and cast Hattu back to dangling from the rear lip of the vehicle.

'Die, Hittite scum!' the Azzi snarled, bashing his spear butt against the side of the chariot again. This time, the right wheel skidded and skated on the shale right on the track's edge. Hattu swung out like a bob on a string, legs kicking out over the drop – now a deadly plunge onto a dry ravine bed. He held on with the fingers of one hand, seeing their rightmost chariot wheel on the cusp of slipping over the edge, seeing Rage's hooves scraping and sliding to keep away from the precipice. But he growled and drew on all of the hard-won muscles his few summers of training had bestowed upon him, pulling himself back onto the carriage. He scrambled onto his burning, flayed knees on the rawhide floor and grabbed his sword, just as the Azzi warrior stabbed out with his spear at Dagon, over Hattu's crouched head. The strike was brutal, and well-placed to pierce Dagon's ear and burst his head like a ripe pomegranate, until Hattu lurched up to bat the spear away with one palm then cut upwards with his sword, cleaving the foe's face off. The man's fingers moved to the pink cross-section of bone and flesh that had once been his face, at once robbed of all his senses. Hattu saw the enemy driver gawp in alarm, and his hands twitch to try and barge them from the side again. In a flash, Hattu snatched Dagon's whip and lashed it past the bewildered, faceless Azzi warrior so the end raked across the eyes of the driver like a cat's claws. The driver screamed, his hands going for his face, one rein pulled unintentionally tight, one dropped. The enemy horses sped up in confusion, the Azzi car shooting ahead of Hattu and Dagon towards a sharp left bend in the path. The enemy chariot slewed to the right and shot off the edge of the path. The screams and whinnies were shrill and unbroken, until a cacophonous crunch of flesh and timber dashing on stone echoed up from the drop.

Hattu panted, spitting sweat from his lips and blinking it from his eyes, scouring the ever-rising path ahead for Pitagga's chariot. 'Where is he?'

'Not far, look,' Dagon panted.

About a quarter danna ahead, approaching the next bend in the track, they saw Pitagga's chariot – marked out by the grim head-topped pole that jutted vertically from the car. He was speeding ever higher into the mountains. Speeding, then slowing, then crawling. Pitagga lashed and lashed the whip at the two exhausted white stallions, not over their heads, but at their backs, flaying the hair and flesh from them. The Kaskan Lord slipped round a blind bend at a mere trot, but Hattu knew they had him.

'He's alone,' Hattu said as they approached the bend. 'He is strong and well-armed, but we have each other.'

'But damn, we do,' Dagon said immediately.

'When he abandons his chariot,' Hattu said as they drove round the bend, 'we can outfox him. He is strong but he will ti-'

Hattu's words ended as they rounded the bend where the path opened out on a high, wide table of rock, splashed with molten sun and long shadow, open to a drop left and right before it became a winding path again on the other side. Pitagga's chariot rested there, driverless and stationary.

Hattu saw the slumped form in the car. *Atiya?* And poor Sarpa's head. But no Pitagga.

'Wher-' Dagon started, just as, from the rock-face at the left side of their slowing chariot, a shape leapt from a niche, a flash of bronze catching the sunlight.

'Dagon!' Hattu yelled, throwing his friend out of the way. But the flat of the axe smacked into Dagon's temple. Knocking him from the chariot and onto the track where he lay, motionless. Hattu leapt back as the axe came around again, splintering the wall of the now halted chariot car. Rage and Thunder whinnied and reared up, fetlocks thrashing. It was enough to drive Pitagga back. But he laughed, withdrawing just a few steps onto the table of rock to stand wide-legged before his own chariot.

Hattu, shivering with exhaustion, stooped to check on Dagon –

keeping his eyes on Pitagga the whole time. Dagon's neck pulsed and he let out a weak moan. Hattu stood, curved sword in hand. He stalked forward, ahead of Rage and Thunder and onto the flat, circular table of rock. Silence reigned bar the gentle mountain breeze. After the relentless din of the battle and the chase, it was an eerie contrast. Pitagga squared his bulky frame, making it clear that none would get past him.

'Atiya, I'm here,' he shouted past Pitagga.

'Ha-Hattu?' she mumbled, her legs and arms tightly bound.

'You'll be free soon,' he assured her.

'Will she? You know I have killed hundreds of warriors, don't you?' Pitagga chuckled.

'But none today,' Hattu remarked, noticing how Pitagga's lion-helm was undented, how his rusty beard and locks, his fine black vest and fierce axe were untainted with blood.

'Many older and far stronger than you,' Pitagga continued, ignoring the comment.

Hattu glowered at Pitagga, standing between him and his tortured love, standing between him and the dishonoured skull of his long-dead brother. 'Then your head will be some prize,' he said flatly.

Pitagga laughed fiercely, pointing at Hattu's short curved sword. 'You do not even have a proper weapon, Prince.'

'Stand aside or I will show you its edge, up close,' Hattu said, his body pulsing with cold, anticipatory dread. But the fear was harnessed, his feet poised to spring, fingers flexing on his sword hilt, eyes on the Kaskan Lord.

'Very well,' Pitagga said with a smirk. The dark mirth faded though as he hoisted his double-headed axe and swung it around his head, leaping forward and roaring as if taking on the spirit of the lion whose skull crowned his head.

Hattu and Pitagga's blades clashed. The Kaskan Lord's axe-blow was mighty, and Hattu's sword edge could only deflect it, the axe head streaking along his arm, making a shallow but lengthy and stinging cut.

'I killed a man like that once,' Pitagga chuckled as they stumbled past each other and came round once more, 'a hundred such cuts and he bled to death.'

'Then his wraith will be waiting for you in the Dark Earth tonight,' Hattu growled.

Pitagga swung his axe again, this time for Hattu's midriff. Hattu ducked back, his heels scuffing the edge of the table of rock and the death plummet as the pair circled. Hattu jabbed his dirk up for Pitagga's ribs, but the Kaskan Lord threw an elbow down, batting the strike away. His breath came in rasps now – his throat unwatered since noon. His limbs felt weak and his blood like tar.

'That's the trouble with young warriors,' Pitagga purred. 'They are over-eager, and tire themselves early in the day. When I walk in the ashes of Hattusa, I will be sure to have my bards tell stories of your foolishness.'

'Your bards already compose tales of your efforts today. The brave lord with the unsullied sword... fleeing alone from a catastrophic defeat.'

Pitagga's lip twitched. 'Enough play,' he said with a low growl and lunged forward, the axe swinging and chopping in a blur. Hattu leapt and rolled, the mighty blade crashing down in his wake. He tried to score his sword across Pitagga's calves, only for the axe to chop down and cut the blade in half. Weaponless, Hattu scrambled back. Pitagga's axe hacked down again and again, and it was all Hattu could do to roll clear each time.

'But damn, you are a bothersome foe,' Pitagga said, steadying his breath. 'Can't you stay still for a moment so I can cleave your skull?' He glanced at the chariot, then grunted in amusement, stalked over there and plunged his hand into the car, then wrenched Atiya up by her hair. Bound and thrashing, Atiya cried out. 'Perhaps this will bring you closer?' He tossed Atiya down like a trussed hog. Her head dashed on the ground and she fell limp as Pitagga brought his axe up over her neck.

Hattu saw the axe rise, saw Pitagga's face twist with effort, saw the bronze edge plunge towards Atiya. In an instinctive blur, he dragged the chariot whip from his belt and lashed out with it. The leather strap licked out, across the gap between Pitagga and him. It coiled around the Kaskan lord's right wrist, snatching the axe from his grip. The great weapon clattered to the ground and Pitagga staggered a few steps to one side, crying out.

There was a brief hiatus of disbelief, before Pitagga roared, drawing out his straightsword and sliding to his knees and raise it over Atiya. Hattu felt his heart thunder as the very ether around him crackled. He lunged forward to take up the fallen axe, then swept it up, batting the sword from Pitagga's hand with one strike, then bringing it down upon the Kaskan's head with the other. With a thick clunk like a breaking slab, Pitagga's lion-skull helm was cloven and his head too. His shrewd and dark mind was scattered across the high, wide stretch of mountain path like a pot of rotten offal. The axe-blade sank deep, cleaving right to his neck. His eyes rolled in his head and some hollow grunting sound escaped from his riven throat, the mighty axe wedged tight. Hattu let go of the weapon haft and Pitagga swayed there for a moment, near the cliff's edge, before he slumped to his side and plummeted, soundlessly, into the shadowy abyss of the mountain gully.

'And so ends the reign of the Lord of the Mountains... ' Hattu panted.

He fell to his knees, taking Atiya in his arms and hugging her, kissing her forehead. She groaned – as did Dagon nearby – as he set about untying her ankles. 'I'm so sorry, Atiya. I should have been there to protect you. I should have freed you long before now, I... '

The grinding of more chariot wheels echoed up the mountain path. He looked up, seeing a single vehicle ascending. When he saw the driver, all of the emotion of the day – the hatred, the anger, the spite – rose in him again.

Muwa...

He stood, taking up Pitagga's dropped straightsword instinctively, letting the blade hang by his side.

***

The dying sun dripped fire, casting long, weary shadows across the plains of Nerik – shining a harsh light across what had only hours ago been a silvery meadow, and was now a bruised, scarlet fen, decorated with riven men: twisted, trampled corpses, gaping, lifeless faces and blue-grey innards. Shards of white bone, arrows and broken spears jutted. A frenzy of flies swarmed and an army of feasting carrion birds tore at corpses.

King Mursili saw from his sick bed his famous and feared army, limping like a broken thing. Victorious… but at an incredible cost. Men stumbled to and fro amongst the dead, shaking, shivering, clutching shattered arms or stumps, holding mortally gashed bellies and pressing dirty rags to torn faces. Propped in his wagon, he heard the panting, croaking reports of many officers, saw from the corner of his rheumy eyes the concern on their faces as they stood by the wagon window, slick with sweat and blood.

'Four whole regiments have been annihilated, My Sun,' a Captain of the Blaze said darkly. 'Another five have lost half their men or more. All told, nearly five thousand men met the Dark Earth today and another three and a half thousand will never fight again.'

A clatter of wood rang out here and there as pyres were thrown together. The scrape of spades seemed unending as others dug graves – there was simply not enough wood in the surrounds of Nerik to burn so many corpses. Mursili felt a bead of rheum spill over one eyelid and scamper down his cheek.

'But the divisions still retain their strong core, My Sun. The Storm, the Blaze, and the Fury – the veteran regiments within each fought like lions,' Colta said without a trace of triumph. 'Pitagga's trap was a wily one, but the masses he gathered were simply not strong enough to break the bronze shoulders of the Hittite army. The Kaskans lost three men for every two of ours. They *are* broken, My Sun.'

Mursili felt a swell of urgency. 'Pi…' he croaked weakly. 'Pitag… ' The poison Volca had fed him a short while before had been potent, and he could almost feel it seizing his already wasted muscles, turning them grey and useless.

Colta's face lengthened. 'Pitagga escaped,' he said.

The Hurrian knew as well as the king: so long as Pitagga roamed to whip up dissent, the Kaskan War remained alive, the Hittite realm could afford no attention to the badly neglected and gravely threatened eastern and western frontiers… and the Grey Throne remained curtailed, tangled with its own near north, a great power in name only. His vision changed, darkening around the edges.

'But Prince Hattu took chase after him,' Colta added, his eyes alight again with an ember of hope and fear, 'into the mountains on a chariot.'

'Prince Muwa set off after him too, in a chariot with Volca,' another officer added.

The shadows drew back and Mursili's body seized up for an instant.

He remembered Volca's last words to him: *The princes need my help, it seems...*

'M... my... bo... boys?' he said with ever-more distress. He felt his weak heart bang like a drum.

'Aye,' Colta said uneasily, 'we haven't seen either of them for some time. Scouts are heading up there now, but... '

The shadow-veil closed in, and Mursili saw in the darkness the swaying, curvaceous form of the winged goddess, her talons clacking as she stalked around him.

High in the Soaring Mountains, they chased the Kaskan lord,
They turned upon each other, and both did draw a sword...

Mursili felt a part of his heart blacken and crumble away. *No... please!*

***

High within the Soaring Mountains, Muwa's chariot ground to a halt by the circular table of rock.

'The young prince has done it again,' Volca gasped, leaning keenly over the front of the chariot, agape. 'This is *his* victory.'

Muwa's mind was in strips. The battle rage pounded in his veins still. The ignominy of leading the army into Pitagga's trap flayed at his pride.

'The Mountain Lord died at his hand – he will surely be the toast of the army... the toast of all the lands, now.' Volca continued, pointing at the shard of broken lion skull from Pitagga's helm. 'And the young priestess, his true love, lives only because *he* saved her. Is it not a wondrous thing?'

Muwa felt the words like hot pins in his chest.

'Though you should be careful, *Tuhkanti*,' he said, his tone changing to that of a cautioning tutor, 'for although it is a good thing when men of the royal line are thought well of by the people and the armies, it can become dangerous if they think him... the *best* of the royal blood. For that is your place surely, is it not?'

Muwa's dark face creased even more. 'My Father is ill, not dead. *He is the best of the royal blood.*'

'Of course he is,' Volca said. 'But all can see he is not far from the Dark Earth. He cannot continue to rule in his weakened condition. Another will have to rise to rule in his stead. When that happens, I fear you will be pushed aside... in favour of the Son of Ishtar... and his beautiful priestess. Look... *look* how he watches you approach... with a sword in his hand – a drawn sword!'

The hot pins became glowing lances. He threw down the whip and leapt down from the chariot, striding towards Hattu. The lonely mountain path was otherwise deserted bar Volca and the unconscious Dagon and Atiya. He heard a million chattering voices in his head, felt shame, greed, lust and fury broil in his heart. He realised then that he too held his curved sword in his hand. Had he drawn it a moment ago or had it been there for some time? He did not know.

This must end, he realised, *now.*

***

Hattu glared at his brother.

Muwa strode towards him. His face was streaked with red, as if a giant cat had clawed him, and the famous shining silver cuirass was clad in battle-filth. The stiff mountain wind cast his hair across his face, set in a rictus. His ice-bright eyes were fixed on Hattu. Utterly fixed. His hand hung by his waist, clutching his jewel-hilted dirk firmly, his white knuckles trembling and his arm stiff. He strode towards Hattu at an unnerving pace. Hattu felt as he had in those moments before the Kaskan horde had smashed into the Hittite lines.

Fear, anger... hatred?

His oath with Father echoed in his mind. *Then you believe Ishtar?*

That it is me who will slay princes and kings? That it is me who will seize the throne?

Darkness and light waged war in his heart.

Suddenly, it seemed all too clear what he had to do.

Hattu strode towards Muwa, matching his pace. His arms shot up and so did Muwa's. A clatter of swords sounded as both blades were dropped to the ground and the pair came together in a fierce embrace. The wind leapt from Hattu's lungs. Muwa pressed his face into the side of Hattu's head. 'I love her too,' he said, his voice thick with emotion.

'Brother?' Hattu whispered, confused.

'Atiya. I love her with all my being, and it drove me to think dark thoughts,' he continued with a weak sob. 'Forgive me, Brother. For now I know,' he said, withdrawing a little to look his brother in the eyes, tracing his thumbs over Hattu's bloodstained cheeks, 'now I understand that she loves you.'

Hattu's mind raced back over the darkness that had enshrouded his brother. It had all begun with his first dalliances with Atiya. 'I did not think anyone could feel for her what I feel... but... you love her too?'

Muwa smiled weakly, it was a look that took Hattu back to their early days of carefree play. 'Who could not, Brother? And I always will love her. But as my brother's woman and soon his wife. As my sister.' He traced a finger over Hattu's feather cloakpin. 'And I heard it from one of my men that Arrow had died. I am sorry, Brother. I did not know about it and my words and harsh treatment of you and your men in these last days must have seemed insensitive.'

'Then it wasn't... '

Muwa frowned.

Hattu did too. *Of course it wasn't Muwa. But then who? Who killed Arrow?*

'Hattu... Muwa?' Atiya groaned, lifting her head groggily. Both looked to her. She smiled weakly, and they crouched by her side. Suddenly, her face twisted in horror, looking past them. 'He's here!'

'Who?' they both said, eyes searching her.

'Look out!' she cried.

Hattu and Muwa turned to see Volca the Sherden, Gal Mesedi,

Protector of the King, lurching towards them, trident levelled, set to plunge into them and drive them off the side of the rocky table. Hattu pushed Muwa back and threw himself aside too. Muwa threw out a leg to trip the Sherden, who tumbled over on himself, his horned helm falling from his head and off over the edge of the path, into the void. Now both Hattu and Muwa took up their swords again and stalked towards him.

***

Volca's outstretched hand shook in vain over the drop, as if clawing at the memory of the helm. His cloak and the ring of hair around the back and sides of his head billowed in the mountain breeze and he felt the cool wind lick at the scabrous crown of vein, sinew and bone.

Behind him, the priestess continued to reveal his secrets. 'He was Pitagga's man. He has been poisoning the king. He lured the army here. He is a traitor.'

He turned to face the two approaching brothers. He recognised the look in their eyes. He had seen it before, on that day when the ingrates he had liberated on the Isle of the Sherden turned upon him and peeled off his scalp. Before he had broken free of their dungeon and escaped the island. He saw in the brothers' eyes and in the priestess', the revulsion at his disfigurement. He saw the whiteness of the princes' knuckles, the sharpness of their swords.

He felt his heart rattle against his ribs and his step grow uneven as he backed away. He retreated slowly until he came to Muwa's chariot, then flicked his trident across the reins and led the nearest stallion from under the yoke. Climbing onto its croup, he trained the end of the trident on Hattu and Muwa, his eyes darting beyond them to the far end of the table of rock and the continuing mountain path there. It was the only way: behind lay the Hittite army and on either side was a death plunge.

The two princes crouched like warriors, challenging him to try. With a shriek, he heeled the stallion into motion, spearing into the space between them. Muwa's blade struck across his green scale vest. Hattu's sword clashed with the trident with a resounding *clang*. The blows nearly threw him from the stallion's back, but he clung on and broke past the pair, charging on up the path.

'Ya!' he cried, tasting the momentary glory of escape, then feeling a crushing sense of disgrace: another throne he had worked so hard to make his own had slipped away.

***

Mursili trembled in his wagon-bed.

High in the Soaring Mountains, they chased the Kaskan lord,
They turned upon each other, and both did draw a sword,

Mursili's lips trembled. *No… please…*

Ishtar crouched so her lips hovered by King Mursili's ear, continuing her poem:

But from the depths of hatred, something golden grew,
The swords fell onto the earth, and they were brothers anew.

Mursili's thumping heart slowed, and he heard something. A distant rumble of hooves. A murmur of surprise from the men around the wagon...

'My Sun!' Colta yelped as if a boy again.

Unable to move his head on his pillow, King Mursili saw from the corner of his eye a young, plague-scarred soldier riding a white stallion from the direction of the Soaring Mountains. Dagon, he recalled, recognising Hattu's army companion. 'Pitagga is dead!' Dagon cried as he rode through the sea of battle-stained Hittites. The bustle and nervous chatter grew into a barely contained clamour.

Then a single chariot streaked into view behind Dagon. Muwa and Hattu stood upon it, lashed with the red paint of battle, each held one hand aloft, clasped together.

The sea of soldiers gawped, then exploded with an almighty cry: 'Pitagga is dead!' they echoed Dagon's news in disbelief then again in triumph, falling to their knees by the stream, casting up water with their hands and singing words of praise to the Gods and the spirits.

'The *Tuhkanti* has slain the Kaskan lord!' men yelled in delight and relief, casting proud salutes at Muwa as the chariot weaved through their masses.

But Muwa's free hand patted Hattu's chest. 'The Lord of the Mountains lies still and cold. But it was the doing of the Son of Ishtar!' Muwa howled.

A cheer exploded across the men once again as the chariot circled. Mursili saw that the slight, pretty priestess, Atiya, was aboard the chariot too, clinging to Hattu's waist. The sight sent a thick, warming sensation through his frail body.

'*Tuhkanti*!' they yelled at Muwa. 'Son of Ishtar!' they cried to Hattu. 'Tarhunda's favour follows you!' the men wept and sang, beating spears on shields. In those few instants, the charnel plain had been transformed into a scene of triumph. A war piper struck up a frenzied tune of victory.

'I knew he could do it,' a voice said quietly. Mursili saw General Kurunta, resting one elbow on the carriage window, talking to the king but watching the events on the plain.

Strange, Mursili thought, the gnarled old veteran seemed young again – his face crease-free and both of his eyes present.

'I know why you doubted him,' another voice said. Old Ruba was there now too. 'And I understand why you tried to hold him back, but I know there is greatness in him, My Sun.'

'Loyal, noble, greatness,' Nuwanza added. The trio reached down and squeezed Mursili's hand. Then, they were gone, and Mursili realised they would not be back.

The king felt his eyelids droop. Behind his closed eyes, he saw that she was still there, as she always had been.

Ishtar? he asked her.

She simply continued to pace carefully around him, seductress and huntress as one.

The sound of hands slapping on the wagon's window ledge scattered the vision and he opened his eyes.

'Father?' Hattu and Muwa gasped. 'Did you hear? Pitagga is dead, dashed in the mountain gullies. The shame of the Lost North is gone with him,' Muwa panted. He held up a leather sack, tightly tied. 'Sarpa's dishonour is over also.'

'Nerik, Hakmis, Zalpa… they are all ours once again. The Grey

Throne rules the Soaring Mountains once more,' Hattu said. 'Old Ruba would have been so proud. Lady Danuhepa awaits you back in Hattusa. Think of these good things... *golden* things.'

Both boys held his arm as they spoke. Only now Mursili realised one who had gone into the mountains had not returned. 'V...' he tried to speak. 'Volca...'

'Volca was a treacherous cur,' Muwa said flatly. 'It was he who was responsible – in league with Pitagga throughout it all – for the missing healers, for the death of Sarpa, of Ruba, of Nuwanza, of Kurunta, of Hattu's falcon... and for what has happened to you, Father. He has been poisoning you all this time.

'I... know,' Mursili whispered. A tear crawled from his eye and blotted on the pillow.

'But Volca lives still. He fled,' Hattu sighed. 'Through the mountains and on to the south.'

'We have already put scouts on that road. Word will reach the corners of our lands,' Muwa insisted, 'and he will be brought before you. Though I fear there is not punishment grim enough in our tablets of law to subject him to. His two kinsmen have been arrested, taken from their places in the Mesedi and bound in chains. Yet they are merely worms – he was the serpent.'

But he is gone, Mursili thought, the effort to speak those words too great. *The Kaskan threat has been seen off, and my boys are in harmony – true brothers.*

Yet when his eyelids drooped again, he saw that still, Ishtar remained, waiting... for what?

CHAPTER 24

GODS OF NERIK
SUMMER 1300 BC

'Father?' Muwa said in a gentle voice, shaking him softly.

King Mursili woke to see that several days had passed. The noonday sun shone brightly and the plains of Nerik had been cleared of corpses. The plagues of flies and vultures were gone. His sons were in the carriage with him, one either side, each holding a hand. And the young priestess was there too, clasping Hattu's free hand. He smelt a sweet scent of summer blooms and realised he had been washed and anointed with perfumed waxes and oils, and his garments had been changed. Equally, the princes wore clean robes, Muwa in black, Hattu with the forest green cape over a fresh white tunic. Outside the wagon windows, he saw many Hittite soldiers, garments washed of battle-filth, wounds bandaged or sewn together with sutures of thin bronze wire. Hardy, proud, chests puffed out, heads high, left hands raised in clench-fisted salutes, they formed a corridor along which the carriage rumbled.

'We're going to ascend the mound of Nerik, Father,' Muwa said. 'To tell the Gods that their shame is over.'

'You will be remembered for this,' Hattu said. 'After three hundred years, you will be the first Hittite King to worship the Storm God on this hallowed mount.'

Mursili's lifeless flesh was suddenly charged with a shiver of wonder. The carriage tilted uphill and he realised this was not a dream. He heard the chanting of the blue-robed priests as they neared the top of the Nerik mound, and smelt incense sweetening the air up there. As the carriage tilted level again, he saw the grey, broken remnant of old Nerik. But the men had been busy, it seemed. The site of Nerik's Storm Temple had been cleared of tumbled stonework, leaving just the neat outline of its foundations, within which benches and an altar had been erected. And the rescued statue of Tarhunda had been raised, stripped of Kaskan adornments and cleaned with oils. He saw an Elder Priest holding the tall, thorned helm – the crown of the High Priest of the Hittite Empire.

The wagon door swung open and Hattu and Muwa helped to lift him into a waiting chair and carried him over to the altar, where a libation jug of wine awaited, along with a cup in the shape of a terracotta bull. Hattu and Muwa stood by the king's side as the corridor of soldiers dissolved to ring the summit of the Nerik mound, watching on as the Elder Priest placed the high helm on the king's head. In Mursili's stead, the priest read the lines of a prayer to the Storm God, and the watching ranks repeated them in a low, cantillating tone.

Two clay vases were brought before Mursili, then planted in the ground. One contained the cremated remains of Prince Sarpa's head, and the other the ashes of the fallen lion, General Kurunta.

'In the name of fallen heroes, this city will rise again,' Muwa spoke in the king's stead. 'The ruins will grow into fine halls, temples, homes and strong barracks. For too long, hallowed Nerik has lain desolate. Now, under my father, our Sun, it will again become the glory it once was.' The campaign scribes tapped out the statement furiously on their soft clay and wax tablets as the men of the army exploded in a joyous chorus.

Later, when the worship was over, the soldiers enjoyed wine and beer bread by the firelight to a chorus of pipe music and raucous, ribald banter. Mursili remained in his seat, watching them, his sons seated by his feet, looking over the celebrating soldiers and chatting between themselves as they enjoyed wine of their own.

'The... world... is yours now, my sons,' he said. The effort nearly knocked him out. 'Never... quarrel...'

Hattu looked up, rising on his knees to be level with the seated king. 'Ishtar was wrong, Father. We have proved that, have we not?'

Muwa looked up too, rising to the other side of the chair. 'Hattu's blood is mine and mine his. We are as one.'

Mursili felt his vision darkening once again, and this time he realised it might be forever. *Is this it? Is this the Dark Earth coming for me?* He knew he did not have much longer, and had to be certain of one thing. *Why are you still here?* He asked the dark ether.

Ishtar's mien appeared in the blackness, long and mournful. *Because I too wish to revel in Prince Hattu's feats. I truly believed he would slay his brother today.* She finally halted her relentless circling of him. *And, because... it has changed nothing. The course of history has been altered... but the confluence of time will bring him to the same, dark place.*

She reached out with one hand, placing it on his forehead. It was like the kick of a mule. With a flash of golden light, he was suddenly alive, spry, sprinting from one edge of the land to the other faster than any man or beast, then soaring through the sky across mountains and seas, through blizzards and arid desert winds. Time, days, moons, seasons, years – whole lifetimes – shot past him in an angry fury. And at last he saw that she was not tormenting him, but speaking with candour:

A burning east, a desert of graves,
A grim harvest, a heartland of wraiths,
The Son of Ishtar, will seize the Grey Throne,
A heart so pure, will turn to stone,
The west will dim, with black boats' hulls,
Trojan heroes, mere carrion for gulls,
And the time will come, as all times must,
When the world will shake, and fall to dust...

And he saw it all played out with her flat-voiced verse. Amongst the flames, the dead and the bloodied throne, stood a shadowy warrior in a dark green cloak with a falcon perched on his shoulder. He realised his body was trembling.

'Father?' Hattu said, his voice tight with concern, one hand on the king's. Muwa clasped the same hand also.

But Mursili, *Labarna,* Great King of the Hittite Empire, the Sun, realised that Volca's foul brew had penetrated deeply, turning parts of his body cold and useless. These words might well be his last, so he was determined to make them sweet. Young Hattu deserved this much after so many years of coldness... and especially given what lay ahead for him. He thought of the hollow with the soaring birds, the cascading falls and the blue tarn, of Queen Gassula, young and smiling, lying by his side on the summer grass there. He remembered the warmth of her caress, the sweetness of her every touch. The rheum in his eyes thickened and a single bead stole down his cheek, splashing on his, Hattu and Muwa's hands.

'The high hollow was truly... wondrous, wasn't it?' he whispered. The words had no sooner parted from his lips than the blackness closed over forever. In the void, Ishtar waited. But she was receding, stepping away at last, after so many years. She gazed heavenwards, her great wings extending. Up, she rose... and was soon gone from view. Mursili found himself alone in the eternal, empty darkness.

***

The king slumped, head lolling back, eyes staring into eternity. Myriad healers ran to the king's side and many soldiers dropped their drinking vessels and clamoured there too. Hattu, pale with shock, backed away to give them space to work. He heard their panicked shouts, saw their grieving looks, felt Atiya's hand on his arm, heard the Wolves rush over too, concerned for their king, but felt himself withdrawing from the scene. Something was beckoning him... something within.

He backed against a smooth, long-ruined column of stone and slid down to sit there. A stinging, blinding light flashed through his mind and he clasped his hands to his temples, screwing his eyes shut tight.

Darkness. Darkness with no form or sense of direction. He heard a sound of a bird landing, gathering in its wings. Then there was silence until, before him, something glimmered in the shadow. It was coming closer. He heard a low, ominous growl of not one creature, but two. Then he saw the eyes. Two pairs of eyes glinting like opals, low down, and another pair in between, much higher, a good few heads over him. He reached for his curved sword, but it was absent in this netherworld.

From the blackness, two lions prowled into view, their fangs dripping with saliva, faces wrinkled in anger. Between them strode an apparition: a curvaceous woman, bare-breasted, impossibly tall, but with wings and the feet of a hunting bird!

'Ishtar?' he stammered.

She smiled, and began pacing around him.

'Let me sing you a song, Prince Hattu...'

EPILOGUE

DEEP WINTER 1300 BC

Snow battered the Kizzuwadna coast, white streaks fighting against the blackness of night. A lone figure stood in the lee of a cove by the sandy waterline, swaddled in a red cloak. The hooded head tilted back and sniffed the perishing, salty air. At last after years marooned inland, *at last*, he had reached the sea – that unforgiving, vicious mistress with which he was still very much enthralled.

A fishing boat rode the spume-peaked, choppy waters, its square sail snapping in the night gale, taking an age to come to him. But coming it was – just as the Egyptian merchant-spies had arranged with him. And what was another hour or so? He had been waiting six moons for this chance after all – hiding in woods, sleeping in caves, eating roots and berries to flee the Hittite heartlands and steal across these southern vassal states – all the time hearing stories of the reclaimed Hittite north, of the power of the Grey Throne and its fierce, doughty army. The truth was far more bleak, he knew: King Mursili lay in complete torpor, mute and staring in his palace bed; the empire was effectively in the hands of his young, inexperienced son, Muwa; the royal bloodline was thin, with just Muwa and the curious young Prince Hattu remaining; the armies were greatly depleted and the harvests of that summer had been neglected.

The flat-bottomed boat ground onto the sand, stern first. A shaven-headed, dusky-skinned fellow with a squared beard leapt over the edge, shooting a sour glance at the local crewmen then turning, shivering, to the cloaked figure.

'Volca?' the Egyptian asked, his kohl-rimmed eyes searching within the shadows of the hood, his teeth chattering and his beard flecked with snow.

Volca looked him up and down and chuckled. The fellow's linen shawl was wholly inappropriate for the harsh Anatolian winter. 'Namurot? If your kind hope to one day call these lands your own, you had best learn how to dress to survive in them.'

The Egyptian's nose wrinkled. 'Come, we must be swift. The crew say if we put to sea now we might reach the fishing village along the coast before morning. The Pharaoh's warships are docked there, waiting to take you across the sea.'

Volca arched an eyebrow. 'He sent ships for me to Hittite lands? Ships bearing his own standards? His crewmen are brave,' he mused as they waded into the perishing waters then and boarded, sitting across from one another on the thwarts.

Namurot sneered and scoffed. 'Is it brave for the wolf to wander into the lamb's pen? The Wretched Fallen Ones – those who clamber across the grim rocks of this land like flies, foraging rotten berries and chewing on raw goat meat – don't even have a navy of their own.'

Volca smiled, thinking of the many ships and warrior-seamen in his homeland. Sherden and Shekelesh in their thousands. Such rich plunder awaited them in these lands, if only they had possessed the courage and wisdom to follow him.

Namurot fell quiet for a moment, then asked: 'My brother, Sirtaya the envoy, he still lives?' Hope and hatred battled on his tight expression, his fingers flexing on his sheathed dagger as if imagining vengeance.

Volca shrugged. In his time in Hattusa, he had heard remarks made about the brazen diplomat. 'He lives. In the eternal darkness of the Well of Silence, I believe. They feed the curs in there offal and mud,' he replied flatly. Namurot drew his dagger and stabbed it, hard, into the boat's timbers. Volca masked a disdainful snort; this wretch's brother was of little concern to him. He turned his thoughts to his own future. 'Tell me again: what does Pharaoh want of me? He already has a troop of mercenary Sherden in his armies, does he not?'

Namurot pulled his shawl tighter around himself as the wind grew fierce and the boat took to the water again. 'They are but fierce sea-warriors. Useful, but only with a sword. He wants you for what lies up here,' he tapped his temple, leaning forward so the dim reflected light from the water's surface reflected in his inky eyes. 'You have lived in the Hittite court for three years. He wants to know everything: about their ways, their weaknesses, their armies, their garrison-strengths on the vassal borders of Retenu... *everything*. And Retenu is key – the throat through which tin pours. Bronze armies can be forged only when kings have tin. Pharaoh intends to press his boot on the throat of the world... and choke the life from the Wretched Fallen Ones. Then, the world will be his!' Namurot wagged a finger at Volca. 'That is why Pharaoh wants you by his side.'

Volca stared at Namurot in silence. He saw in his mind's eye the golden chair of the King of Egypt, saw himself standing by it. He laughed once, short and barking, then again, long and loud. The wind keened, blowing his hood back, revealing the wiry lattice of sinew and scab in place of a scalp, his ring of blonde hair around the back and sides rapping behind him. The Egyptian and the crew gawped in fright, some dropping their oars, but Volca's blade of a nose bent over a feral smile and he stood up on the rocking boat, his old sea legs coming back to him at once as salty spray and snow stung his flesh, casting his cloak up like the wings of a bird. He planted one foot on the edge of the boat, dunted the haft of his trident once on the timbers and gazed across the roiling sea.

'Pick up your paddles, sailors, for we must make haste to Pharaoh's side: glory and fortune await!'

THE END

The _Empires of Bronze_ series continues with 'DAWN OF WAR':

Two great empires on the brink of war, one last hope for peace...

1294 BC: The fragile accord between the Hittite and Egyptian empires is crumbling. The ancient world braces itself for war on an unprecedented scale. Prince Hattu, the greatest of the Hittite generals, suffers dreams of terrible consequences – conjured by the Goddess Ishtar. But Hattu refuses to accept her prophecies, adamant that there is one last chance for peace.

This fragile hope lies in the borderlands of the east, where the two rival empires touch. Hattu gathers a chosen band and sets out for this distant, blistering desert land, determined and defiant. Yet the further he ventures, the darker and more twisted his mission becomes. Old ghosts rise around him and Ishtar haunts his every move.

The Goddess' divinations cannot be avoided, men say. Hattu will walk through fire to prove them wrong.

Empires of Bronze: *Dawn of War* is available at all good online stores!

AUTHOR'S NOTE

Exploring the Hittite era has been a journey riddled with shadows and studded with revelations. The Hattusa excavations are constantly unearthing new tablets and changing our understanding of their world with accounts of gods, kings, wars and treachery.

I found myself drawn towards their so-called 'New Kingdom' – the era in which the Hittites were at their strongest… and the time in which the greater world slid towards the edge of oblivion. It has been a delight and a challenge to understand these denizens of ancient Anatolia and their strange ways (as epitomised by their punishment of eating faeces and drinking urine!). Any Greek or Latin preconceptions had to be dispensed with as I tried to put shape to their way of life. I had to mine detail meticulously and where it was absent – and there are many gaps in our understanding of their world – I enjoyed applying speculation to bridge the gaps.

Firstly, I should comment on people and place names. Early in my research I became acutely aware of the rather tongue-twisting nature of certain names from the ancient Near East. To illustrate, I give you: Tawagalawa – the painfully multisyllabic name of a character that will come into play later in the saga. I aim to tell a snappy, entertaining tale, and as such, certain names have been truncated or altered to spare my readers from awkward (to the modern tongue) names and to avoid alliterative similarities. The table at the end of this note lists the places where I have done this. Also note that my use of the term 'Anatolia' (to refer to what is modern-day Turkey) is anachronistic for the Hittite period. However, I felt it was probably the most succinct way of referring to the geographical region.

The rest of this note serves to outline my major choices in crafting this tale – the places where the fabric of history holds good and the points where fantasy laces the fragments. To begin with, the term 'Hittite Empire' is a debate in itself. The Hittites actually called their realm 'The Land of Hatti' (the Hatti/Hattians being the original native population of the land), and referred to themselves as 'The People of the Land of Hatti'. The term 'Hittite' is technically an anachronism, coming from the Hebrew Bible, which refers to a group of relatively insignificant tribes living in the hills of Syria during biblical times – long after the era of this story and the fall of the Bronze Age. Modern Archaeologists, realising that these biblical tribes were the fragmented remnant of 'The People of the Land of Hatti', thus took to using the term 'Hittite' to refer to the Bronze Age superpower as well. And as for the Hittite *Empire*? It was not an empire in the modern sense, more a proto-empire: a kingdom that enjoyed a loose hegemony over a band of vassal states around its borders.

The Hittite Empire was also known as 'The Land of a Thousand Gods', and it's easy to see why (in fact, the title is probably an understatement!). Their system of deities is perplexing, non-linear and unfamiliar to the modern theological eye. It seems that their chief deities were Tarhunda the Storm God and Arinniti, Goddess of the Sun. That said, each major city had a storm god, a sun goddess or some specific deity of its own, rapidly expanding the godly ranks. More, the Hittites worshipped the ether around them, believing every spring, tree, rock and meadow was watched over by gods and spirits. They also practiced syncretisation (the custom of integrating foreign gods into their own pantheon), and one such divinity was Ishtar, Goddess of Love and War – a very ancient deity present in various forms across the civilizations of the ancient Near East.

Now, on to our hero...

The Hattusa tablets record that young Hattusili III was a sickly baby. When Ishtar came to King Mursili in a dream (supposedly in the form of Prince Muwatalli), she offered to save the baby if the king promised to name her as Hattu's protector. I have added a rather dark twist to this with the choice she also forces upon him (save your Queen or your boy).

Hattu's exact birth date is uncertain. We only know from his own later writings that he was 'only a child' around the time of Queen Gassula's passing (perhaps 1313 BC). This is as precise as most Hittite dates get, and so I have speculated that it might well have been Hattu's birth that caused Gassula's death. Little is known about Hattu's early life, thus his wretched time as the Cursed Son is conjectural but ties nicely into the words of Ishtar and brings him to the famed Hittite military, where he went on to excel.

The Hittite military academy existed somewhere in the countryside near Hattusa. The 'Fields of Bronze' as I have titled this complex, would have been the training ground for new recruits. One of Mursili's attested and most trusted generals, Kurunta, would most likely have had a hand in overseeing the raising and training of young men. Hattu's status as a son of the king would have afforded him little leniency by his trainers. Hittite princes were expected to inspire awe in their soldiers, and it is likely he would have had to push himself further than the rest to prove himself worthy.

The Hittite army is thought to have numbered ten or twenty thousand, or possibly far more. There is limited information on how they were structured, other than that they consisted of a standing army, complemented by 'shepherds' when extra numbers were required and that they were organised into regiments of one thousand, companies of one hundred and troops of ten. There is evidence that there were four main infantry generals, and this is the basis of my four divisions – the Storm, the Wrath, the Fury and the Blaze (evocative but entirely fictional titles).

Regarding weapons technology: popular conception has it that the Hittites 'possessed' iron weapons that were harder than bronze and that this gave them a martial edge over their rivals. This view is very simplistic and the truth is too complex to be covered in this note. But, concisely, iron was 'known' to the world well before the Hittites and all throughout the Bronze Age. The problem was that in this era, almost all of the Earth's iron was locked inside stone in the form of iron ore, and the technology to smelt (liquidise and extract) iron from ore had not yet been developed (or was in its infancy). Thus, pure or close-to-pure iron came almost exclusively in the form of meteorites which plunged from the sky – a rare commodity indeed. The cuneiform texts of Assyrian merchants translated by Prof. Klaas Veenhof support this rarity, showing that iron was hugely expensive (upwards of *forty* times the cost of silver!). The Hittites certainly never fielded an army equipped throughout with iron super weapons – if they had they would have flattened all of their opponents. The likelihood is they had a very small amount of precious iron blades reserved for kings or men in high stations. These blades may have been worked with emerging techniques to give a small advantage over bronze – or they may have been brittle and purely ceremonial as described in this volume. It is also worth noting that the Hittite and other Anatolian Kings preferred their thrones to be fashioned from iron. For those interested, I'll be investigating the iron debate in more depth on my blog (my web address is at the end of this note).

While the Hittite infantry was hardy and feared, the Hittite chariot wing was the dread of the battlefield. These were the lancers of Bronze Age warfare – fast, striking in appearance and lethal in the fray. The horses of the chariot wing were bred and trained by the famed Hurrian, Colta (real name Kikkuli – but this is thought to mean 'Colt' in Hurrian). I've named the Hittite chariot wing 'The Lords of the Bridle', but this was actually the title of an Arzawan chariot wing captured by an earlier Hittite King and brought back to Hattusa to serve their conquerors. It is unlikely that the Hittites adopted the 'Lords of the Bridle' title as their own, but the name is an evocative one with a firm root in the era. It's also worth pointing out that the lack of conventional cavalry (i.e. armed men fighting on horseback) is an accurate reflection of Bronze Age warfare. Horses of this time were smaller and had not yet been bred to produce the likes of medieval destriers or modern racehorses. They could not be expected to walk with armoured soldiers on their backs for any great distance, let alone charge with such a burden during battle. Horses *were* ridden, but only by light scouts or messengers.

The city of Hattusa, despite its striking location on a craggy hill, was assailed several times throughout its long spell as capital of the Hittite realm. On the majority of these occasions it was the Kaskans who committed the assault, forcing the kings to move the royal seat to the safety of other cities. The raid I describe in 1303 is speculative – no such event is recorded on the Hittite tablets for that year (the closest such raid happened in 1318) – but is representative of the constant, mortal threat of the Kaskan tribes.

The Kaskans are something of an enigma. Described as pig-herding mountain men, they appear all too easily in the mind's eye as rough, rugged 'barbarians'. Some scholars theorise that instead, they might actually have been an offshoot or remnant of the native Hattians. Regardless, they were famed for their warlike tenacity and their pervasiveness – plentiful and uncontrollable, a true bane to the Hittite King.

Pitagga (Pitaggatalli) is but a shadow in the annals of history. It seems most likely that he was a Kaskan 'Lord' of some sort, and spearheaded the raids on northern Hittite territories around 1303-1300, including a raid on Wahina (Takkuwahina) in 1303 and on Tummanna & Pala in 1301.

Around this time, King Mursili suffered what historians believe was a stroke. During a thunderstorm, his speech became slurred and his body sagged on one side. I have portrayed this happening during Hattu's 'Chariot Ordeal', and woven in the influence of the deplorable Volca as a possible cause. You might be wondering what was in Volca's root brew for it to have had such a terrible effect on the king? Warfarin is a drug that can be used as a means to thin blood and prevent clotting (useful to alleviate DVT risk) or – in significant doses – as rat poison. As a poison, symptoms include shortness of breath, chest pains, hair loss, general wasting and fatigue and ultimately bleeding on the brain (i.e. a stroke). Of course, Warfarin was only discovered in the 20th century just before WW2, when cattle suffered the above symptoms. Investigations found that their illness had been caused by decomposing sweet clover mixed in with their feed. It is from the elements of that plant that modern Warfarin is derived. So I went for the speculative angle that the people of ancient times might well have noticed or discovered the effects of ingesting rotting sweet clover.

Volca is a fictional character, but his people, the Sherden were all too real. Onomastic theory and archaeological finds suggest the Sherden might have originated from the Island of Sardinia. They, the Shekelesh (from modern Sicily, perhaps) and many other peoples at this point hovered on the edges of the ancient world. But that would soon change, as this saga will show...

In 1300, the Hittites marched north with the intention of finally retaking 'the Lost North' from the Kaskans. On their way, they had to deal with an uprising in the allied lands of Galasma (Kalasma), and a small force including General Nuwanza quelled the revolt. They then marched on through the Soaring Mountains (my speculative title for the modern Pontic massif) to take back a region known as Hatenzuwa and, most famously, they reclaimed the ruins of Nerik. The Hittite annals tell of King Mursili giving prayer there – the first time a Hittite king had done so since the city's fall to the Kaskans three hundred years previously.

Hattusili's part in the 1300 campaign is uncertain. Most agree he was there. Some speculate that he was even leading a division of the army for his father by then and possibly it was he who seized Nerik for the king.

With 'the Lost North' found again, Nerik, Hakmis and Zalpa were re-built, re-populated and re-integrated into the Hittite domain once more. But despite these landmark achievements, the Kaskans were never truly defeated, they remained as abundant and rowdy as ever, roaming the highlands as a presence that meant the future Hittite Kings could never truly consider the problem of the north 'solved'. Worse, the Great Powers of east, west and south had used the diversion of Hittite efforts shrewdly. Egypt, Assyria and Ahhiyawa would not remain quiet for much longer... as the next book in the series, 'Dawn of War', will attest!

Yours faithfully,
Gordon Doherty
www.gordondoherty.co.uk

P.S. If you enjoyed the story, please spread the word. My books live or die by word of mouth, so tell your friends or – even better – leave a short review on Amazon or Goodreads. Anything you can do in this vein would be very much appreciated.

Also, I love hearing from readers – get in touch via my website: **www.gordondoherty.co.uk/contact-me**

The *Empires of Bronze* saga continues with…

EMPIRES OF BRONZE
DAWN OF WAR

THE CITY OF RA, EGYPT
SPRING 1294 BC

An Egyptian vulture sped low across the eastern desert, coasting on the white heat of the dune sea, its frill of pale feathers shuddering and its yellow head and purple-beak sweeping in search of prey.

'See how the carrion bird flies,' whispered Pharaoh Seti, his kohl-lined eyes tracking the creature.

'The sacred hunter,' said Ramesses, his youngest son, beside him on the temple balcony. 'It is coming this way.'

Indeed, the bird sped over the last dune and onto the green, fertile stripes of land hugging the mighty River Iteru. It rose to soar over the palm-fringed banks, swaying rushes and crop fields, its head switching this way and that, captivated by the myriad fawn-skinned people at work there. Finally, it tilted towards the sculpted, burnt-gold jewel on the river's eastern banks: The City of Ra, a vast complex of mud-brick pylon gates, temples, towering pillars and statues of gods and ancient kings. Young Ramesses stretched on his toes for a better look as the vulture sped closer to the temple, gripping the marble edge of the balcony and leaning out a little *too* far.

Seti felt a weakness in his veins – a need to protect the lad as a father should, to pull him back from the precipice. But when the vulture shrieked, Seti's eyes snapped up, seeing the bird banking around the head of one mighty statue – a likeness of Pharaoh Thutmosis, unforgotten despite the passing of many generations. A warrior-king, a conqueror, a victor, a god. The great statue's shadow stretched across the city, blanketing half of the balcony too. Seti forgot about his son's welfare in that moment. He stepped clear of the shadow, a shaft of sunlight falling across his axe-sharp cheekbones and lantern jaw. *I will match and outshine your legendary achievements,* he mouthed, staring at Thutmosis' stony eyes.

A strange noise sounded behind the pair. The creaking of a bow. Seti swung on his heel, tearing a dagger from his belt and bringing it round on the assailant.

'Chaset?' he raged at his eldest, the adolescent prince who would one day succeed him.

Prince Chaset did not even notice his father's dagger, halted just a hand's-width from his heart. The young man was too busy training his arrow-tip on the vulture. 'I will teach the bird its final lesson.'

With a swish of one hand, Seti snatched the bow from the prince and threw it across the room behind the balcony, where it clattered, knocking over a wicker stool and a vase of wine. 'Choose your enemies more carefully, you fool.'

Chaset's hooded eyes flared open for a moment. 'You told me to be the greatest warrior I could be: with the sword, the spear... the bow!'

Seti stood his full height and glared at Chaset – and Ramesses too for good measure. Snapping his fingers, he strode past them both. The two princes followed, obedient and afraid. 'You train not so you can shoot sacred birds and offend the Gods, boy, but so you might share my destiny.'

He led them into a grand chamber at the far side of the temple. White, sweet-smelling ribbons of frankincense and myrrh smoke rose from the sconces affixed to the chamber's pillars, the stone floor was polished to a sheen, and the high walls were adorned with reliefs of bird and snake gods. Most striking of all, however, was the set of stairs at the chamber's far end – as wide as the hall, streaked with sunlight and guarded by black-wigged, white-kilted spearmen on the edge of each and every step, leading up to the temple's roof terrace. Seti halted in the middle of the floor, lifting his arms while a pair of slaves helped strap to his chest a cuirass of crossed bronze-wings, gleaming even in the cool shade of the room. Another placed a coruscant and bulbous sapphire warhelm on his bare scalp. Two more handed him each a sceptre and a fanged flail, and another tied a lion's tail to his belt. Armed and armoured, he strode on and up the steps, shafts of sunlight passing over him as he ascended. 'It is to the north we will find our destiny. Conquest and glory, just as mighty Thutmosis once knew.'

'The north,' Ramesses muttered. 'Retenu, the vassal lands?'

Seti looked down at his youngest. Ramesses had a keen mind. Sometimes he wished for Chaset to have such a thirst to learn. But his eldest was a fine warrior, at least. 'The vassal lands, at first,' he said as they emerged onto the rooftop and into the full power of the sun. The savage heat bent and warped the air around them, giving life to the statues of jackal, falcon and baboon-headed deities lining the roof's edges. 'There, I will press my foot on the throat of the tin routes. None will have that precious metal, none but I. Yet that is only the beginning, for the world stretches beyond those parts, and much greater rewards wait beyond.'

He stepped over to the semi-circular platform jutting from the front edge of the temple roof and threw out his arms, his sapphire helm sparkling like a dark sun. At once, a wall of noise hit him from below, and the sight down there set his heart alight with pride.

The Army of Ra cheered on and on in adoration: ten thousand voices, guttural and strong, rising from the huge, white-flagged square. The bare-chested, white-kilted *menfyt* stood in countless blocks of two hundred and fifty – each unit of these veterans known as a *Sa*. They pumped their gleaming, sickle-like *khopesh* swords and tall spears skywards, pale blue and white linen headdresses fluttering in the hot wind. The thousand-strong, bronze-coated crack corps known as the Strongarms simply fell to one knee – devoted, invincible, shimmering like treasure behind their zebra-hide shields. A huge host of coal-skinned

Medjay archers, clad in leopardskin kilts and armed with stave-bows and twin quivers lined the left of the square and another swarm of bowmen stood on the right – paler-skinned Libyans, naked but for giraffe skin capes and dangling penis-sheaths, crying out to the skies in veneration. To the rear, a five-hundred strong wing of bright and majestic chariots glittered, the warrior and driver aboard each encased in armour and draped with weaponry, the feather-crested horses snorting and pawing at the ground. From the rooftops around the palm-lined square, trumpets keened and drums rumbled.

Chaset and Ramesses came to stand by Seti's sides at the roof's edge and another wave of adulation rose.

'Army of Ra,' Seti boomed.

The clamour of adulation fell silent instantly. Even the masses in the city streets beyond the square and all around the city's hinterland seemed to halt and look up. All quivered and trembled with awe, entranced by their God-king.

'It has been a long winter of preparation,' said Seti. 'Of whetting blades and fashioning armour.' He let a moment pass to reinforce his authority and to choose carefully his next words. Oddly, they seemed to be stuck in his throat. Was it the presence of his two boys at his sides distracting him, directing his thoughts elsewhere, to weaker places, to thoughts of being a mere father?

Just before the silence stretched a little too long, a voice whispered, behind him: 'Now it is time. Time to march north to the lands of Gubla at the edge of our realm.'

Once more, Seti felt his dagger arm stiffen and his body tense, ready to swing round on the other, until he realised who had crept up behind him and his boys. His alarm faded as fast as it had risen. 'Now it is time,' he repeated to the crowd. 'Time to march north to Gubla at the edge of our realm.'

The voice whispered to him again and Seti repeated this next line: 'Then we will march *beyond* Gubla, and smash the petty kingdoms who do not bend their knee to Egypt.'

The army was rapt.

'At the last, we will come to face... *them*,' the voice said in a strained hiss, Seti repeating the words and the hesitation.

He heard some men down below murmur to one another: 'The Hittites,' said one. 'The Wretched Fallen Ones,' agreed another. 'They grow their hair long like women, scrape the beards from their chins and they live on windswept crags – like *animals,*' said a third.

'We will dash their armies,' Seti continued, prompted by the voice, 'topple their crude cities, their wretched capital high on the hills of their cursed heartlands... *all* will fall, *all* will be razed to dust. When it is done, the Hittites will be no more.'

The army seemed set to erupt with fervour, barely containing their hubris, a few yelps of zeal escaping mouths here and there. Now they just needed their Pharaoh to give the command that would begin it all. They took to drumming their swords and spears against their pale hide shields in a frantic rumble, knowing the moment was almost upon them.

But Seti was again plagued by that irritating doubt. He felt his hands slide up and over the shoulders of his boys, a mewling sense of concern for them once more pricking and jabbing at the golden promise of conquest. Next, he turned his head from the massed army and to the man who had helped choose his words: Volca.

The pale-eyed, fair-skinned Sherden islander had come to his lands six years ago from the Hittite court, pleading for shelter, telling his story – of how he had devoted himself to the service of their old king, Mursili, only to be turned upon by the ailing Hittite leader's sons. Volca had been pathetic that day, snivelling at Seti's feet. Not so now. Tall and lean, with collar-length, flaxen hair and plate-sized copper rings dangling from his ears to frame his handsome, narrow face. He wore a red cloak and a green-painted, armless scale corselet with a wide gold band clinging to his right bicep, and a trident strapped across his back. His horned-helm was remarkable, adding to his already considerable height. But the most striking aspect of the man was the part that the eye could not see, thought Seti – the thorny vines of hatred coiled around his heart. Volca despised the Hittites even more than most Egyptians did. On the day news had arrived of King Mursili's death, the Sherden had shed tears of delight. Most crucially, he knew almost everything about those strange, northern people: how they lived, how they traded, how they made war. As such, he was more vital to the coming campaign than any champion down on the square.

'The Hittites may be hardy, but they are weak in numbers,' Volca said calmly – the words intended for Seti alone. 'More, the two brothers who chased me from their lands are weak leaders: King Muwa is but a shadow of his father; and as for Prince Hattu,' he spat the name and paused for a moment, his lips twitching, face sliding into a look of pure malice, 'every night I dream of his death. It will be slow and it will hurt like the fires of the Gods.'

Disquiet crept across Seti's shoulders, seeing the Sherden's right fist coil and uncoil as if flexing around the hilt of an invisible knife. His eyes were like coals, blazing into the ether. Such intense hatred...

'This is your time,' Volca continued, snapping from his trance, 'Lord of the Two Lands, Son of Ra, Horus of Gold,' he gestured to the square and the crescendo of rumbling weapons on shields. 'This is the moment for you to rage like a panther... to etch your name,' he leaned towards Seti, clenching and shaking a fist, his face pinching into a rictus, spittle flying from his gritted teeth, 'into *eternity.*'

Seti's skin shivered with fervour. Charged with belief and a rampant sense of entitlement, he barely noticed his hands sliding from his boys' shoulders. He turned his gaze back to the army, lifting his sceptre overhead like a sword, drinking in the sight of his forces. 'It is time to march.'

The Army of Ra roared until the city itself shook.

'To the north,' Seti cried as the drums boomed and the trumpets blared, 'to *war!*'

Hope you enjoyed the sample! **Empires of Bronze: Dawn of War** is available at all good online stores!

GLOSSARY

Arinniti; Hittite Goddess of the Sun and protector of the Earth. The Hittites believed she spent each night in the underworld beneath the earth and the seas, then rose as the sun to cross the sky each day. She was the spouse of the Storm God, Tarhunda, and the protective deity of the Hittite city of Arinna.

Aplu; Hittite God of the Underworld (known as the Dark Earth).

Arma; Hittite God of the Moon.

Arzana House; A tavern, usually outside the city walls. Men would go here for food, music, prostitutes and wrestling. Soldiers particularly favoured these places. There is evidence that Hittite princes would be taken there for cultic festivals and for puberty rites/inductions.

Asu; Medical expert/healer.

Bel Madgalti; 'Lord of the Watchtowers' – a prestigious post that involved presiding over a region of Hittite frontier forts or towns as a governor and commander of sorts.

Danna; Measure of distance, somewhere between a kilometre and a mile.

Gal Mesedi; Chief of security and commander of the Hittite King's bodyguards. Usually a highly trusted man – often a close relative of the king.

Haga: A ferocious two-headed eagle from ancient Hittite mythology. A symbol of power that would one day become the emblem of the Byzantine Empire.

Hasawa; The 'Old Women' (or Wise Women as I have called them) who performed religious and magical rites to heal, protect and strengthen the Hittite people.

Hurkeler; A sexual deviant – one who performs an act of *hurkel* with an animal. The Hittites believed bestiality was a sin punishable by death… unless it was committed with a horse, in which case it was perfectly alright.

Illuyanka; The winter rival of the Storm God, Tarhunda. Every spring the Storm God had to defeat this sacral serpent, who ruled the nature in wintertime. Tarhunda's annual victory ushered in the spring rains, allowing the crops and pastures to flourish.

Ishtar; The Goddess of Love and War. Also known as Shauska, Inanna and many other names.

Kamrusepa; Hittite Goddess of Birth and Protector of the Herds.

Lelwani; Hittite Goddess of the Underworld.

Labarna; The Great King and High Priest of the Hittite Empire. Steward of the Gods. Alternately known as *Tabarna.*

Mesedi; The bodyguards of the Hittite King. A select group who were armed ornately and would travel with the king everywhere.

Namra; Prisoners of war. These formed a big part of Bronze Age war booty. They would often be put to work in their captor's crop fields so that native men could be freed up to serve in the armies. Sometimes they were integrated en-masse into the Hittite army.

Panku; The Panku is thought to have described a council or proto-senate of some sort in the Hittite court – a sounding board to aid the Hittite King in making his decisions of law.

Sarruma; Hittite God of the Mountains.

Tarhunda; Hittite God of the Storm, spouse of the Sun Goddess Arinniti and principal male deity of the Hittite pantheon.

Tuhkanti; The Tuhkanti was 'the second commander' and intended heir to the Hittite throne. Usually a son of the king.

Name Alterations

Person Name in Story	Person Name in History
Hattu	Hattusili III
Muwa	Muwatalli II
Gassula	Gassulawiya
Pitagga	Pitaggatalli
Colta	Kikkuli (Means 'Colt' in Hurrian)
Shahuru, Viceroy of Gargamis	Shahurunuwa
Sirtaya, the Egyptian envoy	Zirtaya
Place Name in Story	**Place Name in History**
Wahina	Takkuwahina
Galasma	Kalasma
Gargamis	Carchemish
Nuhashishi	Nuhashi

If you enjoyed *Empires of Bronze: Son of Ishtar*, why not try:

Legionary, by Gordon Doherty

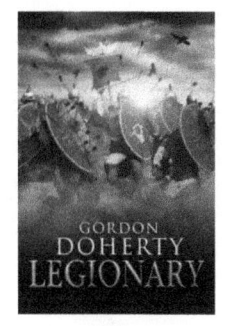

The Roman Empire is crumbling, and a shadow looms in the east...
376 AD: the Eastern Roman Empire is alone against the tide of barbarians swelling on her borders. Emperor Valens juggles the paltry border defences to stave off invasion from the Goths north of the Danube. Meanwhile, in Constantinople, a pact between faith and politics spawns a lethal plot that will bring the dark and massive hordes from the east crashing down on these struggling borders.
The fates conspire to see Numerius Vitellius Pavo, enslaved as a boy after the death of his legionary father, thrust into the limitanei, the border legions, just before they are sent to recapture the long-lost eastern Kingdom of Bosporus. He is cast into the jaws of this plot, so twisted that the survival of the entire Roman world hangs in the balance…

Strategos: Born in the Borderlands, by Gordon Doherty

When the falcon has flown, the mountain lion will charge from the east, and all Byzantium will quake. Only one man can save the empire . . . the Haga!
1046 AD. The Byzantine Empire teeters on the brink of all-out war with the Seljuk Sultanate. In the borderlands of Eastern Anatolia, a land riven with bloodshed and doubt, young Apion's life is shattered in one swift and brutal Seljuk night raid. Only the benevolence of Mansur, a Seljuk farmer, offers him a second chance of happiness.
Yet a hunger for revenge burns in Apion's soul, and he is drawn down a dark path that leads him right into the heart of a conflict that will echo through the ages.